KNIGHT

New York Times
Bestselling Author

LORA
LEIGH

USA Today
Bestselling Authors

ALYSSA
DAY

VIRGINIA
KANTRA

SHIFTER

FOUR ALL-NEW STORIES OF PARANORMAL DESIRE

BERKLEY
SENSATION

$7.99

ISBN 978-0-425-22035-1

9 780425 220351

5 0 7 9 9 >

S EAN

SHIFTER

Angela Knight
Lora Leigh
Alyssa Day
Virginia Kantra

B

BERKLEY SENSATION, NEW YORK

THE BERKLEY PUBLISHING GROUP
Published by the Penguin Group
Penguin Group (USA) Inc.
375 Hudson Street, New York, New York 10014, USA

Penguin Group (Canada), 90 Eglinton Avenue East, Suite 700, Toronto, Ontario M4P 2Y3, Canada
(a division of Pearson Penguin Canada Inc.)
Penguin Books Ltd., 80 Strand, London WC2R 0RL, England
Penguin Group Ireland, 25 St. Stephen's Green, Dublin 2, Ireland (a division of Penguin Books Ltd.)
Penguin Group (Australia), 250 Camberwell Road, Camberwell, Victoria 3124, Australia
(a division of Pearson Australia Group Pty. Ltd.)
Penguin Books India Pvt. Ltd., 11 Community Centre, Panchsheel Park, New Delhi—110 017, India
Penguin Group (NZ), 67 Apollo Drive, Rosedale, North Shore 0632, New Zealand
(a division of Pearson New Zealand Ltd.)
Penguin Books (South Africa) (Pty.) Ltd., 24 Sturdee Avenue, Rosebank, Johannesburg 2196,
South Africa

Penguin Books Ltd., Registered Offices: 80 Strand, London WC2R 0RL, England

SHIFTER

A Berkley Sensation Book / published by arrangement with the authors

PRINTING HISTORY
Berkley Sensation mass-market edition / March 2008

Copyright © 2008 by The Berkley Publishing Group.
"Mad Dog Love" by Angela Knight copyright © 2008 by Julie Woodcock.
"A Jaguar's Kiss" by Lora Leigh copyright © 2008 by Lora Leigh.
"Shifter's Lady" by Alyssa Day copyright © 2008 by Alesia Holliday.
"Sea Crossing" by Virginia Kantra copyright © 2008 by Virginia Kantra.
Excerpt from Sea Witch by Virginia Kantra copyright © 2008 by Virginia Kantra.
Cover illustration by Tony Mauro.
Cover design by Rita Frangie.
Interior text design by Tiffany Estreicher.

ISBN: 978-0-425-22035-1

BERKLEY® SENSATION
Berkley Sensation Books are published by The Berkley Publishing Group,
a division of Penguin Group (USA) Inc.,
375 Hudson Street, New York, New York 10014.
BERKLEY SENSATION and the "B" design are trademarks belonging to Penguin Group (USA) Inc.

PRINTED IN THE UNITED STATES OF AMERICA

10 9 8 7 6 5 4 3 2 1

CONTENTS

MAD DOG LOVE

Angela Knight

ONE

R ance Conlan prowled his cell like the caged wolf he was, anger boiling through him with every long stride. There was nothing to divert his rage, since the cell held only a cot built into the floor and a toilet unit that thrust from the wall. Both were stark, white, and rounded, without so much as a sharp corner he could put to bloody use.

Not that it mattered. All he had to do was shift, and he'd have fangs, claws, and two meters of werewolf muscle at his disposal. Trouble was, the slave collar wouldn't let him shift.

One of the new slaves sobbed in her cell on the other side of the bulkhead, her voice thick with despair and aching grief. Her tears scraped at Rance's Freeworlds-bred instinct to protect and comfort. Adding to his frustration, the doorway of his cell lacked either bars or barrier field, creating the illusion that escape was possible.

Unfortunately, Rance knew better. If he so much as stepped over the threshold, agony would cripple him.

Bloody collar.

He glared at the empty doorway in brooding fury. All his life, his nanobot system had provided him with absolute control over his body. The molecule-sized robots traveling through his blood-stream gave him the ability to heal any illness, tap superhuman reserves of strength, communicate over vast distances, access any fact he needed to know. Even change into something not quite human.

On the savage world he called home, a man had to be more than a man to survive.

Rance's nanos had given him that kind of power—until slavers had captured him three months ago. The collar they'd locked around his neck had reprogrammed his nanosystem and turned it into the instrument of his enslavement. If he attempted rebellion now, the 'bots would plunge him into a screaming red hell.

But that wasn't going to stop him. Nanos or no nanos, he'd find a way to escape. The traitor who'd handed him over to the slavers was damn well going to pay.

"Mad Dog!" The voice rang down the corridor, arrogantly nasal. The sobbing from the cell next door cut off as if a switch had flipped.

Smart girl.

"Mad Dog, I've found a potential buyer." The slaver strutted through the cell doorway with two hulking cyborg bodyguards at his heels. "An aristo courier looking for a werewolf bodyguard. And you'd better not space the deal, or you'll curse your mother for birthing you into hell."

Ortio Casus had a taste for melodramatic threats. Trouble was, he also liked carrying them out.

Rance ignored the little bastard, all his feral attention focused on the two 'borgs. They were as powerfully muscled as their boss was thin, dressed in steel-gray nanotium body armor and black-visored helmets that concealed their faces. And they were entirely too alert, apparently well aware of just what Rance was capable of.

Bloody hell. All he needed was a moment's inattention. Even a little boredom would do. Too bad they were so well-trained. Probably ex-Imperial Marines. Especially the leader of the two, Captain Aaren, who'd first hacked into Rance's nanosystem . . .

"Did you hear me? I said I've found a potential buyer." Casus glowered, jerking his weak, bearded chin upward in irritation. As usual, he was dressed like the aristo fop he longed to be: gaudy velvet and too much lace. But what interested Rance was the glittering array of rings he wore on every finger. One for each slave in the cells.

Rance suspected the big ruby on Casus's right hand controlled his particular collar. It'd be interesting to bite the ring off that spidery finger and find out. A quick shift to wolf form, a snap of razor fangs, and—

The pain slammed into his groin so fast and brutally, his knees buckled. Rance crashed to the floor, his body jerking into a helpless fetal ball. He gagged, struggling to breathe despite the sensation of a big fist slowly twisting his dick with sadistic strength.

Fucking nanobots.

He must have met Casus's gaze again. The little prick hated it when he did that. Probably because he could see the patient death waiting in Rance's eyes.

The pain abruptly ended, leaving him to collapse in sweating nausea.

"If you ruin this deal for me, I'll see you dead!" Casus snarled, red-faced and quivering. "You'll scream for days, Mad Dog. Days, do you understand me?" He raised the riding crop. "Do you?"

"Yes . . . master." Rance gritted his teeth, because to do anything else would bring more punishment and accomplish nothing. Slavery had taught him he couldn't afford empty gestures, no matter how satisfying it might be to spit in the bastard's face.

He had to pretend to submit, regardless of the humiliation. With any luck, a new master would be less wary than Casus. Rance would only need an instant's inattention to do his killing and make his escape.

Mollified by Rance's pretended submission, Casus drew himself to his full height—such as it was—and straightened his lace cuffs with a fussy jerk. "Good. My guards will prepare you now. But if you dare meet her gaze with those yellow mad dog eyes, you're a dead man. One way or another, I want you out of my stable. Either she buys you, or—"

Rance concealed a frown. *She?*

Zarifa Lorezo pushed the heavy gold drapes aside and stared out the porthole beyond. An imperial courier maneuvered to dock at one of Market Station's other arms, its thrust nodes glowing blue as it edged into its assigned slip.

Was her vicious fiancé aboard? Gerik often used courier ships on his secret missions for the regent.

Zarifa sent up a silent prayer that he wasn't on that ship. She'd tried so hard to lose him. The course she'd flown had been almost ridiculously intricate, making orbit at one world only to immediately blast into superspace headed for another. Her trip here to Market Station had taken more than a week longer than it would have by direct flight.

Still, she was only delaying the inevitable. Gerik Natalo would catch up to her sooner or later. They didn't call him the

Regent's Fist for nothing. He served his father's whims with fanatical devotion, and Umar Natalo wanted her back.

Zarifa's right hand tightened on the hilt of the sword that hung at her hip. As she shifted her booted feet restlessly, a thin knife of agony stabbed her ribs. She stifled a hiss. The wound was almost healed, but the pain remained, a silent reminder of Gerik's last attempt to bring her in.

Her new system had been worth every imperial she'd paid for it. Less than a week had passed since the bastard had driven his sword into her side. She'd have bled to death if not for the nanos that had accelerated her body's healing. Yet she had no illusions: if her fiancé hadn't been intent on taking her alive, she'd be a dead woman now. The Regent's Fist was simply too powerful, too skilled. Too deadly.

She had to make sure she had a protector before he caught up to her again.

"Lady Selan?"

Zarifa whirled, damn near drawing on Casus before she managed to stay her hand. She slid the sword the inch back into its sheath and wiped the feral determination off her face. "Yes?"

The slaver gave her an oily smile, gaudy in his yellow silk waistcoat and green velvet jacket. *A tradesman with pretensions,* her father's ghost whispered. Casus's eyes flicked nervously to the white-knuckled grip she had on her sword hilt. She wondered how quickly he'd sell her out if he knew who she really was. *He'd call the palace before I was halfway out the door.*

Luckily, the image her nanos projected would keep him from recognizing her. Between that and her cover identity of slightly shady aristo courier, she should be relatively safe.

Unless Gerik showed up with a warrant for her arrest . . .

Casus sketched an elaborate bow. "The slave is ready for your consideration, milady."

"Good. Show him in, please." Zarifa squared her shoulders and braced her booted feet apart as the slaver turned to gesture at one of his men.

The thought of buying a slave set her teeth on edge. If she'd had her way, she'd have outlawed slavery years ago. If it was illegal to enslave imperial citizens, it should be just as unconstitutional to kidnap and collar Freeworlders. Unfortunately, the regent had ignored all her arguments. She suspected he was probably involved in the slave trade himself.

Umar did love his money.

And wouldn't it be ironic if one of those slaves turned out to be her salvation? Too bad she couldn't afford more of them. She'd be happier with a whole phalanx of werewolves to escort her on her mission. Unfortunately, buying the ship had left her funds so drained, one shifter was all she could afford.

Frowning, Zarifa used her thumb to twist the diamond ring that rode her right hand, a nervous habit formed in the last stressful month. The intricately engraved band felt cold on her finger, heavy with old debts and lost honor.

The door whispered open. Zarifa looked around just as one of the guards led the slave in on the end of a silver chain.

And she forgot everything else.

The shifter prowled between the overstuffed pseudo-Victorian furnishings, naked except for a gleaming black collar around his neck. One sweeping glance branded him on her senses: the hard, angular features, the broad, powerful curve of his chest, the ripple of brawny arms and legs. The swing of his heavy sex between his thighs . . .

She looked away, feeling her cheeks burn. Right into Casus's amused, faintly contemptuous gaze.

Alarm jolted through her. *I'm blowing my own cover.* The jaded aristo she was pretending to be was not the kind of woman who'd blush at the sight of a big cock.

But my lover was nothing like that, a tiny voice protested.

Zarifa ignored it. She had a role to play.

She started toward the shifter with as much swagger as she could manage. He didn't meet her stare, even when she stopped barely centimeters away.

Her eyes were on the level with his small, dark nipples. She looked down, along the rippled plane of his hard belly, deliberately forcing her gaze to his sex. *Sweet Lady, how big would it be fully erect?*

She ordered her nanosystem to cool her cheeks before they could heat again.

Zarifa looked up into the shifter's face. His eyes still refused to meet hers, but she saw now they were the color of ancient coins, a bright gold that was not entirely human. His hair was a rich, deep sable that gleamed like fur, cut ruthlessly short, yet still showing a hint of curl. She could almost feel the smooth silk of it against her fingers.

God, she craved the touch of another human. Entombed in her fortress of fear, she hadn't dared let anyone close. Especially a man.

Especially a man like this.

True, he wasn't the most handsome male she'd ever seen. The aristocracy habitually sent its most beautiful sons to her court in hopes of attracting her eye. Despite the breathtaking power of his body, the shifter's features were too rough for that kind of perfection. His nose was a bit too flared across the nostrils, his deep-set eyes too feral, his cheekbones not quite knife-edged enough, his chin a little too stubborn.

But it was his mouth that fascinated. His lower lip was full with the promise of lush eroticism, yet his upper lip was thin, with a faint twist that suggested pain and bitterness.

Gold-coin eyes darted up to meet hers. For an instant, they blazed hot with male interest as those beautiful lips curved into a knowing smile. Then he looked away, leaving her heart pounding in desperate lunges as she remembered everything they said about shifters.

She could have him. Have him as she'd not dared to have a man since the regent had ordered her lover's murder. Six years, she'd lived like a Lady's nun, not daring to allow so much as a stolen kiss from the beautiful men who surrounded her. Fearing what the regent would do to protect his power and keep the way clear for his son's claim. Only Gerik had touched her, and his hands had not exactly been welcome.

But she could have this wolf. Buy him. Own him. Take him to her bed.

You're letting him distract you, her father's ghost whispered. *You're not buying him for sex. He's a means to regain our lost honor. That's all.*

Zarifa forced herself to step back. Forced her eyes not to drop to his lengthening cock. "I need a protector. Can you fight?"

White teeth flashed in a hard, reckless smile with just a hint of viciousness. "Yes."

She flicked a glance at the guards in their gray nanotium armor. "Show me."

"Now, Lady Selan . . ." Casus began nervously.

But the shifter was already moving, spinning, one bare heel lashing out to slam into the nearest guard's armored belly. It must have hurt, but he didn't even break step, pivoting to ram a fist into the man's faceplate, following up with a series of furious hammer blows to the 'borg's head and body. Blood flew in a crimson arc, but it was from the shifter's own splitting knuckles.

Yet he didn't seem to feel the pain, his face twisted in an animal snarl as the guard stumbled back from the fury of his attack.

The second cyborg dove at him with a roar. The shifter ducked the charge and danced back, throwing another brutal punch. And then another, and another. More blood flew from his hands.

Zarifa caught her breath. The rage in him, the fury boiling to the surface to spill from his pounding hands and savage kicks—it was as if the Lady herself had given Zarifa's own frenzied, angry frustration human form.

But human as he was, he couldn't hurt his guards, could only break himself against their armored bodies.

"Shift!" she snapped, feeling wild and reckless. "Shift now!"

Gold eyes flicked to hers. He bared his teeth.

"No!" the slaver gasped.

But sable fur was already spreading over the shifter's bare skin, his body bulking even larger, his face lengthening into an elegant muzzle. His ears rose into lupine points as his big hands and feet grew deadly, curved claws. He turned his feral golden eyes on the guards.

"Down!" Casus roared.

The shifter roared in agony and dropped to the ground as if he'd been shot. The fur melted away as his body returned to human form, writhing and kicking in anguish.

Zarifa knew exactly how that felt. The pain. The helpless, searing rage. The black shame of being a puppet to callous men.

Her gaze shot to the slaver, who wore a smile of grim satisfaction now. "I told you what would happen, Mad Dog," Casus spat. "I warned you."

The next thing Zarifa knew, her sword was in her hand and pressed hard to the slaver's throat. A tide of red washed over her vision. It seemed she could almost see the slaver's blood streaming under her blade. Casus's thin lips pulled into an O of terror.

She bared her teeth. "Let. Him. *Go*."

TWO

Rance peered through the fog of pain to see the woman's sword digging into Casus's neck. "Stop torturing him," she growled. "Now."

An aristo was *defending* him?

The slaver's hand jerked, ready to drop the stiletto he wore in a wrist sheath down into his palm. Rance prepared to drive a kick into the man's groin, knowing even as he did that he'd pay for it.

"Draw on me and die," she snarled, angling the sword upward to press it deeper into the skin. A bead of bright blood rolled down Casus's throat. The man's hand fell limp at his side.

"Mr. Casus, what is your order?" Captain Aaren demanded, obviously torn between fear of laying hands on an aristo and allowing her to threaten his boss.

Rance rolled to his feet despite the pain still fisting his balls. He was damned if he'd let a woman be threatened while he lay on his ass. Even if he couldn't quite stand up straight.

Aaren shot him a warning look and edged toward the aristo.

Her eyes narrowed as she flashed him a glare. "Dare to touch me, and I'll see you executed."

And she could, too. The penalties for a commoner committing violence on an aristo were severe. On the other hand, Lady Selan could cut Casus's throat without incurring so much as a slap on the wrist.

Rance grinned through the knife-blade pain. He'd never thought that particular law would ever work to his advantage.

A fresh tide of pain hit, buckling his knees. He barely held himself upright.

Casus apparently hadn't appreciated the grin.

The aristo titled her blade, forcing the slaver's chin higher. "I said *release him*."

"He threatened my guards!"

Her voice was calm, level, as if she could cut Casus's throat with no more concern than slicing a grapefruit. "He was demonstrating his skills on my order, as you well know. I will not tell you again."

"He is dangerous, lady!"

"So am I." Her eyes narrowed, took on a fixed, cold gleam. "And I grow impatient."

The hand with the ruby gestured, and the pain abruptly faded. Rance slumped with a grunt of relief but forced himself to keep his feet. His rescuer might need him.

The aristo's voice was brisk and cool when she asked, "How much do you want for him?"

Casus promptly lost his sense of ill usage in greed. His narrow face lit with calculation. "I don't know that I can sell him, not in good conscience. He's more dangerous than I thought."

"If I wanted a lap dog, I'd go to a pet shop. How much?"

"He should be destroyed."

She peeled her lovely lips back from her teeth. "So should you, slaver. How much?"

Rance swallowed a snort of laughter as the two began to dicker in earnest.

He had to admit, if he had to have a mistress for a few hours, he could have done worse. There was an arrogant purity to the aristo's features, to the clean, straight line of her nose, the high jut of her cheekbones and curve of her chin. Her eyes were large and liquid, a rich forest green, and her blonde hair gleamed like a crown in a tight, smooth upsweep.

She wore one of those vaguely historical costumes fashionable among aristos. The tight red velvet jacket and snug white pants tucked into black boots, as if she should be off hunting foxes from horseback. She certainly didn't look like an assassin-dodging interstellar courier. Which was probably the idea.

There was a certain kinky temptation in the idea of being owned by her. Though, eyeing the length of those exquisite legs and the high, sweet rise of her breasts, he decided he'd much rather own her.

An aristo slave. What a delicious thought.

"Then we have a deal?" Casus demanded. The slaver was all but drooling in anticipation of all those imperials.

The lady's green gaze flicked to Rance again. Considered him for a long moment while his heart skipped a beat. What if she said no?

He'd be a dead man. The slaver's cyborgs would kill him before she was halfway down the hall.

"Yes," the aristo said at last. "We have a deal."

Zarifa could feel the weight of the shifter's intense golden eyes on her as Casus presented her with the control ring. It was damned uncomfortable, having a man watch you accept the instrument of his torture.

Especially when she knew all too well what it was like to be on the receiving end of that kind of pain.

"I don't need that," Zarifa said shortly, waving aside the offered ring. "Just give me the code for his controls."

Casus frowned at her. "Freeworlds nanosystems like Mad Dog's are too different from ours to access. You need a translator to control him." He held out the ring again.

Zarifa grimaced but reluctantly accepted it. Slipping it on, she gestured at the ring the slaver wore. "Yours, too."

Casus paled slightly, his gaze flickering to the shifter, who had come to feral attention. "I don't think that's a good idea."

"And I don't want anyone else controlling my slave." She gave him her father's best silky smile. "Unless you'd rather cancel the transaction now . . ."

His expression sour, the slaver jerked the ring off his finger and handed it over.

Zafira tucked the ring into a jacket pocket and thought, *Nanos, reencrypt and password Mad Dog's system. I don't want anybody accessing him but me.*

Done, said the system's chiming mental voice.

She relaxed. They wouldn't be able to use him against her now.

"You're going to need the maximum pain setting to control him." Malice filled Casus's eyes as he added, "Applied to his dick. That's about all that makes an impression on him."

"I'll take that under advisement." Apparently her icy displeasure showed; the slaver visibly flinched.

One of the cyborgs spoke in a basso rumble. "Mr. Casus, a delivery cart is here. It says it has something for Lady Selan."

"It's the armor I ordered," Zarifa said. "Is there somewhere Mad Dog can change?"

Casus sniffed. "He's already naked. It's not as if he needs privacy."

"But I do." She stared coldly at the slaver until he dropped his gaze. "And I expect to get it. Any recording devices will be turned off."

Casus dipped a low bow. "Of course, milady."

The nanotium cuirass was a deep, rich crimson, accented with slashes of black. The armored greaves, gloves, and bracers were in the same color scheme, while the thigh plates and boots were black piped in red. Each piece gleamed under the overhead lights, though they could go dark and dull if needed for stealth.

Rance held his arms out as his new mistress fitted the chest plate around his torso. "You know, I can put on my own armor."

She gave him a faint smile and went on settling the cuirass into place. "I know. But you're my man, and I want to be sure it's properly fitted. If not, I want to be able to tell the armorer exactly what to change."

My man. There was something faintly medieval in the way she said the phrase, like an ancient lord claiming responsibility for a vassal knight. Something about the words sent warmth expanding through his chest, and he frowned.

I'm not her "man," he told himself fiercely. *I'm getting the hell away from her as soon as I get the chance.*

The traitor owed him a blood debt, and he was damned well going to collect.

The cuirass shifted to accommodate his width, then sealed with a soft hiss. Rance smoothed his hands over the slick, gleaming surface. If he knew combat armor—and he did—this was quite possibly the most expensive suit he'd ever worn. It seemed to weigh no more than a thin tunic and moved with him easily as he twisted his waist and swung his arms.

One thing was for sure; the lady wasn't cheap.

He watched her lift the next section of the suit from its gleaming black case. She rose gracefully and fitted it over his biceps, her long fingers skilled and competent, as if she were no stranger to armor herself.

Rance mentally totaled the imperials she must have spent, between buying him and the armor. He frowned. "Just exactly how much danger are you in?"

Her pretty face went grim. "Enough." She bent and picked up the right bracer. Rance fought not to focus on the curve of her ass.

The last thing he needed right now was a hard-on. "There's a very good armorer on this station," she said in a blatant change of subject. "When Casus told me he had a shifter, I ordered this fabricated. The woman tells me it will change when you do, but you'll want to test that. I don't want any ugly surprises in the event of an ambush."

A dozen questions crowded Rance's tongue, but he kept his mouth shut. He needed to play the obedient slave until Lady Selan dropped her guard.

Though he hated to contemplate what he'd have to do to this pretty, delicate creature in order to make his escape. She wouldn't want to let him go—and he couldn't let himself be kept.

Lady Selan picked up the groin section and crouched at his feet. He stiffened, suddenly, painfully aware of her face so near his cock. *Don't,* he warned it. *God, don't.*

All she'd have to do is lean forward to take it into her mouth . . .

Groping for a distraction, he said, "You realize Casus is probably recording this?"

Her teeth flashed up at him in a feral smile. "Oh, he tried. I put a stop to it. I've got a pretty good nanosystem."

Rance blinked. "You disabled Casus's cameras? He's not going to like that."

"Do you truly think I care?"

He laughed. "Not really."

But any sense of amusement faded as she paused, green eyes on his cock. The shaft promptly began to lengthen under her attention. He heard her swallow. She leaned forward . . .

And fitted the hip section around his groin. Rance gritted his teeth as it sealed, pressing into his growing erection. The fact that she'd obviously been tempted was no help at all.

"There." She rose to her feet and tilted her head, studying him as he towered over her in a suit that could have stopped a star tank blast. "You look quite formidable."

"I *am* quite formidable."

"We'll see. Now shift. I want to make sure that suit accommodates the change."

Since he wanted to know, too, he sent a mental order to his nanos. The shift surged through him as the 'bots realigned cells, altered bone and muscle and flesh. He shuddered at the hot, familiar pain. The room blurred.

When his sight sharpened again, all his senses seemed to explode to vivid life. He looked down at her. And down even farther, since he was almost half a meter taller now.

She looked so delicate, so fragile. And she smelled deliciously feminine, like distilled sex. Like everything he'd ever craved in a woman.

His kind had been created to protect the colonists of a savage world filled with predators that would have slaughtered an ordinary human, no matter how well-armed. Instincts bred into his every cell drove him to speak despite the dictates of common sense.

"Why did you do that, lady?" His voice emerged in a deep, alien rumble. "Ordering me to transform like that? I could kill you before you even had time to activate your collar."

There was a hint of icy warning in her smile. "I think you underestimate just how fast I really am."

He doubted that. "You shouldn't take such risks."

"Perhaps." Selan shrugged. "My father used to say you never know whether you can trust a man unless you give him a chance to betray you. It's better to watch what he does than be unpleasantly surprised when you're not expecting it."

Rance stared at her, appalled. "This was a test?"

"And lucky you, you passed." Her eyes dropped to the ring on her hand. "My father knew all about betrayal. He was good at it." Pivoting on one booted heel, she started toward the door. "Change back, Mad Dog, and let's go. We have a schedule to meet."

The nickname carried a surprising sting it had never possessed before. "Rance. My name is Rance Conlan."

She gave him a siren smile. "Rance, then."

Grinding his teeth, he let the power roll through him again, then slipped ahead of her like the loyal guard dog he definitely wasn't.

She's playing into my hands, he told himself. *She doesn't know as much about betrayal as she thinks she does.*

The thought left a surprisingly bitter taste in his mouth. Betraying women was for aristos and slavers, not for Freeworlds shifters.

Too bad he didn't have a choice.

THREE

It wasn't easy to keep her mind on business with her body thrumming in a sweet, electric buzz. *I can't afford this kind of distraction,* Zarifa realized with a grim jolt of alarm. *What if Gerik shows up? He'd have me in chains before I saw him coming.*

And yet . . . Her gaze slid up to the shifter's towering shoulders as he preceded her through the door. Yes, she'd needed to test him, but if she were honest with herself, she'd insisted on helping him don his armor simply because she'd wanted to touch him.

His tanned, smooth skin had felt like velvet over steel. And the way his cock had grown under her gaze . . . *Stop it. Get your mind on the job.*

Casus looked up as they walked into his office. He was seated behind an ostentatiously massive desk, his 'borgs flanking him like bookends. As Rance fell into a snappy parade rest just behind her, all three came to full alert. Even the guards looked nervous. And Casus was one deep breath from panic.

Not that she could blame him. Rance had looked intimidating stark naked, but fully armored he was huge, a gleaming human weapon. But it was more than just the armor. He exuded a calm, deadly confidence that nobody in the room had a prayer against him.

Zarifa turned her head to watch as he gave Casus a long, cold look that suggested he was remembering every time the other man had tortured him. He smiled, slow and chilling.

Casus went dead white.

Oh, sweet Lady, Zarifa thought, fighting a panic surge of her own. *Can the nanobots take Rance down before he kills the little idiot?*

If he murdered a man who hadn't attacked her, he was dead. And Zarifa herself would be detained, which meant officials would discover her true identity in short order. Gerik would arrive to haul her back to Throneworld within hours, and everything would be lost.

Just as she started to activate her nanobot control ring, Rance spoke, his deep voice as smooth and courtly as any knight's. "Milady? You said we're on a tight schedule."

He wasn't going to attack. The relief was dizzying. Zarifa managed a nod. "Yes. Yes, we are." She turned to the slaver, who had frozen in his chair like a bird hypnotized by a snake. "I believe that completes our transaction."

"Yes." Casus blinked and swallowed with a visible dip of his Adam's apple. "Yes, fine. Your funds have transferred. Take him."

Rance didn't even give the man a second look as he walked from the room. Suppressing a relieved grin, Zarifa followed him down the corridor past the slave cells and out into the space station beyond.

C asus slumped as the outer door closed behind Mad Dog and his aristo bitch. Sweat slicked his underarms beneath his expensive velvet jacket, and his heart hammered like a volehare's. For a moment there, he'd thought the fucker was going to tear him apart.

But then, Casus had been having nightmares about wolf fangs sinking into his flesh since he'd acquired the hulking bastard three months ago. Doing favors for the regent could be lucrative, but sometimes it wasn't exactly safe.

He turned toward Aaren, the chief of his guards. "Did you get past Selan's image shield?"

The big man shook his head. "I couldn't crack her system defenses. Hell, I couldn't even get proper readings on her true height and weight, much less what her face looks like."

Casus felt his jaw drop. A former stellar guard, Aaren could make a slave's nanos dance to his tune like no one else. "Why the seven hells not?"

"I can't be sure because of her shielding, but I suspect she's got an Imperial Combat-grade nanosystem. Those bastards are designed to be unhackable." He frowned. "But an aristo courier wouldn't have a system like that. I'd expect her to top out around a Nova grade. And I've hacked those before."

"Think she's military? Maybe some kind of special ops

agent?" Though everyone had nanos—for communication and emergency healing if nothing else—it was illegal for civilians to possess the same systems the Empire's warriors used to enhance their speed and strength.

"Could be, but I've met elite forces soldiers before, and she's a little too jumpy. The lady does ice bitch aristo better than anybody I've ever seen, but there's just a hint of fear underneath. I think she's running from somebody—and it's not some corporate rival after whatever file she's carrying."

Casus came to full alert, smelling the profit of his dreams. "You think she's the fugitive?" The one whose name they dared not even mention.

The guard shrugged. "Maybe."

"All right." Casus drummed his fingers nervously on his desk. "I'd better report in. Just in case."

"That would be wise," Aaren said in such a mild tone that Casus knew he'd damned well better get on the comm to Throneworld.

I t was midshift on Market Station, and the main concourse was crowded with shoppers. Spacers and elaborately dressed aristos strolled along under the massive transparent dome, while tourists stopped to gape upward, shameless in their awe. Rance couldn't blame them. Overhead, the Cordovo Nebula gleamed against the black of space like a woman's silk scarf, a shimmering veil of purple and red dotted with gemstone stars.

The view inside the concourse wasn't nearly that elegant. Merchants pushed massive antigrav carts displaying wares from a hundred worlds. Spidersilk in countless shades, robot toys that pranced and sang, even spices from the Freeworlds that gave Rance a pang of homesickness. A naked slave girl danced in front of one of the dealer shops, her voice musical and lilting as she invited passersby to sample her wares. Yet despite her bright smile, there was desolation in her eyes.

Fucking aristos.

Selan glanced at the girl as they passed, and a spasm of pity—and oddly, shame—crossed her face. Pity he could understand, but what the hell did she have to be ashamed of? She hadn't made the girl a slave.

Frowning, Rance eyed his new mistress, then turned to scan the surrounding crowd with all his senses, both wolf and nano. He spotted no one who seemed to have an assassin's unhealthy interest in her.

Good. Still, he didn't dare relax.

As they'd left Casus's shop, Selan had returned most of his nanobot functions to his control, which said a great deal about how much danger she thought she was in.

"You know," Rance said aloud, "I'd find it a lot easier to protect you if I knew what I was protecting you from."

Selan shot him a cool look, one hand riding the hilt of her sword. "Not here. Once we get to the ship, I'll brief you."

"Yes, mistress."

She lifted a brow, no doubt detecting the edge of sarcasm in his voice. He hid a wince, half expecting her to give him a nanobot jolt for his impertinence. Instead she went back to scanning the surrounding crowd, tension visible in the set of her slim shoulders. *She may be paranoid, but at least she's not a bitch.*

It might have been easier if she were.

Still, bitch or not, nanos or no, he had to escape. He had a traitor to kill, and he needed to warn Kuarc Lorezo about the mole in his organization. God knew how much damage the spy had done to the Rebellion.

Rance frowned in worry at the thought. He'd known Kuarc for years and considered him a friend. Though an aristo, he'd sworn to abolish slavery once he became emperor. Which was why Conlan Shipping had been providing his rebels with weaponry and armor for the past ten years.

It was damned sure Kuarc would make a better ruler than his drunken excuse for a sister. As far as Rance could tell, the only thing Zarifa Lorezo had going for her was that she was legitimate while her brother wasn't. Yet the man they called the Bastard was far more honorable.

So if Rance had to hurt Selan to escape, there really was no choice. Friendship, honor, and his own thirst for revenge gave him no alternative.

On the other hand, I could always seduce her . . . The thought came from out of nowhere, with the particular ring of something that had been percolating in the back of his mind for a while. Rance blinked, then narrowed his eyes in interest.

Seduction had always been an effortless skill for him. Women were fascinated by shifters, who had a reputation for animal sexuality and inhuman endurance.

Unfortunately, though sex came easily, romance was a bit more difficult. An arms-smuggling run to the Empire might be profitable for Rance, his company, and his crew, but it also meant months away from home. More than one of his partners had fallen in love with someone else by the time he returned.

Still, Rance knew women, and he knew Selan wanted him every bit as much as he did her. He could get her into bed, romance her, make her care about him. With a little patience, he might even be able to convince her to let him go.

And if that didn't work, he could always get ruthless.

G erik Natalo stalked into his father's privy chamber, the heels of his boots clicking on the gleaming gemstone tiles.

He found the regent crouched over his royal compdesk like a heron hunting in the shallows of a swamp, long nose pointed downward, narrow face fiercely intent as he stared at screens of data.

Umar Natalo was almost as tall as Gerik himself but weighed a good fifty kilos less, his skin stretched taut over bone and sinew. The shoulders of his black velvet coat were padded in a vain attempt to make him look as if he had some meat on his frame. Black lace spilled around his narrow hands, and a ruby gleamed like a pool of blood on his intricate black cravat. The dark, rich clothing only called attention to his pale skin, making him look rather like a vampire from some ancient myth. Which, knowing Umar, was probably his intention.

The regent didn't even look up when Gerik came to attention before his battleship of a desk. Gerik wasn't surprised. His father had yet to forgive him for letting Zarifa slip through his fingers.

Well, he'd find her eventually, and she'd pay dearly for humiliating him. They didn't call Gerik the Regent's Fist for nothing.

Waiting for Umar to deign to notice him, Gerik drummed the fingers of his right hand on the hilt of his sword and let his eyes drift around the richly appointed room. It barely missed gaudy with its gilded furniture, red upholstery, and golden statues of naked slaves. Umar's common blood had a way of showing in a certain lack of taste.

It was fortunate Gerik's mother was a member of the royal line. Not only did she compensate for his father's multitude of sins, her ancestry made Gerik an acceptable candidate for Zarifa's hand. At least in the eyes of the nobility.

Zarifa was another matter. The ice bitch hated him—and it was mutual.

"She has been found."

Gerik jolted. "Zarifa?"

His father lifted a coal-black brow under hair styled in an elaborate tumble of black curls. "Is there another fugitive who has escaped you?"

Stung, he glowered. "I'm not the only one she escaped, Father. Have you discovered how she managed to break your control?"

Umar's icy gaze narrowed. "It seems you were right. She has gotten her hands on an Imperial Combat nanosystem."

He'd suspected as much from the way she'd fought, so different from every previous time she'd tried to stand against him. "Have you found out where she got it?"

The regent shrugged. "Black market, no doubt. She had the money for it. I've found evidence she transferred three hundred million imperials out of her personal accounts."

He cursed. "She could have bought a battleship with that much cash."

"Among other things. It seems she's also purchased a certain werewolf slave."

"Conlan?" Gerik ground his teeth. "I told you we should have had that bastard killed!"

"And I felt slavery was a far more galling punishment."

"No, you were just looking to line your pockets!"

"Watch your tongue!"

Gerik subsided, glaring at his father. "I don't understand how she even managed the independence to have the system installed to begin with. When did she break your control?"

Umar shrugged and leaned back in his massive thronelike chair. "The money transfer was three weeks ago. One assumes just before that."

"On her birthday." Gerik raked his hands through his hair and gave it a frustrated jerk. "Must have been one of the gifts."

"Probably. There were several things her father's will specified she receive when she reached her majority."

Gerik glowered. "And you *allowed* that?"

Umar drummed his ringed fingertips on his desk. "Apparently the emperor's lawyer was more determined than I expected."

"Have the bastard killed."

"Oh, I did."

A new thought struck him, drew his belly into a sick knot. "Do you think she knows?"

Umar shrugged. "We must assume so."

"If she tells the Bastard—"

"She won't get the opportunity." His father's voice was hard and icy.

"She'd damned well better not. Where is she now? I'll—"

"You'll stay right here." Umar's voice could snap like a slaver's whip when it suited him. "I have put a plan into action. We'll have her back in hand shortly. In the meantime, you will best serve me here. The Bastard is planning something—I can almost smell it on the wind." His long nose twitched, as if catching Kuarc Lorezo's scent.

"Don't worry about Kuarc." Gerik's hand tightened on his sword. "I'll deal with him."

Umar lifted that brow again. "You'd better. If you fail this mission, my son, there will be no others."

FOUR

Zarifa could feel Mad Dog walking behind her, pacing like a great animal. Something about him seemed to broadcast raw sex. She could feel his intense sensuality in every hair that stood on the back of her neck, in the nipples that rose to hard, tingling attention, in the tension that clenched between her thighs.

We're going to make love. Then she corrected the thought with the brutal self-honesty her father had taught her: *No, we're going to fuck.*

The idea shimmered in her mind, dancing on the waves of heat that surged in her blood. It had been six years since she'd known a man's touch, six years since she'd dared risk the fumbling rush and furtive pleasure of sex. After watching her lover's execution for treason, she'd had no taste for risking another man's life. Not when Umar had made it so viciously clear that he'd do anything to control her and keep his grip on power.

A grip she was damned well going to break. Escaping him and his son had been only the first stage of the plan. There would be more to do later, but for now she was free—free to sample her seductive Mad Dog.

Unfortunately, she had no idea how to go about it. Asking him to make love to her seemed a bit too bald, but her personal experience didn't extend to seduction.

Still wrestling with the problem, Zarifa led the way down the vast, echoing corridor that was the Gamma Deck, past the endless rows of airlocks that led to umbilical docking tubes. Each tube held a ship at a precise distance from Market Station. Some of the tubes were scarcely wide enough for two people to walk abreast, while others—those for cargo vessels—were as big around as some ships.

Spotting the 'lock she wanted, Zarifa sent it a silent message through her nanobot communication system. "This is my ship," she told Rance as the thick door slid open with a chirrup of greeting.

They stepped inside and paused, waiting for the airlock to cycle and let them out into the tube. She stole a glance up at her slave's stern profile. He looked grim and tough, more wary warrior than sex toy.

He met her eyes. Heat leaped between them like a flame, so searing she had to catch her breath. He studied her, his eyes wolf-fierce, with an elemental hunger that had nothing to do with sub-mission and everything to do with pure, male demand.

The airlock slid open, breaking the hot tension. He stepped through as Zarifa followed.

He stopped just inside to stare around at the cramped passage-way with an experienced eye. "This is a Phoenix class transport, isn't it?" In contrast to the sexual heat he'd exuded a moment be-fore, the question was sharp, clipped, thoroughly in professional bodyguard mode.

"Yes." She watched curiously as he prowled the corridor. "How can you tell?"

"My family owns Conlan Shipping. We had a Phoenix class or two."

"So you're a trader?"

"I'm a captain." He shot her a defiant look, as if expecting her to remind him he was only a slave now. When she said nothing, he relaxed. "I am surprised your company assigned you a Phoenix class, though." The model was notoriously underpow-ered and slow, which made it an unlikely choice for a courier ves-sel. "Any armament?"

"Definitely. She isn't your average Phoenix class." Zarifa rat-tled off weapons systems and engine enhancements until Rance's brows began to climb.

"Sounds like the previous owner was a smuggler."

She grinned toothily. "Does sound like it." He looked in-trigued as she turned to lead the way toward the bridge. "Wel-come to the *Empire's Hope*."

W ho *was* after his new mistress? And who the hell was she, anyway? He studied her as she led him through the cramped confines of her little ship with every evidence of pride. Each time he thought he had her pegged, she morphed on him like a Drago chameleon, changing shape and color and mood, keeping him constantly off balance.

"Lady Selan," my ass. That's not her name. Hell, that's probably

not even her face. A good nanosystem could create a three-dimensional disguise image to make you look like anybody. Or for that matter, anything.

Was she really a courier? True, that *was* a job aristos sometimes gravitated to—usually bored and adventurous younger daughters and sons without the prospect of inheriting. But somehow he had trouble picturing her as some company's minor underling. She had too much authority in her manner.

Besides, she hadn't hesitated to drop two million imperials on a werewolf slave, which didn't suggest a minor anything.

Could be a government agent, though, in which case he'd better watch his step. Or one of Kuarc's spies. She was certainly idealistic enough.

He needed to get her talking if he wanted to find out which she was. The seduction he'd been contemplating sounded like a great place to start.

M ad Dog was making her nervous. From the moment they'd stepped aboard, he'd been watching her like one of his furry brethren staring at a particularly fat fawn gamboling in the forest.

Why in the Lady's sweet name had *anyone* thought they could make that man a slave?

Zarfia sat in her control chair, fighting to concentrate with Rance sitting next to her in the copilot's seat. Her hands rested on the manual controls, ready to dance if the autos failed. She'd linked her nanosystem with the *Empire's Hope*'s computer in order to guide the transport out of dock.

Three months before, she would have had no idea what to do—but that was before she'd upgraded. Her new nanobot combat system had taught her the piloting skills she'd needed to make her escape.

Now the three-dimensional control display flashed bright blue and green as it orbited their seats. Its stylized schematics showed the other ships clustered around Market Station's docking arms. And she knew exactly what to do.

Zarifa guided the *Hope* around a massive passenger liner then veered away from a speedy little courier less than half the transport's size. It took more than an hour of nerve-racking navigation to clear Market Station's traffic, then zip up beyond the orbital disc of the surrounding star system and into empty space.

Clearance from station command came minutes later, and she punched into super-C.

The engines didn't so much howl as thrum, in a subsonic growl felt more in the base of the brain stem than the ears. For an instant, reality slid sideways with a nauseating little jolt. Everything acquired a rainbow aura . . .

And then they were through into superspace, and the auras vanished, along with that nasty little psychic thrum. She sighed in relief.

"Nice piloting." There was something in his voice, a note of experience, that told her he knew exactly what he was talking about. But then, a merchant captain would.

Zarifa blinked. Whenever she emerged from an intense flight session, there was always a moment of disorientation, like waking from a particularly vivid dream. Rance waited patiently while she brought her consciousness back to the here and now. "Thank you."

He rose from the copilot's seat, all gleaming armor and male strength. "Think you'll need to link again, or are you free for the next few hours?"

"I'm free." She scrubbed both hands over her face. "The ship's comp will be piloting until we reach our destination."

"And how long will that take?"

Zarifa shrugged. "About three weeks, assuming we don't encounter any ugly surprises." Like the Fist, looking to drag her back to Throneworld.

"Good." A wicked smile curved his lips. Armored hands closed over her shoulders and pulled her gently from her pilot's chair. Drew her full against smooth, cool nanotium. "I know just the way to occupy our time."

Surprise had her stiffening. Slave that he was, she hadn't expected him to be so bold.

He hesitated for just a heartbeat, reading her eyes. *Making sure I'm willing* . . . She caught her breath and licked her dry lips.

His eyes followed her tongue. Flared like molten gold.

Despite his sudden aggression, there was nothing of the marauder in his kiss. His lips were warm, surprisingly soft, sweetly seductive, a gentle wooing of lip and tongue.

This bore no resemblance to the clumsy boy's kisses she'd known from her lover or even the rape of the mouth Gerik had always practiced. Rance dazzled, enticed with every soft brush and lick, with every gentle breath.

He went on kissing her, slowly, patiently, as his armored hands came to rest on her waist. Not grinding her against him but holding her in a lover's clasp. It was more like something she'd seen in an entertainment simmie than anything she'd ever known in real life.

Zarifa found herself relaxing into the kiss, opening for the soft petition of his tongue along the seam of her mouth. He tasted of mint mouth cleanser, but under that was something dark and wild, a hint of forest and rain.

Impossibly delicious. And just as dangerous.

She kissed like a virgin. Sweet, untutored, a little unsure, yet with a delicious, trembling need that made him rock hard inside his armor.

He was breathing hard by the time he lifted his head. "I think," Rance said hoarsely, "we're both overdressed."

Her eyes went wide as he pulled off his gauntlets. They made a heavy, metallic sound when he dropped them on the deck.

He reached for the tie of her cravat, and she froze, watching him with those big, lovely eyes. Her lips parted, tempting him with the thought of kissing her again. He could easily learn to crave her taste.

Fighting his body's clawing demand for haste, he slowly untied the length of white lace from around her slender throat. He tossed it across the copilot's chair and reached for the gold buttons marching down the front of her scarlet jacket. As each button popped free, a bit of thin silk shirt appeared beneath it, warm and fragrant from her body.

He was dying to taste her. To bury his face against the elegant curve of her lovely breasts, take her nipples into his mouth. Savor each silken centimeter.

It had been months since he'd had a woman. Dehumanizing months of deprivation and torture, of grinding frustration and humiliation.

God, he needed this. He needed *her*.

The tiny pearl buttons of her blouse parted, revealing a thin lace chemise. Rance resisted the impulse to simply rip it in two. Instead, he drew it over her head and let it slide from his hands.

She looked up at him, biting her full lower lip, as if uncertain of his reaction. As if he could feel anything but desire at the sight of her perfection.

Her breasts were sweet and pale and curving, tipped by pretty pink nipples, furled tight with her hunger. They reminded him of candy.

"You're beautiful," Rance told those hesitant green eyes.

As shy pleasure filled her gaze, he reached for her. Her skin felt as soft and fine as the silk he'd just stripped away. Her breasts rode high on her narrow torso, not quite large enough to fill his hands. He stroked a thumb over one velvet nipple and watched it rise and peak even more, silently begging for his mouth.

He bent and licked it. Swirled his tongue over the fine-grained nubbin. Suckled.

Her moan was the sweetest thing he'd ever heard.

FIVE

Zarifa grabbed for Rance's shoulders as he picked her up as easily as if the gravity had been cut. He laid her down on the pilot's chair and seized one of her boots in those big, strong hands. Tugging it off, he dropped it with a thump and attacked the other boot with equal determination. It hit the deck an instant later, and he went after her skintight trousers.

She watched him, dizzy with rising excitement. He still wore full armor, and every time he moved, light rolled over the shining nanotium like water. There was something shockingly erotic about being naked when he was dressed like an invading conqueror.

His hard, angular face wore an expression of feral hunger, yet his strong hands were careful and warm as he stripped away her trousers.

Zarifa shivered. She could feel herself tightening, growing slick and eager.

Finally he stepped back and just looked, towering over her with that blatant male lust in his eyes.

Zarifa licked her lips. "You're still dressed."

He lifted a dark brow. "Does my mistress command me to strip?"

Her mouth felt dry as sand. "I want to see you."

"You saw me." His gaze went a little distant.

Naked. Collared. Humiliated. "No. I want to see you as you are."

It was the right thing to say. A faint smile curled his lips as he reached for the seal of his cuirass.

Zarifa watched, aching, as he removed each piece and set it aside with a warrior's care for his equipment. She caught her breath at what he revealed: the long flex and play of his torso as he bent, the powerful bunch of biceps and triceps, the ripple of thigh and calf.

And the thick jut of his cock, brash and male and eager. There was nothing subservient in that demanding thrust, in its long satin length, flushed dark rose with need. His balls were full and drawn delightfully tight, dusted in the same silken hair that snaked in a line up his belly to form a cloud over his chest.

"You're beautiful." The words escaped her without her conscious intent.

A flash of discomfort lit his eyes, but instead of denying it, he inclined his head. "Thank you."

She couldn't help but smile. "I know this isn't the first time a woman's told you how handsome you are."

He grinned. "Well, no. But I have noticed they're always naked at the time."

"So they're, what? Under the influence of your powers of seduction?"

"Something like that." Rance moved closer to the pilot's seat and dropped to his knees. "I have a face like a z-boxer, and I know it."

Before she could object to the description, he caught her ankles and draped them over his brawny shoulders. Zarifa gaped, bracing on her elbows to look at him. "What are you . . . ?"

"What do you think?" He dipped his head with a white and wolfish grin. The first dancing stroke of his tongue across her outer lips almost catapulted her out of the pilot's chair.

Even as she cried out, he did something to the chair controls, leaning the seat back while keeping the leg rest tucked tight. Then he scooped his long fingers under her backside and lifted her into his mouth.

And feasted.

There was really no other word for the slick dance of his tongue over and around her inner flesh, for the way his teeth gently caught her clit, her labia.

Her first lover had attempted to give her this pleasure, but it hadn't felt anything like this. Delight seared her with every wet tongue flick, each lazy circle and stroke. Her legs tightened convulsively over his back. He made a low, rough sound of satisfaction.

Something probed her opening, slid inside. She writhed, gasping helplessly, her hands grabbing for him, fingers tangling in the thick silk of his hair. He pumped that single finger deeper and swirled his tongue around her clit, laughing deep in his throat as she yelped.

"How's that, mistress?" There was just a trace of mockery in that last word, but Zarifa didn't care.

"Oh, sweet Lady!" She clenched her eyes shut against the storming pleasure. "More!"

"Your wish"—he nibbled gently—"is my command."

As he slowly plunged a finger in and out in that maddening tease, his free hand found her breast, cupped her in warm strength, tugged and stroked her nipples. Pleasure rushed through her in a burning tide that had her muscles twitching. She tightened her grip on his hair, clinging. Drowning.

And intoxicated.

R ance loved the way she felt writhing against his mouth, her long, slender body arching under his hands.

His. She might own him, but just now, he owned her. Her body danced to his tune, her breathless voice begged for the pleasure only he could give.

He was hard as stone.

"Mad Dog," she moaned, rolling her hips against his face. "Sweet Lady, please!"

He lifted his head, suddenly hating that name with a passion. "Rance. My name is Rance."

"Rance! Rance, you drive me insane!" There was a note of genuine desperation in her voice that had him grinning in dark pleasure.

Oh, yeah. She was his. Taking his time, he savored her, enjoyed every whimper, every twitch of long, muscled legs, every roll of her hips. He cupped her breast with his free hand, squeezing and teasing her nipple, driving her hunger higher and higher.

She jerked, making a desperate, pleading sound.

And he could take no more. He had to have her.

Now.

In one hungry move, he pulled away from her, grabbed her slender hips, and lifted her. She gasped an incoherent protest, but he'd already moved between those long legs. Catching his aching cock in one hand, he positioned himself at the opening of her sex.

That first thrust was a long, liquid slide that tore a shout from his mouth. She cried out in chorus and convulsed. Her legs wrapped around his butt in a fiercely strong clasp.

Bracing one arm against the back of the chair, he began rolling his hips, grinding hard, taking her. Enjoying the hot, creamy clasp on his cock.

And as he rode her, he watched her face, loving the way she threw her head back in ecstasy. Loving the blushing curve of her mouth as she gasped in time to his thrusts.

Mine.

It was an irrational thought, and he knew it. She wasn't his, couldn't be his. He didn't even know who she was, what kind of game she was playing.

And yet his body, buried deep inside hers, insisted this was just where he was supposed to be. And God, it was so sweet.

Rance closed his eyes, letting the burning delight take him, feeling it pulse and tighten in his balls. On the verge of spilling over.

She cried out sharply and convulsed. He opened his eyes to watch her orgasm flood her. Her tiny inner muscles drew tight around his cock, each delicate convulsion sending another jolt right to his balls.

The convulsion took him by surprise, tumbling him with a bellow into climax.

Mine, that primal something roared in his head, caring nothing for logic. *Mine!*

Long minutes went by before he recovered enough to drag himself off her, pick her up, and take her place in the pilot's seat. She moaned in sleepy protest but subsided as he arranged her across his lap. Slender arms wrapped around his neck, and she nestled her face against the underside of his jaw.

Rance sighed and wrapped his own sweating arms around her. He let himself relax, float in the aftermath.

God, how could he have forgotten how damn good this felt? After so many weeks of helplessness and humiliation, it was delicious being a man again. Being treated as a man again.

The sweet pleasure lay on him as weightless and dreamy as a feather spinning in the breeze. Until she spoke.

"Mad Dog? I mean, Rance?"

"Hmm?" He wished she'd settle down and let them both sleep.

"I think it's time to tell you what's happening. Why I need you. What I'll give you for helping me."

He jolted from the sweet lassitude and opened one wary eye, then lifted his head to look down at her. His muscles grew taut. "I'm listening."

She took a deep breath. "My name isn't really Lady Selan. This isn't even really my face. My nanos are broadcasting a simmie disguise."

"I suspected something like that." He studied her cautiously. "So who are you?"

"That's . . . a long story. It would be easier to show you." Then, as he watched, change spilled across her face. It wasn't a big change—largely the color of her hair and eyes. The shape of her nose, the curve of her mouth, the high, proud angle of her cheekbones remained the same.

Yet the instant her hair went to blazing flame red and her eyes a deep violet, a sense of disorientation rolled over him. Rance knew that face. He'd seen it on news documentaries and entertainment simmies so many times, it was branded on his consciousness.

"Zarifa," he breathed. "You're Empress Zarifa Lorezo."

Fury spilled over him in a blazing wave. She'd played him for a fool.

Zarifa knew that look. Recognition. Contempt. She'd seen it so many times on so many faces.

She'd hoped a Freeworlds werewolf wouldn't be quite so informed about Empire gossip, but apparently she was juicy news even light-years away. So much so that he'd instantly forgotten how she'd kept Casus from torturing him.

"So this was a game after all." Rance's voice was cold, distant. His arms dropped from around her. "You were never in any danger."

Bitter disappointment rolled over her, so intense she itched to slap his arrogant face for it. She rolled off his lap and started gathering her clothes. "I assure you, Mad Dog . . ." She used the name with a sneer. ". . . I'm not playing games."

He didn't bother to rise as he watched her. "Why would a woman with her own palace guard need the protection of a shifter slave?" It was obvious he thought this was another drunken, scandalous lark, the kind Throneworld's simmie reporters adored.

The kind Umar regularly ensured she supplied.

"Maybe it's the palace guard I need protecting from." Zarifa jerked on her shirt and buttoned it with hands that shook with temper. She should be used to this now. And to a certain extent, she was. An hour ago, it wouldn't have bothered her to see that look in Rance's eyes.

But that had been before she'd made love to him. Experienced his breathtaking tenderness. Felt almost as if he'd cared.

Why in the hell did I ruin it? But he'd had to know what they faced, and she'd been afraid if she waited much longer, she'd lose the courage to tell him.

"Your own guards tried to kill you? Why didn't you tell Umar?" His lip curled when he said the regent's name.

"Because they do what Umar tells them to do." His face went so stony with disbelief, she swore and snatched up her pants. "I don't have the patience for this. Do you want to be free or not?"

Rance blinked, surprise replacing contempt. *Didn't see that coming, did you?* Golden eyes narrowed in suspicion. "You'd free me? Why?"

Because I know what it's like to be a slave. Not that he'd believe her. "I need to get back to Throneworld and meet with Kuarc Lorezo." She jerked her trousers over her hips and buttoned them, then grabbed the nearest boot and sat down on the copilot's chair to put it on. "I've got some information he needs. Your job is to protect me from the regent's men while I find him."

Rance rose from the pilot's chair and stared down at her, big fists braced on his naked hips. "You expect me to believe you want to help the Bastard—when you're the one he's rebelling against?"

She jerked the boot on and grabbed its mate. "Umar's the one he's rebelling against."

"And if your brother kills you, Umar's screwed. His son loses his chance to be emperor, Kuarc takes over, and the first thing he'll do is order the regent's execution."

Was that an expression of actual concern for her on that hard, wolfish face? *Probably thinks he'll die trying to keep me alive.* "Kuarc won't kill me."

"He can't afford to do anything else."

She remembered the laughing older boy she'd adored as a child. "My brother's not a murderer." Standing, she stomped to settle the boots on her feet.

Rance watched her, his expression impatient. "There's a war on, Zafira. Killing's what war is all about."

Zarifa bent forward and stared hard into his eyes. "So keep me alive and get me to him, and I'll emancipate you. I'll strip the control codes off your nanosystem and issue an imperial decree making you a free man. You can go home to all the other werewolves and forget any of this ever happened. Even kick Casus's ass on the way home."

"If you live that long." His blatant sneer told her he didn't believe a word out of her mouth.

"You'd better make sure I do. Or *you* will die a slave." Unable to take any more, Zarifa turned toward the door. Before she stalked out, she snapped, "Go take a shower. You smell like sex."

So did she. And she refused to let it hurt.

SIX

Naked, Rance left the bridge and stalked aft, looking for the head. Her Imperial Highness was right; he needed a shower. What the hell kind of game was she playing?

Assuming she was playing a game at all. He couldn't reconcile the woman who'd come to his defense against Casus with the feckless party girl he'd always believed Zarifa to be.

And why was she so determined to talk to Kuarc? What information could be so important that she'd risk her life to communicate it? And why not just get on the comm and call the man? Going to him in person virtually ensured she'd end up dead or a hostage, and there was damned little one werewolf could do to protect her.

Unless she was trying to set some kind of elaborate trap, with herself as bait. Which, frankly, struck him as nothing short of stupid.

Even if Kuarc didn't kill her, the regent was going to be out for her blood. Whatever she had to tell the Bastard was guaranteed to be something Umar wanted kept secret. He'd send every man he had after her.

Frowning, Rance found the ship's main head and walked in, rubbing at the ache he could feel growing between his eyes. A transparent cylindrical shower stall occupied the center of the room, and he headed for it. Its door slid open, and he stepped inside. "Ship, full jets, thick foam, thirty-eight degrees Celsius."

Hot soapy water sprayed from the stall's countless tiny nozzles, hitting his body from all directions. Rance sighed in pleasure. He'd had nothing but sonic showers since his capture, and he'd missed the pounding heat of real water.

He'd missed so many things.

An image flashed through his mind: Zarifa's slim body rising against his, meeting his thrusts with an endearing, clumsy eagerness. Rance frowned. She certainly hadn't made love like the borderline slut she was reputed to be. More like someone who was all but a virgin.

Which made no sense at all. The media had linked her to countless men, including her fiancé, Gerik Natalo, the regent's son. A woman like that would know her way around a man's body. Why would she pretend otherwise?

Rance stayed in the shower, brooding, until the nozzles started blowing hot, dry air over his skin, sending his hair whipping in the miniature windstorm.

By the time he stepped out, he was clean and dry again. No trace of Zarifa's scent remained on his body. To his surprise, he found himself regretting the loss.

He padded into the next room, which turned out to be the captain's quarters. Zarifa's, judging by the suit of female armor that stood in one corner.

Again, the room wasn't what he'd expected. Instead of clothes strewn over every surface, the cabin was as neat as a nun's cell and about that stark. A bunk barely wide enough for one curved from the deck, covered in a walnut veneer that gleamed softly under the overhead lights. The bed had been made with such obsessive neatness, he could have bounced a gold imperial off the dark blue spread.

A matching desk and chair occupied the opposite corner from the suit of armor, both seeming to grow organically from the deck in curving walnut shapes. In the center of the room hung a simmie globe, currently projecting a superspace image of streaming stars in a rainbow of colors.

Rance ignored the globe in favor of the suit of armor, which featured the same striking red and black color scheme as his own. The chief difference was the heraldic coat of arms that marked the suit's right shoulder. Though the imperial arms featured a lion gripping a starship between its paws, this design was unfamiliar: a dragon rampant on a field of stars.

"Ship," he said aloud. "Whose coat of arms is that?"

"The arms of House Lorezo."

Not the kind of suit you'd wear in an effort to hide who you were, then. So why not wear the imperial arms?

A flash of gold along the suit's right glove caught Rance's attention, and he crouched for a better look. Something was written up the length of the gauntlet in a language he suspected was Latin; like their nineteenth-century role models, the aristos were big on ancient languages. "Ship, translate the sentence on her glove."

" 'I will no longer endure dishonor.' "

Interesting. "Is that the motto of House Lorezo?"

"No."

Rance straightened from his crouch and turned to sit down on the bunk. If the empress took exception to his making free with her cabin, he'd find out soon enough.

In the meantime, he intended to make the most of the opportunity. "Ship, display the most recent media file concerning Empress Zarifa Lorezo." The Empire's media reported on every move she made with an obsessive interest.

Two gossiporters appeared in the simmie globe, clad in velvet and lace in cheerfully eye-straining colors.

"Any word on our party girl empress, Corvin?" the female of the pair inquired brightly. Her eyes were surrounded by an intricate pattern of glittering blue face paint that shimmered against her pale skin.

"According to the palace, she's in deep seclusion preparing for her wedding to the regent's son, Gerik Natalo." Corvin, a burly man in lime-green stripes, gestured with beefy fingers. An image appeared: Zafira, standing next to a hulking man who wore his long blond hair tied back in a club.

Despite his massive, powerful build, her escort dressed like a fop, in dark purple silk with black lace spilling around his wide cuffs. There was cruelty in the sharp lines of his face, and his eyes looked too small, despite the eyeliner apparently intended to enhance them.

"They're a gorgeous couple, aren't they?" the woman said, her smile blinding.

"Not really," Rance muttered. Zarifa's expression was flat, almost doll-like compared to her normal intelligence and animation, and her smile looked strained. She might be engaged to Natalo, but she didn't seem to like it.

"Maybe Lord Natalo can get some of her more outrageous behavior under control," Corvin sniffed.

Yet another image flashed on screen: Zarifa, laughing hysterically, staggering as she climbed over the lip of a marble fountain. The spray splattered over her, dancing off her neck and shoulders.

"That's cold!" she yelped, jumping up and down under the pattering water as it quickly soaked through her thin clothes.

Bouncing in dizzy circles, she grabbed the hem of her silk shirt and jerked it off over her head before throwing it aside with a whoop. Her naked breasts quivered, white and full under the lights of the city square.

"Well, it *was* the empress's twenty-fifth birthday," the woman gossiporter trilled. "In accordance with her father's will, she'll officially take the reins of power this year on Our Lady's Day."

Corvin laughed. "Lady help us all. Good thing she'll be marrying Lord Natalo the same day. She won't have time to do much damage."

The globe went black as the words "End File" flashed up.

Rance frowned and lay back on the bed, crossing his bare feet at the ankle. "Next file."

The next story featured Zarifa sunbathing naked on a Throneworld beach, her red hair not quite covering her lovely backside. The gossiporters made all the appropriate sounds of scandalized titillation.

The third file was an interview she'd apparently conducted while under the influence. She kept giggling, and she couldn't seem to construct a coherent answer to the gossiporter's questions.

"Freeze image," Rance snapped.

Zarifa cut off in midgiggle. Despite the silly grin on her face, there was something different going on in her eyes, something that had caught his attention.

Helpless rage and frustration.

It was as if she hated what was coming out of her own mouth, yet she couldn't seem to stop what she was saying.

Rance ran a thumb across his lower lip, staring at the simmie image. Drunk or not, she sounded nothing like the capable, intelligent woman who'd confronted Casus on his behalf. He wouldn't have even known it was the same person.

But what really bothered him was the fact that the empire didn't have freedom of media. If she'd wanted, Zarifa should have been able to censor these broadcasts. God knew Throneworld was quick enough to censor any other media report that was even remotely negative. Yet these stories had been permitted, despite the fact they made the empress look like a drunken slut.

That suggested someone in government wanted her reputation ruined. And there was only one man with that kind of clout: The regent.

The reason for that was obvious. If the public believed their empress was a drug-addicted idiot, nobody would complain when the regent continued to run the government—or when his son married her. What had the gossiporter said? "Good thing she'll be marrying Lord Natalo the same day. She won't have time to do much damage."

"And if she dies in a tragic, drunken accident six months after the wedding, no one will ask too many questions," Rance said aloud.

"You put that together fast," Zarifa said from the doorway. "I have advisers who still have no clue, even after all these years."

Apparently she'd taken advantage of one of the ship's other heads. She was dressed in a one-piece, dark blue uniform, stark and plain compared to the red hunting jacket she'd worn to buy him. Even so, the suit made the most of her lean, intensely female body.

He watched as she walked in and sat on the bed beside him. "They've been drugging you, haven't they? You're not the type to play into their hands by drugging yourself."

She snorted. "The regent didn't have to drug me. He controlled my nanosystem."

Nanos could induce intoxication, even hallucinations, without any drug use at all. It wasn't unusual for people to become addicted to misusing them.

But to force such intoxication on someone else was supposed to be practically impossible. "How did he hack into your system? You're the empress, for God's sake. Your security should be better than anyone's." Elaborate antivirus and firewalls were a necessity for everyone with a nanosystem. Otherwise an attacker could paralyze or even murder you by having the nanos attack your central nervous system.

"I was fifteen when my parents died and Umar became my guardian." Zarifa stared up at the simmie of her own frozen, enraged face with brooding eyes. "He had my system stripped and reprogrammed so I couldn't defend myself. I've been his puppet ever since."

"He did that to a child?" Rance stared at her, appalled. "Why would your father make a man like that your regent?"

Her laugh was short and bitter. "Lodur had his own questionable secrets. Umar made a profession of keeping them for him."

"He was blackmailing the emperor? With *what*? And why didn't Lodur have him killed?"

She rose restlessly to her feet, rubbing the back of her neck with both hands. "My father wasn't an evil man, Rance. He just wasn't very good."

"Are you going to elaborate on that?"

Zarifa snorted as she began to pace. "Not likely."

Meaning that whatever secret Umar had used to blackmail the old emperor still had power over her. And yet, she'd done all this. Escaped from Umar and his son, bought both this ship and Rance himself. "Umar's not controlling you now, or you wouldn't be here. How did you free yourself?" He remembered the comment she'd made about disconnecting Casus's cameras: *"I've got a pretty good nanosystem."* "You upgraded your nanos. A combat system? Something they can't hack."

She stopped her pacing to shoot him a look. "Good guess."

"Where does Kuarc fit in all this?"

"He's going to be emperor."

Rance shook his head. "The aristos will never let him take the throne, and you know it. He's a bastard."

"But he's a bastard with an army." She smiled grimly. "And I'm going to help him."

Unable to sit any longer, Rance rose to his feet. "Zarifa, I know Kuarc. He's a friend of mine. He believes you were involved in your father's death, and he's sworn to kill you for it."

She stopped pacing to stare at him. "He honestly believes that ridiculous conspiracy theory? For the Lady's sake, I was fifteen!"

He leaned a shoulder against the nearest bulkhead. "You wouldn't be the first teenage murderer."

"No, I suppose not." Zarifa twisted the diamond on her finger, restlessly turning it back and forth, then sighed and dropped her hand. "I'm going to have to take the chance anyway. Besides, I've set up a meeting with one of his advisers. I think he'll be able to convince Kuarc to see me."

Rance straightened away from the bulkhead and frowned at her. "That may not be a good idea. There's a traitor in Kuarc's organization. That's how I ended up in this damned collar."

She nodded. "Dallon Izac, one of Kuarc's chief lieutenants. Umar got to him last year."

Rance came to full alert. "Dallon Izac—that's the son of a bitch's name?"

She lifted a red brow. "You don't know?"

"He didn't introduce himself. I met the fucker in a bar on

Market Station to arrange delivery of a shipment of weapons. The minute I sniffed him, I knew he was a lying spy. He had that stench."

Zarifa cocked her head, interested. "You can tell someone's lying by smell?"

He nodded. "Werewolf senses. Anyway, he realized I was onto him. Must have seen it on my face. I started to shift, but he shot me with a dart gun before I could take him out. Next thing I knew, Casus was fitting me for a collar."

"Wonder why he didn't just kill you?"

Rance bared his teeth. "Bad judgment."

She laughed. "Oh, I'm sure you'll make him rue the day."

"I will; believe me." Rance frowned and moved over to lean a hip on her desk. "In the meantime, I need to get to Kuarc and warn him about that bastard. Who knows how much damage Izac's done?"

"More than enough. According to what I've overheard, he's been funneling information to Umar for months." She gave him a reassuring smile. "But don't worry too much. I've already gotten word about him to Kuarc. I just spoke to Edin, my father's cousin, who's also Kuarc's chief adviser. He's skeptical, but he did agree to meet us at one of Kuarc's Thronesystem bases. If I can convince him I'm sincere, he'll arrange a meeting."

Rance grimaced. "Assuming he doesn't decide to kill you first."

SEVEN

Zarifa went off to check the ship's engines, leaving Rance to dress. He ordered the ship to fabricate a dark blue uni in his size and waited until the wall unit produced the one-piece suit and a pair of boots.

Finally, dressed in normal clothing for the first time in months, he went looking for Zarifa.

The *Empire's Hope* was designed with its cargo hold and passenger deck forming a single fat egg shape that hung suspended under the long cylinder housing the super-C engines. The exotic fields the engines generated didn't get along well with the ship's artificial gravity, so the two had to be kept separate.

Rance kicked through the circular hatch into the engine room to see Zarifa floating midway up the vast central pylon in the dimness. Her long red hair waved around her head like a halo as she watched the violent blue crackle of super-C fields inside the neutronium glass tube. The light painted the delicate contours of her face in an otherworldly glow.

With a captain's automatic caution, Rance studied the tube as he kicked off from the hatch and sailed up the length of the core. The energy patterns looked normal—no flashes of scarlet that might indicate a field rupture. "The engines okay?"

"Fine." She didn't look around. "I just like watching them. All that destructive power, all that energy . . ."

Rance caught one of the handholds jutting from the tube and brought his weightless body to a halt. "I know what you mean." Clinging to the handhold, he watched the hot blue and green light dance inside the tube. "It is beautiful—even if it could wipe us out quicker than the fist of God."

Silence fell between them, filled by the low, bone-deep thrum of the generators. Rance turned to watch her watch the fields. Even with him right next to her, there seemed something profoundly alone about her.

No surprise, he thought. *She's been betrayed by everyone she was supposed to be able to trust.*

Even him. He'd made love to her—and promptly turned on her the moment he found out who she was. The thought sent a stinging prickle of guilt through him.

"I keep thinking about my uncle." Her thumb twisted the diamond band around and around on her index finger.

"The one we're supposed to meet?"

"No, not my father's cousin—my father's twin."

A dim memory from some history class reared its head. "Sevan of the Hundred Days."

Zarifa nodded. "He was just five minutes older than Lodur. Raised all his life to be emperor, only to end up murdered by terrorists one hundred days after taking the throne."

Which resulted in her father's becoming emperor instead. Lodur had been dogged by rumors he'd killed his brother all sixteen years of his reign, just as many now whispered that his daughter had been involved in *his* murder.

Rance was contemplating the irony of that when Zarifa said, "Before he became emperor, Sevan fell in love with a commoner."

He looked over at her in surprise, digesting the implications. "I can imagine how well that would have gone over with the aristos."

She snorted, a delicately inelegant sound. "Grandfather would have disinherited him on the spot if he'd known. To tell you the truth, I think that's exactly what Sevan had in mind. He never wanted to be emperor."

"I can't imagine why," Rance said dryly. "Who wouldn't want to live with a target painted on your back?"

"Exactly. But then Granddad died, and there he was. Emperor. He could have both the crown and the woman he loved. And a hundred days later, he was dead. Killed by a sniper on his way home to her."

Rance studied her pensive expression in the dancing light. "You think your father had something to do with it?"

"No, he wouldn't stoop quite that low."

Which begged the question. "So how low would he stoop?"

Zarifa turned in midair to give him a tight smile. "That, my shifter friend, is a bit of knowledge that would get you killed."

"Besides, you don't trust me."

"Oh, I trust you," she said lightly. "I gave you the chance to rip out my throat today, and you didn't take it."

Rance was surprised by how much that stung. "Is that as good as it gets for you? You give somebody the chance to kill you, and they don't?"

Zarifa turned toward the core again. "Depends on the day."

Pure instinct had him catching her by one shoulder and tugging her into his arms. She looked up at him in surprise.

"That shouldn't be good enough for you, Zarifa." Her violet eyes looked dark and mysterious as he lowered his mouth to hers. "It's sure as hell not good enough for me."

She seemed to resist the kiss for a moment, but just as he started to pull away, she moaned. Her body relaxed into his, her arms slipping around his shoulders. Surrendering.

No. Trusting. Despite her hardened royal cynicism, despite the betrayals she'd suffered, for some reason she trusted him.

And God, he hungered for that trust as if it filled an elemental need. Never mind that only hours before, he'd been willing to hurt her in order to escape.

In some dim corner of his consciousness, he wondered what was happening to him. What was she doing to him?

The rest of him didn't care.

Five seconds into the kiss, Zarifa realized something had changed. Rance had made love to her the first time with a seducer's easy skill, but this was different. She could feel it in the faint tremor in his body as he anchored her against him with tender strength.

He kissed her softly, endlessly, then nibbled his way down her chin to the underside of her jaw. She let her head fall back as he tasted her there in tiny, seductive nips.

"Open your suit," he whispered against her skin. He had both hands occupied: one wrapped around her waist, the other hanging on to a handhold to keep them from tumbling in weightlessness.

Zarifa obediently wrapped both legs around his waist and leaned back to find the seal of her uni. His eyes flared as she opened it. He nuzzled the edge of the suit aside and closed his mouth over one nipple, sending an intoxicating sizzle straight to her core.

"Rance," she sighed.

He rumbled deep in his throat, a purr more tiger than wolf. His tongue circled the pink bud, flicked and teased. His teeth raked with such precise delicacy, Zarifa quivered.

She needed to touch him. Had to. Reaching between them as he continued his lazy ministrations to her breasts, she found the seal of his uni and raked a nail down it. The seal parted obediently. Zarifa grabbed the edges of the suit and tugged, but he still held her, and she couldn't get it down his arms. She growled in frustration.

"All right, all right!" With a low, sexy laugh, he let go of his anchoring handhold. They promptly started a weightless tumble. Both legs wrapped around him, Zarifa ignored the spinning room, intent on dragging the suit off.

Rance went to work on hers at the same time, and her elbow clipped his chin as she pulled at a sleeve.

"Ow!"

"Sorry!"

Writhing in midair in a hopeless tangle of clothes, arms, and legs, they only tumbled faster. Rance laughed as he grabbed for her head to keep it from knocking against the side of the core, then yelped as he barked his knuckles on the neutronium glass.

"Are you okay?" She slapped a hand against the glass, trying to slow them down.

"Yeah, but this isn't—ouch!" His shoulder thumped against the housing. With a growl, he shot out a booted foot and kicked, sending them floating away from it. "This isn't one of my more suave seductions."

"You give suave seductions?" Zarifa blinked in mock innocence. "I thought you just kind of pounced and nibbled."

He narrowed his eyes with mock outrage. "I'll show you pouncing!"

Her giggle became a yelp as he ruthlessly jerked her uni down her hips and off her legs, then sent it sailing across the chamber. Before he could grab her again, she released the grip of her legs, kicked against a passing bulkhead, and shot toward the opposite side of the chamber.

Naked, still laughing, she steadied herself with a handhold and watched as he ruthlessly attacked his own uni. Hard muscle rippled as he bent double to drag off his boots, then pulled the suit down his thighs.

"Have I mentioned I love your ass?"

The suit went flying as he gave her a glittering look, braced his bare feet on the bulkhead, and sprang toward her. Zarifa yelped and kicked off, but Rance was more practiced in zero gravity, and he snagged her ankle before she could escape.

"Come here, you." He dragged her into his a

Zarifa pretended to swat at him. "Bad dog!"

"And I'm about to show you exactly how bad." One
found her breast as the other slipped between her thigh
laughter became a gasp as a long finger slid deep.

"I'm not the only one who's bad." His grin turned smugly
wicked. "Your Imperial Highness is wet."

Zarifa reached down and closed her fingers around the thick
length of his cock. "And that's a very nice bone you've got there,
doggy."

His golden eyes narrowed in offense. "Keep it up, and I'll
paddle the royal ass."

Then she stroked, and his eyes went wide and a little dazed.
Deciding to try something she'd seen in one of her more for-
bidden simmies, Zarifa caught his hip and pulled herself down
his body. The rosy head of his erection bobbed, tipped with a
single bead of arousal. Still clinging to him, she licked the little droplet away.

His gasp was so gratifying, she opened her mouth and took
the head inside.

"Zarifa!"

She ignored his strangled cry, far more interested in the velvet
texture of his cock and the long, thick veins snaking up its length.

Rance must have been a veteran of zero-gravity sex, because
he resisted the urge to squirm as she licked and suckled. Instead,
he grabbed two handholds on the side of the core and held his
body rigid. Zarifa rolled her eyes up at him, curious. His eyes
were closed, his lips parted in pleasure.

The sense of power was immediate—and irresistible. She
licked him slowly, loving the way he quivered against her. She
gave him a gentle, testing nibble, and he jerked.

"You're living dangerously, Zarifa." The growl was low,
menacing—and deliciously arousing. She looked up to find his
golden eyes narrowed to feral slits as he stared down at her.

Daring, she took his balls in hand and gently caressed them in
her fingers. He rewarded her with a groan that made her inner
muscles clench in need. God, she wanted him.

And she was going to have him.

Catching hold of his waist with one hand, she pulled herself
into position and wrapped her legs around his thighs. "Oh,
yeah . . ." he purred, rolling his hips. "That's it, darlin'."

Zarifa aimed his cock with her free hand and curled her legs tighter, slowly impaling herself. He felt impossibly hard, impossibly endless as he slid inside one sweet centimeter at a time.

She gasped. "Rance!"

"Yeah." His head rolled back, baring the long, muscled arch of his throat. "Again . . ."

Licking her dry lips, she braced both hands on his chest and pushed off just far enough, then screwed herself back onto him again. "This is hard!" she panted.

He grinned, white and wicked. "You're telling me."

Sex in zero gravity took a lot of effort. If they tried to go too fast, they'd bounce apart, so they had to take it slow.

And it was the single most arousing thing she'd ever experienced in her life.

They surged against each other, hips circling, grinding. Maddening each other with every teasing thrust. Pleasure gathered and pulsed as she watched his face, loving the wild glitter in his eyes, the fine muscles that clenched with effort, the fiercely gritted teeth. Until he arched against her with a shout, spinning her off into fire.

She screamed as she came.

Zarifa curled in his arms, listening to the wild thump of his heartbeat. He'd released his grip on the handholds, and now they floated together lazily. She felt at peace for the first time in . . .

Well, actually she couldn't remember the last time she'd felt this peaceful. It had probably been while her parents were still alive.

With a murmur of contentment, she tightened her hold on his broad back and snuggled down. It would take them another three weeks to get to Thronesystem and the rendezvous with Kuarc's adviser, Edin.

Three weeks. Rance was hers for the next three weeks. After that . . . Well, after that it would be over.

Pushing away that thought, she closed her eyes and tightened her grip on his sweating body.

And basked in the sense of peace she knew would be all too brief.

EIGHT

Zarifa sat back in the pilot's seat with a sigh. Her head ached with the sullen intensity that came from hours of effort. She looked around to find Rance watching her with concern.

"Are we in?"

"We're in."

Around them, the three-dimensional control display showed the asteroids that surrounded the *Empire's Hope*. Some were no bigger than grains of sand, others the size of star liners, but all of them tumbled erratically from frequent collisions. It was probably the most dangerous place for a ship in the Thronesystem, with the possible exception of the core of the local sun.

"I don't like this." Rance studied the display with a dark frown.

"I'm not exactly thrilled myself."

It had been a nerve-racking flight. First they'd come into Thronesystem under heavy shielding to avoid being detected by the Empire's security forces. Next she'd spent three hours maneuvering into the asteroid belt that lay on the outer edge of the system—all that remained of two planets that had collided a couple of billion years before. She'd then had to find the right enormous chunk of rock, match its tumbling spin, locate its hidden airlock, and perform a nightmare of a docking maneuver.

It was a kilometer-long asteroid that was no asteroid, but rather one of the Rebellion's hidden bases. Zarifa had no idea how many such bases Kuarc had, or where they were located, but she figured they'd all be as tough to get to as this one. Otherwise, Umar and the Imperial Marines would have found them by now. Lady knew they'd looked.

Now that the *Hope* was docked, she silently ordered the ship to issue a short-range communication squirt. "*Hope* to Centurion."

The response was instant; he must have been standing over the com. "I see you found the place." Edin sounded so much like her father, it hurt.

"Barely. You folks don't much want visitors, do you?"

"Depends on the visitor. I'm looking forward to seeing you. It's been a long time."

She smiled. "Too long. Where do you want to meet?"

"Come on down the main corridor into the warehouse. We'll talk there. Centurion off."

Zarifa cut the connection and took a deep breath, trying to ignore her stomach's unhappy little jitter. She'd been working for this moment for weeks, but now that it was here, she almost wished she could put it off. So much could go wrong . . .

She turned to find Rance watching her, his gaze all too perceptive. "Zarifa, just stay on the ship. Let me meet with Edin. I'll give him the message, whatever the hell it is. You don't need to—"

"Thank you for the offer, but we both know I can't take you up on it." She swung her legs off the pilot's couch and reached out to cup his cheek. They'd spent the past three weeks talking and making love, and she suspected she now knew him better than she'd ever known anyone in her life. Being protective came as automatically to him as breathing. "This is something I have to do myself. It's a matter of honor."

Frustration flared in his eyes. "Look, *this is a trap*. You know it, I know it—"

"And you seriously think I'm going to send you in alone?"

"I can turn into a two-meter werewolf. I'm a hell of a lot less killable than you are."

"And I'm empress. I know my duty, Rance. If Edin's setting me up, Kuarc will be somewhere around. I'll tell him what I need to tell him, and he'll back off."

"What the hell makes you think that?"

Hanging on to her temper with an effort, she gritted, "Because he won't have a reason to kill me anymore."

"You're assuming he needs one!"

Frustrated with the argument, she stood and fisted her hands on her hips. "Are you going with me or not?"

"Well, I'm sure as hell not letting you go alone." Growling, he got up and stalked toward the airlock.

The base's airlock door opened on a dimly lit corridor that seemed to have been cut through the asteroid's rock with a laser. Zarifa started to step through the 'lock, but Rance grabbed her armored wrist. She stopped and looked up at him, her violet gaze questioning. He'd shifted to werewolf form, so she looked even more delicate to him than usual.

"Let me check it out first," he told her.

She frowned, looking along the corridor. "My nanosystem sensors aren't picking up anything."

"Neither are mine, but my wolf senses aren't as easy to fool." He inhaled deeply, scenting. "A standard human male came this way a few hours ago. Alone."

"Edin. Coming to our meeting solo, just like he said he would."

"Which doesn't mean an ambush team didn't come in through another airlock." Rance prowled through the opening, his every sense on high alert. Zarifa's boots scraped on the corridor's stone as she followed him. Like him, she was wearing full armor, a nanoblade great sword sheathed across her back.

At the end of the corridor lay a pair of enormous double doors that probably led to the warehouse Edin had spoken of. After a cautious scan, Rance drew his sword, triggered the doors open, and walked in.

The room was cavernous, filled with stacks of crates that towered meters high. Rance spotted one that still bore the logo of Conlon Shipping. He'd probably brought it over himself years before.

A man stepped from behind one of the stacks. Tall, rangy, he wore the stark black uni favored by Kuarc's men. His hair was thick and red, and his eyes were the distinctive violet of the Lorezo clan. Rance noticed a strong resemblance to Kuarc in the aquiline shape of his nose and the thin line of his mouth, but he looked even more like Lodur, the old emperor. He gave Zarifa a slight smile. "Greetings, child."

"Edin!" Zarifa started forward, a grin of pure happiness lighting her face.

Rance clamped a hand over her wrist, not taking his eyes off the older man. "No closer, Zarifa."

She looked around at him, startled. "But—"

"He smells dirty. And I don't think it's just that he set you up for an ambush by the Bastard's men."

A bitter smile twisted Edin's mouth. Steel hissed as he drew the sword sheathed across his back. "Fucking werewolf. Kuarc always said you could scent a lie."

Suddenly far too many things became far too clear. Rance spun his sword in a circle and started forward, a snarl twisting his werewolf muzzle. "I always wondered why I'd never met Kuarc's second-in-command."

Zarifa shot him a look as she drew her own weapon and fell into guard. "Wait—he's working for Umar?"

One of the crates slid open with a hiss of escaping air. A warrior in imperial armor stepped from it. "Edin's never worked for anybody but himself."

"Gerik!" Zarifa took a step back, the scent of her fear acrid to Rance's wolf senses. Not surprising; she'd told him how the bastard had terrorized her for years.

With a lupine howl of pure rage, Rance swung up his sword and charged.

The two armored men collided with the thunderous crash of steel meeting steel. Zarifa heard Rance's ripping wolf snarl and Gerik's furious curses. The Fist's massive blade blurred in a glittering arc, and she sucked in a breath.

Rance met it with a ringing parry, then pivoted into his own ferocious attack. She realized that as powerful as Gerik was, he might have met his match.

A blur of motion in the corner of her eye jolted her into awareness of her own peril. She spun aside and brought up her sword for a parry that rattled her teeth.

Edin's too-familiar face sneered across their locked weapons. "You know, don't you? My fucking cousin got word to you from beyond the grave."

"Except for the part about you being a traitor." She disengaged her sword from his and brought the weapon up in a furious slash that forced him to leap back. "So what nasty role did you play in our sorry family story?"

He laughed in her face and tried to take off her head. Zarifa leaped back, parrying strike after strike as he chased her. Finding her rhythm at last, she retaliated with a blurring combination of strokes that drove him back. Daring a glance over her shoulder at Rance and Gerik, she found them hacking at each other like madmen, with grunts and curses of effort and a display of inhuman speed. In werewolf form, Rance towered over the cyborg, but she knew Gerik's viciousness made him a match for his opponent's greater size.

Beyond them, in the shadows of a stack of crates, Zarifa

thought she saw a flicker of motion. For just an instant, a pale face stared back at her.

Casus? What the hell was the—

Edin's sword came whirling at her face. She ducked and forgot the slaver as she focused on staying alive.

Zarifa's fiancé might be an aristo, but he was also a hulking, powerful cyborg who was fast on his feet, strong as a Centarian dragon, and mean all the way to the bone.

"You're not bad, for a mongrel slave," Gerik sneered as the two men circled, each looking for a weakness in the other's defenses. "But you're still a dead man."

"You first," Rance sneered back, even as he used his nanosystems for another scan. Besides Gerik, Edin, Zarifa, and himself, there were three other people in the room, which begged the question of why they were just hanging back watching. But why only three? Why not an army?

Unless somebody's minimizing the number of witnesses to the empress's assassination . . .

Not good. Not good at all.

He parried another teeth-rattling attack and danced around Gerik on the balls of his feet before launching a lethal swing at the cyborg's chest. Gerik's parry was a fraction late. Rance's nanoblade sliced through that black imperial cuirass, then tore free in a rain of scarlet drops.

He grinned at the sweet copper scent of blood. "Bet *that* hurt."

Gerik spat an obscenity that had Rance laughing as he stepped in close for another swing. He lifted his blade—

The pain came out of nowhere in a blinding, sickening explosion that cut Rance's legs out from under him. He went down hard, shooting a terrified look at the legs that must have been hacked off at the knee.

They were whole. No sign of blood, no wet slash in his armor. But sweet God, the pain—

He threw himself into a roll to avoid Gerik's savage downward chop at his head. The sword struck the deck with a grating shriek.

Fresh agony detonated in the center of his chest, freezing his lungs, tearing a strangled gasp from his lips.

A big, booted foot smashed down on the center of his cuirass, pinning him to the floor. Gerik's sword pressed against the side of his throat before he could knock it aside.

"Surrender, Zarifa!" the cyborg bellowed. "Or I'll cut off your mutt's head!"

Rance lay writhing on the deck under Gerik's armored boot, pain twisting his lupine muzzle in a grimace.

Zarifa looked frantically for blood on his armor but saw nothing. Then again, the armor was black and red . . .

"Throw it down, or he dies," Edin snarled, thrusting his sword at her.

"Don't you dare!" Rance yelled, his voice hoarse. "Don't let these bastards win!"

Block his pain, she ordered her nanos. *Get him up!*

Unable to comply. We have been locked out of his system.

Horrible understanding flooded her. Oh, sweet Lady—they'd seized control of his collar!

Casus swaggered out of the shadows, one of his 'borg bodyguards at his heels. "I told you there isn't a slave's system Captain Aaren can't hack," he told the big man beside him.

"So you did," Umar said. He gave Zarifa a terrifying smile, looking massive in the gold and black nanotium armor of the Imperial House. A cadre of bodyguards in the same armor trailed behind him. "Assuming you want to keep your furry friend alive, isn't it about time to surrender?"

NINE

Fangs gritted, Rance surged under the boot that held him down, trying with everything in him to throw Gerik off. Though he was stronger than the cyborg in wolf form, whatever they'd done to him had drained his strength. He could barely lift his head, much less heave this armored monster off himself.

"You're not going anywhere, puppy." Gerik's blade dug deeper into Rance's throat as he lifted his voice. "Except to hell, if Zarifa doesn't drop that sword."

Steel clattered on the deck. "Don't hurt him."

Rance tried to wrench free again. Failed. "They're going to kill me anyway, dammit!"

"No, they're not." Her voice sounded surprisingly steady, surprisingly calm. "Not if they expect me to marry Gerik."

His despair turned to sick horror. "Zarifa!"

She turned her back on Edin and strode toward the regent, wrapped in royal arrogance like a cloak. "You don't control me anymore, Umar. If you expect me to cooperate, you're going to have to give me what I want."

Umar lifted a sooty brow. "And what would that be?"

"Remove Rance's collar and let him go."

Rance grabbed Gerik's boot, but his fingers had no strength. "They'll kill you the day after the wedding!"

Gerik grinned maliciously and said in a low, suggestive voice, "Oh, not quite that soon. It would look bad."

Rance stared up at the man as a tide of raw hate rolled over him. "I'm going to rip out your throat."

The regent's son laughed.

As Rance stewed in his frustration, Umar turned to murmur something to his guards, who turned reluctantly and marched out, presumably to stand watch outside. *He must not want any witnesses to this conversation,* Rance thought grimly. *Which is a very bad sign.*

"So if we release your werewolf," the regent said after they were alone, "you'll marry my son?"

"Yes." Zarifa spoke with no hesitation at all. "But only after Rance sends word from the Freeworlds that he has arrived safely home."

"You drive a hard bargain, my dear. But yes."

He must think she's an idiot. Rance ground his teeth in fury as he glared up at Gerik. A new thought struck him, and he went still. *Of course he does. He's controlled her every move for years. He has no idea what she's capable of.*

But Rance did. Zarifa was intelligent, determined, and capable. She knew who she was dealing with, and she knew they'd break any agreement they made. What's more, she wouldn't let them get away with it.

Which meant she had something in mind. He had to be ready to move when she put her plan in action.

Rance let his body go limp and dropped his head to the deck. Pretending submission to these bastards went against every instinct he had, but he knew his woman. She wouldn't fail him. And he wouldn't fail her.

"Yes, that's right, dog. Give up." Gerik smirked down at him in triumph. "You can't win."

Umar's smile was so smug, hate threatened to choke Zarifa. The fact that he wore the arms of the emperor splashed across his cuirass only added to the insult. She ached to see his blood fly, but years of practice let her keep the rage off her face. Instead, she widened her eyes in the guileless, earnest expression she'd learned to wear like a mask.

Umar didn't realize it, but he'd made her a very good actor.

"You'll let Rance take my ship, and you're not going to interfere."

Through his open visor, he gave her that benevolent look he wore whenever he was planning a betrayal. "Of course."

"That's not all." She started reeling off further conditions, making them up as she went along as she moved into position.

Casus stood beside the regent, visibly basking in his role of trusted ally. Idiot. He was a dead man. Umar didn't leave witnesses to his more flamboyant acts of evil, which was probably why he was using Casus and Aaren instead of his own valuable hackers. Knowing Casus, he'd probably been stupid enough to volunteer their services in bringing the werewolf in.

Captain Aaren stood behind him, his expression abstracted through his visor. Probably trying to make sure Rance didn't break free of his control and kill Gerik.

Perfect. Still rattling off conditions, she stepped in close to the slaver and flicked her right wrist. The nanoblade dagger dropped into her hand even as she drove her left fist at Casus's face.

Just as she expected, Aaren automatically jolted forward to defend him, swinging up a huge, armored hand to block her blow.

Zarifa drove her dagger into the underside of the bodyguard's jaw, right in the seam between his helmet and throat guard. Aaren choked and went down, dead before he hit the ground.

And so was his control over Rance's nanosystem.

Drop all controls on Rance.

Done.

Rance roared in a throaty blast of sound more lion than wolf.

Both Rance's hands clamped hard around Gerik's ankle before the 'borg even had time to react to Umar's shout of alarm. As Aaren went down, Rance tossed his opponent into the air like a playing card.

Gerik hit the deck in a rattling crash of armor. Rance flipped over and sprang at him with a snarl. His armored fist hit the 'borg's faceplate so hard, the tough visor spiderwebbed like glass. He hit it again, then a third time, intent on breaking through and killing Zarifa's tormenter. His lips peeled off his teeth . . .

Gerik slammed both big hands into his chest and sent him flying with a heave. Rance hit the ground rolling and bounded to his feet before the stunned 'borg had time to rise. As he started back toward his enemy, something clattered against the toe of his boot. Rance bent, scooped up the sword he'd dropped, and began to stalk the man who'd abused and threatened Zarifa.

Gerik slapped his own faceplate, clearing away the broken visor. To Rance's satisfaction, blood flowed from countless cuts on his face. "You're dead, mongrel," he hissed, his eyes wide and wild with rage. "And then I'll fuck Zafira before I kill her."

"No." Rance swung his great sword into position. The anger

that filled him was a cold, pure thing, as focused as a laser. "You're just going to die."

U mar swung his great sword at Zafira's belly, but she leaped clear and began to circle him. "You're a fool, thinking you can take me," he sneered. "You don't even have a sword!"

No, she'd had to drop it when Gerik threatened Rance. But she did have a dagger—and more importantly, her Imperial Combat nanosystem. Umar, judging from the arrogance on his face, had forgotten all about that.

From the corner of one eye, she saw Edin standing off to one side, watching the fight with the casual interest of a man at a z-boxing match. Casus, meanwhile, stood over Aaren's body and wrung his hands, visibly longing to run.

"Bitch!" Umar charged, swinging his sword in a furious arc. Zarifa coolly stepped into his charge, catching the descending sword with her dagger. She twisted and wrenched upward with all her nanobot-enhanced strength. The sword flew out of Umar's hand. He grabbed for it frantically, but she snatched it out of the air.

For an instant, their eyes met. The regent's widened in shock and disbelief. She bared her teeth and whirled the great blade in a vicious arc. He tried to stumble clear—

The impact jarred her arm to the shoulder.

Umar's body toppled as his helmeted head hit the deck with a rolling clatter. The monster was finally dead.

"Father!"

She whirled as the big man spun away from Rance and plunged toward her, his sword lifted. "*You're dead, you little whore!*"

Zarifa had time for an instant's icy fear. She'd already learned her combat system was no match for his cyborg power. Bracing herself, she lifted her sword and prepared to parry.

Gerik stopped in his tracks with an odd, gasping sound. He looked down.

Zarifa followed his gaze and saw three inches of blade protruding from the center of his chest.

Behind him, Rance said, "I told you you're a dead man." He jerked the sword free.

"No," Gerik wheezed. "I'm not supposed to lo—" He never finished the sentence. His eyes rolled back as he fell.

Her nanos warned her. Zarifa whirled, her sword swing taking

Casus in the belly the instant before he could bury his dagger in her back.

"I wanted to do that," Rance said, watching the slaver topple.

"And I'd rather have let you." Zarifa grimaced and swallowed bile. She badly wanted to sit down. As many times as she'd practiced swordplay with her trainer, she'd never killed a man before. Now she'd slain three.

Rance reached for her, but before he could take her in his arms, the warehouse's double doors slid wide.

Oh, sweet Lady, Zarifa thought, her heart stuffing its way into her throat. *Not more of them . . .*

They turned to see Kuarc Lorezo saunter in at the head of a small army of armored men, two of whom were dragging a badly battered Edin. Evidently he must have tried to slip out when he realized which way the fight was going.

Every one of the rebels was covered in blood and breathing hard. Apparently they'd run into Umar's bodyguard—and it hadn't gone well for the guards.

Kuarc bared his teeth in something she didn't mistake for a smile, his eyes assessing the bodies lying around the room. "Well, Sister, you have been busy."

Weariness and shock kept her from choosing her words more carefully. Anyway, she was tired of pretending. "I'm not your sister."

Kuarc laughed, but a dangerous anger flared in his violet eyes. He looked like a younger version of her father: big, broad-shouldered, with a mane of red hair tied back in a club. "I've got blood tests that say differently."

"They *were* identical twins." She tugged off her gauntlet and dropped it on the deck. "That's the only reason my father was able to pass you off as his bastard."

"Zarifa," Rance hissed, "what the hell are you doing?"

"The girl's drunk again," Edin put in. "That, or she's gone mad."

"Shut up," Kuarc snapped. "You're in this up to your neck." He bared his teeth at his second-in-command. "Did you really think I wouldn't notice what you were up to? Did you really think I wouldn't have you followed?" He turned his attention to Zarifa and lifted his sword. "As for you, I'd strongly recommend you start talking sense, if you can. I'm running out of patience."

"It's simple, Kuarc. You're not a bastard." She fought to drag the big diamond off her finger. It had, of course, never fit particularly well, since it wasn't her ring. "You're the legal son of Emperor Sevan Lorezo, who married your mother before his death. This is her ring—and the proof of their marriage." The diamond finally slid free, and she dropped to one knee, extending it to her stunned cousin. "You're the rightful emperor, Kuarc. You always were."

As she brushed a thumb over the diamond, it triggered the simmie recording the stone held. The three-dimensional image flashed into being, showing a handsome young redheaded man standing next to a slender blonde who wore an expression of giddy joy. "Would you kiss the bride already, Sevan?" a voice called in the background. "I'm in the mood to get drunk."

Like most modern rings, the diamond had recorded all the significant events of the couple's marriage, from the wedding ceremony to their son's birth.

Kuarc extended his hand, his expression dazed. She dropped the ring in his palm. "They were married in a secret ceremony not long before the old emperor died. Your mother was pregnant with you at the time," Zarifa explained softly. "She was a commoner, and Sevan was hoping to present his father with a fait accompli. But the emperor died, and Sevan had to leave her to take up his duties. He apparently planned to announce their marriage once he had the nobility under control. He was on his way back to claim her when he was killed."

Kuarc blinked the eyes so like her own. "And your father knew all this?"

She nodded. "He'd planted Umar in Sevan's entourage as a spy. After the assassination, Umar convinced Lodur he could be emperor. All they had to do was conceal the fact that you were Sevan's legitimate son. Then Umar spent the next fifteen years blackmailing my father."

"Lodur always claimed my mother was one of the maids. Said Grandfather got rid of her." He looked stunned. "What really happened to her?"

"She's still alive," Zarifa told him. "But Umar programmed her nanosystem to ensure she could never tell anyone about the marriage or about you."

"Why didn't they just kill me?" He stared down at the ring, visibly struggling to take it all in. "It would have been easier all the way around."

"You were an infant, Kuarc," Zarifa told him. "Umar floated the idea, but my father wouldn't have it."

"Lodur wasn't evil," Rance murmured, repeating what she'd said weeks before. "He just wasn't very good."

Mechanically, Kuarc thumbed the diamond. "Would you kiss the bride already, Sevan?" the recorded voice repeated. "I'm in the mood to get drunk." He thumbed it again. "Would you kiss the bride already, Sevan? I'm in the mood to get drunk."

Kuarc frowned. "That's Edin's voice."

"You're right." Zarifa rose to her feet. "I hadn't spoken to him in ten years, so I didn't recognize it."

Kuarc turned to stare at Edin. "You knew about all of this, but you never said a word." His eyes narrowed in sudden realization—and a growing, deadly rage. "It was you. It wasn't some madman who killed Sevan—it was you all along."

Edin's mouth worked, his eyes darting from side to side as he visibly considered whether to lie. Until the truth exploded from him. "Yes! Because I should have been emperor! My blood is as royal as yours—and I'm not a naive fool!"

"So you spent years betraying my father, betraying me, even betraying Umar—playing all ends against the middle." Kuarc shook his head, a bitter twist to his lips. "You even had me believing Zarifa was involved in Lodur's murder."

"It wasn't hard," Edin sneered. "As I said, you're a fool. Like your father, like your uncle, like your bitch cousin. None of you deserved to rule!"

"That's just too bad, because now I am emperor." His gaze was cold and regal. "And my first official act will be to discover just what kind of treason you've been committing all these years."

TEN

Rance walked onto the elegant marble balcony and stopped in his tracks to gape in mingled awe and pain.

Zarifa stood silhouetted by the setting sun. She wore an exquisite dark green velvet grown with a long train, the fabric intricately embroidered in gold and gems. Her red hair was piled on her head in a cascade of silken curls. The sunlight slanting over the palace grounds painted her exquisite face in gold.

She looked every inch the empress she no longer was.

Zarifa had abdicated the throne today at Kuarc's coronation ceremony. Her last act as empress had been to award Rance the Order of the Lion, the crown's highest honor in recognition of civilian heroism. The heavy gold medallion hung around his neck from a crimson ribbon, glinting against the black silk jacket he wore.

He felt like an idiot.

Being in the center of a media hurricane hadn't helped his acute discomfort. Just hours after Umar's death, Kuarc and Zarifa had given a joint press conference from the asteroid base. Together they'd laid out all the events of recent imperial history with merciless honesty, including Edin's murder of Sevan and Lodur's usurping the throne from his then-infant nephew.

Shock waves would still be blasting across the empire for years to come.

A week had passed since then. Zarifa had ordered the marines to stand down so that Kuarc and his men could land on Throneworld. Umar's cronies might have kicked up a fuss about that, but they probably feared calling attention to their own dubious activities.

Now she'd brought Rance here, to this intimidating palace of hers. He was a free man in truth, his neck bare of the slave collar, his nanosystems under his full control again. Best yet, Kuarc had announced his intention to abolish slavery.

Rance had everything he'd worked for all these years. Yet he was afraid the one thing he really wanted was beyond his reach.

Why should a woman who had all this trade it in for the Free-worlds and life with a werewolf?

Zarifa looked around as he walked across the balcony toward her, his black boots ringing on the marble tiles. She turned to face him, leaning back against the carved balustrade. "You know, I always wondered why my father trusted Umar. I knew they'd served in the marines together, and Umar had supposedly saved his life once, but . . ." She shook her head.

They were back to that again. He was frankly getting sick of the subject, but he knew it bothered her still, so he was willing to play along. "Well, if Umar was blackmailing him—"

"I don't think it was ever that overt. If Umar had ever actually come out and said, 'Make me regent or else,' my father would have had him arrested." She turned to gaze across the rolling green gardens of the palace grounds. "But my father still didn't completely trust him. According to what Edin said under Kuarc's . . . questioning, Lodur was counting on Edin to protect me from Umar if something happened to him."

Rance leaned a hip on the balustrade and curled his lip in disdain. "Edin was only interested in protecting himself."

"Exactly. Yet still, my father didn't completely trust him either, because he left me Sevan's ring, to be handed over when I reached my majority on my twenty-fifth birthday. And it was the ring that broke Umar's control."

"I wondered how you did that."

She stepped closer and looped an arm around his waist. "Apparently, my father realized that since Umar had used Kuarc's mother's nanosystem to control her, he might alter mine and use it the same way. So the minute I put the ring on, it injected my nanosystems with a routine that blocked Umar's control."

He smiled at the triumph in her voice. "And you were free."

She gave him a dazzling smile. "Not quite. *Now* I'm free. Umar and Gerik are dead, Edin will stand trial for my father's murder, and the Empire is Kuarc's to run."

An opening. Rance's heart started pounding in irregular thumps, but he fought to keep the tension off his face. "So what are you going to do now?"

Zarifa looked up at him, uncertainty flaring in her beautiful eyes. "Mostly I want to get the hell out of the Empire. I'd never have anything like a normal life here. I've spent the past ten years as media fodder, and somehow I don't think it's going to stop just because I'm not empress anymore."

To hell with tiptoeing around this, Rance thought, suddenly impatient. *I'm just going to damn well ask.* He caught her hands in his. They felt surprisingly cool, as if with nerves. "Come to the Freeworlds with me. I don't know if you'd consider living with a werewolf a normal life, but . . ."

Violet eyes flew so wide, he could see his face reflected in them. "Are you sure? You've seen the way the media hound every move I make. Even relocating to the Freeworlds may not stop them. And they've got a talent for making my life a living hell."

He bared his teeth. "Oh, I can safely say they wouldn't try that more than once."

Zarifa laughed. "I don't doubt it." She sobered. "But it still wouldn't be easy."

He slid his arms around her waist and drew her closer. "When I was lying on the deck under Gerik's boot with my nanosystem frozen, I knew you wouldn't let them win. I knew you'd get us out of it. And I trusted you enough to wait until you made your move." He brushed the pad of his thumb against her mouth. "That's when I realized I love you."

She caught her breath. As he watched, a slow, blinding smile spread over her face. "It took you that long? I fell in love with you when you believed me about Umar's smear campaign to make me look like a drunk."

He smiled as his heart picked up that hard beat again. "Will you marry me?"

"Sweet Lady," she breathed, "yes!"

Her mouth tasted of champagne and strawberries. He groaned into her lips, instantly hard.

Rance swept her into his arms, kicking aside the velvet of her train as it tried to tangle his legs. Zarifa looped her arms around his neck as he carried her into the bedroom.

He looked breathtakingly handsome in his aristo black jacket and snug black trousers, a stark white cravat tied around his powerful throat. The Order of the Lion hung around his neck from a crimson ribbon that provided the one splash of color against all that monochrome starkness.

He lowered her to the thick red silk counterpane of her bed—the same bed she'd cried in so many nights for so many years. Straightening, he surveyed her with a frown.

Feeling suddenly uncertain, she frowned back. "What?"

"How the hell am I supposed to get you out of that dress?"

She laughed. "Come here, and I'll show you."

He grinned and lowered himself to her side. "Your wish is my command, mistress."

Velvet whispered. Buttons yielded to impatient fingers with a gentle pop, corset strings sighed from their eyelets. His hands felt strong and warm on the bare skin of her thigh. His mouth met hers, licking, tasting, as she untied his cravat. His jacket dropped from broad, silk-clad shoulders.

He growled, the sound impatient. "Aristos wear too damn many clothes."

Plucking at his buttons, she could only rumble her own growl of agreement.

Finally the edges of the shirt parted, revealing his broad chest, dusted in rich, curling hair. She smoothed her hands over the rise of his pectorals and listened to his groan as she thumbed his small, tight nipples.

Her corset yielded to his demanding fingers at last, spilling her breasts free for his mouth. She caught her breath as he bent to suckle in sweetly fierce tugs. "Rance . . ."

He rumbled something hot in reply, his fingers cupping and kneading with gentle skill. Her eyes drifted downward and found the massive ridge behind the fly of his trousers. She attacked the buttons with a greedy sound, hungry to touch him, taste him.

With every button, his cock pressed a bit more free, a long, rosy shaft, thickly veined and eager. She curled her fingers around his satin heat and groaned as he jolted in her hand.

Rance pulled away and hurriedly stripped his trousers down his thighs, pausing just long enough to drag off his boots before jerking his pants the rest of the way off.

He turned, magnificently naked, his cock thrusting from a thick nest at his groin. Zarifa caught her breath at the sight of him, tall and powerful, sculpted muscle lying in beautiful ridges along torso and thighs and brawny arms. He looked down at her, and his eyes seemed to catch flame.

Zarifa lay in creamy nudity atop the green velvet gown and red silk of the counterpane, her hair a crown of flame that matched the soft thatch between her legs. Her eyes looked fathomless as she gazed up at him, her soft lips parted. Her nipples peaked, rosy and lovely, on the full, soft mounds of her breasts.

"In all my life," Rance said hoarsely, "I've never seen anything as beautiful as you. No woman, no mountain, no sunset, no nebula. Nothing as beautiful."

Her violet eyes widened and blinked. She ducked her head, the gesture oddly shy. "I . . ." Her voice trailed off.

He'd rendered his bold empress speechless.

Of course, he had to kiss her again after that as he covered that strong, slim body with his. She kissed him back, her mouth just as eager and hungry as his own. When she curled her long legs around his waist, his head swam. He could feel her heart beating against his, hard and fast.

Violet eyes met his as he lifted his head. "I love you." And the truth of that was stark in her exquisite gaze. A single tear spilled free to roll down her elegant cheek. "You gave me back my life."

"No." He brushed away the tear. "You'd have found a way to beat them even without me. That's why I love you."

She lifted her head and took his mouth with a warm, sweet hunger. They surged together, skin to skin, her breasts soft against his chest, his cock hard against her belly.

Rance began kissing his way down her body, lingering to taste the delicate hollow of her throat, then trailing gentle bites to the budding crowns of her breasts. She gasped as he paused to circle the tight peaks with his tongue and rake his teeth carefully across them. She tasted sweet, heady, impossibly delicious.

"Sweet Lady," she moaned.

He started to smile—just as long, delicate fingers closed around his cock. His back arched in pleasure as she stroked and explored him.

"Let me taste you." She cupped his balls in her hand, caressed him with a gentleness that stole his breath.

"Only if I get to taste you, too."

She laughed, breathy and seductive. "You talked me into it."

They rearranged themselves, him shifting until he was head down along her body. The scent of her sex hit him in a pure wave of intoxication, and he groaned as he lowered his head.

She was already deliciously wet. He shuddered in pleasure as he swirled his tongue through tender folds.

Then her hot mouth closed over him in a breath-stealing rush. He gasped at the laser-bright pleasure. And gave himself up to her.

Closing her mouth around the head of him was a pure, delicious pleasure all by itself. She loved the way he felt filling her mouth, loved the shudder and jump of his powerful body as he reacted to her touch.

And she adored every slow, tormenting lick he gave her in sweet retaliation. The pleasure burned her like a brand, hot as Terran whiskey—and just as quick to go to her head. She wrapped one hand tighter around his thick shaft and took him deeper inside, digging her nails into his ass to hold him there.

Sweet Lady, he felt so good.

She licked, tasted, teased, fighting to concentrate despite the exquisite sensations he inflicted with his clever mouth and pumping fingers.

Until it wasn't enough. She needed the thick cock she teased buried inside her as far as he could get it. She jerked her head away and gasped, "Now. Lady, Rance, now!"

He didn't need to be told twice. Pulling away from her, he moved between her thighs and lifted her ass in his hands. Aiming his glistening length for her swollen sex. Zarifa rolled her hips up, fierce and needy. He plunged inside in one hot sweep. With a helpless gasp, Zarifa grabbed for his brawny shoulders, half blinded by that first luscious burst of pleasure.

Bracing both hands against the mattress, he began to thrust, slowly, carefully. She met him, rolling her hips, taking him so deep he shuddered.

He felt thick and endless in those slow, deliberate digs. Muscle surged and flexed in his powerful torso as he braced himself over her, and his ass rolled under her calves, all gentle strength.

Pleasure bloomed through her like an exotic rose with each burning entry, each delicious retreat. She shivered helplessly as she watched his face, staring into those tender golden eyes.

She'd never felt like this. Never felt such heat, such passion. Never known herself loved with such sweet certainty.

The orgasm took her by surprise, drowning her in a tide of fire and cream. She gasped as it rolled over her, hot and inevitable, driven by his long, pumping thrusts.

He growled as she convulsed. And lunged, so deep his pelvis ground against hers. Then again, faster and faster, harder and harder, gentleness lost in the frenzy of his need. And each slap of flesh on flesh drove her pleasure higher, wilder.

Rance roared, throwing his dark head back, arching hard against her as he came. She screamed, her cry ringing over his as the pleasure flamed like a star.

Tangled in velvet and silk, they lay together, breathing hard, hearts still pounding.

Tomorrow, Zarifa knew, they'd take her ship and head for the Freeworlds. She didn't know what she'd find there on those wild planets, didn't know what kind of acceptance she'd find among his people. But it didn't matter.

Home was wherever he was.

With a sigh of pleasure, Zarifa let her eyes slip closed and settled into Rance's strong arms to sleep.

A Jaguar's Kiss

Lora Leigh

For Natalie.

*For your friendship, your willingness to listen,
and your patience in the face of so many
different versions of one story.*

But most of all, just for being you.

FOREWORD

They were created, they weren't born.
They were trained, they weren't raised.

They were taught to kill, and now they'll use their training to ensure their freedom.

They are Breeds. Genetically altered with the DNA of the predators of the earth. The wolf, the lion, the cougar, the Bengal: the killers of the world. They were to be the army of a fanatical society intent on building their own personal army.

Until the world learned of their existence. Until the Council lost control of their creations, and their creations began to change the world.

Now, they're loose. Banding together, creating their own communities, their own society, and their own safety, and fighting to hide the one secret that could see them destroyed.

The secret of mating heat. The chemical, the biological, the emotional reaction of one Breed to the man or woman meant to be his or hers forever. A reaction that binds physically. A reaction that alters more than just the physical responses or heightens the sensuality. Nature has turned mating heat into the Breeds' Achilles' heel. It's their strength, and yet their weakness. And Mother Nature isn't finished playing yet.

Man has attempted to mess with her creations. Now, she's going to show man exactly how she can refine them.

Killers will become lovers, lawyers, statesmen, and heroes. And through it all, they will cleave to one mate, one heart, and create a dynasty.

PROLOGUE

Natalie Ricci stared at the tall, imposing figure standing on her doorstep and reminded herself to breathe. A woman who fainted over a dark, arrogant, exceptionally handsome man deserved whatever happened to her while she was out cold. And anything this man did, she would want to be awake for.

"Can I help you?" She brushed back the dark bangs that grew over her forehead and tried to restrain the nervous jitter playing patty-cake in her stomach. Tall, dark, and handsome was good, real good, but that gleam of powerful male assurance in his eyes warned her this man would be impossible for any woman to ever comfortably control.

"Natalie Ricci?" Even his voice was worth shivering for.

There was no discernible accent, and she was fairly good at identifying accents. His voice was well modulated, perfectly pitched, and stroked over her senses like black velvet.

Black hair, thick and lustrous, was pulled back from his face and bound at the back of his neck. His fallen angel features were composed, almost emotionless, but those eyes, eyes like emeralds, gleamed with intelligence, sensuality, and a spark of primal intensity from within his sun-bronzed face.

There were shadows in those eyes as well. A latent, hidden pain that a part of her, the feminine, caring side of her that she wished she could ignore, longed to ease.

Dark jeans cinched low on leanly muscled hips while a dark blue chambray shirt stretched across his powerful chest. And he wore boots. Well-worn, scarred, and totally masculine boots.

"I'm Natalie Ricci." She had to clear her throat to answer him, had to tighten her stomach to stop the little flutters of longing that attacked her womb.

Whew, if ever there was a man to tempt her hard-won self-control, she was betting it would be this one. What he was doing on her doorstep she had no idea, but whatever he was selling, she was certain she was ready to buy. Empty bank account notwithstanding.

It was really too bad, too. She had sworn off men. Until she could figure out how to play the game, how to protect her heart and her independence, then men were out.

As luscious and sexual as this man looked, she had a feeling he would be just as controlling, domineering, and arrogant as any man born. Probably worse than most. Definitely more than her ex-husband, whose control tendencies had managed to destroy their marriage.

"Can I help you?" she asked again, wishing she had worn something other than old faded jeans and her brother's too-big, paint-spattered T-shirt.

He inhaled slowly, as though he had caught the scent of something that intrigued him.

"Ms. Ricci, I'm Saban Broussard, liaison to the Breed Ruling Cabinet. I'm here to discuss your application to teach in Buffalo Gap." He pulled the slender identification wallet from the back of his jeans and flipped it open. The Breed law enforcement badge, his photo, and pertinent information were all displayed.

She froze in shock. Well, shock and the sound of his name, or the way he said his name, Saban, a soft little sigh of the *S*, the subtle *a*, and the *bahn* at the end. But what caught her, what had her senses standing to complete attention, was the vaguest hint of a Cajun accent in his voice after her certainty that there had been no accent.

If he was Cajun, she was just lost. If there was any sexier accent created, then she couldn't think of it at the moment.

It took several breathless seconds for her senses to stop reeling, to focus on who he was and where he was from. When she did, her eyes widened in shock.

"Did I get the position?"

She wanted that position with a desperation that had left her shaking when she filled out the application more than a year ago. She had known, had been warned that there were thousands upon thousands of applicants on the waiting list for a teaching position in the small town just outside the Breed headquarters of Sanctuary.

She had taken the chance, filled out the application, and sent it in, praying. She had prayed for months, and when nothing came of it, she settled back into her own routine and tried to make other plans.

"May we speak inside, Miss Ricci?" Saban Broussard turned

his head, stared along the tree-lined street, and lifted his brow at the residents that had managed to find one reason or another to come to their porches or to work on their lawns. She should just charge admission and have done with it.

She bit her lip, knowing the questions that would be coming before the hour was out.

"Come in." She stood back, holding the door open and allowing him to step inside the house.

He brought the scent of the mountains with him, wild and untamed, dark and dangerous.

"Thank you." He nodded as she led the way into the small kitchen off her living room.

The living room was almost empty, filled with taped boxes rather than furniture as Natalie packed her belongings.

"Have you already taken another position?" He stopped in the center of her kitchen and stared at the boxes there.

She shook her head. "I haven't. Simply moving to an apartment closer to the school where I currently work. My ex-husband gets the house and all its glorious payments. I get an apartment." And hopefully a little peace.

He stared around the kitchen again, his jaw bunching before turning back to her.

"I was sent to inform you of the opening of the position and to escort you to a meeting with our pride leader, Callan Lyons," he said then. "I'll then stay to help you get things in order before escorting you to Buffalo Gap."

She really needed to sit down, but she had given the table and chairs to a distant cousin that had recently made the monumental mistake of getting married.

"How did I get the position?" She shook her head in confusion. "I was told there were thousands of applicants just waiting for one to open."

His lips quirked. "I believe the pride leader, Callan Lyons, stated it was close to forty thousand applicants. You hit the short list on the first stage of the selection process and managed to gain the position by what I'm told was a very long, tedious, and exacting investigation into the backgrounds of those on that list. Congratulations, Miss Ricci. You'll be the first teacher hired in the county in close to seven years."

Natalie blinked back at him. He stood confidently, his arms held loosely at his sides, his eyes seeming to take in everything as she stared back at him, certain she must look like a complete lunatic.

"How soon can you be ready to leave?" He stared around the house once again. "Callan Lyons of the Breed Ruling Cabinet will be flying into the capital, Columbia, tomorrow evening, if this is convenient for you, to outline the position and discuss the specifics of the job, though we do need to arrive ahead of him to complete other matters and sign the endless forms, contracts, and so forth that will go with the job."

Natalie shook her head in confusion. "I thought the Breeds didn't interfere in Buffalo Gap? I heard that somewhere. Wouldn't I be meeting with someone from the Board of Education instead?"

"Not if you're being hired to teach Breed children. Those children are very well protected, and any hiring done in that regard comes under the sanction of the Breed Ruling Cabinet. Until that decision was made, the Board of Education has allowed the Breed Ruling Cabinet to select any additional staff required." He tilted his head and watched as she gripped the small bar she stood beside to keep herself from falling. "You are still interested in the job, are you not?"

She nodded slowly. "Oh yeah," she assured him. "I would say that's an understatement."

"Very well. I was hoping we could make arrangements to leave for Columbia this afternoon, if possible?" He stared around the kitchen, his gaze touching on the boxes. "Sanctuary's heli-jet is waiting on the private airfield outside of town to escort us there. Is that agreeable—"

His words broke off at the sound of the front door slamming open, hitting the wall in the small foyer she had led Saban Broussard through and echoing through the near-empty house.

Before she could do more than gasp, she was pushed behind the bar and within a blink Suban was across the room, weapon drawn from somewhere as he slammed her ex-husband's body against the wall and jammed the muzzle of his weapon beneath Mike Claxton's jaw.

Mike's pale blue eyes widened as his face blanched in terror. Saban's lips were drawn back in a snarl, lethal canines flashing as a growl rumbled in his throat.

"Call him off," Mike gasped, his gaze latching on Natalie in desperation as he wheezed out the plea.

"For God's sake, let him go!" Natalie stalked across the room, glaring at the Breed. Obviously a Breed. Only they had the unique, terrifying, wickedly powerful canines such as this one had. "He's not dangerous, he's just stupid. Dammit, do I have to be plagued with stupid males?"

Saban drew his weapon back, but only reluctantly. He wanted to pull the trigger. He wanted to rip the bastard's neck out and watch him bleed, taste his blood, feel the terror that filled him as he knew death was coming.

Because his scent was in this house and to a small extent, lingered around the woman. The reaction was an anomaly. It wasn't a part of who or what he was. He cared for no woman, and he certainly didn't care which male touched them. Until this one, this Natalie Ricci, whose brother called her Gnat. Whose mother laughed at her childhood antics with loving amusement.

Until this woman, Saban had never known a time when he would have killed a man over his possession of a female. But this one, he knew he would kill man or beast over her.

The possessiveness had grown over the past weeks, during his surveillance of her. He had seen her on her back porch shedding tears after this bastard had stalked from her home. He had heard the screaming, stood outside her back door and prayed for the control to restrain the violence that rose inside him.

Brown-haired, weak, full of his own self-importance, Mike Claxton had no business near Saban's Natalie, no reason to breathe her air, to be here in this house, as she attempted to leave the home he had stolen from her in the divorce.

"Let him go before I kick you both out of the house and end up costing myself a job I wanted. You won't like me much if I have to do that."

Saban glanced at her from the corner of his eye, aware of the weak-minded fool gasping for air, his hands clawing at Saban's wrists as he was held securely to the wall.

The feminine ire, frustration, and promise of retribution filled her gaze and did something council soldiers, scientists, or rabid Coyote assassins couldn't do. It caused a small core of wariness inside him to awaken.

If he was going to charm her, tempt her, and steal her heart, then starting out with her upset with him, possibly frightened of him, may not be the wisest course of action.

She looked furious and fierce, eyes the color of molasses, dark and gold swirling together as she glared up at him, demanding the release of a man whose scent of dishonor was cloying and offensive.

He released Claxton slowly, uncertain why he did so when he wanted nothing more than to crush him, and reluctantly holstered his weapon.

"Consider it your lucky day," he told the other man as he collapsed against the wall, fighting for breath. "I'd leave if I were you. I'm not known for mercy or for my patience where fools are concerned. The next time you enter her home, I would suggest knocking."

"You know," Natalie commented, her tone stern and perhaps just the slightest bit concerned, "I have a feeling you and I are not going to get along if this is your normal attitude."

Saban smiled. A flash of canines, the expression of innocence he had seen other males adopt around their mates when they had managed to test their women's patience.

"We'll get along fine, *cher*," he assured her before turning, locking his gaze with Claxton's, and praying the other man read the silent warning there. "This one, though, he may have cause to worry."

"Natalie, what is this?" Claxton massaged his throat as he glared at Saban.

There was fear in his eyes though, and Saban let himself be content with that for now. Maybe later, he told himself, perhaps once he'd secured his place in Natalie's heart, then he would take care of this bastard.

"This is Saban Broussard," she bit out as she moved away from both of them and went to the counter across the room to pour herself a cup of coffee.

He could feel the anger pouring from her now, the uncertainty, and he flashed Claxton another hard look before letting a hard growl rumble in his throat. Because of this son of a bitch, she was mad at him, and if Claxton weren't very careful, Saban would take it out of his hide.

He was satisfied to see Claxton pale further, but when his gaze slid to Natalie, he nearly paled himself.

What an interesting reaction. Saban felt the clench of his chest, the awakening knowledge that he cared if this woman were upset with him. And she was very upset with him.

"He's a Breed enforcer, if you haven't guessed," she snorted, a cute little feminine sound that he found he liked. "He's here to escort me to meet with members of the Breed Ruling Cabinet. I've accepted a job with them."

Ah. Saban's gaze slashed to Claxton as fury, rich and satisfying, poured from the man. Perhaps this fool would give him the reason he needed to slash his throat after all.

Evidently he was doomed to disappointment. Claxton narrowed his eyes, his lips thinned, and his weak hands tugged at the polo shirt he wore, but he made no move toward Natalie.

She moved to the end of the bar with her coffee, leaned her hip against it, and regarded both of them rather curiously as she sipped from her cup.

Was she weighing the differences between them or seeing similarities? There were no similarities, Saban decided. Better she see that now rather than later.

"We need to be going," he told her. "I arrived in time for you to contact Sanctuary or your local law enforcement for confirmation of my assignment and the arrangements that were made to transport you to Columbia. We're running out of time."

She sipped at the coffee again, her gaze going between the two of them.

"I can't just run out of the house with you, Mr. Broussard. Even Callan Lyons should know that. I do intend to contact Sanctuary as well as the police department, my parents, and the principal of the school that I've been teaching in. I'll then shower, dress, pack, and get ready to go. That won't be accomplished in a matter of minutes."

His body tightened; lust slammed through every bone and muscle that comprised it as he stared at the defiance in her eyes. When was the last time anyone had dared to defy him, to make him wait?

"I'm not leaving you here alone with him," Claxton snapped, but there was very little heat in his voice.

Saban slid his gaze to the other man. "Bet me," he murmured, letting his gaze meet the pale blue orbs and allowing the lust that fired his body to gleam in them.

Better this bastard knew up front that Saban intended to claim what the other man had so carelessly thrown away. Some men were just smarter than others, it appeared.

"Bet me." Natalie's cup struck the counter, jerking Saban's gaze back to her.

She didn't bother to shoot Claxton that gleam of anger burning in her eyes, but Saban felt it clear to the soles of his feet. It made him horny. Made him want to show her exactly who she would belong to, who would control all that fire and passion inside her.

But that wasn't going to happen if he let her remain angry with him.

What had those dating books said? The ones little Cassie Sinclair had heaped on him the year before? Charm, soft words, praise, and the ability to compromise would show a woman his innate ability to please her on both the emotional as well as the mental level.

He could do this.

"Cher." He let the soft breath of his accent free and tried to keep from strutting as her eyes widened, her face flushed, and a hint of aroused heat flowed from her body. "I apologize for this. He came in threatening." Explaining himself nearly had him clenching his teeth in irritation. "I thought he had come to harm you or perhaps even myself. I am a Breed." He shrugged, knowing it was self-explanatory; Breeds were attacked on a daily basis. "My only thought was to protect you and myself as well." He smiled at Claxton. All teeth, sharp canines and the male promise of future payment. "Pardon my reaction to your entrance, but perhaps you should have knocked first."

Silence filled the kitchen for long moments.

"And here I thought my day couldn't get worse," he heard Natalie mutter then. "I was so wrong."

ONE

Years before, Natalie could have sworn there was no one harder to get along with than her brother. Ill-tempered, over-bearing, and certain of his place in their mother's affection, he had tortured her. Tormented her. Pulled her hair, hid her dolls, flushed her goldfish, and generally kept her in a state of distress.

She was of a mind to forgive him now, because she had found someone more overbearing, more ill-tempered, and much, much harder to get along with.

So would someone tell her, please, why she could feel herself being charmed rather than irritated? Why it was becoming so damned hard to maintain her distance and not smirk at his antics?

She was pissed, she told herself. It was all a game—she could feel it, sense it—but his efforts to get her attention were begin-ning to draw much more than her interest. She was beginning to like him. No, not just like him, and that was the scary part.

She'd been in Buffalo Gap less than two months, and she had tried, she knew she had tried not to be charmed with the arrogant, conceited, smirking Jaguar Breed that Jonas Wyatt had saddled her with, but God help her, it was getting harder by the day.

She should be angry with him, because to tell the truth, there were times she just didn't know what to do with him.

Such as the time he had followed her to the doctor. Had he stayed in the waiting room? Of course not; he had tried to breach the examination rooms. Had become so threatening that Natalie had been forced to ask the nurse to allow him to stand in the hall-way.

Not so much because of his protective determination to be there, but because of his eyes. She almost sighed at the thought of that. The shadows in his eyes had been bleak, and Natalie knew if she had forced him outside the doctor's office entirely, then the animal DNA that had somehow decided she needed protecting would have pushed them both over a line they were delicately balancing on, even then.

It was distracting though, even a little embarassing. Even her ex-husband hadn't attempted anything so forward as to try to horn in on her examinations.

That had just been the first week. The first week. It had been one frustrating episode after another.

She understood that they were still acclimating themselves to the world. She really did. It had to be hard, even now, ten years after the Breeds were first discovered and adopted by America and all its enemies and allies. They were the unknown element in the world now, a different species, kind of like aliens. There was speculation, rumor, prejudice, and pure human spite. It couldn't be easy functioning normally. But this . . . this was impossible.

She needed groceries, but after less than ten minutes in the store, she was ready to leave her cart sitting, the Breed standing, and forget about eating. He had her hormones racing in arousal and her frustration level rising as she fought to ignore his surprisingly endearing antics.

"I believe you need more meat," he whispered from behind her, his voice suggestive as he leaned toward the cooler and picked up the thick, rolled roast from inside. "This one looks promising." He held the meat up for display, and she felt her face flame as the butcher smirked at her from behind the cold display case.

Natalie jerked the roast out of his hand, thumped it in her cart, and kept going.

"*Boo*, surely you aren't gonna continue in this silent campaign," he sighed behind her. She could hear the amusement, wicked and insidious, vibrating in his voice as thick as his accent. His Cajun accent.

She really wished he wouldn't call her *boo* or *cher* or *chay* or *petite bébé*. He could call her by her name, just once, couldn't he? So her heart wouldn't thump so hard in excitement.

Except, the few times he had, the syllables had rolled off his tongue like a caress and sent a shiver spiking through her body. And she liked that too damned much.

She continued through the aisle, picked up milk and eggs, a package of processed cheese, then watched as he picked up a package of Monterey Jack. She managed to glare over her shoulder at him.

"I've never tried it," he said softly, suggestively. "But I've heard it's quite good."

Saban Broussard was wickedly handsome. Too damned handsome for his own good with his long, black hair, gleaming emerald green eyes, and patrician features. He looked wild and wicked, and he was irritating, frustrating, and driving her insane.

He refused to give her a moment's peace, and Jonas Wyatt, the director of Breed Affairs, flat-out refused to give her a different bodyguard.

Not that she had really tried too hard for that one. She restrained her sigh of self-disgust. She kept putting off forcing the issue, afraid she would miss him if he was gone. Even if he was driving her crazy, there was something about him that drew her. And she hated that part the worst. She could have handled the rest if she could be assured that she could handle the forceful personality she knew he was holding back.

As the first teacher for Breeds in a public school, Jonas said he considered her a resource and a liability, so he gave her the best to protect her.

A Jaguar Breed. A Cajun who had been buried in the swamps for most of his life, a Jaguar that he had promised was as antisocial as any Breed living. She wouldn't even know he was around.

Fat chance.

"You shouldn't eat that." He took the TV dinner that she had picked up out of her hand and replaced it in the freezer. "Fresh meat is much better for you."

Her teeth clenched tighter as a young mother giggled across the aisle, and her dimple-cheeked baby waved shyly at Saban. Evidently, he was social. The young mother blushed prettily, and the little girl's smile widened as Natalie jerked the dinner back from the shelf and plopped it in her cart before moving on.

This wasn't going to work. She was going to end up jumping his bones, and if she did that, she might as well shoot herself. Why wait for those sneaky Council soldiers she was told still lurked in the shadows? She'd take care of it herself.

"That boxed food will give you a heart attack before you're forty," he murmured as he followed her. "Are you always so stubborn?"

She clamped her lips tight and moved on.

All she wanted to do was buy some groceries, go about her business in relaxed comfort, and get ready for the coming school year. She didn't want to deal with a Breed who didn't have an antisocial bone in his tall, hard, handsome, too-damned-arrogant body and made her heart race, her lips tingle for a kiss, and her thighs weaken in need.

"You are going to hurt my feelings, *boo*, if you keep refusing to talk to me." He sighed as she moved into the checkout lane and began lifting her purchases to the counter.

He moved to her side and began taking items out of her hand and placing them himself with an amused quirk to his lips and laughter gleaming in his dark green eyes.

That laughter was almost impossible to ignore. Bodyguards were to be seen, not heard, she told herself.

Who could have known that the normally taciturn, sober, somber, *quiet* Breeds could have a complete anomaly in their midst? This breed was a maniac. He drove a twenty-year-old four-by-four black pickup that sounded like a monster growling. She couldn't even step in it by herself for God's sake.

He flirted. He cooked food so spicy hot the fire department should be put on call, and he watched cartoons. He didn't watch action movies or the news, hated the world events channel, and flat-out refused to watch any of the documentaries concerning the Breed creation.

If he wasn't watching cartoons, he was watching history or baseball. He watched baseball with such complete absorption that she wondered if he would notice a Council soldier walking in front of him.

He was taking up more room than her ex-husband had and invading her life more fully. It was going to have to stop before she lost her heart.

As her cart emptied, she moved forward, paid for her purchases, and smiled at the young man bagging and loading them back into the cart. That smile froze on her face as she heard a growl behind her. The lanky young man loading the bags paled, fumbled the bag that held her eggs, and swallowed tightly, his Adam's apple bobbing in his throat.

Yeah, that was something else he did. He growled. He growled at the delivery guy, he growled at the mailman, and he actually snarled when one of the other Breed males had stopped to talk to her while she was in a department store in town.

Natalie wiped her hand over her face and took her cart after paying for her purchases. She stalked outside to her car, fury pumping through her system.

This was supposed to have been an independent move. Away

from friends and family and her ex-husband. Away from precon-
ceived notions of who or what she should be so she could just be
herself for a change. Instead, she was babysitting a snarly Breed
male who made zero sense to her and threatened to invade her
heart as well as her life.

"Here, *boo*, let me." He took the keys from her hand as she
pulled them from her purse and moved to open the back of the
compact SUV the Breed Ruling Cabinet had given her to drive
while employed to teach their children.

She was the first teacher to be allowed to teach Breed children
who wasn't a Breed. This was also the first year a Breed child had
been allowed in a public school. And she was going to have a nervous breakdown before the news of it ever hit the world.

"I'll follow you back to the house. I have one of those barbe-
cue grills that I saw on television the other day. I could fix steaks
tonight." He gave her a mocking yet hopeful look.

"You didn't buy steaks." She broke her silence, it was just too
much. A Breed who was going to grill steaks, and he hadn't even
bought any.

He smiled, satisfaction curving lips that were too damned eatable for her peace of mind. She wanted to take a bite out of them.
Taste them. Devour them. And there wasn't a chance in hell she
was going to allow that to happen.

"They're in the cooler in the truck." He nodded to the black be-
hemoth parked beside her little dove gray front-wheel-drive SUV.
It gleamed, black and sinister. She almost smiled, almost softened.

Natalie shook her head, jerked her keys from his hand, and
stalked to the driver's door of her own vehicle. She hit the lock
release on the key and pulled the door open before stepping into
the sweltering confines of the interior.

She didn't check to see where he was; checking meant she
cared, and she wasn't giving in to it. She drove back to the little
two-story house just outside town, pulled into the driveway, and
stormed to the house. She didn't bother with the groceries; he
was just going to beat her to them anyway.

Instead, she left the door open and entered the house, aware of
the disapproval that followed her inside. She wasn't supposed to
enter the house without him; she wasn't supposed to breathe
without him testing the air first; and by God, she was not supposed to melt inside because he did it with such subtle moves that
she felt cuddled rather than smothered.

"*Chay*, you and I are gonna have a talk." Just as she suspected, he stomped into the house, six feet four inches of irritated male, decked out in denim and boots as he plopped the groceries on the table.

Natalie stared at the bags and wondered if her eggs had a hope in hell of having survived intact. Anger surged inside her, but it was at herself more than at him. Anger that she was letting another man close, risking her heart and her independence on a man she knew would be impossible to get out of her system.

"You know," she finally said carefully, "I do have a name."

She lifted her gaze to him, adopting her most severe expression. The one she reserved for the most difficult of children. And it didn't even seem to faze him.

He glowered down at her, his head bent, his shoulder-length, straight black hair falling around the face of a fallen angel. Green eyes glittered with sparks of irritation, and his expression was too damned sensual to be scary in anything but the most primal of ways.

Oh yeah, Saban Broussard terrified her. She was scared to death she was going to lose control and jump his bones one night when he was parading half-naked around her house. Wouldn't that look good on her résumé?

"I know your name, *boo*," he growled. "As well I know who your bodyguard is. Me. You do not run from me like a scared little rabbit scurrying from sight. I won't have it."

"You won't have it?" She widened her eyes in amazement. "Excuse me, Mr. Broussard, but you do not have a leash around my neck or ownership papers with my name on them. I do as I please."

"You do not." His head lowered, his nose nearly touching her, as anger sparked inside her like wildfire flaring out of control.

Her hands pushed out, flattening against his chest and trying to push him back. Trying, because he wasn't budging an inch.

"You're fired," she snapped.

"You can't fire me; you can only quit." He smirked. "Until that time you will obey the precautions made for your safety, or you will deal with me."

"I'm just real scared of you!" Her hands went to her hips, her lips flattened. "What are you going to do, growl me to death? Make me watch baseball until my eyes fall out of my head? Oh no, wait, you're going to take all my TV dinners." Mock fear rounded her eyes. "Oh, Saban, I'm so scared. Please don't."

He growled. It wasn't a hard vibration of sound, rather a subtle rumble that had the more cautious part of her brain urging wariness. And she might have paid attention if she weren't so damned mad.

"You are in my way." She lifted herself until her nose touched his. "Get out of it."

His expression changed then, shifted. His eyes narrowed, and the savage, remorseless determination she'd heard all Breeds possessed flashed in his eyes.

She should have run then and there. She should have turned tail and run as fast as those rabbits he'd mentioned earlier.

The minute his hands latched on her upper arms, the second she realized his intention and his head lowered, she should have slammed her knee into his groin and had done with it.

If she'd had time.

Between one second and the next his lips covered hers, his tongue pushed between her lips as they parted in surprise, and oh hell in a handbasket, she was lost.

Those eatable, kissable lips were devouring hers. His tongue stroked inside her mouth as the taste of heated spice filled her senses.

His kiss had a taste. Not the normal tastes a kiss had, but the taste of a wild promise, a desert afternoon, heated and filled with mystery and hunger.

Natalie found herself melting against him. She shivered. That hard, luscious body braced her weight as his hands cupped her rear and lifted her closer. His head slanted, the kiss grew deeper, a hard growl rasping his throat as she let her lips surround his probing tongue, and she sought more of his taste.

It was there, each time she caressed the tongue twining with hers, subtle, urging her to consume more, to hold him closer, to devour this kiss.

And it terrified her. She felt her independence, hard-won and imperative, fighting beneath the claiming she could feel coming, screaming out in warning until she jerked back, struggled, stumbled from his grip as she stared back at him, panting from the need suddenly tearing through her.

She lifted her hand, touched his lips. Lips that mesmerized

her, left her aching, a miracle of pleasure, just as she had known they would be.

"You're mine." There was no sexy teasing in his voice, no flirty seductiveness. His dark eyes glittered with predatory awareness and with triumph.

Her hand dropped away from him.

"You're insane," she gasped.

"Mine."

TWO

Saban watched as Natalie's eyes grew wider, a hint of fear flashing in the molasses depths, mixing with the anger and the arousal.

He knew what he had done. Knew he had spilled the potent mating hormone to her system in that kiss, and he knew he should feel guilty. He should feel remorse pounding through his head rather than satisfaction.

"You feel it now, don't you, Natalie." He drew her name out, tasted it on his tongue and relished the sound of it.

He had kept himself from using it, held it back, knowing he couldn't say it without the breath of ownership in his tone, as it was now.

And she heard it, as he had always known she would.

"I feel your insanity." She moved quickly away from him, wariness tightening her body.

Saban watched her, letting his gaze track each movement as he inhaled the scent of her, tasted her against his tongue. He could still taste her; beneath the taste of the mating hormone was the taste of her passion, of the needs she kept tightly bottled inside her and the battle she waged to hold it all in.

His Natalie, as intelligent as she was, as softly rounded and sensual as the feminine core of her was, was disillusioned, hurt, all because of one weak-minded, inept man that hadn't the good sense to see the gift God had given him.

And now he faced that woman, knowing he had committed the ultimate crime in her eyes once she learned what that kiss actually meant. He had taken her choice from her. He had begun something which tied her irrevocably to him and thereby took away the control she so highly revered.

"I'm not insane," he finally sighed. "At least no longer." He swiped his hands through his loose hair and stared around the kitchen.

Damn, he should have known better than to listen to Cassie

and her lectures on women who did not possess Breed DNA. He had taken advice from an eighteen-year-old, had seriously considered every word she had said, and now he'd pay for it.

"What do you mean? No longer?" Her eyes were narrowed, and her body was burning.

The sweet, spicy scent of her desire wrapped around his senses and had him clenching his teeth at the need to taste it, to taste her.

"What I mean doesn't matter now." Saban rubbed at the back of his neck before lowering his hand and staring back at her.

She had the width of the kitchen between them, the scent of her coffee mixed with the soft fragrance of the apple pie she had baked yesterday morning and the scent of the woman herself. It was as powerful an aphrodisiac as the mating hormone.

She watched him closely, perhaps too closely. He could see her mind working, see her sorting out the odd heat that came from his kiss, the taste of the hormone in her mouth and her need for more. And he watched as she began to suspect the truth.

His chest actually ached, and regret shimmered in his soul as his Natalie swallowed tightly, and her eyes darkened.

"The tabloids aren't all bullshit, are they?" she whispered. "There is some kind of virus that you spread with a kiss."

Saban snorted at the simplicity of the statement.

"The tabloids are the ones who are insane." He shifted his shoulders, uncharacteristically nervous in the face of this explanation. "It's called mating heat," he finally said softly, wishing he was holding her, that he had just taken her, that he had bound her to him more fully before he had to explain this. "There's no explanation for it, and so far, it seems it happens only once. Only one woman was meant to be my mate, and that woman is you."

She crossed her arms over her breasts, her lips pouting with instant denial, though she only said, simply, "Go on."

Go on. Hell, he was no good at this.

"Simply put, you are my mate. The mating hormone ensures that you won't deny me or my claim instantly. It's rather like an aphrodisiac. Like an addictive aphrodisiac."

Her lips flattened. "It's not a sickness? A virus?"

"You will not become ill," he snapped, more to distract her from this line of questioning than for any other reason. "Merely aroused. Very aroused." *Damn.* He growled that last word, his anticipation thickening in his voice as he felt the need inside him burning hotter than before, flaming across his nerve endings.

She was his. She may as well resign herself to this now. He would give her as much explanation as he had been cleared to give, but no more.

"And if it's not what I want?" Slow and precise, the words dripped from her lips like a death knell. He was very certain this was not what she wanted. And in ways, he couldn't blame her, but unlike those who did not carry the Breed DNA, Saban had a very healthy respect for Nature and all her choices.

"Once the heat begins, it can't be reversed." It could be eased, but he didn't have to tell her that yet. There were many things he couldn't tell her yet.

"So anyone you kiss—"

"No! Only my mate. Only one woman, Natalie, only you."

"I knew this was a bad idea!"

Saban almost jumped back at the sharp, furious words and the sparks that lit her molasses eyes.

"What was a bad idea?" he asked carefully.

His senses were already prime to claim her, his teeth ached to mark her, and she stood, her angry, defiant, slender hands propping on her hips as her expression became outraged.

"Letting you stay here. Listening to that insufferable, arrogant Jonas Wyatt, and allowing, for even one second, for your impossible, frustrating, completely insane ass to stay here." Her voice rose, but it was the flush on her face, the scent of heat, both anger and arousal that whipped through the room that held him mesmerized.

She was like a flame burning with incandescent beauty; even her dark, nearly black hair became brighter, shinier.

Damn, there went his chest, clenching again, those emotions he hadn't yet figured out rioting through his system.

"So it would appear you were right." He inclined his head in agreement. "But I wouldn't have left, and Jonas knew it. Now, we can deal with this."

"Deal with this?" Her brows arched in angry mockery. "Oh Saban, we're going to deal with this all right. Right now."

She stomped to the phone, jerked it off its base, and her finger stabbed at the button programmed to ring in Callan Lyons's main office.

Saban frowned. "Callan has nothing to do with this."

The look she flashed him would have silenced a lesser man. Hell, it almost silenced him.

"Mr. Lyons." Her voice was sugary sweet and lifted every hair on the back of Saban's neck. He could only imagine Lyons's expression and the frustration that would be twisting his savagely hewed features.

"Oh yes, we do have a problem," she said politely, her smile tight. "You're going to have a dead Breed in, oh, I'd give him twenty minutes, if someone from Sanctuary doesn't pick him up. I do believe he's rabid. Someone needs to save him, or I'm going to put him out of his misery."

As she listened, the sides of her nose began to twitch, and Saban had to restrain his grimace.

"I don't care if Coyotes are swarming Sanctuary with grenade launchers. Get some of those badass Breeds you prize so highly out here to collect him, or I'm going to kill him. And after I kill him, I'll hang his mangy, worthless hide in my front yard to show everyone else exactly how it's done. Twenty minutes." She slammed the phone down.

"One of your handlers will be here to pick you up soon. Don't let the door hit you in the ass, and don't find yourself anywhere near me after that."

She stalked across the kitchen, her pert little nose in the air, her face set in lines of rejection, denial, and fury.

His mate was denying him. Not that he had expected anything less, but with a spirit as strong as his Natalie's was, there was only one way to combat it.

He caught her as she attempted to brush past him, swung her around, surrounded her with his arms, and before more than a gasp could pass her lips, he had them in a kiss.

His arms tightened around her, lifted her, bore her through the doorway until he was able to find the couch and fall into it, one hand cupping the back of her head and holding her lips to his.

She wasn't fighting it.

She was furious, enraged, but she wasn't fighting his kiss. Her greedy lips were suckling at his tongue, and it was heaven. Her hands were in his hair, twining in it, tangling in it, and pulling him closer as a ragged female sound of hunger tore through his senses.

She was like a flame burning in his arms, blistering with her kisses, with the ragged sound of her pleasure, tightening his cock, his balls, hell, every muscle in his body with the need to possess her, to claim her so deeply that she could never deny him again.

"I hate this!" Snarling and filled with outrage, her voice stroked over him in shades of arousal and need as his lips lifted from hers.

Saban framed her face, his hands relishing the feel of her flesh as he stared into her eyes, read her inability to deny the pulsing desperation of his touch.

"I thank God for this . . . and for you," he whispered, allowing his thumb to brush over her swollen lips, his tongue to taste her on his lips. "Hate me as you please, Natalie. Curse me, revile me until hell freezes over, but it changes nothing. It can change nothing. You're mine."

Natalie struggled beneath the statement, fighting to refute it, to find some way to counter it. But how was she supposed to fight anything when desire clawed through her system with talons of fiery lust and pulsing heat?

She had wanted him before; God knew she had. Fighting that need night after night had made her insane, snappy, frustrated. But now—now it was like some demon of lust clawed at her womb, tore at her clit, and tightened bands of wicked, agonizing heat around each.

She arched, totally involuntarily, against his hips as they pressed between her thighs, the ridge of his erection digging into the tender flesh of her pussy as the subtle flexing of his powerful thighs stroked the denim-covered ridge against her.

She could feel her juices spilling from her sex, moistening her panties and preparing her for him. Preparing her for something she knew would tie her to him forever.

That was the warning her brain had been screaming for weeks. To get away, to escape while she could still run, and to put as much distance between her and the luscious Jaguar as possible.

"You can't do this," she gasped as one of his hands smoothed down her neck and gripped the slender strap of her camisole top.

"I was born to do this," he growled.

The feel of the small strap sliding over her shoulder had her lungs pumping for oxygen, her lips parting to draw more in. How was she supposed to breathe? He surrounded her, sucked all the air out of the room, and he was touching her. Undressing her.

"I have dreamed of nothing but this since the moment I laid

eyes on you." He traced the rising flesh of her breasts as they spilled over the top of her lacy bra. Her nipples hardened violently, becoming so sensitive she wondered if she could orgasm from the rasp of the lace against them.

"Saban." She licked her lips, tasting him, needing more of him.

The hormone, as he called it, was worse than addicting. Already she could feel the need for it overtaking her senses, battling with her common sense, and topping it with little struggling.

"Ah, here, how pretty is this." He smoothed the strap of her bra over her shoulder, then eased one cup away from a straining breast.

Her nipple was cherry red, swollen and needy. She was almost embarrassed at the state of it. A testament to how long it had been since she had been touched? Or a testament to the power of that freaky hormone he was talking about?

She needed his lips there, needed his mouth suckling her, stroking her past the point of sanity.

"Look how sweet, *cher*." He touched his fingertip, strong, calloused, to the hard tip.

Natalie felt the breath rasp from her throat. Her back arched, driving her nipple into his touch as her head fell back and she let her eyes close. She just wanted this touch. Just this once. Right now.

"Please, Saban." Was that her? Her voice? Her begging for something she knew would destroy the independence she had fought so hard for? Was she insane?

"*Cher*, sweet petite *bébé*," he groaned. "Anything. Anything you need."

She felt his lips first, brushing against the violently sensitive puckered flesh. Then his tongue, swiping over it, hot and wet and wringing a cry from her lips a second before she lost the ability to breathe.

His mouth surrounded the tip as the fingers of one hand caught its mate. He covered the heated flesh, burned it, licked it, sucked it into his mouth, and fed from the hunger that began to pour from inside her.

Natalie was unaware of time, place, or reality. Nothing mattered but the hunger. Nothing mattered but his touch. One hand on her other breast, the other pushing the elastic waist of her cotton pants down her hips, delving beneath them.

She knew what was coming. Natalie was no virgin to be seduced, so she knew where he was headed, and she knew the worst thing she could do was let him actually get his hand in her pants. She would be lost. Any more pleasure, and she would never tear free of him. He would try to own her, control her.

She whimpered at the thought and fought for the strength to pull free, to drag his lips from her breast, to pull free of the hand moving closer, closer to the saturated flesh beneath her panties.

It was hard to tear him away though when her hands were tangled in his hair and trying to pull him into her flesh. When her thighs were sprawled open, her hips arching, her desperate mewls urging him on.

She sounded like a cat in heat, which might be fitting, considering what he had told her, and when his fingers met the humid, blistering need spilling from her pussy, she knew she was lost.

Natalie's hips arched, a cry tore from her throat, and rich, sweet, overwhelming lust spilled from his kiss as he took her lips once again.

"I thought she said she was going to kill him. Are you sure you didn't get that message mixed up, Callan?"

THREE

It was a science fiction nightmare, and Natalie was caught in the middle of it. The director of the Bureau of Breed Affairs, Jonas Wyatt, and the pride leader of the Breed Ruling Cabinet hadn't come to whisk their irritating Breed back to Sanctuary. To the contrary. They had brought the heli-jet and whisked Saban as well as her back to the estate and far belowground, where the Breed laboratories were now set up.

It was definitely a nightmare. Hours of tests, drawing blood, examinations that shouldn't have been so uncomfortable, and questions so damned personal Natalie kept blushing.

The explanations were even worse than the examinations and the questions, though. The explanations were nearly more than her mind could comprehend.

Natalie liked to think she was a fairly intelligent person. She was always open to the paranormal; she questioned everything that confused her and tried to understand. She even believed in psychics and reincarnation for pity's sake. But this?

A pheromonal, biological, chemically based reaction that resulted in the swelling of tiny, normally hidden glands beneath the Breed's tongue. Those glands then filled with a hormonal aphrodisiac, addictive and potent, ensuring that those affected actually had sex.

When Natalie asked if there was a cure, Elyiana's only answer was that they were working on it. Does it go away? They were working on it.

They were working on it. The day was over and edging into night when the doctor was finally finished with her, and she knew no more then than she did when she arrived, but she was fairly certain there was a truckload of information they weren't giving her.

By the time the heli-jet landed in the wide side yard beside her house and she and Saban were reentering her house, she was angrier than she had been when she first called Callan Lyons.

Fat lot of help he had been. He and Wyatt both refused

emphatically to change her bodyguard, and they refused to keep Saban away from her long enough for her to understand what the hell was going wrong with her own body.

And it was wrong. It had perspiration beading on her forehead, her womb clenching, and the aches at her clit and in the hidden depths of her vagina were nearly too much to bear. She felt off center, uncertain, and scared.

In her life there had been few times she had actually been frightened, but she admitted that she was definitely scared now. She was tied, bound to a man that she was certain she might not even like.

Well, she didn't actually dislike him, she thought as she stood back voluntarily and let him open the house, let him smell the air then step inside to be certain it was safe while checking the security system wired into it.

"It's safe, *cher*." His voice was gentle, patient, as he returned to the door.

"Someone could have shot me from the road while you were checking the place out," she informed him, her voice so brittle she nearly winced as he closed the door behind her and locked it.

"The chances were slimmer. My senses are degraded a bit tonight; I wanted to be certain you weren't walking into an ambush before you came in. The sensors on the heli-jet would have detected weapons in the area or hidden assassins."

She shook her head. She didn't want to talk about the heli-jet.

"I'm going to take a shower and go to bed." She turned away from him and headed for the stairs.

"Cold water won't help the heat. You won't be able to sleep through it; you won't be able to make sense of it or to apply logic to it. But we could discuss it."

She turned back to him, her jaw clenching as she fought the emotions rising inside her.

Damn him, as frustrating as he was, she did like him despite her reluctance to admit it. She had liked him playful, she had liked him teasing, but this part of him, the part she had sensed he was hiding, this she doubted she would like.

He stared back at her, calm, self-possessed, determined. That determination was like a silhouette over his entire body, a shadow he could never escape.

Fortunately, he wasn't ordering her to discuss it. It was the only thing saving his life at the moment.

Natalie met Saban's eyes. Just for a second, she had been scared to do that, afraid of the satisfaction, the triumph she would have glimpsed there. There was none. Those dark eyes were somber, brooding. And she thought, for a second, she might have glimpsed regret.

"And what would we discuss that I haven't already learned?" She kept her voice low, though she knew the fear inside her was throbbing through it.

Breeds were amazingly perceptive. Hiding emotions from them just didn't work.

He breathed out deeply before raking his fingers through his hair and stepping one step closer toward her.

"I endured the tests today as well," he said.

Natalie flinched, those tests had been more than uncomfortable; they had bordered on too painful.

"The heat has advanced further inside me, the hormone building in it." He came closer. One step. "Weeks, from the moment I first saw you, I knew what you would be to me. Each day that the heat builds inside, the harder it is to endure another's touch, no matter male or female, until the effects of the heat begin to ease. My flesh is sensitive, my distaste at another woman's touch nearly violent."

Natalie jerked her gaze from his and stared over his shoulder, fighting the tightening of her throat, the tears that wanted to rise.

"Natalie," he drew the sound of her name out, as though he were relishing each syllable. "I can cook. The steaks are in the freezer. Let me care for you this evening and answer your questions."

One step closer, his hand reached out, touched her cheek. "Let me care for my mate, if only briefly, if only in this small way."

"I hate what you're doing to me. What this is doing to me," she muttered, feeling the defenses she had been building through the day crumble. He wasn't demanding anything, he was asking, and it wasn't a ruse. He wasn't pretending.

Saban grimaced, his nostrils flaring. "In this moment, I don't blame you for hating me, *boo*. Perhaps, at this moment, I hate myself as well. Let me take care of you." He held his hand out to her. "Just a little bit."

Natalie stared at his hand, fighting herself now as much as she was fighting him. This was a side of him she hadn't seen. There was no teasing, no flirting, no deliberate male innocence, which hadn't gone over well with her at all.

She wondered for a moment who this man was, this Breed whose eyes were so somber, whose expression wasn't dominating but rather filled with quiet pride and confidence.

She lifted her hand and placed it against his, feeling the roughness of his palm, the strength of his fingers as he clasped it and led her to the kitchen.

"A young Breed teenager, the daughter of a mated pair, she knew you were coming into my life," he said as he led her to the kitchen table and held her chair out for her.

Natalie sat, uncertain now what to say.

"She's psychic or something." He shrugged. "Cassie Sinclair has gifts none of us have really been able to determine, but sometimes she knows things. She told me more than a year ago that you were coming into my life." He turned from the freezer and cast her an amused, baffled smile. "I didn't believe her. But she pushed dozens of books off on me: *How to Charm Today's Woman, Sex and the New Generation.*" He shrugged before pulling the steaks from the freezer and moving to the counter. "Asinine."

"But you read them?" Natalie pushed her hair back from her head and tried to breathe through the flash of heat that suddenly tore from her.

And he knew. His head jerked around, a frown pulling at his brows as his eyes suddenly flashed with primal awareness.

"I read them." His voice was harder, thicker. "If you were going to arrive in my life, then I wanted to be ready."

The heat tore through her vagina then, causing her to tighten her thighs and hold her breath against it.

Saban's fists clenched on the counter as his body tightened.

"Saban, I need to go upstairs."

She moved to rise from the table.

"You need me." He kept his back to her, but he snarled the words, a declaration, an agonized certainty.

"Not like this." She breathed out roughly, then tried to draw enough breath into her lungs to breathe through the building contraction of heat tightening in her abdomen. "I trusted you enough to allow you to stay in my home. I trusted Lyons and Wyatt enough to make certain nothing happened to me. You've forced me into this."

He shook his head slowly.

"You know you did," she whispered, tears finally thickening her voice. "You knew when you kissed me what you were doing."

"You belong to me." He turned then, his eyes glowing in his face, hunger and need tightening his features into savagely hewn lines. "You've had one day to feel what has grown inside me for weeks. One fucking day, Natalie. I've burned for you through the days and the nights. I've ached for your touch, and even that you would not give me. I flirted, I teased. I did everything those fucking books said a man should do, and nothing worked."

Natalie stared back at him, confused, uncertain. "And you thought throwing me into this would?" she finally asked bitterly. "That forcing my compliance was the only step left? You forced this on me, Saban. How is it any different from rape?"

How was it different? His lips opened, fury pounded in his head that she would think such a thing, that she could ever believe he would force such a choice from—

Saban felt it then, the knowledge, the certainty, from her point of view, that it was exactly what he had done. He had given in to his own frustration, his anger at her defiance, his hunger, and he had unleashed it on her in a way she could never fight, one she could never escape.

He had never raped a woman in his life. The Cajun swamp rat who had raised him would have been horrified that the young man he had such pride in at his death, had done something so vile.

The sickness of it clogged his throat, tore at his conscience.

"Ely gave you the hormonal treatment, didn't she?" he finally asked.

"That injection? Yeah, she shoved something up my veins and slapped a bottle of pills in my hand before we left. Wyatt didn't give her much of a chance to explain them though."

He nodded quickly. That sounded like Jonas. Jonas would do that for him, but he had done Saban no favors, no matter what he thought.

"They ease the heat." His throat was so tight he could barely speak now. "They adjust the hormones during this phase, allow you some ease." He grabbed the steaks and stalked to the door. "I'll fix your dinner. Take them. Bath, shower, whatever you need."

He slammed the door behind him and took a hard breath of fresh air, fighting to push the scent of her need and her anger from his head.

God help him, it was the same as rape.

He slapped the steaks in their protective containers on the

narrow table beside the new grill before bracing his hands on the wood and staring along the forests that bordered the house.

He needed to run. He needed the mountains and the silence, he needed the peace that came with it to clear his mind, to think.

God in heaven, he hadn't meant to do this to her. To make her feel this way. She was everything he had dreamed of for so long. Gentleness, sweetness, intelligence, and determination—and his. Something meant just for him. A gift, an affirmation that he wasn't a freak of science but instead a product of nature and God's mercy.

He had waited for her for so long.

Deep into the darkness of night his arms ached for her, even when another woman had lain within them. His heart had beat for her, his soul had burned for her. He hadn't known who she was, where to find her, but he had known she was there. Known that she belonged to him.

And what had he done to this gift he had so wanted to cherish?

He had taken her will, her control, with a kiss that he still remembered with the greatest of pleasure. A kiss she had met with equal force. One she had been waiting for; he knew she had been waiting for that kiss. But it didn't excuse it. He had known what he was doing, what would happen; she hadn't.

"I'm sorry." The back door opened, and the scent of her wrapped around him then.

"For what?" Rather than looking at her, he lifted the lid to the grill and ignited the flames that curled over the ceramic briquettes inside.

"It's not the same as rape."

Saban clenched his teeth and fought the need to fist his hands.

"You decided this for what reason?" He lowered the grill lid and watched it, as though in watching it he could make it heat and burn away the shame inside him.

"Because I already suspected the truth of it," she finally said. "I knew it existed, and I pushed anyway because you were frustrating the hell out of me. It wasn't rape, Saban, but neither was it right. And now we'll both have to deal with this. But I won't deal with it with lies between us. Not from either side."

FOUR

How could she have said something so vile to him?

Natalie felt everything inside her cringing, searing from the knowledge that she had struck out in the most unacceptable way and accused him of something so vicious.

This man, who had set aside his pride to read those stupid dating books, who had tried to charm her, tried to ease her into his arms rather than taking what he wanted.

And it had almost worked. Hell, it was working, and she had known it; it was the reason she had been confrontational. It was the reason she had fought each overture he made so fiercely. Because he was making her feel, making her want things she told herself didn't exist.

She had suspected, in some ways she had known after she met Callan Lyons and his mate/wife, Merinus, that the rumors of a strange mating hormone/bond, and the deceleration of aging that the tabloids ran such stories around, were true.

Neither Callan nor Merinus had aged so much as a year in the past ten years; the same went for the others who had played prominent roles in the Breed freedoms and had married. Or mated, as the Breeds referred to it.

He stood stiff, still, in front of that grill, struggling, she knew, with his own emotions. She had seen the struggle in his expression before and saw it now in the tense set of his shoulders.

She wanted to touch him, ease him, and yet the fear of pushing her own arousal to that point terrified her. But she couldn't leave him hurting, believing she felt that. She moved to him, laid her head against his back, and felt his hard indrawn breath, the minute easing of the tension.

"I'm sorry," she whispered again.

His nod, a hard jerk of his head, was enough.

Moving back, Natalie sat down in the padded chair that was next to the patio table. Saban's back was to her, his arms spread until his hands rested on the wooden table sides of the large grill.

The muscles of his back were tense, his head lifted as he stared into the forest. She could almost feel his need to run.

Just as she had felt it before over the past month. A unique tension that gripped him despite his usual teasing manner. She wondered how much of it was an act and how much was truly a part of Saban Broussard.

"Most of what you know of me is a lie then." He shrugged, his back still to her. "I'm snarly, I'm arrogant, I hate jokes, and baseball fascinates me." He glanced down then. "I do like to cook."

"The teasing and flirting?" Parts of it she had liked; others she realized she had somehow known were all an act.

"I'm not much of a lady's man, *cher*," he grunted. "I'm a killer. I was created a killer, raised as one, and once I escaped, I killed to stay free."

Natalie watched as he turned to her, his expression still and composed; only his eyes raged with emotion.

"I know what the Breeds are, Saban," she murmured. "And now I know why you tried to be something you weren't." She shook her head stiffly.

God, this arousal stuff was killing her. It was bad enough before that kiss, but now it was tearing through her system, nearly making her ill.

And he knew it, he could smell it, he could feel it.

"Natalie, take the hormones," he said, his voice gravelly as she watched his fingers form fists against the wood. "Go inside. I'll fix the steaks, and I'll be in in a bit."

"Has it been like this for you since the beginning?" She needed to know what she was dealing with, who she was dealing with.

"A week before I came to your door and introduced myself, I watched you." She jerked in surprise, watching as his head lifted to the soft breeze that fell from the mountains around them. "You were alone in the house, your bedroom window was open, and the scent of your arousal drifted down to me. You were masturbating."

Natalie felt her face flame and had no chance to hide her embarrassment as he swung around and crouched in front of her chair.

"I could taste your sweet scent on the air," he growled, his face only inches from hers. "Needy, aching, your pussy throbbed for satisfaction, and you found none." His lips pulled back from his teeth in hunger, his eyes burned with it as his voice lowered. "And

I knew I could ease you. I knew I longed to ease you with a strength that overcame even my need to kill the bastards who hunted us for so many years. And I knew, tasting the scent of your juices in the air, that you were my mate."

"How?" Desperation filled her, longing, fear, so many emotions, so many needs she couldn't make sense of. "How could you have known, Saban?"

He took her hand before she could draw back and flatted her palm over his heart. "That night was the first time in my life that I realized my heart beat. In my life I have never known fear, nor excitement, or nerves. I was always calm. Always steady. But that night, Natalie. That night, I felt all those things, *cher*. I felt them rip inside me, tear through my soul, and fill me. Without control. Without volition. I had no choice, because you're the other part of me. My soul, *boo*. My mate."

He should have looked ridiculous, kneeling there in front of her, her hand pressed into his chest, unfortunately, he looked anything but ridiculous. He looked arrogant; he looked like a man determined to claim his woman.

Sexy, savage, hungry. He wasn't pleading, he wasn't asking permission for her heart. He was claiming it, and as far as he was concerned, it was that simple.

"It doesn't work that way." She could feel his heart beneath her hand, strong and steady. "Just because you want it—"

"Doesn't make it so." His lips twisted with an edge of bitterness. "But the mating heat does make it so, Natalie. What you said, about the choice being taken from you, may be true from your perspective, at this moment. But it isn't true of mine. If you weren't meant to be my heart, and I yours, then it would not have happened."

"Saban, there are no guarantees in life," she snapped, frustrated, feeling the pressure his certainty brought her. "I just walked out of a marriage that nearly destroyed me with one controlling man. I don't need to jump out of the frying pan into the fire."

As the last word left her lips, heat bloomed in her womb, between her thighs. Her teeth clenched on the agonizing pleasure. It wasn't pain. It was a need for pleasure, and it was sharp, intense, destructive to her self-control.

"I took the damned pills," she groaned, wrapping her arms around her stomach, pressing, fighting against the clenching, spasming need that tore through it.

"The hormone in the kiss raises the arousal level," he said softly. "The hormone in the male semen eases it somewhat."

He pushed her hair back from her face, his hard hands stroking pure pleasure along the sides of her face.

"I suspected." She shook her head. "The tabloid stories, all those silly articles. When I came to Sanctuary and met Callan and Merinus, I suspected parts of them were true."

And she had been intrigued, curious about the Breed who watched her with hungry eyes and pretended to be something, someone he wasn't.

"Parts of them are true," he agreed. "Let me ease you, Natalie. Let me take away the pain."

His lips touched hers, a butterfly kiss that had her own lips parting and a breath of need escaping her lips.

"I'm going to regret this." She knew she was.

Natalie opened her eyes and stared back at him, desperation, need, and fear roiling together inside her. "I can't handle shackles, Saban. I can't be controlled." The fear of it was ripping through her mind, destroying the balance she had found after her divorce.

Because she was being controlled. By the mating hormone he had spilled into her system, by her own body, by needs she couldn't deny because everything inside her was demanding his touch.

"I'll call Ely," he growled. "She can strengthen the pills."

Natalie shook her head, her hands jerking up to cover his as he moved to straighten away from her.

"Touch me. Just touch me." She could feel the perspiration pouring from her face now, the weakness invading her body. "Saban, this is worse than she predicted. Oh God, this is bad."

Dr. Ely Morrey had explained what she could expect in the first stage of the mating heat. But she'd said it only got worse after mates had sex that first time. Before that, the arousal would stay steady, a little uncomfortable, until she and Saban actually had sex.

If it was worse than this later, then she didn't know if she would survive it.

She stared back at Saban, seeing the agony in his eyes, the knowledge that he hadn't expected this either.

"*Cher*, Natalie." His thumbs smoothed over her cheeks. "Go inside, away from me. I'll finish this meal for you. You can eat."

She shook her head.

"If we stay out here, *bébé*, we'll end up fucking out here." He was breathing hard, his chest moving fast and hard as his hands tightened around her face. "The scent of your arousal is making me insane. My control is thin enough as it is."

She licked her lips nervously. "Come in with me."

The fact that she had made the decision, that she was actually considering having sex with him at this point shouldn't have surprised her, but it did. This arousal wasn't painful, not in the sense of levels or degrees of pain. Instead, it was imperative, desperate; her skin was crawling with the need to be touched, her mouth watering for the taste of him.

"Go in," he said tightly. "I'll bring the food back in and come to you."

She shook her head.

"Get away from me, Natalie," he snarled, jerking to his feet, surprising her with his vehemence. "Go inside. Five minutes. Give yourself five minutes away from me, make certain without me that your wisest choice isn't to call Ely first."

"You started this." She jumped from the chair and faced him, anger rising inside her, pounding through her blood and spearing through her senses as it strengthened along with the lust. "You shot this freaky hormone into my system; now you can take care of it."

If she could just get past the need, just for a few minutes, just long enough to think again, then she could figure it out. But she knew, until he touched her, until he took her, there wasn't going to be a clear thought in her head.

A growl rumbled in his throat. "It's too strong right now," he grated. "I won't take you easy."

"If you tried to take me easy, I might have to kill you," she raged back, her hands fisting in his shirt as she felt the flames of need licking over her flesh. "Saban, please, just touch me. Do something, anything so I can think."

"So you can figure a way out of this?" Bitterness filled his voice, but he was touching her, easing her backward into the house, the steaks forgotten.

"So I can figure out how to handle this." Maybe she was accepting there was no way out of it, but she didn't accept what she knew was coming from it.

She liked Saban. She hadn't realized how much she liked him

until she had to think about it, had to categorize the relationship that had developed. She cared for him. She would miss him, God, miss him so bad if he wasn't here, but she didn't love him. She didn't want to love him. And she didn't want to be controlled by him or some damned hormonal aphrodisiac.

The door locked behind him, and Natalie found herself lifted against him, his arms like steel bands around her as his kiss became a tease. He licked and nibbled at her lips, giving her just a taste of the spicy, storm-laden essence of his kiss. He made her crave more. Made her moan, her arms tighten around his neck, her tongue dip past his lips to taste more of him.

"We won't make it to the bedroom if you keep this up," he warned her, his voice dark, rough, a growling rasp that sent a shiver racing through her as one hand pushed beneath the elastic band of her pants to cup the curve of her cheek.

"So?" She didn't care.

As he held her against him, her hands slid from around his neck to the buttons of his shirt. She wanted to feel him, wanted to touch him. The weeks he had followed her through the house that image had played out in her mind. Turning, ripping the buttons free and jerking the material from his body before rubbing against him like a cat. Like he had a habit of rubbing against her every chance he had.

She wanted him. She didn't have to fight that want now; something had forced her into it, taken the choice out of her hands, and she suddenly wondered if that wasn't a good thing. Would she have ever gone after the powerful, sexual beast this man was on her own?

Natalie tore her lips back from him, the teasing little tastes driving her insane. Her hands locked in the front of his shirt, and she ripped. Buttons scattered as a snarl left his lips, savage, animalistic, but his chest was finally bare. Sun-bronzed, hard, and tough, and free of hair except the nearly invisible, incredibly fine pelt that covered him.

"Oh, God." This was better than chest hair. Perspiration gleamed on it now, making the soft hairs easier to see, and Natalie realized nothing could be more sensual. The thought of it rubbing against her sensitive nipples made her pussy clench, her juices spilling between the swollen folds between her thighs.

She had to taste him. As he carried her through the kitchen to the short hallway and the stairs, she licked his chest. His muscles jumped beneath the caress, his arms tightening as he stumbled against the wall.

The taste was there, and she lapped at it, kissing and licking her way to the flat, hard disc of his male nipple. Her teeth raked it, nipped at it. Natalie wondered vaguely if she had needed the hormone to become addicted to him, to hunger, to ache for his touch until she thought she'd die without it. Saban could be addictive on his own, she decided.

"Yes. Sweet mercy, *cher*." He pressed her against the wall, his head falling back as she tongued the hard disc, licking at the stormy taste of perspiration, the heat and hardness of tough male flesh.

"You taste like your kiss," she whimpered, licking over his chest again, little small laps that tasted his flesh and fired her blood. "Kiss me, Saban. I need your taste."

The growl that came from his lips should have been frightening; it should have caused at least an edge of wariness to cool the lust burning inside her. Instead, it tightened her stomach, caused wet heat to spill from her vagina again. And when his lips covered hers, his tongue pushing inside, there was no room for wariness or for thought, only for hunger, only the desperate need inside her to replace the shadows in his eyes with light.

That thought pierced her as she felt him stumble up the stairs. She had seen those shadows when she first met him, wondered at them, ached for them.

She stroked her hands over his bare shoulders as her head bent, her lips suckling at the storm-ridden taste of his kiss. She loved storms. The smack of thunder, the flare of lightning, and it was all there in his kiss, in the desperate hunger she knew no other man had felt for her.

"Not gonna make it to the bed," he groaned, tearing his lips from hers to pull at her shirt. "Take it off."

She took it off and flung it behind them as he shed the scraps of his shirt and went to his knee on one step.

Natalie's eyes widened as she straddled his thigh, the heated muscle pressing into her pussy, the force of her weight against him applying a teasing pressure against her clit. And when he moved her—oh Lord, his hands rocked her on his thigh, stroking her clit as his lips covered an inflamed nipple.

"Yes!" She hissed the word, her head falling back as she rode him in slow, undulating movements.

The rasp against her clit was exquisite, if she could just get the right pressure, the right position.

It was shockingly ecstatic, poised on the pinnacle of orgasm, certain when it came, it would take the top of her head off.

"Not like this." Hard hands gripped her hips. "Inside you. I'll be inside you when you come for me, *cher*. I'll be damned if you'll go without me."

FIVE

He had to make it to the bed. God, he couldn't take her here on the stairs. He had promised himself, the first time, when he completed his claim on her he would do so in the bed he had made for her. The one he'd made certain was in place before she came to this house.

The king-size bed made of heavy cypress posts, carved and detailed, made especially for the woman who would one day hold his soul.

He dreamed of claiming her there. Not here, not on stairs where she couldn't possibly know the comfort of soft sheets and the finest mattress he could provide.

Growling, his lips still holding the tight, sweetly succulent flesh of her nipple captive, he forced himself to his feet then nearly lost all strength he possessed as her legs wrapped around his hips and the heat of her pussy seeped through his jeans to his cock.

He locked his hands on her ass, and he forced himself down the short hall to her bedroom. He pushed his way through the doorway, slammed the door closed, and barely remembered to lock it before he stumbled across the room to the bed.

He felt the power of it the minute he collapsed to the mattress with her. The comfort, the peace. Entwined with the prayers of the swamp rat that had saved him, carved into lightning-struck cypress were ancient symbols of protection and peace. It was a work of art by an artist the world had never known as he taught the craft to the strange boy he had rescued from the hurricane-ravaged bayou.

It was the bed Saban had dreamed of building at an age when most boys were still tied to their mother's apron strings. The bed where he knew he would one day create his family.

"Here," he sighed, lifting from her, giving her nipple one last lick before levering himself from the curvy sweetness of her supple body.

He pulled her legs from around his waist, gripped the band of her capris, and pulled them quickly down her legs. Disposing of her strappy little sandals was easy, as was removing the silk of her damp panties.

And then he paused, held himself still, and stared down at the perfection of the woman who was his mate.

Her breasts that filled his hands perfectly, the flare of her hips, the gentle weight of her thighs, the smooth, curl-less folds of her sex. Her pussy was bare, silken, and beautiful. But how much more beautiful, he thought, if he could convince her to allow those soft curls to return?

All the sweetness in the world was held there, and he was a man who thrived on his sweets.

His head lowered, his tongue distending, and he swiped through the soft cream, a rough growl leaving his throat as he found the swollen little nub of her clit and her soft, needy cry filled the air.

Sugar and cream, that was her taste, and he could become drunk on her. He licked through the slick juices, nectar, the wine of the gods, it had to be. His lips opened, and he kissed the delicate folds of flesh, licked at the taste of her, devouring the passion that flowed from her.

And she loved it. He could feel the pleasure twisting, climbing through her body as she writhed beneath him. He had to clamp his hands on her hips to hold her still, but she lifted herself to him.

Her knees bent, her feet pressed into the mattress as he knelt beside the bed. Her hips angled, and his tongue found paradise. Rich, heady, living passion flowed to him as he heard her cries sinking into his head.

He had never known lust this hot, this wild. He fucked his tongue into the gripping, heated depths of her pussy and growled. An involuntary sound, wild and primitive, as he fought to slake his hunger for her taste.

The scent of her arousal had filled his head for weeks. Heated and mesmerizing, it had built a hunger for her that he feared he would never sate.

Mating heat be damned. This woman had consumed him long before the mating heat had begun affecting him. And now he would consume her, become so much a part of her that she could no longer run, that she realized they were bound: bound in ways she didn't want to escape.

"I want you!" Natalie clawed at his shoulders as his tongue

pumped into her pussy, driving her to the point of madness with the wicked, incredible pleasure tearing through her.

She wanted to touch him, wanted to give him the same pleasure he was giving her, but she couldn't think. She couldn't push herself away, and she couldn't help but beg, to plead for more of his wicked tongue and evil fingers.

Fingers that were pressing inside her, filling her as his lips moved to the hard knot of her clit and surrounded it.

Her eyes jerked open, stared down her body, met the dark green fire in his as he licked and suckled at the violently sensitive flesh.

She was going to explode. She could feel it. She was right there. So close.

"You taste like a dream." He kissed her clit, once, twice, then licked around it slowly, his slumberous eyes locked with hers. "I could eat you forever."

She could barely breathe.

"But I want to be inside you when you come for me the first time." He pulled back, despite her attempt to tighten her legs and hold him in place.

"I've dreamed of this, *cher*." Anticipation filled his voice, his slumberous gaze as he jerked at the laces of his boots and quickly pulled them free.

Licking her lips, Natalie moved as his hands went to his belt. She rose, sat on the side of the bed, and brushed his fingers away.

"I want you now." She slid the buckle free then went to work on the metal buttons, pulling them free, the hard, thick ridge of his cock making the task difficult at first.

As the material parted, Natalie drew it down to his thighs, left it there, and cupped her palm over the thick flesh hidden only by the cotton briefs he wore.

She heard his breath hiss from between his teeth as she gripped the band of the underwear and drew it slowly over the swollen length of his erection.

Weakness flooded her. Her juices pooled on the ultrasensitive folds of her flesh, and she swore her womb was clenching in trepidation. Because he wasn't a small man in any way.

"*Cher*, leave me a little control, eh?" His voice was strained, but his hands were gentle as he brushed the hair back from her face.

"No." She gripped the hard flesh with both hands and brought it to her parted lips.

He said something. Something foreign, thickly accented, but she didn't catch it. The blood was thundering in her ears, rushing through her body, and her mouth was surrounding the wide, hot crest of his cock hungrily.

She had dreamed, too. Dreamed of him taking her in this big bed, dreamed of taking him, just like this.

She stared up at him, tasted the heat and male lust, the hunger and the need on his flesh. Sweat gleamed on his chest, ran in small rivulets along it, and added a subtle male fragrance to the air.

It was his eyes that held her though. A green so dark now she wondered if they weren't closer to black. They glowed in his face, as startling as the wicked white canines that gleamed at the side of his mouth as his lips pulled back in a desperate snarl.

Hard hands were in her hair, twisting in it, tangling in it as she sucked his cock head inside and swirled her tongue over it slowly, tasting him.

He wasn't watching her in detachment, he wasn't analyzing her performance, he was enjoying it. Enjoying it to the point that she moaned at the additional pleasure that the expression on his face brought her.

Savage pleasure tightened his expression, pulled his lips back and had growls leaving his throat. It was the most exciting, erotic sight she had known in her life.

"Ah, *cher*," his voice whispered over her. "Sweet *bébé*."

She sucked him deep, tasting the subtle essence of pre-cum and wild, desperate lust.

She tasted and teased, tempted and tormented until she felt the control she had always sensed inside him break.

Between one second and the next she was pushed to her back, his jeans and briefs discarded, and he was moving purposely between her thighs. The length of his erection was iron-hard, throbbing, the prominent veins ridging the flesh, the engorged head darkened and pulsing in lust.

"Saban, please—" She bit her lip, holding back her words. She wanted to ask him to go easy, to take her slowly at first, but she could see the hunger raging in him, brewing into a storm of lust that darkened his emerald eyes.

"Do you think I would hurt you?" His jaw clenched, his chest heaved as he fought for breath, and the thick head of his cock tucked against the folds of her pussy.

His voice lowered to a primal growl. "Do you think I don't

know, Natalie? That I didn't feel more than your sweet, slick heat?"

His hips bunched, tightened, pressed forward as his lips lowered, and he lifted her hands to his shoulders. "Hold on to me *cher*. I'll take care of you, I promise."

Small, stretching thrusts did just that. Eased inside her, parting the snug tissue gently, working his cock into her with fiery, delicious strokes that were both pleasure and pain.

Ecstasy whipped through her system, fiery trails of lashing pleasure tore across sensitive nerve endings, and as Natalie stared up at Saban, she saw something she had never seen in her marriage to Mike: shared pleasure. The need to please her as well as to be pleasured.

Saban wasn't rushing. He wasn't intent on pushing boundaries as much as he was intent on sharing the burning need, which was more erotic than any boundary she'd ever had pushed.

"What are you doing to me?" It was more than pleasure. With her gaze locked with his, the patience in each thrust, the taut hunger on his face, sweat gleaming and running in slow rivulets down the side of his neck, he was the picture of a sex god at work. But his eyes. Emotions glowed in his eyes, emotions she didn't want to face, didn't want to battle, within him or within herself.

"I'm loving you, *cher*. Whether you want the love or not." He leaned forward, nipped her lips. "Just loving you, *bébé*."

One last thrust, slow and measured, buried him inside her as his lips took hers in a kiss that fired her soul. Her body she could have understood. The heated hormone spilling from his tongue hit her system like a fireball and began speeding through her bloodstream. But her soul? It should have been protected, closed away from any and all male influence.

But she felt her chest tightening, her heart racing from more than excitement, and the almost hidden acknowledgment that this was more than she had ever dreamed loving could be.

The growl in his chest deepened as his thrusts began to increase. His cock stroked once-hidden nerve endings, buried to the depths of her, and stroked there before beginning again. Natalie became a creature of sensuality, of pleasure. Thought, caution, and fear receded beneath the agonizing pleasure burning through her body.

Her hands gripped and caressed sweat-dampened muscles. She writhed beneath him, thrusting back, needing the fierce, hard thrusts now that she had grown used to the width and length of the erection buried inside her. She twisted beneath him, gasping, crying his name as she felt the heat burn hotter, the pleasure flame higher. Each stroke of his flesh, no matter which part of her body it touched, drove her higher. She was flying. Oh God, she had never flown.

"Saban!" She screamed his name, fear suddenly coalescing inside her, the sensations building, burning, rising to a crescendo that threatened to terrify her.

"I have you, Natalie." His lips moved over her jaw, her cheek. "Give to me, baby. Give to me. I'll hold you here. I swear it."

Husky, rough. His lips skimmed over her neck, her shoulder, those wicked canines scraped against the tender flesh between neck and shoulder, and his thrusts became stronger, hard, driving into her, fucking her with such complete abandon that the waves of ecstasy building inside her began to crash over her.

Her orgasm exploded, ruptured, imploded. It tore through her with a force that she was certain destroyed her mind as she felt those canines rake her flesh again, then a hungry growl left Saban's throat.

She couldn't have anticipated it. She should have. His teeth pierced her shoulder, his mouth clamping over the wound, his tongue stroking, laving, as his body jerked in its own release.

She felt the head of his cock swell, throb, then she felt *it*. The extension swelling from beneath the head of his cock, moving inside her, stroking her, locking his cock in place as his semen began to spurt inside her.

The second orgasm that shook her stole her breath and her sight. Her nails locked into his shoulders, her muscles trembled, shook, and she swore she saw the flames racing over both their bodies as her wail filled the air.

She had never known, never believed so much pleasure could exist. That she could orgasm, from her vagina and her clit at once, that the orgasm could race through her body and explode through every cell, every molecule of flesh. Or that in that orgasm she could feel herself, a part of herself she never knew existed, finally awakening.

SIX

There were times in a woman's life when she didn't have a choice but to admit that she was in over her head, and Natalie admitted the next morning that this was one of those times. She didn't like it, didn't like having to reprioritize her life, or acknowledge that she had no choice but to deal with a relationship that she had been certain was highly ill-advised.

Saban, despite his easygoing manner, was no pussycat, and she knew it. She sensed it clear to the core of her being and had no idea how to handle waiting for the other shoe to drop where he was concerned.

And she didn't like the fact that the mating heat had forced this, rather than human nature alone. Of course, how she could expect a Breed to be ruled by human nature, she couldn't imagine.

He had proved beyond a shadow of a doubt in the bed the night before, throughout the night, and into the morning that he was much more than a man or an animal.

He had been tireless, but then, so had she. The hunger that had driven them had kept them going at each other well after midnight before throwing them into an exhausted slumber, only to bring them awake hours later, hungrier, more desperate than ever before.

She wanted to blame it only on the hormonal reaction. Unfortunately, she clearly remembered awakening, that abnormal heat finally sated, only to have her curiosity and her needs aroused once again without that stupid hormone coming into play.

She had wanted to stroke him. Stroke him, kiss him, hear those primal growls that rumbled in his chest, and feel the strength of him when he finally had enough and tumbled her beneath him.

Now, as morning began to edge into afternoon, she found herself trying to find sense in something she knew she didn't have a hope in hell of making sense of.

What the hell had she managed to get herself involved in? But even more to the point, why wasn't she angry over it? She should be furious. She should be screaming at Lyons, threatening Wyatt and the Bureau of Breed Affairs with all manner of legal actions for not informing her of the hazards of consorting with Breeds. Instead, she was standing in her kitchen as she watched a shirtless Saban frown down at the grill he was currently attempting to figure out.

It had worked perfectly last night. This morning, it seemed to be intent on driving one Jaguar Breed insane. That, or he was trying to buy time the same way she was, by focusing on something other than the situation at hand.

She had finally given up on that herself an hour ago.

She glanced at the steaks lying on the counter, the potatoes ready to go into the microwave, and pushed her fingers through her hair before forcing herself to turn away from the sight of it. All that luscious, bronzed flesh displayed was too much for any woman's senses to deal with for extended periods of time.

She was on edge, uncertain, and trying to deal with something totally out of her realm of understanding.

The ringing of the doorbell had her jumping, swinging around, and staring through the house as the back door opened, and Saban strode in, jerking his shirt over his shoulders as he glanced at her.

His eyes were cold, hard, causing something inside her to chill as she followed him through the house. He hadn't pulled a weapon, so she assumed he knew who was at the door.

She moved quickly behind him, pulling at the hem of the long shirt she wore, drying her palms on the sides of the denim shorts.

Saban paused at the door and stared back at her as the bell rang again.

"Remember one thing," he suddenly growled, causing her to tilt her head and stare at him in surprise. "You're mine now, Natalie. I won't tolerate another man in your life. Or in your heart."

Her teeth snapped together a second before her lips parted to sling a searing retort his way. He chose that moment to jerk the door open and face the sheriff and her ex-husband, Mike Claxton.

Mike looked frustrated, furious, his blue eyes snapping in anger as the sheriff of Buffalo Gap shot Natalie a resigned look before turning to Saban with an edge of wariness.

Sheriff Randolph had the broad, heavy build of a linebacker, dwarfing Mike's smaller, leaner frame. His dark hair was cut military short, his dark eyes sharp and intelligent.

"Sorry to bother you, ma'am, Saban." He nodded to Saban. "But it seems we have a complaint."

"Mike, what are you doing here?" Natalie stepped forward, only to pause as Saban sliced a hard, warning look her way.

She almost rolled her eyes, but something about the set of his expression, the ready tension in his body, warned her that he wasn't quite ready to shelve the whole protective, possessive male thing.

She hated the thought. Hated the thought that the trust and the independence she needed could be wiped away so easily in his mind.

"Look at her, Sheriff," Mike suddenly snapped. "I told you something was wrong with her. Are you ready to listen to me now?"

Shock had Natalie backing up a step as Mike turned his enraged gaze on her. This was one of the reasons their marriage had been doomed from the first month. Jealous rages, an almost fanatical certainty that Natalie was always looking at other men, lusting for them.

She shouldn't have been shocked, much less surprised.

Natalie shifted her gaze from Mike to the sheriff. "Sheriff Randolph, it's good to see you again." She gave him an uncomfortable smile. "You haven't caught me at my best this morning."

"I apologize for that, ma'am." He shifted on his feet uncomfortably. "Mr. Claxton here seems unwilling to accept the fact that you're hale and hearty though."

"Look at her, she's pale. She looks drugged," Mike accused as he started to step into the house.

"You have not been invited inside." Saban stepped forward, his low voice dangerous.

"Get out of my way, Breed." Mike was shaking now, his voice holding a nervous tremor as Natalie watched him fight stepping back. "I want to talk to my wife."

"Ex-wife." Natalie didn't wait for Saban to answer to that one. She turned back to the sheriff instead. "I'm sorry you were bothered."

"Dammit, Natalie. Pack your things, you're coming home. This foolishness has to stop somewhere," Mike bit out virulently, his fists clenching at his sides as he was forced to stare around Saban rather than walking through him. "I'll take you home."

"Your new friend has a death wish, Ted," Saban told the sheriff. "Get him out of here."

"Now, Saban, let's be reasonable about this." The sheriff pulled his hat from his head and swiped his hand over the short cut of his hair. "Mr. Claxton just wants to talk to her. Let him see her, see she's not under any undue influence, and then he'll leave."

Saban's body jerked tighter as a ready, dangerous tension filled him.

"What sort of undue influence would I be under?" Natalie turned back to watch Mike suspiciously. He could be paranoid, he could be a bastard, but he wasn't normally insane.

Normally. She was starting to revise her opinion of that. He had that bulldog look on his face that assured her he was about to go off the deep end on her with one of his paranoid accusations.

"I want to talk to her away from him," Mike snapped at the sheriff then.

Sheriff Randolph grimaced as he glanced at Saban almost hesitantly. "Mr. Claxton, I can't make her talk to you alone." He glanced at Natalie then, his dark brown eyes intent, somber as he studied her. "It's up to you, ma'am."

"What the hell are you pulling here, Ted?" Saban snarled then. "Take your friend and get the hell out of here."

Sheriff Randolph wasn't buying something here. Natalie could see the suspicion in his eyes as he glanced from her to Saban, and she could see Mike's anger growing.

"Saban, that's enough." The tension in the air was thick enough to choke on. "Why don't you and the sheriff go get coffee—"

"You think I'll be relegated to the kitchen like a recalcitrant child and leave you alone with this madman?" He turned his head, his fierce green eyes pinning her with cold fire. "I don't think so."

She breathed in deeply and prayed for patience.

"I think you're going to take the sheriff to the kitchen for coffee, and you're going to do it without growling like a temperamental five-year-old." She smiled back at him, a thin, furious curve of her lips. "Don't make me think of an 'or else.' That's just so tacky, and I do hate appearing tacky."

Sheriff Randolph cleared his throat, obviously fighting a chuckle as Saban glowered back at her, one side of his lips curling back to display those wicked canines.

Canines that had pierced her shoulder, holding her in place more than once through the night as his tongue laved, and the hormone burned the wound.

He was a part of her. In a way no man could ever be a part of her. He was in her head, her blood, and she very much feared he might be a part of her heart. A part that would be destroyed if he continued to try to smother her.

"I don't like this," he growled. "He's not stable."

"I'm not stable?" Mike burst out, his eyes glittering with rage as he pinned her with his gaze. "For God's sake, Natalie, look at what you're shacked up with and tell me anything about that is logical. He's an animal."

"Enough!" Natalie swung to him, instinctive, heated anger filling her at the accusation. "If you want to discuss anything, Mike, then keep a civil tongue in your head."

His lips flattened as the sheriff watched both of them with flat, hard eyes. He had his own agenda, Natalie thought. Questions he couldn't ask, so instead he watched.

"And I'm to leave you in the same room alone with this man?" Saban questioned her with an edge of disgust.

"Listen to me, you rabid bastard!" Mike tried to push into the house, rage burning in his face now, splotching his cheeks as the sheriff grabbed his arm and Saban blocked the doorway. "Let me in there. You've done something to her, and I know it. Look at her. She's pale and scared. Look at her, Sheriff. He's done something to her. He's a fucking animal. He shouldn't be here with her. He shouldn't be around her."

Natalie stepped back from the doorway as Saban's hard body blocked Mike's furious attempts to get past the door. She had never seen him like this, so enraged that his own personal safety wasn't uppermost. Surely he knew Saban could break him like a matchstick if that was what he wanted.

"Mike, that's enough!" She snapped out the order, firming her voice, hardening it. "For God's sake, have you lost your mind?"

Saban was struggling not to hurt him, Natalie could see that. He was blocking the doorway with his own body, holding Mike back as the sheriff gripped his arm and dragged him forcibly away from the door.

"Get him out of here, Ted. Jonas will be in your office within the hour to file a complaint. I want him kept away from her."

"Fucking animal! You don't make that decision." Mike struggled against the sheriff. "That's my wife in there. You don't touch my damned wife."

Mike fell back as Saban snarled, a primal, dangerous, feline sound unlike anything Natalie had heard as he rasped. "Ex-wife, bastard."

"My God, this is insane." Natalie pushed past Saban, slapping at his hard stomach as he tried to hold her back. "Take your hands off me and stop this crap. Are all of you insane?"

"Natalie, listen to me." Mike reached for her, his hands closing around her arm, his fingers biting into her flesh.

The sensation of his touch caused an immediate reaction, one she didn't understand, couldn't make sense of. Her skin felt as though it were shrinking, physically trying to draw away from his touch as shards of brittle, sharp distaste filled her brain.

A shocked, hoarse cry came from her lips as she tried to jerk away from him, staring at where his fingers wrapped around her flesh just below the elbow.

A vicious snarl sounded behind her, and before Natalie could process the lightning-fast events, Mike's neck was gripped in Saban's powerful hand, his fingers loosened from her arm, and he was tossed, physically, through the air into the yard beyond the porch.

She stared down at her arm, then back to Mike before she rubbed at her skin slowly, trying to wipe away the feel of his touch. It was still there, the sensation of his skin on her, causing a sickness to roil in her stomach as nausea rose in her throat. She felt invaded, molested, as though Mike had touched an intimate part of her flesh rather than merely gripping her arm. The sensations had bordered on agony, unlike the mere feeling of distasteful discomfort when the Breed doctor had examined her.

Shock slowed reality, had her head lifting, watching as Saban jumped to the ground, lifted Mike from the lawn, and nose to nose snarled furiously, flashing the sharp canines in his mouth as his fist struck with lightning quickness into the soft padding of Mike's belly.

The sheriff tried to tear them apart, tried to force himself between the two men, but Saban was too enraged.

She heard her own voice screaming his name as she jumped to

the ground, rushing to the fray and gripping Saban's arm as it came back for another round.

Mike's eyes had rolled back in his head, his body slumped as Saban stilled, his head whipping around to Natalie, his eyes slicing to where she touched him.

"Let him go." Thin and reedy, she had to force her voice to work, force herself to think. "Let him go now."

She stared back at him, shaking, shuddering with the force of the knowledge tearing through her now. Whatever he had done to her had more far-reaching effects than an arousal gone haywire.

"Let him go." She lifted her other hand, wrapped it around the wrist where his fingers were still clenching Mike's neck. "Please."

Mike was gasping for air as Saban opened his fingers slowly and allowed him to collapse to the ground where the sheriff jerked him back up and hustled him back to the cruiser.

Natalie stood beneath the hot summer sun, distantly aware of the neighbors that had come from their houses to watch in horrified curiosity.

"What's happening?" she whispered. She could still feel Mike's touch echoing painfully through her arm. She couldn't wipe it away, couldn't stop the churning in her stomach.

Saban grimaced, turned to her, then wrapped one hand around the nape of her neck and lowered his lips to hers. His tongue speared past her lips, tangled with hers, and in a second she was devouring the taste of him, suddenly, horrifyingly craving the dark taste of lust that spilled from his tongue.

It was a brief moment in time, no more than a touch, a taste, but when his head lifted, Natalie felt as though the energy had been sapped from her body, but so had the pain. She laid her forehead against his chest, her breath hitching in fear.

"What have you done to me?" she whispered. "Oh God, Saban, what have you done to me?"

Mike watched the scene in the front yard. That animal touching her, kissing her, his arms going around her as he pulled back and Natalie rested her head against his chest.

She leaned into the Breed, let him support her, let him hold her through whatever pain she was feeling, and he hated it. He wanted to rip the bastard apart, cell by cell. The son of a bitch had what should have belonged to Mike. He was stealing it, had been stealing her away from him for God only knew how long.

This was the reason she had been so all-fired determined to divorce him, to walk away from him. This was the reason she never depended on him, never leaned on him and let him guide her, because of this Breed, this animal.

He wiped his hand over his face, feeling the sweat building there, running down his temples. The soldier that had come to his apartment just after she left town was right. Mike hadn't believed it, couldn't believe that those bastard animals could have the control over a woman that he was told they had.

But he was seeing it with his own eyes. He had seen her, unable to bear his touch, her face going white, the shock of it darkening her eyes a second before the Breed had torn him away from her.

And now the animal was holding her rather than the husband she should have never divorced.

God. What was he going to do? He had to get her away from that bastard. He had to get her to the doctor the soldier had waiting so they could fix this.

This was why she divorced him. He shook his head in amazement. He hadn't understood it at the time. He was her husband, he had the right to have her home when he wanted her home, the right to protect her and look over her. To keep her safe from bastards like that animal Broussard.

He let his eyes lock with the glowing green of the Breed's and swallowed tightly at the promise of retribution there. Broussard would kill him if he had the chance. Mike would have to make certain he didn't get the chance. There would be a way; he would find a way to draw Natalie away from this, to save her, to get her to that doctor so he could cure her. So he could wipe the effects of whatever had been done to her out of her mind.

He knew her. The Breed didn't. He could do it.

"Man, you have a fucking death wish." The sheriff got into the driver's seat and glanced back at him pityingly.

Pityingly, as though Mike didn't have a chance. He did have a chance. He just had to get Natalie where they could help her, that was all.

"She's my wife," he snapped.

"Ex-wife," the sheriff reminded him with a sneer.

Mike glared back at him.

Shaking his head, the other man turned and started the vehicle before pulling out of the drive.

Mike continued to watch Natalie. She was arguing with the Breed now. He knew that look on her face, had become intimately acquainted with it in the year before their divorce.

He had wondered what had happened to his wife. The woman who loved him, who obeyed him. This was what had happened to her. This Breed. And Mike was going to have to fix it.

SEVEN

He should feel guilty, he should have a conscience, shouldn't he? He should feel pain: the same pain she felt that she was bound so irrevocably to him that even the touch of another male brought her distress.

But he wasn't. And the true problem lay in the fact that he couldn't hide that he wasn't. That was why he had to rush to keep up with her as she stormed into the house, nearly slamming the door in his face before he could get past it.

"You know, *cher*, I'm a man," he stated as she whirled to confront him in the living room. "I am a Breed male. Possessive, confrontational, and territorial. You can't ask me to be any different."

"I could ask you not to drag me into it. I could ask you not to show your ass on the front lawn simply to stake your pitiful claim, and I could ask you not to commit murder while the sheriff is watching. For God's sake, some things should just be private." Her voice rose as she spoke, anger spiking each word, clipping them until they rolled off her lips like a curse on the head of the unwary.

"He touched you." That was enough for Saban. "He caused you pain."

"Oh yeah, and he knew that gripping my arm was going to cause that freaky hormone you infected me with to send knives slashing into my flesh." Disgust colored her words.

Her molasses eyes were hot, boiling with temper, her face flushed with her fury, and he swore even her hair seemed to have picked up fiery highlights. She was like a dark flame burning before him, searing him with the wonder of her. That and pure male ownership.

She was his woman. His. The one thing nature had created solely for him. If she thought for even one second he would allow another to touch her, to claim her, then she had best think again.

"I should have warned you of that perhaps," he grunted,

though he was certain that warning her of it would have done no good. "I would have thought Ely had taken care of that."

"Expect discomfort." She pushed the words past her lips like some filthy curse. "Expect a few side effects. Tell me, Saban, what the hell else should I expect now that you've actually fucked me?"

He felt his teeth clench at the derogatory tone of voice.

"Don't push me, Natalie," he warned her softly. "My own temper hasn't yet cooled from watching that bastard attempt to claim you."

"No one claims me." Her fists balled at her sides, and he could have sworn she nearly stamped her foot.

How interesting. It was definitely a sight to be wary of, because he could smell the pure violence simmering inside her. Her patience with him, with Breeds, with males in general was rapidly reaching its limit. He wondered, though, and couldn't help but be fascinated with the idea of her losing that patience and temper.

There was a warrior inside her; he could feel it. A woman ready to take on the world when it counted and to flay a Breed at twenty paces should he deserve it. And he definitely deserved it; hell, he was almost looking forward to it. From what he had seen of his pride leader, Callan, and Callan's mate, makeup sex could be damned satisfying.

The books Cassie had pawned off on him had assured him that it was satisfying. Often the best sex of any relationship. Though, to be honest, if it got better than last night and this morning, he may not survive it.

"Did you hear me, Saban Broussard?" Her voice roughened, rasped with her anger. "No one claims me."

"That mark on your neck proves otherwise." He shrugged as he stared back at her calmly. "I've claimed you, *cher*, for better or worse. There is no divorce, there is no separation, and there will be no ex-husband believing he can rescind that claim."

Saban kept his voice calm though firm. He had a feeling that if he lost control of his hot Cajun temper, then he would have lost this battle from the beginning. Because with the temper came a resurgence of the heat, hotter and brighter than before, as he knew Natalie was now learning.

Nature did not allow the breed mates to confront each other without a safeguard in place. They may fight, they may rage, but they would not deny each other.

In the face of her anger, he could feel no guilt. He wasn't a man to do anything by half measures; he had been trained to know what to do, how to do it, and not question himself over every decision made.

But as he stared back at Natalie now and saw the flash of hurt and fear beneath the anger, he wondered at the ache in his chest. Guilt? Perhaps. He'd never known that emotion either until Natalie, so it was hard to be certain.

Her independence had been hard-won, and now she felt it threatened. He didn't blame her for her anger, but he would not allow her to deny him or the mark she now carried.

"You should leave." Her voice was thick with unshed tears and unresolved fury. "Now!"

"Well, *cher*, I'll just make certain I do that," he growled. "With your ex-husband prowling around like a demented coyote and that fool sheriff sticking his nose in where it don't belong. Oh yeah, I'm jus' gonna pack up and head on out, eh?"

He was growing tired of being told to leave her.

"I have to get out of here." She shook her head. "I have to get away from you before you drive me completely crazy."

"Until your ex-husband showed up, you had no problems with me." He felt like snarling, like roaring in his own frustration as the thought hit his mind. "Does he mean so much to you that now you have to run from me?"

The look she cast him was so filled with disdain that had he been a lesser man, he may have flinched.

"Don't pretend to be stupid, Saban; you just don't pull it off well," she informed him caustically. "I don't know what your Breed rule book says, but common decency should keep you from acting like a complete moron just because it suits your purposes to do so. You threatened Mike. You nearly killed him. And you shouldn't be standing in front of me as though this mating heat bullshit makes it all right."

"I will protect you." He stepped closer, glowering down at her as the animal part of his brain demanded that he show her, again, just how much she was his woman. "Claxton wasn't being reasonable, Natalie, you know that."

"And you were?" She crossed her arms over her breasts and glared at him. "You were choking him to death. One-handed."

"Would you have preferred I used two hands? I thought it sporting to give him a handicap at least, but next time I'll make certain I do the job right." The next time he would just kill the bastard and have done with it.

The look she flashed him spoke volumes of her fury and her opinion of that statement.

He watched, fascinated, as she restrained her rage. Her arms unfolded, her body tightened, until he wondered if her spine would snap.

"I have things to do today," she informed him then. "Things that do not include you. Excuse me."

She headed for the stairs, dismissing him as though the argument were over, simply because she deemed it over?

"Not so fast, mate," he bit out, moving quickly to slide between her and her destination. "This argument has not yet finished."

"Why? Because you haven't gotten fucked yet?" She flicked a glance at the evidence of his erection beneath his jeans. "I'm not in the mood."

He growled at that. "You damned sure are ready to fuck, but that wasn't on the agenda quite yet. Your anger at the moment is, because it's completely illogical. Claxton was gearing himself up for violence, Natalie, and you know it. Better he found that outlet with me than with you. It ensured his survival."

"Mike wouldn't hurt me." A frown flashed between her brows. "I was married to him for years, Saban, he never touched me in violence."

It was the way she said it, the telltale flicker of her lashes, the scent of deceit. She wasn't lying to him, but she wasn't telling him the entire truth either.

"What did he do then?" he asked her carefully.

The sudden evasion in her eyes was proof that he had done something.

"He never hit me, and do you know what else he never did, Saban? He never started fights with men over something so asinine either."

"No, he likely started them with you." Saban could feel the renewed need to rip the man to shreds, one limb at a time. "Is that why you divorced him, Natalie? Why you fight the mating with me so hard? Did he attempt to control all that wild, beautiful fire inside you? Or did he attempt to douse it?"

"Conversation is over." She said it calmly, but he could sense, smell the hurt and the anger raging inside her.

Like those flames Claxton had wanted to control, she pushed it back, buried it, hid it beneath that mask of calm self-control. She could teach a Breed about self-possession.

She could definitely give him lessons in it, because he wasn't handling this nearly as well as she was, but also, he knew, he had already accepted what she was to him. She still had that journey to make.

"This conversation is not over." He bared his teeth in frustration; he could feel that frustration rising inside him now, threatening the boundaries of his control. "Hear me well, Natalie. It doesn't matter who it is, man or woman; any threat to you will be dealt with. Any strike against you will be retaliated against. So much as a thought, a flicker of threat, and I will be there. Whether you like it or not, whether you want it or not."

"Whether I want it or not." Her voice was bitter, cutting like acid into his soul. "Because you decree it. Stand wherever the hell you want to stand, Saban. As long as it's well away from me."

EIGHT

It hurt. Natalie couldn't stem the hurt rising inside her, the fear, the certainty that the loss of control where Saban was concerned would be her undoing.

"I don't need you to fight my battles." She needed to fight her own battles, dammit. "Especially where Mike is concerned."

She turned to move away from him, only to be confronted by his broad chest once again.

"Get out of my way, Saban."

"So you can run and hide?" he bit out. "Rather than facing this problem and fixing it, you're going to run away."

"There's no fixing it," she pushed between gritted teeth as her fingers clenched at her side. "You think you're right. You always think you're right. Big, bad Breed knows it all."

Silence met her accusation. Natalie lifted her gaze then, met his, and had to fight the thickening in her throat as she saw not anger as she thought she would find, though there was a little of that there. Instead, he watched her broodingly, as though searching for an answer or trying to find the question that eluded him.

"You didn't smell what I smelled," he finally said gently. "The rage, the need for violence that was filling him. You divorced him, Natalie, for a reason, and you know this. Just as you knew that violence was brewing within him before you forced him out of the home."

She wasn't going to let him be right about this. She couldn't. If she did, how could she ever stand up to him later? Mike had done this at first, used logic, used a shield of understanding and patience to tear down her self-confidence.

"How my marriage ended in a divorce is my business. How I deal with Mike now is my business. Not yours."

"You don't truly believe that, Natalie." He shook his head as he shoved his hands in his back pockets, obviously restraining the need to touch her.

Unlike Mike.

Not that Mike had ever hit her, but it came close too many times. His temper could be ugly, hands bruising, his tongue sharp and cutting.

"I said it, didn't I?" She forced past clenched teeth as the irritation and the arousal combined into some funky kind of tingles that radiated from her womb outward to the rest of her body.

She was certain that in another place and time, in any other situation, this could have been amusing. If it was happening to someone else maybe.

"Why can't you do just one thing like a normal, everyday person?" she snapped, wanting to pull at her own hair as frustration began to build in her.

The anger was bad enough. But being angry and dying to fuck that hard body? No woman should have to deal with this.

His expression eased slightly from the predatory determination, and sensual amusement darkened his eyes, lowered his lashes as he bent his head closer to her.

"*Cher*, if you haven't noticed yet, normal is not a part of my genetics. Should I give you another example of this?"

She backed up as his hands came out of his pockets and rested comfortably at his sides instead.

"Sex is not going to get you out of this," she hissed. "There's not enough sex to make up for deliberately attacking someone who hadn't attacked you."

"He touched you. He caused you pain." Saban shrugged, though his expression tightened. "That is all the reason I need."

Then he turned away. He turned away as though it didn't matter, as though his decisions were all that mattered and were all that was important.

"Don't you do that." Natalie could feel herself shaking inside and out.

"Do what? Drop this little spat we're having?" He turned back to her, a smooth, powerful flex of muscle as he faced her once again. "We won't agree on this, Natalie. Whether you want to believe it or not, Mike Claxton means you harm, and I won't allow it to happen. You disagree, and that's fine. That doesn't mean that I'll not put a stop to it. Now, if you're not willing to cool off that heat building inside you with a little therapeutic sex, then I could use a snack. Are you hungry?"

Was she hungry?

Her lips parted in shock. He didn't want to argue? He wasn't going to fight over it?

"Since when?" She followed him rapidly. "Since when do you not want to fight? You're male, right?"

He flashed her a wicked grin over his shoulder. "You should know by now."

Oh God yes, she knew. She knew his hard, calloused hands holding her to him, the feel of his mouth devouring her, his cock destroying her. And she knew the cold, icy fury in his face when he had held Mike's neck in his grip, slowly choking him to death.

"You can't just attack people who piss you off, Saban. Especially men. I have to deal with men daily at work, I can't afford this."

"Then they'd best have the good sense to keep their hands off you." He opened the door of the fridge, bent, and looked inside before pulling free a gallon of milk.

Natalie stood and stared at him, anger shuddering through her body.

"It doesn't work that way, dammit," she cursed.

He set a glass on the counter, poured it full of milk, then, lifting the glass, turned and faced her.

"Bet me." His eyes gleamed in amusement as he lifted the glass and drank.

A man drinking whiskey was sexy. A man with a bottle of beer could be sexy. But a man drinking a glass of milk should not have been sexy. Unfortunately, Saban could make it erotic, especially when he lowered the glass and licked over his lower lip with sensual male awareness.

Natalie felt her stomach tighten, felt her pussy cream furiously as she remembered the enjoyment on his face as he licked her just like that.

"You're being unreasonable." She forced her fingers to uncurl from the fists they were making, to stretch as she strove to make sense of this attitude. He'd been ready to kill Mike. Now he was watching her with amused playfulness.

"You do not attack anyone for something so insane as touching me when they aren't aware of this stupid mating heat," she retorted, feeling off center, uncertain of her own anger now. It was damned hard for a woman to fight with a man when he was watching her like a piece of candy that he was dying to taste.

"We'll see." He crossed his arms over his chest.

"We'll see?" she pushed through her teeth, that anger rising again, along with the need, the hunger. She hated this. It was insane. The madder she got at him, the hornier she got, and that wasn't a good combination. "The next time you attack someone, I'll have you arrested myself," she threw out rashly. "I won't allow it."

His expression changed then. Predatory, arrogant. This was the Jaguar Breed, the frightening, sensual animal she always felt lurking beneath the surface.

"You won't allow it?" His voice rumbled with a growl, slurring the words with just enough primal power that it sent a chill racing down her spine.

"I won't allow it." She felt the shudder that tore through her body as the amusement fled his gaze, and savage arousal filled it instead.

He moved toward her.

Natalie wasn't retreating. She wasn't backing down on this, and she was not going to allow him to railroad her into agreeing that he could attack whenever and wherever he chose. If she didn't put her foot down now, if she didn't stop it now, then there would be no end to it. He would believe he could run over her anytime he wanted, however he wanted.

Start as you mean to go on, her mother had always warned her. She had tried doing that with Mike, tried to stay firm, and he had run over her. He had frightened her, her love for him had excused him, and she had spent three miserable years trying to make a marriage work that was doomed from the start.

"I pulled back for you," he rumbled as he came closer. "I let the bastard go, because you said 'please,' because the pain in your voice for that piece of shit was more than I could bear. Did you see the look on his face when he gripped your arm, when he saw the pain it caused you?"

Natalie shook her head, denying the question.

"Oh, you saw all right, *boo*." His lip curled in anger. "You saw the satisfaction, the glee in his eyes, and I smelled it. I smelled it, and I swore I would kill him for it."

"You can't just go killing people over something like that." She smacked her hands against his chest, tried to push him back.

His hands lifted then, smoothed down her arms, and a shiver raced across her flesh.

"He still breathes," Saban snarled.

"Barely!" she bit out. "Do you think that makes what you did okay?"

"I think it made it very dissatisfying," he said softly, dangerously. "Killing him would have been preferable at that time, but losing you over it wouldn't have been worth it. That doesn't mean I'll allow him to get away with it. He'll be more careful in the future, and so, mate, will you be more careful. The next man that comes at you in anger, get the hell out of my way. Because the more harm he causes you, the greater his chances of meeting his eternal maker." Each word shortened, roughened, until he finished with a harsh, furious growl.

Natalie opened her lips to blast him, to argue further, though the words tumbling in her head refused to find coherency. Before she could speak, his head lowered, his hands jerked her to his body, and he nipped at her lips.

It wasn't even a kiss. He nipped at them, then licked them, watching her through narrowed eyes as her tongue jumped to the lower curve of her lips to taste him. To savor the spicy, stormy essence that lingered there from the hormone that infused it.

A broken little groan came from her throat.

"You taste me." He licked her again. "You feel me, Natalie. Tell me, tell me you know I'd do nothing to harm you. Including killing that miserable little bastard unless he actually endangered your life."

"You'd hurt him." She tried to shake her head, tried to fight the need beginning to burn in her blood.

"Oh, *boo*, for sure I would. I'd hurt him bad." The Cajun slipped free, lazy, guttural, spiked with hunger and dangerous intent. "I'd make him run crying to his momma for daring to harm, to believe he could ever take what is mine alone. And you know, *cher*, you are mine alone."

His.

Her lips parted, and his covered them, a weak, whimpering little moan leaving her lips as she tasted him fully. As he sucked her tongue into his mouth and then gave her leave to play. To lick at him, to tease until his tongue came to her, until she could suckle it, sweeping her tongue over it, drawing the taste of him into her mouth.

"No!"

Natalie jumped around him, ignoring the little growl that sounded behind her.

"Don't tell me no, mate," he retorted heatedly. "I smell your need, and even more, I smell the fact that you know I'm right. You'll not run from this or from me."

"I'll run whenever or however I want to." She pushed her fingers through her hair and backed out of the kitchen. "Leave me alone, Saban. Just leave me the hell alone."

She turned and stalked to the steps. She had to make sense of this; she had to find a way to balance the things she was learning about him.

He couldn't just attack people. This mating heat stuff was bad enough. How would either of them survive it without some control? Without one of them thinking sensibly, and it was real damned clear that the one thinking clearly wasn't going to be him.

All she had to do was get away from him, just for a little while. Away from the sight of him, the remembered taste of him, the aching need for him.

She hit the stairs almost at a run, aware, so very aware that he was behind her, moving with lazy speed, gaining on her, his expression taut, hunger burning in his eyes.

Her breath hitched in her throat; a ragged moan left her lips as she felt his hands grip her hips halfway up the steps, stopping her as his hands moved quickly to the front of her jeans and began working the snap and zipper loose.

"What are you doing?" she screeched, scrambling to capture his wrists, his hands, to stop the quick release of her clothes even as he jerked the material over her hips. "Dammit Saban . . ."

She went to her knees as a large hand pressed into her back, pushed her forward, and he came over her, dominant, forceful, his lips covering the wound he had left on her shoulder the night before.

Natalie froze as pleasure streaked, exploded, tore through her from that single caress. The area was so sensitive, so violently receptive to his lips, to his stroking tongue, that it stole her breath.

"This won't solve anything," she gasped as the head of his cock pressed between her thighs, slid through the slick moisture there, and found the entrance it sought.

He didn't move his lips; instead, he growled against the wound as his hips pressed forward, burying his erection inside her as Natalie felt needle points of ecstatic pleasure begin to attack every nerve ending he stroked.

"This doesn't change it," she panted, fighting the pleasure, fighting her inability to refuse it. "It doesn't make it right."

Her back arched as a mewling cry left her lips, and his cock pressed to the hilt inside her, filling her, overtaking her.

"Tell me you're mine." He nipped at the wound, causing her head to jerk back against his shoulder, one hand to reach back for him, clamping on his hip as he held her to him.

"I won't let you control me."

"Tell me," he snarled, licked the bite mark, sucked at it with a hungry growl.

"I won't let you do this." Her cry was weak, a pitiful, pathetic attempt to defy what she knew, even now, was the truth. A certainty as nothing else in her life had ever been.

His hips flexed, causing his cock to stroke her internally, to rasp against her inner flesh, the swollen, flared head caressing, enflaming tender, sensitive flesh with small thrusts. His lips grazed the wound at her neck once more, then his teeth raked over it, sending violent shudders to race down her back as her senses became overwhelmed, her common sense lost beneath the rush of pleasure.

"Tell me." Insidious, flavored with dark sensuality, rough and primal, his voice stole through her mind, as his touch stole her reason.

"Yours." Her cry was rewarded, her submission accepted, and the animal within him broke free.

It was burning, pleasure-pain; each thrust was hard and heavy as control was lost for both of them. As though her admission of his conquest was all he needed to allow his own pleasure free rein.

It was more pleasure than she could process; it was heated and liquid; it burned through flesh and bone and filled her soul where she hadn't known she had been cold. Cold and lonely and searching for that something more, that reason to give her inner self to another.

She didn't have a reason, but that didn't matter. She felt it melting, felt it flowing through her body, pouring from her cells, wrapping around him and drawing his essence into her. And breaking her heart.

In the moment between agonizing pleasure and climax, Natalie admitted it to herself. It wasn't Saban she was fighting; it was herself. Because she was losing herself in him, giving him parts of her soul that even Mike hadn't known existed. Giving him parts of her that she hadn't believed she could share.

And when the climax exploded through her, when it sang through her senses and quaked through her body, she knew she was lost.

Behind her, Saban jerked, snarled. The head of his cock throbbed, the barb, that thumb-sized extension, became erect, pushing past the underside of his cock head and stroking areas too sensitive for touch, already primed, already enflamed as his semen spurted inside her.

He had marked her. Taken her. He possessed her. And unlike Mike, Natalie had a feeling Saban truly could destroy her.

NINE

There was a wariness between them, days later, that Natalie couldn't figure out how to overcome. She didn't know if she even wanted to overcome it at this point.

The mating heat had her off balance; her emotions, her independence, and the fear Mike had instilled in her through their marriage of being controlled again all battled within her head and within her heart.

A part of her wanted to reach out and take everything Saban seemed to be offering her, yet the other part held back, watched and waited. Nothing could be as easy as this. The mating heat, the sense of everything coming together when his body moved within hers.

The new school season was coming closer by the day. Classes were on a year-round basis, but the six-week break between the final semester and the beginning of new classes gave students and teachers a much-needed vacation before classes began. And it was during that time that the Breed Cabinet had given Natalie a chance to get used to the town and to review the files she had been given on the students assigned to her.

The classroom she had been given was one of the finest she had seen. The computers were state-of-the-art, the room was bright and airy, the tinted windows that lined one wall looked out on the green, well-manicured grounds that surrounded the school.

She knew the glass to those windows was specially made to ensure an assassin's bullet couldn't find its way through. Just as she knew that the Board of Education had approved a variety of security measures that would place Breeds in close proximity in and around the school to ensure the protection of the Breed children who would be attending classes.

It was a chance of a lifetime. She would always be known as the first non-Breed teacher to be a part of the education of the exceptional children rumored to have been born of the unions between Breeds and non-Breeds.

That had been part of the excitement of having been chosen for the job, until she met Saban.

Natalie paused in inputting the class schedules she was making up into her personal PC at that thought. Yeah, Saban had changed things. From the day he had arrived at her home, she had known he would change things within her, and because of it, she admitted, she had fought the attraction rising between them.

She had fought him, snapped at him, acted like a shrew and a spoiled brat, searching for ways to irritate him past the wickedly sexy looks he had given her.

A part of her had wanted nothing but to run from him, while another part of her had held on to every look, every word, every second of attraction sizzling between them.

Until she found herself here, staring sightlessly at the half-finished class schedules and the room prepared for incoming students as Saban rechecked the security control room that the Breed children's bodyguards would use during class.

She looked to the open door, aware of the murmur of his voice, too low to make out what he was saying, but comforting nonetheless. Comforting just because she knew he was there, close, protective.

God she was totally losing her perspective here. The same protectiveness that terrified her when he was defending her against Mike was now comforting.

She shook her head at the thought, just as she mentally kicked herself for not having anticipated what Mike would do. He had been fine with the divorce and the mistress he'd had on the side the last year of their marriage until he thought she might have someone else in her life.

Then it was all over but the screaming, the fighting, and the accusations. She was well acquainted with all of them.

The surprising part had been that he had actually stayed away from her since the confrontation at the house. She had been terrified he would try to get in again, that he would bring his insanity back to where Saban could choke it out of him.

As she dragged a hand wearily through her hair, her gaze still on the doorway, Saban stepped through it. Tall and rugged, dressed in jeans, a T-shirt, and boots, a black Breed Enforcer badge clipped to his belt on one side, his weapon worn comfortably in a shoulder holster.

He looked like what he was, a badass Breed ready to fight if the situation warranted it. Ready to love if she would give him half a chance.

He strode across the room, powerful legs eating up the short distance, his brilliant green eyes eating her alive despite the forbidding line of his mouth.

The flat, severe expression was a warning, and one she knew she wasn't going to like.

"What's happened?" She rose slowly from her chair, all manner of nightmare visions flashing through her head. Heading it was the fear that Callan Lyons, pride leader of the Ruling Cabinet, had changed his mind about allowing the children to attend the public classes.

He moved to the front of her desk, his brooding gaze flickering over her face before he propped his hands on his hips and scowled. The irritated, aggravated look took her aback.

"I've just been informed that your ex has attempted to order Callan Lyons to have me removed from your home based on his suspicions that you have been unduly influenced by me and therefore not in possession of your full mental faculties. He's threatening to sue me, the Ruling Cabinet, and the Board of Education for being conspirators in my evil designs upon your very luscious body and demanding that you be released from your contract and escorted immediately to his location where he will then return you to your home and get you medical care."

As he spoke, Natalie felt her lips parting in shocked amazement.

"He wouldn't dare," she breathed.

"Oh, he's dared," Saban snapped. "Now, tell me again why I shouldn't kill the son of bitch and put us all out of our misery."

She only wished he was joking.

"Because it would piss me off?" She flattened her hands against the desk and glared back at him. "Do you think I want bloodshed over someone's insane jealousy? For God's sake Saban, why the hell do you think I divorced him?"

"I'm wondering what possessed you to marry him to begin with," he snorted irritably before running a hand along the back of his neck. "He's out of control, Natalie. I'm warning you now, the Breed Ruling Cabinet is considering a measure to have him arrested and barred from the area. If he ignores the injunction, he'll be jailed."

"Saban—"

"Don't Saban me," he growled. "Do you have any idea the

threat he poses to the very tenuous agreement the Ruling Cabinet and the Board of Education came to here? Or the threat he poses to you, personally? I've warned you, he's not sane, and this merely proves it."

"Mike is a little intense sometimes." She grimaced. "He'll get tired of this and go away." She hoped.

He leaned forward. This time he was the one that flattened his hands on the desk as his nose came within inches of hers. "You are fooling yourself."

Perhaps she was. Shaking her head, Natalie moved away from the desk and walked to the windows. She stared out onto the lush grounds, the tall, thick trees that bordered it, and wondered what she would do if Mike managed to destroy this chance for all of them.

"You should let me talk to him." She turned to Saban, knowing, even before she did, what she would see.

His eyes narrowed on her, denial reflecting on the hard, savage lines of his face.

"Not gonna happen," he informed her with a menacing purr. "Do you remember the last encounter? Did he look as though he would listen to you then?"

No, he hadn't. She breathed out roughly.

"He's not a bad man," she finally said softly. "He just wasn't a good husband."

"He's insane. Stop trying to defend him. He'd cart you out of here physically no matter your wishes, if you gave him only half a chance. I don't intend to give him that chance."

No, she didn't either. But Mike had never been dangerous, not really. He was suspicious, paranoid, and sometimes a little over the top, but she couldn't believe he would hurt anyone.

"When are you going to stop defending him, Natalie?" He crossed his arms over his chest and glowered back at her.

"I'm not defending him." She hunched her shoulders against the accusation. "I just don't want you killing him."

"And if I promise not to kill him?" he rasped coldly. "What then? Will you accept that he's fucking crazy and at least allow me the satisfaction of throwing him over the county line?"

Her lips almost twitched. He might be a Breed, but at the moment he was pure arrogant, irritated male.

"You should let me talk to him," she said again, shaking her head. "You have to know how to reason with him, that's all."

"Well evidently you don't know how to do it either, or you wouldn't have ended up divorced, now would you?"

"Yes, I would have." She met his gaze without flinching. "Reason or not, Mike couldn't accept my need to be myself, and I couldn't accept his need to control me. It was that simple, Saban. Everything else aside, that was what destroyed our marriage."

"You loved him." And he hated it. She could see it for the barest second, flashing in his eyes, the knowledge that she had felt something for another man.

Natalie nodded slowly. "When I married him, I loved the illusion he gave me. I loved the man I thought he was."

His nostrils flared; if it was in anger or in an attempt to scent the truth of her statement, she wasn't certain.

His arms dropped from his chest as he shook his head then, turning from her and running his hand along the back of his neck as though to rub away the tension there.

"I had a life before you, Saban. Just as you had one before me," she reminded him.

"I never loved until you." He turned back to her, that arrogance stronger, tightening his features, brightening his eyes. "But I don't blame you for the emotions you had for him. Sucks, but there it is. My problem with this is your refusal to admit how dangerous he is."

"A danger to himself." That was the sad part, and what Natalie had admitted to herself before taking that final step to divorce him. "He's not a danger to me, Saban. If he hurt me, he couldn't continue to be the martyr he sees himself as. The world is against him." She spread her hands helplessly. "That's how he sees it. Use force or violence against him, and it's only going to make him worse."

She moved then, not certain why the memory of that had her moving to him, walking into the arms that opened for her. Why did she even need to be held? Mike was out of her life, at least for the most part. She didn't need comforting, and she knew Saban sure as hell didn't need it. He was arrogant enough for a dozen men.

But there she was, folded against his chest, his hands rubbing against her back, his warmth enfolding her.

The arousal that had remained a low throb inside her all day wasn't building; the hormonal adjustments the doctor had made the day before had made it safe for her and Saban to actually leave the house for longer than five minutes. So it wasn't overwhelming hunger driving her.

She felt his lips press to the top of her head, though, and couldn't stop the smile that tugged at her lips.

For two days they had avoided the subject of Mike, as though he were a grenade in danger of exploding between them.

"Something will have to be done about him, Natalie," he said softly, one hand curling beneath her chin to lift her face to allow his eyes to meet hers. "This won't continue."

She nodded slowly, regretfully. Yes, something would have to be done, and she knew she would have to do it. She couldn't allow Mike to be hurt. He wasn't a bad man, as she had told Saban. He was just a very needy man, a man who refused to accept that things couldn't always go his way. Once he accepted he had lost, though, he would give up, lick his wounds, and torture some other poor woman who didn't have the sense to see through the sad stories he wove.

She had seen through them a long time ago, and now, as she stood in Saban's arms, she was willing to admit that she didn't want Mike's accusations and his paranoia to damage what she was finally admitting to being between them.

She had a chance here for the love she had dreamed of, for the life she wanted. She couldn't let Mike destroy that. She couldn't let herself destroy it, because she was learning that Saban just might be a man she could depend on. A man she could be free with.

TEN

She was up to something. As the day went by, Saban could watch the gears working in her mind. It was fascinating, watching her, sensing her turning the problem of her ex-husband over in her mind until he wanted to snarl in jealous fury at the knowledge that she was thinking about him.

He didn't want her thinking about another man. He wanted to wipe Mike Claxton with his smarmy smile and avaricious gaze completely out of her memory.

Knowing he couldn't grated at his temper. Knowing she was trying to figure out how to do his job and get rid of the bastard only made things worse.

He watched the process, though, and cataloged each shift of expression, each changing scent of emotion as she worked in the schoolroom, and later as they ate dinner at one of Buffalo Gap's better restaurants.

The hormonal adjustment Ely had given her the day before, as well as the adjusted capsule she took that morning had eased the heat enough to allow Natalie to think rather than to fuck with instinctive abandon. He would have preferred the abandon, he had to admit, because there was no hormonal treatment for the males.

The effects were different, the agonizing heat not nearly as uncomfortable. Or perhaps it wasn't as noticeable as pain. Saban had known pain. Pain so agonizing, so brutal that the need to fuck, no matter how vicious, was more pleasure than agony.

But it was bordering on intensely irritating as he checked out the house. He went over the security diagnostics and then ran the secondary sensors for electronic listening devices, explosives, and a variety of threats.

His dick was spike hard and threatening to rip his zipper from his jeans, but if he was going to fuck in peace, then he had to make damned sure the house was safe first.

Moving back to the living room, his gaze moved instinctively to his mate. She was curled in the corner of the couch, watching him, molasses eyes dark and hot, her body vibrating with arousal.

She was perfection to him. It didn't matter that another had taken her, that she had loved another, he told himself. But did she still love him? Were there emotions that had carried over from her marriage that now hampered her ability to see her ex-husband as he was?

"You're watching me with that predatory look in your eyes again," she announced, her voice husky, edging into passion.

God, he loved the sound of her voice when she desired him. When the heat was building and her pussy was creaming.

"Perhaps I'm considering dessert." He moved closer to her, his teeth clenching at the needs suddenly rocking through him.

The heat building in her wrapped around his senses, intoxicated him, made his blood boil. It had been like that the moment he had laid eyes on her, watching her from afar. She had been an assignment when he landed in Nashville, where she had worked in a small public school as a teacher. Within hours she had become the most important thing in his life. In the weeks since, she had become even more. She had become his soul.

That knowledge made his need for her harder, sharper. It made him all too aware that his position in her life was precarious, despite the mating heat. As much as he hated it—and he did hate it—there had been another male in her life at one time, and that male was encroaching on his territory.

Saban had been created and trained to deal with such irritations with maximum force. He had been raised by an old man he called Broussard to know compassion and to follow something far greater than death.

As he stood there, staring at his mate, he wondered which would win. The training or the upbringing, because at this moment he wanted nothing more than to shed blood and to protect his mate. Because something inside him—that primal, primitive part of him—warned him that his mate needed protecting against Mike Claxton.

"You don't look like a man considering dessert." She unfolded herself from the couch, a sinuous, sexy move that had his nostrils flaring to both draw the scent of her into his head and to maintain control. The scent tested the control, but he resisted for the moment.

"I'm a man considering many things." Foremost, he was considering the best way to maneuver his very intelligent, very confrontational little mate.

Her low laugh was knowing, sexy. The scent of her was like sunrise, like spring and innocence, and like a woman moving slowly, confidently into her place in her mate's life.

He liked that scent. He liked all the feels and the textures of watching her claim what was hers alone.

Perhaps Claxton wouldn't be such an issue. Not that he would ever let her confront the man herself, but perhaps he could not shed blood. And maybe he didn't have to worry about securing her heart. She was coming to him, the scent of her was mixing with his, his scent was mixing with hers.

Her fingers slid under his belt.

Saban's head jerked down. His gaze slashed to those graceful fingers, curled as they were between his jeans and the shirt tucked into them.

The heat of her fingers branded his flesh through the shirt and flashed to his balls, drawing them tight.

It was a first for them. The first time she had come to him. He lifted his head back to her, saw the flash of vulnerability in her eyes, and took a firm hold on the hunger tearing through him.

"I'm yours," he told her. "Do as you will, mate."

"Mate," she whispered the word almost questioningly.

"Much more than a wife." He kept his arms still at his sides rather than touch her as he wanted to. "The most important part of who I am."

Her expression softened, though her gaze gleamed with nervousness and with a twinge of uncertainty. It didn't stop her need, though, and it didn't stop that small step into awareness of her power over him.

And she had a great amount of power over him. He would do more than kill for her—he would die for her. But even more, he would fight to the very limits of his training to live for her.

"I want you." She said it simply, and with that she stole any remaining part of him that he may have held separately from her.

The breath literally stalled in his throat as she worked at the buckle of his belt. Slow, sure movements, her slender fingers easing the belt loose then slipping the metal button free to slide the zipper down, over the heavy ridge of flesh throbbing beneath.

He growled involuntarily, the muscles of his abdomen flexing violently as her fingers gripped the hem of his shirt and pulled it up his torso.

Saban lifted his arms, bent enough to allow her to pull the shirt free, then nearly roared out his pleasure as her head bent and her sharp little teeth raked his chest.

"*Mercy*, my *cher*," he growled, forcing his hands to merely skim along her back.

She was fully dressed. He wanted her naked, and he wanted her naked now.

He gripped the hem of her shirt and drew it off when he wanted to rip it off. He forced back a hungry snarl as he felt her satiny flesh, and then a roar as her hot lips moved down his chest to his abdomen, then to the straining length of his cock.

He stared down at her in amazement as she went to her knees. Her breasts were framed in black lace, pale and swollen and pretty as hell. Nothing could be as pretty as those pale pink, luscious lips surrounding and consuming the head of his cock though.

Damn. Nothing could be as good.

His fingers slid into her hair. The warm strands tangled around his fingers like living silk. She sucked the head of his cock deep inside her mouth. She sent his senses exploding.

Saban felt his head fall back on his shoulders then forced himself steady to stare down at her. He felt the rumbling growls that came from his chest, and he growled her name. He snarled his need for her, and he fought for control. He prayed for control, because he wanted this to last. He wanted this touch, the way her eyes blazed up at him, the sight of his flesh held intimately in her mouth seared into his memory.

A shattered groan ripped from his chest as her tongue swirled around the head, caressing the swollen crest with wicked licks. And there, just beneath the crest, her curious little tongue probed at the flesh that covered the barb. The extension wasn't erect, but it throbbed beneath the flesh, ached with the need for release.

"I'll not stand much more," he groaned as she sucked the head back into her mouth and whispered a moan over the thick crest.

"Natalie, *cher*." His thighs tightened against the need to come, his balls drew up in agony.

With one last, slow lick, she pulled back slowly.

"I want to take you."

Saban stared down, dazed, sweat forming on his forehead as she rose to her feet, her slender fingers stroking over his erection.

"I want to take you right here." She toed off her shoes as she unsnapped her jeans.

"Here?" He swallowed tightly, watching as she wiggled from the snug denim like a fantasy present, unwrapped one slow inch at a time.

"Here." Her smile was pure sex, pure need. "Do you have a problem with here?" She kicked her jeans free before reaching behind her and unclipping the bra.

The cups fell away from the firm, sweet flesh of her breasts, and control was suddenly the last thing on his mind. Sweet, succulent nipples topped the flushed mounds, and he was lost.

"Here works."

Hell, he didn't care where it was, as long as he was inside her, holding her, her holding him, a part of each other.

Saban sat back on the couch, watched in wonder and pleasure as she straddled his thighs and came to him.

His hands shackled her hips as he reclined into the back of the couch.

She flowed over him like hot honey. Soft, saturated, slick flesh enclosed his cock head, then by slow, agonizing inches took the shaft of his erection. Tiny, whimpering cries left her lips. Her sharp nails bit into his shoulders, and her dark eyes were nearly black in her pleasure.

"I'll not last long. I'll make up for it." He was fighting to breathe.

He could feel the sweat beading on his flesh, feel the wildness invading both of them.

"You can make it up all night." She leaned into his chest, her hips lifting, dragging the tight, clenching flesh of her pussy over his cock, and he lost it.

Who cared about control? This pleasure, the touch of her, the taste of her, the feel of her was all that mattered. Gripping her hips, Saban shifted and began to move inside her with hard, desperate thrusts. Nothing mattered but fucking her now. Fucking her so hard and deep, with such pleasure that she never forgot what it meant to belong to him.

Natalie was wild above him, meeting him thrust for thrust. Sharp little nails pierced his back as her teeth bit into his shoulder.

The tiny pinpricks of pain were nothing, more pleasure than anything else, but enough to tear away that last strip of control he had kept reined in. He gripped her hips harder, his cock shafting into her with furious strokes as he felt her orgasm rip through her body.

He laid his mouth over the mark he had given her, his teeth scraping it as he gripped her flesh and let go his own release. The barb beneath the head of his cock thickened, hardened, the pleasure-pain of it drawing a snarl from his throat as ecstasy poured through him. Sweet heaven, the pleasure of it. The feel of her pussy against flesh so sensitive the agony was too much for him. He felt it pulse, throb, spilling more of the hormone into her even as he spilled his seed inside her.

The barb locked his cock in place, caressed hidden flesh, and sent them both hurtling into a brilliant, burning sphere of pure pleasure.

He would figure the rest of it out later, he promised himself as he bore her back against the couch cushions and came above her. As his release spilled inside her and the aftershocks of rapture tore through them both, he swore he would hold onto her, no matter the cost. Jealousy be damned, it wasn't worth losing the faith she was finding in him. And it wasn't worth losing the loyalty he could feel growing between them, a loyalty born of emotion and, he prayed, of love.

He didn't want to shackle her to him with sex. He wanted to hold her to him with love. Nothing more.

ELEVEN

Natalie had tried desperately not to think about Saban or the emotions twisting inside her where he was concerned. She'd used frustration and aggravation, she'd tried to hide, and she'd tried to deny them. She'd wanted to deny feeling anything for him, because otherwise she would have had to face the fact that within a matter of weeks, less than two months, she had let a man steal a part of her heart that even her ex-husband hadn't possessed.

And here she had been the one to promise herself she would never let another man affect her again.

She almost snorted at the thought the next morning as she put on coffee and began preparing breakfast. Saban sat at the small kitchen table, dressed in his Breed Enforcer uniform.

Strapped to his side in a shoulder holster was his weapon, to his left thigh a sheathed dagger. He would have more weapons hidden on him, she knew. Weapons she couldn't see, weapons he knew how to use with deadly efficiency.

And why that brought her comfort rather than freaking her out, she wasn't certain. She should have been frightened of Saban from the day she learned he'd be living in her home with her, following her, protecting her.

It was one of the reasons she had fought him so far, she realized as she finished the bacon, eggs, and toast. It was why she hadn't wanted him here. Why she hadn't wanted him to be a part of her life. Because she had known he would become a part of her heart.

And he was. Right there in living color, bronze muscle covered by the military-type black uniform with the Jaguar insignia on his shoulder.

She almost shook her head at herself as she poured two mugs of coffee and moved to set his on the table. Turning away from him, she couldn't help it, she just couldn't help but to let her fingers skim over the thick, black silk of his hair.

"Hey." He caught her hand, his head jerking up, his gaze connecting with her in lazy awareness of her. "You don't have to try to sneak and touch me."

He placed her palm against his cheek, turned a kiss into it, then went back to work on the small electronice notepad he had attached to the palm Internet link he carried.

Natalie threaded her fingers through his hair, a smile twitching at her lips as he leaned into the caress, even though his brow was furrowed with concentration.

He didn't mind being touched. And he didn't think a light caress meant running straight to the bed as well. Mike hadn't wanted to be touched unless he was ready for sex.

She let her fingers linger a moment longer then moved back to the stove and breakfast.

Strange, how easily Saban has slipped into her heart. She hadn't wanted it, she had given it the good fight, but he was there.

She paused at the stove, felt the sharp blow to her heart, and realized she loved it. It stole her breath, when she knew it shouldn't have. It shook her to the core, even though she realized she should have known all along what was happening.

She had fallen in love with a man a hundred times more dominant than her ex-husband had been, and he had managed to slip so much deeper inside her soul than Mike ever could have.

She stared sightless down at the bacon and felt the anger that began to build inside her. It wasn't an anger toward herself or toward Saban. But toward Mike.

He had come to Buffalo Gap to destroy not just her independence but what she had found with Saban. He had left his bimbo, his job, and the home he had stolen from her to make certain she lost anything she could have found in this small community.

He would do it, too, she realized. He wouldn't physically hurt her, but he would destroy the respect and the good standing she was building here. He would make it impossible for her to teach the Breed children before he would make himself appear as a threat to her and to them.

And he knew what he was doing. And she knew she was going to have to stop him before he destroyed this chance she had at happiness.

"I need to check a few things in the truck." Saban rose from his chair as she turned to him. "I'll be right back."

He strode quickly from the room as she drew in a slow, hard breath. As she heard the front door close, she jerked the phone from the wall and punched in Mike's cell phone number.

She was going to take care of this between her and Mike. She wouldn't have Saban's hands bloodied because of her ex-husband's stupidity, and she wasn't giving him the chance to nearly destroy her career again.

"Natalie, thank God you called." He answered on the first ring. "Are you okay?"

The pseudo concern in his voice was nearly too much.

"Go home, Mike," she snapped. "I divorced you for a reason. To get you out of my life. Don't make me get another restraining order on you. You know how bad that's going to look if you have to actually get another job."

"You didn't used to be so hard, Natalie." There was a wealth of sorrow in his voice. God, didn't he ever see what he was doing to himself?

"You didn't used to be so stupid," she hissed. "I left Tennessee to get away from you. I'm happy here, Mike. Happier than I ever was in our marriage. Go back to your bimbo and leave me the hell alone."

Silence filled the line for long moments.

"I just want to see you first," he finally said, his voice soft, regretful. "Is that so much to ask?"

"Yes, it is." Way too much to ask, because she couldn't blame Saban for being concerned, and there wasn't a chance in hell he was going to agree to this.

"Five minutes, Natalie. Anywhere. I don't care. Just give me five minutes to say good-bye."

"And you'll leave?"

"I swear, I'll leave."

"Five minutes," she retorted. "I'll be at the mall later today sometime around four. I'll meet you at the outside entrance to Sally J's." Sally J's was one of the women's-only clothing stores in the large mall just outside town. "You'll have five minutes. I'll call you right before I step outside."

"Will your furry friend be with you?" he asked bitterly.

"He'll be around," she finally sighed. "But I'll talk to you alone. Be there at four, Mike. And remember, five minutes. That's it."

"Five minutes. That's all I need, Nat."

She hung the phone up and moved back to the stove as the front door opened once again, and seconds later Saban strode back into the kitchen.

As Saban sat back down at the kitchen table and took a healthy sip of the decaffeinated coffee he'd slipped into the canister days ago, he drew in a slow breath.

Sometimes his sense of smell was a curse rather than a blessing. Times such as moments before, when he had smelled the emotion pouring from Natalie. Rich and saturated with arousal, tempestuous with need, and overlaying it all, the deep, heady scent of love.

Love had a scent, though it varied from person to person and couple to couple. It wasn't easy to detect and often wasn't even apparent except in high-stress, personal moments.

What was she thinking of? he wondered. What had caused that well of emotion to open inside her and break free and then to touch him. To touch him of her own volition, as though testing her ability to do so or his patience in allowing it.

God help them both—he would lie at her feet until hell froze over to feel again what he had felt when she had touched him so timidly. Sensation, like an electrical current had run over his scalp and sizzled down his spine. He'd barely restrained a weakening shiver, and he cursed himself for it. For a second, he'd been like the pitiful cub he remembered himself as, so long ago. Staring at the scientists from his metal pen, hungry for something that went beyond the need for food. And now he knew what that hunger was, not for just a touch, but for one filled with emotion.

That touch had set his nerve endings on fire, and now, long moments later, it had him on edge, off balance, and filled with his own emotions.

"I'd like to postpone the trip to the mall that you planned for today," he told her, keeping his voice level as she set the plate of food in front of him. "There are still some safety issues I'd like to have taken care of first."

His control not withstanding, the report Jonas had sent out via the eLink wasn't happy news.

"I can't postpone it."

Saban's head snapped up. Her voice was carefully bland, non-confrontational, but he heard the nervousness behind it. The same nervousness he sensed every damned time she disagreed with him. Did she think he was going to beat her for disagreeing with him? That son of a bitch, Claxton, had a lot to answer for; unfortunately, Saban had already come to the conclusion that he would have to allow Jonas and his team to take care of getting the bastard out of town, rather than taking care of it himself.

Natalie might not like his methods.

As he watched her, he noticed that she didn't meet his eyes. She took her seat, salted and peppered her food, sipped her coffee, and said nothing more.

He could see the pulse beating a ragged rhythm in her throat though, and he could smell her trepidation.

"Very well." He lowered his gaze to his own breakfast and dug in. "I'll contact Jonas and have a few extra men assigned around the mall just to be on the safe side. An enforcer caught sight of a suspected Council soldier in town last night. The Council has been attempting to capture Breed mates for years, so we need to be careful."

"Why?" She lifted her head then, suspicion flickering in her gaze.

Did she believe he would lie to her? Saban wanted to growl, he wanted to throw something, wanted to beat her ex-husband until he was nothing but bloody pulp.

"Why are they attempting to capture our mates? Or why do we need to be careful?"

Her lips pursed as mocking patience filled her expression. "What do you think?"

Saban smiled, making certain to add just enough wicked sensuality to the look. "Many things, but I'll concentrate on your question. They want our mates to experiment on the phenomenon, which by the way, they saw as early as the first Breed's creation more than a century ago. Unfortunately for them, that first Leo escaped in his twenty-seventh year of creation. The mating hormone and the genetic viruslike condition it creates is of interest to them."

"What sort of interest?" She was eating, but her attention was caught, he could see.

Natalie was a curious little thing, and that curiosity was rarely a problem. Until now.

He finished his breakfast, pushed back his plate, and stared back at her coolly. "It creates a condition that decreases aging in both the Breed and his or her mate. In ten years, Merinus and Callan have aged perhaps a year. There are rumors the first Leo, who should be nearing the age of one hundred and thirty, is still alive and still in his prime. And that, my dear, is the reason the Council scientists would do anything to capture our mates."

TWELVE

It was hard to take in. Hours later, as Natalie entered the huge, two-story indoor mall just outside the town's limits, she felt as though she had been sucker punched with the information.

Saban had answered all her questions, he had even offered to take her to Sanctuary to allow her to discuss some of the more advanced effects of the mating heat. Nothing dangerous, he had assured her. There was nothing life threatening in being a mate. Why, hell no, just an advanced life span and only God knew what problems in the future. Not to mention mentally defective, in her opinion, Council scientists and soldiers drooling for a chance to slice into a body verified as a mate, Breed or human.

It amazed her at odd times, the destructiveness that men could force on each other. The horror and cruelties didn't exist in the animal world. It was survival of the strongest there, and in some ways, that was how the Breeds saw living now. Survival of the fittest.

Did nature see it that way as well? Was that the reason for the mating heat? The reason for the advanced life span once mated? She knew that women, Breeds and those who were married or mated to feline Breeds, conceived quickly without the hormonal treatments Dr. Morrey had worked up. But after the first conception, it then became much harder to conceive. And Saban had told her that the Wolf Breeds had had an even harder time of it until only recently, when their doctors had detected additional hormones, so far unknown, within one of their mates.

The whole mating process was confusing as hell, but according to Saban, the one constant in it all was the emotion the mates shared. So far, in over eleven years since the announcement of their existence, a mating had always resulted in love. And the look he had given her as he related that information had been filled with heat, emotion, and the unvoiced question she wasn't ready to answer yet.

Yes, she loved him, and knowing it terrified the hell out of her.

As they neared Sally J's, Natalie checked the watch on her wrist surreptitiously and glanced around at the crowds mingling from store to store. She had ten minutes to meet Mike on the other side of the store.

The restrooms were on the other side, with two entrances and exits into them. She was hoping she could enter from one side and move quickly to the exit on the other side, beside the doors that led to the outdoor parking.

Five minutes. That was all she was giving Mike, and she intended to do that talking. Enough was enough. They were divorced, they had divorced for a reason, and she wasn't going to turn the new life she wanted for herself into an international incident. Which was what it would become if he became the first recorded non-Breed to die from jealous rage.

She trusted Saban, she did, with her own life. But Mike's, she wasn't so certain of.

"I'm going to the ladies' room." She paused by the entrance. "I'll be out in a few minutes."

She had to force herself to tamp down nervousness, to hold back fear, which she was terrified was damned near impossible. But after one narrow-eyed look, Saban nodded slowly before leaning against the wall with all the resigned patience of any put-upon male.

She almost smiled.

Moving into the ladies' room, she picked up her steps, walked quickly past the stalls, then out of the exit on the opposite side of the curved room. It was only a few steps to the outdoor exit through two sets of double doors and onto the sidewalk that surrounded the mall.

Mike was waiting for her directly across the small road, arms crossed over his chest, his expression causing her chest to clench with a spurt of familiar panic. He was angry. Mike wasn't always rational when he was angry. He didn't care if he caused a public spectacle of himself or her, and he rarely listened to reason. She almost turned and walked back into the mall.

Instead, she glanced at her watch then back at Mike, a silent declaration that she wasn't walking over there. At least this close to the doors, there was a handy escape route if one of those Council soldiers was lurking around the mall.

She looked around just to be certain and saw no one suspicious. The parking lot was busy, the traffic fairly thick.

She watched Mike curse before he moved across the street, his shoulders thrown back, his expression pugnacious.

"We couldn't do this in the shade?" He sneered. "You always have to be difficult, don't you, Natalie? Big-time Breed teacher has to call all the shots."

"I can go back inside, and we can forget this," she retorted. "Saban's waiting just inside the doors, Mike. Make this fast."

"I want you to come home. Dammit, you have no business here. You're my wife."

A sharp, amazed laugh left her throat. "Drop it, Mike. We both know this has nothing to do with you wanting me back and everything with losing control of me. I'm not your wife. I'll never be your wife again, and if you don't get that through your thick skull, then you're going to end up dead."

"Siccing that rabid animal of yours on me, Nat?" Disgust filled his voice. "How can you let that thing touch you?"

Natalie wanted to roll her eyes but knew it would only make this little fight run longer.

"Mike, I agreed to meet you so you'll see this isn't happening with me." She tried to keep her tone soft, gentle. Sometimes it worked. "Our marriage was over the first year; I just didn't want to admit it. Now, let it go, and go back to Tennessee. Don't make this harder than it has to be."

His lips flattened, his face flushing with anger.

"Don't you see what those Breeds have done to you, Natalie?" He pushed his fingers through his hair as fury flashed in his eyes. "They've done something to you. They drugged you." He reached for her, his teeth clenching violently as she jumped back. "Look at you, you can't even stand to be touched by anyone but that bastard fucking you."

"Stop this, Mike. You don't know what you're talking about, and it's not a discussion we're going to have. You need to leave. I didn't want you before I came here, and I don't want you now."

His nostrils flared, a telling sign. Only at his most furious had Natalie ever seen that. Those were the times he had wrapped his hand around her neck and pounded the wall beside her head. When he had smashed furniture and spent hours accusing her of screwing every man they both knew.

"You're my wife." He advanced a step, and in his eyes Natalie saw something she had never seen before. A fury so violent she knew Mike would never keep his control.

Had he truly been working his way up to this over the years? How had she not seen it, not suspected that he would retaliate like this the moment he knew he was no longer a part of her life? Forget the divorce, the bimbo; he had still controlled her. She hadn't dated, she hadn't sought out friends, because she knew Mike, and she knew he wouldn't have tolerated it.

And she hadn't even suspected she knew until now.

She stepped back warily toward the doors now, wishing she hadn't slipped away from Saban, that she had just fought it out with him, made him at least let her try. She would have been safe. Or safely in her bed screaming in pleasure as Saban argued his side. Either one would have been preferable to this.

"They drugged you, Natalie. The doctors that talked to me after you left told me all about it. This drug their bodies make. It makes you addicted, dependent."

Oh God. Oh God. She looked around frantically, knowing what was going on, certain Mike had set her up.

She turned to push through the entrance doors into the mall, to run, to escape back to Saban.

"You fucking bitch, you're not running back to him."

Natalie almost screamed as his hand locked over her upper arm, pulling her back as she scrambled to grab the handle to the door, to get away from him.

The pain, though not as severe at first, became mind-numbing as he dragged her back. She felt his arm lock around her waist, his chest against her back as she clawed at his flesh, guttural whimpers leaving her lips as she tried to scream for Saban.

She heard screams, but they couldn't be her own. A haze of pain covered her eyes, filled her brain, and with it came terror.

Mike was cursing, raging. She could hear tires squealing and she knew, oh God, she knew he was taking her away. Taking her away from Saban and the dreams she hadn't known she had.

"You bastard!" Fury, rich with terror and mixed with adrenaline, spiked through her mind.

Her hands curled back, her nails clawing back at Mike's face as she tried to tangle her feet with his legs, throwing him off balance.

They hit the street as horns blared and a siren began to scream through the air. As she rolled to her stomach, she felt hands grab her ankles, pulling at them, trying to drag her back as she kicked, screaming, trying to roll, fighting for release.

There were too many voices. Too many hands touching her, and a second later she froze in a terror so thick, so horrible it nearly stopped her heart.

A feline roar of rage split through the chaos of sound as she heard the rapid, staccato bursts of stunners and bullets ripping around her.

One last kick, and she was free of the manacles at her feet. Crawling to her knees, she lifted her head, fighting to see. There were people everywhere. Black uniforms surrounded her. Someone was screaming from behind the barrier of enforcers, and she swore it sounded like Mike's screams.

"Saban! Oh God, Saban!"

"Stay the hell where you are!" The growling roar from her right had her twisting, searching for him, her mind still dazed, the pain of Mike's touch still ripping through her senses.

But he was there. Through the blur of tears and pain, she saw him, then she felt him, one arm curling around her and pulling her into the mall as the gunfire behind them suddenly ceased.

His eyes were blazing into hers, filled with rage, his expression twisted with it. "If you wanted him that fucking bad, I would have readily released you," he snarled. "Now keep your goddamned ass here, and I'll see if I can save the son of a bitch for you." He turned around, stood aside for the two female Breed Enforcers who crowded into the small area. "Watch her and keep her here if it means shackling her to the fucking door."

Shock froze her, parted her lips on a cry, and left her staring at his retreating back as he left her sitting there between the street entrance and the mall entrance.

She curled her arms around her waist, and as she fought the pain and the need for his touch, she laid her head against her knees and let the tears fall.

She knew what she had done. Without meaning to, certainly without desiring to, she had betrayed her mate.

THIRTEEN

S aban stared at the mess four Council soldiers made as they bled out on the asphalt of the street outside the black panel van they had been attempting to get Natalie into.

The scientist was still alive, a little bit wounded, but he was breathing, and the EMTs seemed certain he would keep living. If it weren't for the information they needed from him, Saban would have finished the job and put a bullet in his head.

Mike Claxton was sitting on the ground, his head in his hands, a bandage wrapped around one arm and another binding his ankle.

The bastard had been damned lucky. The fact that Natalie had managed to trip both of them had saved his life, taking him out of the line of fire when he, Jonas, and the other Breeds swarmed out of the mall into the parking lot.

Saban braced his hands on his hips and stared at the man and wanted to howl in rage. He could smell the weakness, both physically and mentally, that poured from Mike Claxton. He wasn't a fitting mate for Natalie; hell, he hadn't even managed to be a fitting husband to her, and yet she had run to him.

He couldn't even find it in him to excuse her, to find a way to understand it. It simply came down to the fact that Claxton had meant more to her than her own life, than Saban's life, had. And that broke his heart.

Shaking his head, he moved to the man, then hunched in front of him, his elbows resting on his knees, as he stared at Claxton's bent head.

Mike's head lifted. Miserable, damp blue eyes met Saban's.

"You set this up." They knew that. He had arranged with the scientist and the soldiers to take her.

Claxton sniffed back his tears. "They have a cure for her. Whatever you did to her, it made her leave me, divorce me. She loves me, Breed. Not you."

The pain of that was like an open, gaping wound inside Saban's soul.

"I didn't meet her until the day you came to the house to find me there," he told Claxton, striving for patience. "Until that day, Natalie had never so much as breathed air that I had passed through. How could I have harmed her or damaged your marriage?"

Claxton shook his head. "They saw you."

"Did they have pictures? Video?"

The other man continued to shake his head.

"The Council records everything, Claxton. Every investigation, every move they make, one way or the other, is recorded. If they had no proof, then it didn't happen."

"You drugged her," he bit out, his voice rising as he glared at Saban. "She divorced me."

"You cheated on her with her assistant teacher," Saban said cruelly. "You broke trust with her. You betrayed her. You refused to allow her to make her own decisions, to be herself, because you were too frightened she would learn the truth. And when she did, you blamed her."

Saban had had the investigation done. His sister, Chimera, had sent the information via the eLink, carefully organized, brutally concise, days before.

"She would have forgiven me." Claxton swallowed tightly, but his demeanor shifted slightly, lost the aggression and became pathetic rather than furious. "Eventually, she would have forgiven me."

Saban shook his head. "Would you ever forgive her?"

The other man blinked back tears and looked down, shaking his head.

"You nearly died here today, Claxton." Saban stared at the Council soldiers who had lost their lives instead. "But what would have happened to Natalie is beyond your worst nightmares. They would have cut her, studied her, and dissected her . . . while she lived. The horror she would have endured would have been more agony than you could ever imagine."

He shook his head desperately. "They have a cure. You did something to her. She can't even bear my touch."

"Nothing is wrong with her," Saban snarled, flashing his canines. "She was my woman, my lover. Why would she want the touch of one who had betrayed her? One who had fucked her assistant in her own bed? Why would she wish for your touch?"

Claxton flinched at each question, hunching his shoulders against the truth Saban laid at his feet.

"You didn't just break the law today in your attempt to aid in her kidnapping, but you broke Breed law, Claxton." He gave that a second to sink in, and as Mike's face paled, he went on. "Attempting to kidnap the woman of a Breed is punishable by death. Your trial would be a Breed tribunal, not a jury of your peers. You don't even have to be there." He leaned forward. "Justice would be horrifying. Death by the most excruciating pain we could devise. The Council taught us how to cause pain, my friend. Pain like you cannot even imagine."

Claxton's face was white now.

"I wanted to save her."

"You wanted to fucking own her," Saban snarled. "Now, here is what you are going to do. You are going to your hotel, you will pack, and you will leave before night falls. If at any time you are found to be in Buffalo Gap or if you attempt to contact Natalie without her permission, then Breed law will come down on you."

Surprise reflected on Claxton's face. "You're going to let me go?"

"I have never killed over a woman, Claxton." Saban let a growl enter his voice for effect. "But over Natalie, I will rip your guts from your navel and strangle you with them. Do you understand me?"

Claxton nodded slowly. Saban held his gaze, staring back at him, letting him see the savagery, the need for blood rising inside him.

"Why are you letting me go?" Claxton asked timidly, almost hopefully.

"You heaped enough guilt on her head during your marriage." Saban rose to his feet and stared down at him coldly. "I won't let you guilt her with your death."

The hope left his eyes. Claxton nodded again then dragged himself to his feet and stared at the dead soldiers now being bagged, the disabled van that would have taken Natalie away.

"I was trying to help her," he finally said roughly. "I thought . . . I thought she was in danger."

"As long as I live she will be safe," Saban snapped. "Can we say the same for you?" Saban looked at the bloody scene again and then back to Mike.

Mike didn't say another word. He limped across the street to his car and dragged himself slowly inside it. The bloody battle, the knowledge that his death had been so close, and that Saban would do more than kill him, did what nothing else could have. Right now, in shock, Claxton had taken in the truth of what had happened. He had nearly destroyed Natalie rather than saving her, and whether he had known it before or not, right now, he knew this was his last chance to live.

"We weren't trained to have mercy, Brother."

Saban turned to meet eyes identical to his own in a face so delicate, so sweetly curved that at times he couldn't believe she was one of the highly trained, merciless Breed Enforcers the Bureau of Breed Affairs prized so highly.

Long, black hair was braided into a thick plait and fell to the middle of her back, while her slender, doelike body radiated confidence and strength.

"We weren't trained to have it, yet we do." He shrugged carelessly.

"I'll keep an eye on him for a while. Make sure he gets home safe. We'd hate for him to have an accident between here and there." Her smile was cold, hard, her eyes like chips of green ice.

"I gave him his life; take it at your own risk, Chimera," he warned her.

"You're going to spoil her," she stated.

Saban shrugged again.

No, he wasn't spoiling her, he was letting her go. She would keep the job; that had nothing to do with him. Whether she stayed, left, or allowed Claxton back into her life was her choice.

"Tell Jonas to have Natalie escorted home and assign her a new bodyguard," he told his sister as he fought the pain building in his chest. "I'll follow up with the scientist we captured and see to his transport to Sanctuary."

He had to force the words past his lips.

"And if he sends a male with her?" Chimera asked.

Saban just shook his head and moved away from her, knowing she would do exactly as he asked. She had never failed him, not once, not before their escape, not after. And if, as she asked, Jonas sent another male to guard his mate?

God, such pain shouldn't be possible without an open wound. How could his heart still beat in his chest when it felt as though it were ripped from his body?

Love. God, he had waited for this, dreamed of it, from the moment he had learned that Breeds mated, that their one and only would be their natural one and only, he had waited and he had hoped.

And this was what he had hoped for? A woman who, though she may care for him, loved another.

He had to force himself not to look back at the mall, to the doors where he had left her. He had to force himself to the van where the scientist was confined, restrained and awaiting transport.

Saban stepped to the opened back doors and smiled. A slow, cold smile that showed his canines and bore little resemblance to a civilized being. He didn't feel so civilized right now.

"Well now, Dr. Amburg." He greeted the aging scientist with a growl. "How nice to see you here today. I trust you're doing well?"

Beldon Amburg. He had tortured, murdered, experimented on, and destroyed more lives than Saban could count. His file was extensive; the proof of the atrocities committed at the lab he headed was stored in boxes rather than files.

"You've forgotten who your masters are, animal," Amburg sneered. "One day, you'll bow before us again, and we'll know no mercy."

"Oh, you knew mercy before?" Saban widened his eyes in surprise. "Well now, you'll have to jus' tell me 'bout dat lil' thing," he announced sarcastically as he stepped into the van and wrapped his fingers brutally around the thin neck of the scientist known as Bloody Amburg. "Right this way, Doctor. We have a nice little cell just waiting for you."

The scientist gasped for air, but he put up little struggle. Saban dragged him from the bullet-ridden van to the secured security van that pulled up alongside it.

The back doors opened, revealing two Breeds, weapons held ready. The restraints locked into the floor of the van were lifted by a third Breed. And that one, Saban knew, would never leave Amburg alive if he had the chance. Mercury had more reason than most to see this particular scientist dead.

"Mercury, ride up front." Saban pulled his captive in and took the ends of the restraints himself. Snapping them on, he felt the Breed behind him move to the side.

"I'll let him live." The voice was a demon's growl, causing

Amburg to collapse onto the wide metal seat bolted to the wall behind him.

"I'm just going to make sure." Saban shook his head. "Ride up front. I'll ride back here with Lawe and Rule."

He took his seat, another metal bench facing Amburg.

Mercury snarled but moved from the van, allowing the other two Breeds to jump inside before securing the doors.

"We have two escorts front and back to Sanctuary," Lawe announced. "Seems there's a report there could be more Council soldiers in the vicinity. Jonas is expecting trouble."

Saban kept his eyes on Amburg. "If they attack, put a bullet in his head. He's not worth dying for."

Amburg swallowed tightly, terror flashing in his cold, pale blue eyes.

Terror was a good thing, Saban thought, because right now, he was just enraged enough to kill for the simple hell of it. His mate was back at the mall, alone, without him, without the ex-husband she had risked her life to save.

And here he was, guarding a fucking Council doctor. Hell, today just sucked.

As Lawe moved to close the doors to the van, Saban looked out, his gaze moving instinctively to where he left Natalie. There, between the entrances to the mall she stood, one hand pressed to the glass door, her cheeks wet with tears. Her eyes were dark, too dark in her pale face, anguished, filled with pain. With sorrow.

As he watched, her lips moved, whispered his name, and he felt his soul shatter.

Lawe slammed the doors closed and secured, but nothing could erase the sight of her pain from his soul.

How the fuck could he ever live without her?

FOURTEEN

Saban sat outside the little brick house, outside Buffalo Gap, outside period.

Natalie's bedroom light was on. She'd left the curtains cracked just the slightest bit, and he'd warned her about that. Warned her to the point that he had started closing them at night himself, just to make certain they were secure.

Well, maybe not just to make certain they were secure. Her bedroom was like this hive of scents. Everywhere he turned there was another subtle tease of a scent that made up Natalie. Her perfume, the smell of her soap and shampoo mingling, the scent of passion on her sheets, of frustration on her pillows. The smell of the feminine struggle against the male dominant force. Her unconscious, wary battle to hold back her own needs, her hungers, even as the scent of those needs and hungers reached out to him.

Hell. He rubbed his hand over his face in frustration. How could he have been so wrong? Dammit, Natalie wasn't a fickle woman. Fickle had a scent, just as deceit, dishonesty, and depravity had a scent. There was nothing fickle in what he smelled from his mate.

Stubborn. Eh, she had vast quantities of stubborn. Distrust, she had a fairly healthy dose of that as well. But her character was strong, pure.

He leaned his head back against the seat with a rough growl. He remembered clearly his rage when he realized what she had done. She had risked her life, risked the life they could have together, and her own soul with the horror she would have faced if Amburg had managed to take her. All to save the worthless hide of an ex-husband.

But hadn't she also nearly wrecked the vehicle Callan had given her that first week to avoid a lame dog in the middle of the road that couldn't move quick enough? Then, sweet *mercy*, what had that female done? She had gotten out of the car and approached it, despite its terrified growls and dazed eyes.

She had risked herself then as well. And him. He still carried the mark of that mangy mutt's teeth in his leg where it had bitten him. All because molasses-brown eyes had been filled with tears, and his mate's soft heart had decided the bastard deserved to live.

It could have rabies, yet, there he had been, risking his neck for a wounded, enraged animal so she wouldn't risk hers.

Could Mike be no more than a stray that she feared he would euthanize?

Or was he attempting to make excuses for himself and the woman who owned his soul?

He inhaled warily, looked at the digital time displayed on the dashboard of his truck, and grimaced. It was nearly three in the morning. Natalie was still awake; he had seen her shadow pass the slit in the curtains. He knew the enforcers, Shiloh Gage and Mercury Warrant, were still awake.

Two of the most contrary Breeds ever born were Shiloh and Mercury. No doubt they were in different rooms, in opposite corners waiting, like a cat on a mouse, for the unwary.

No wonder Natalie was pacing the floors. When those two were on guard duty, conversation was in very short supply.

Damn. He'd sat out here in the dark feeling fucking sorry for himself long enough. He wasn't going to have the answers he needed until he confronted her, until he asked her why she risked herself for her ex-husband. And he would have his answers.

He was man enough to accept that she had loved before, but he'd be damned if he was man enough to accept that those emotions could still remain for another man.

Pushing the truck door open, he moved from the vehicle, closing and locking it with a flick of the security button on the key before heading to the house.

The front door opened before he stepped to the porch, and Shiloh stepped outside, quietly closing the door behind her before leaning against the doorframe.

Dressed in black, her long, dark hair pulled back tight from her face, her dark gold eyes gleaming in the moonlight, she looked exactly as she was: a powerful predator, a force to be reckoned with.

She was considered the brat of Sanctuary, a bit spoiled, definitely a shade arrogant, but she had a kind heart. And from her expression, she had managed to find a bit of sympathy for Natalie.

"Shiloh." He stepped onto the porch.

"Broussard." She smiled, but it wasn't pleasant.

Shiloh wasn't known for her even temperament, but she was known for her ability to hurt a man. In ways he was sure even the Council wouldn't have approved of.

He stopped and stared back at her evenly. "Are you gonna let me into that house, Shi?"

She looked out into the night before bringing her gaze back to him.

"She's cried most of the evening." There was a hint of a hiss in her voice. "Since when is it okay to make your mate miserable, Saban? This damned place reeks of her misery."

"I'll take care of her," he assured the enforcer. "You have your own things to take care of. I thank you for coming here and taking care of her for me."

She sniffed at the gratitude but moved away from the door before opening it and heading for the steps.

Mercury moved from the darkness beyond, nodding easily to Saban before he followed the other enforcer and disappeared into the night.

Saban stepped into the house, locked the door, and checked the security system before heading for the stairs.

Strangely, it wasn't misery that the house reeked of, it was anger. Hot, brilliant, and definitely female.

He moved up the stairs, slid into the hallway, and approached her closed door. Beyond that door lay ecstasy. The bed he had shared with his mate, the scent of their passion, the knowledge, complete and overwhelming, that this woman belonged to him, no matter the evidence to the contrary.

This insanity where she thought she could save the world and those hapless males drawn to trouble because of their own stupidity was going to have to stop though.

He clenched his teeth as the scent of anger grew sharper here, firing the hormone-laced adrenaline, pounding in his head with a primal urge to show her, to enforce his dominance over her. To ensure this never happened again.

Never, ever, would she take another's side against him. If he felt blood needed to be shed, then he would shed it. He didn't need her standing between him and danger or between him and his own conscience.

She had no idea the blood he had already shed in his fight to survive. Standing between him and one weak-kneed, paranoid little son of a bitch wasn't going to make a difference, and she needed to learn that right quick.

He gripped the doorknob, pushed the door open, and with a quick widening of his eyes ducked to avoid whatever heavy object was sailing through the air toward his head.

"Dammit, Natalie!" He ducked again and quickly sidestepped another projectile. Some kind of white ceramic creature he guessed as it shattered against the doorframe as the door slammed closed. "That's enough."

"I'll show you enough!" The bedside clock flew at his head and struck his shoulder with a resounding whack. The pain was minimal, but he didn't have to give her a chance to perfect her aim. He jumped for her.

She was fast, but she wasn't fast enough. Hooking his arm around her waist, he tossed her to the bed, coming down on her quickly. He straddled her thighs, gripped her wrists in one hand, and held her securely to the bed.

The short robe she wore had worked to her thighs, the loosely belted front slipped open, revealing hard little nipples and swollen, flushed breasts.

The pert mounds bounced as she struggled against him and had his cock straining against his zipper, desperate to be free. The scent of anger and desire filled the room. The heat of it flushed her cheeks and made her eyes darker.

And the scent of pain. It was carefully masked beneath the anger, but he could smell her hurt, sense it in the air around them.

"You dirty bastard, get off me," she screamed. "Get off me, and get out of my house. Go back to wherever the hell you came from. I don't want you here."

Those were tears glittering in her eyes, the damp sheen making her eyes more luminous, darker, sweeter than ever.

Leaning toward her, he let the low, warning rumble in his chest free. The rough, primal sound only had her eyes narrowing, her face flushing deeper.

"That growling thing is not working on me," she snapped. "You left. You left me with Breeds that wouldn't even speak to me. But even worse, moron, you left me hurting!"

He had a feeling she wasn't talking about arousal or mating heat.

"And how, mate, did I leave you hurting?" He snarled. "By not trusting you? By deceiving you and placing my life deliberately in danger? Deliberately choosing another over my mate! Did I do this?"

"What you did was so much worse," she panted, her voice rasping. "You left me, Saban. You left when you swore you would never leave me." A single tear caressed her cheek. "You lied to me."

Yes, he had. He wiped the tear from her cheek with his thumb, feeling the guilt that rode inside him.

"I came back." He wasn't going to be swayed by tear-filled eyes.

"At three o'clock in the morning," she sneered.

Saban almost smiled. She sounded like a wife, and the knowledge filled him with a sense of excitement rather than anger. She could keep a time card on him whenever she pleased.

"Why did you go to him?" He asked the question, hating himself for it, hating the anger that filled him because of it. "I nearly lost you, Natalie. I would have lost my soul if anything had happened to you. Why? Why would you fucking take that risk? Is he so important to you?"

"You're that important to me." She jerked, raising her head until they were nearly nose to nose, flames flickering in her dark eyes. "I wanted him gone. I wanted him to leave, and I didn't want you to have to kill him to achieve it."

Saban shook his head in confusion. The way this woman's mind worked, he would never figure her out.

"What made you think you could make him leave? Even if the Council soldiers hadn't been involved, Natalie. What in God's name made you think he would listen to you?"

She breathed out heavily and glared back at him.

"Tell me." He snarled.

Her gaze became cutting, furious. "Because he knows me, Saban. I threw him out of our house; I divorced him despite his pleas. Once he knew, beyond a shadow of a doubt, that he didn't have a chance, he would have left. He would have hated me, and that was fine, but he would have left."

"And what could you have said to convince him of it when fear of me didn't?" He growled. "For God's sake, Natalie, there's nothing you could have said."

"I could have told him I love you!" she cried, shocking him to silence. "I could have told him that if he didn't leave, then I'd not stand between him and your fists ever again. Damn you. I could have made him see reason."

"Why would you want to?" He shook his head. She had said she loved him, and she meant it. He could see it in her eyes, in her face, he could smell the sweet, burning scent of it now. She loved him.

"Because I can't stand to see animals or fools bloody and dying. Geez, Saban, letting you loose on him would be like letting an alligator free in a chicken house. Complete annihilation."

"You were protecting him," he growled.

She rolled her eyes! Right there, staring right at him, she rolled her eyes at him as though he were an idiot. It shouldn't have pleased him, but it filled him with pride.

"No, asshole, I was protecting you from defending yourself against a murder charge," she snapped back. "If you haven't noticed, you're not exactly rational where he's concerned."

"Because he's consorting with Council scientists," he yelled impatiently, glowering down at her. "For God's sake, Natalie—"

"Well, I didn't know he was that stupid," she muttered. "Intense, yes; paranoid, sure; that's Mike Claxton, but he didn't used to be incredibly stupid."

He shook his head, amazement filling him. "You're serious." He couldn't believe it. "You expected me to be rational when he was clearly violent toward you—"

"He's never hit me."

"No, he would just turn you over to monsters." His voice was rising. "Trust me, you'd have preferred that he try to hit you."

"That's not the point."

"Not the point?" He was going to pull his own hair out.

"The point is," her voice softened, "I love you, Saban. I'd have done just about anything, said anything to get him out of our lives. I thought Mike was smarter than he was. I was wrong. I was wrong, and it will never happen again." Her voice hitched as her eyes filled with tears again. "But it won't change the fact that you left me, that you couldn't even look at me or find out for yourself why I felt I had to do it. Nothing will change that."

"That, mate, is where you are wrong."

FIFTEEN

Natalie would always remember the sight of Saban jumping into the van with that nasty little scientist, refusing to look at her, refusing to give her a chance to explain. It didn't matter that she had realized she had made a mistake even before Mike had attempted to kidnap her. What mattered was his refusal to even ask her why. She would have asked him why. She would have demanded to know why.

Shaking her head, she struggled against him, jerking at her wrists as he held her easily, staring down at her with those brilliant eyes, spiking her heartbeat with the look in them.

Possessive, dominant, everything she thought she would abhor and was now finding herself drawn to.

She stilled beneath him, watching him from under her lashes, growing angrier by the moment. Fine, he was the big, bad, strong Breed, but she hadn't been raised with her brother for nothing.

The minute she stopped struggling, his hold loosened on her wrists, just the slightest bit, but enough for her to jerk her upper torso up and to bring her lips to his. Where she bit him. A sharp little nip to that delicious lower lip before she was back, writhing, twisting beneath him.

"You little hellion." His voice was filled with wonder as a small bead of blood formed on his lip. "That was no love nip."

"How would you know?" she panted. "Maybe you're not the only one who likes to bite."

She managed to free one wrist, and before he could grab it again, she reached out, locked her fingers into the muscle of his chest, right around his nipple, and twisted.

He jerked back with a muttered curse, releasing her wrists, giving her the room she needed to twist away from him.

"I don't need a man who doesn't trust my love," she yelled furiously as she freed herself.

"You need a man to paddle your delectable little behind for

being so damned stubborn," he snarled, rubbing at his chest as he stared back at her almost wonderingly.

"Or a man who isn't so damned filled with pride he can't even wait around for a reasonable explanation." She managed to roll to the side of the bed and jump out of his reach.

She had a feeling he let her, though.

"The explanation would have to be reasonable first," he growled. "Yours wasn't."

"So spank me," she retorted, her voice mocking. "At least I didn't run away from the problem."

She stood on one side of the bed breathing hard as he glowered at her from the other side of the bed.

"I intend to get to that, *cher*, real soon," he drawled, his expression tightening not in anger but in arousal. "And I didn't run far, did I *bébé*? I came right back here to be the one to deliver the spanking."

Natalie felt her ass clench at the tone of his voice. He sounded serious. Maybe he sounded a little bit too serious.

"You wouldn't dare," she gasped, her eyes widening as he stripped off his shirt.

"Watch me." His eyes narrowed on her as her gaze flicked to where he was quickly releasing the closures on his jeans.

"You are not undressing," she snapped.

She couldn't believe it. Did he think this could be fixed with sex?

"Watch me," he repeated.

He sat down on the small, fussy chair beside her bed, unlaced and removed his boots, then stood and shucked his pants.

Oh Lord, she was in so much trouble. He was furiously aroused, his erection standing out from his body, thick and heavy, the ridged veins throbbing with subtle power.

"You can take those clothes off, or I'm going to rip them off you." He moved around the bottom of the bed, each shift of muscle, each flex of his long, corded body sending a flare of heated lust to ignite in the center of her womb.

God, the man was just gorgeous. Maybe just a little bit pissed if the heated flare of emotion in his eyes was anything to go by.

"I'm not fucking you while you're angry," she informed him coolly, or at least, she tried for cool; there might have been the slightest tremor of arousal in her voice. Because he was really turning her on.

"I'm not angry." A flash of strong white teeth in a confident, anticipatory smile. "I've decided something about you, *cher*. As stubborn and independent as you are, you're coming to believe that the reason you do things is not so important as the fact that you be allowed to do them. That the control streak you're adopting be given free rein."

"So?" She watched him warily, backing up as, naked, aroused, and dominating, he stalked toward her.

"Tonight, love, you learn, in matters of your safety, this will not be allowed. First lesson begins now."

Natalie shrieked as she watched the muscles in his chest bunch, but by the time she saw it, it was too late to run. And it was too late to save the robe she had dressed in after her shower.

The material tore and slipped to the floor as the sleeves ripped and the tatters of cloth were tossed away a second later. Natalie stared down at her bare breasts in amazement then up to Saban's narrowed gaze.

"That was just so wrong," she muttered.

"Ah, but was it as wrong as defying me, slipping away from me, and nearly getting yourself kidnapped?" He shook a finger at her before he struck again.

Before Natalie could consider running, she found herself on her back, the light cotton pajama bottoms flying through the air as Saban tossed them over his shoulder.

She was naked now. Naked and hot and wet, and she was damned if she going to let him get away with this.

She jerked to rise from the bed, only to find herself pushed back, rolled to her stomach, and a hard male weight straddling her thighs as one broad, calloused palm pressed between her shoulder blades, holding her to the bed despite her struggles.

"I said I was sorry," she bit out. "What more do you want? I won't do it again."

The opposite hand stroked over the curve of her butt as his fingertips pressed lightly against the narrow crease.

"Saban, I love you. You know I love you. I swear, I learned my lesson already." Okay, she was caving, but she had been wrong, she was big enough to admit to it. "You shouldn't have walked away like that. You shouldn't have left me."

"I'll never leave you again, *cher*." The words whispered over the small of her back a second before his lips grazed the flesh. "Should you ever be so foolish again, I'll spank you where you stand."

His hand landed lightly on the curve of her ass.

Natalie froze, her eyes jerking wide at the incredible streak of burning pleasure that tore through the nerve endings there.

"Saban." Was that weak, whimpering sound actually coming from her lips? She sounded like a sex vamp begging for more.

"You'll be a good girl in the future, will you no, *cher*?" The accent slipped out, cutting words and sounding so incredibly sexy she almost climaxed from the sound of it alone.

"This is ridiculous," she cried out as another firm slap landed on her rear, sending those curling fingers of heat and pleasure to wrap around her already swollen clit.

His hand landed again, again. Oh God, she could feel her flesh heating, blushing, and she knew she should be outraged, furious; instead, she was burning alive with arousal.

She could feel the dampness between her thighs, coating her pussy, spreading along her clit and increasing its sensitivity.

"I'll not walk away again, mate." He leaned forward, his lips pressing between her shoulders, his teeth rasping over her spine. "I'll love you until you know nothing exists in this life for me but you. I'll protect you, sometimes, from yourself." He nipped at her shoulder. "But never will I leave you again."

His hand slipped between their bodies, found the juices gathering along the swollen folds there, and he growled in hungry demand.

His touch was like a flame. She could feel the pleasure burning inside her, her body begging for more. She should be fighting him, but she couldn't find the will to deny herself, let alone him, what she knew he could give her.

What she knew they both needed.

"Come, *cher*."

Natalie turned eagerly as he lifted his weight from her, turning her to him. Her arms twined around his neck, dragging his chest to her breasts and his lips to hers.

She wanted that kiss. She was burning for it, dying for it. When it came, it was filled with the taste of wild lust and stormy emotion. Anger and fear laced each desperate bite of passion, each sip of lips as their moans mingled, their hands caressed.

Oh God, his hands. Calloused and strong, they skimmed over her flesh as his lips moved to her neck, licked, stroked. A frenzy of sensations tore through her. She could feel the heat like lightning, searing her flesh.

"Mine!" He snarled the word against the curve of her breast. "Always mine."

She wasn't fighting it, she couldn't fight it. The hours he had left her alone had given her a chance to think, a chance to feel. She had faced the thought of life without him and found it intolerable.

"Come for me, *cher*." His fingers slipped inside her pussy, stroked with diabolic pleasure, as his lips covered the hard point of her nipple.

And she did just as he asked; she came, shuddering, arching, feeling the pleasure overtake her in gentle, consuming waves.

"Ah, *cher*." He licked her nipple, grazed his teeth over it. *"Ma cher."*

"I love you." She whispered the words against his neck as she held on tight and felt the shudder of response that rippled through his hard body. "I'll always love you."

She would never be able to walk away as she had with Mike. That knowledge was both terrifying and exhilarating, knowing he held that much of her soul.

"I treasure you." He kissed her nipple with suckling little motions of his lips. "I adore you." His head moved to her stomach. "Ah, *cher*, I love you until I feel lost without you." His lips lowered to the swollen, saturated folds of her pussy.

Pleasure became a vortex of sensation. She screamed his name as he licked, sucked, tasted, and growled into the wet heat of her sex.

His teeth tugged at the swollen folds, his tongue licked and probed and wrapped around her clit with rasping little caresses that sent her exploding into the night.

When he dragged his body over hers, his cock nudging at the entrance to her vagina, Natalie forced her eyes open, lifted her lashes, and became lost in his gaze.

"I marked you," he growled roughly. "Mine. Forever."

"Stole me with a kiss," she whimpered, arching against him. "Steal some more, Saban."

With his Jaguar kiss, with the taste of lust and the touch of a conquering warrior, he had stolen her heart and become a part of her soul.

Natalie cried out his name as he took possession of what was his. His erection pressing forward, the silk-over-steel flesh parting delicate tissue, caressing, burning with a pleasure that fired more pleasure and sent her careening into a world where nothing mattered but the pleasure, the touch, the taste of his kiss.

Strained cries echoed around her as she felt the blaze of ecstasy, the pounding strength of his cock shafting inside her forcefully, as sensation became a hunger and hunger became a demand.

She writhed beneath him, arching to him, driving him deeper until the force of the need exploded through her, brilliant, lightning hot, and filled with all the love she had kept inside, locked away, frightened of the pain of losing this man. If she lost him, how much of herself would she lose as well?

As she felt his climax tearing through him, felt the barb in all its burning pleasure extend inside her, locking him in place as his semen spurted hot and fierce into the depths of her pussy, Natalie knew she would lose all of herself.

"I love you more than life," she whispered, tears filling her eyes as she held him to her, her nails pressing into his back, her lips pressed to his shoulder. "Don't leave me, Saban. Never, never leave me."

"Even death won't tear me from you." His head lifted, his green eyes nearly black with the emotions ripping between them, soul to soul. "Even death, Natalie, could not tear my soul from yours."

She lifted her hand to his face, let the tears fall, and let him shelter her in the strength of his arms, in an embrace as freeing as it was protective.

It would never be easy, but right here, sheltered by her Jaguar, loved, protected, held, she knew it was definitely worth fighting for.

And together, one heart, one soul, they whispered, "I love you."

SHIFTER'S LADY

Alyssa Day

This one is for Ann Thayer-Cohen, who gave me the title and who is an extraordinary moderator and a great friend. And, always, for Judd. And to my readers—thank you! Please visit me at www.alyssaday.com for excerpts, free downloadable screensavers, and a free short story for members only—"Atlantis: In the Beginning"—and watch for Lord Justice's book, Atlantis Unleashed, coming soon!

ONE

Moonlight silvered down through the branches of the cypress trees, shadowing the gnarled limbs and trunks into the menacing forms of ogres from a child's nightmare. The blood tracing geometric patterns in the dirt was no specter of childish terror, but the very real damage from a vicious attack.

Swearing under his breath, Ethan circled the fallen panther—the sixth one attacked in two weeks—all the while scanning the chill winter's dark for a glimpse of the unnatural predator who'd attacked it. He'd heard the animal's screams of pain while patrolling more than a mile away and had immediately broken into a full-out run, but the attacker had disappeared into the winter night.

At least for this panther he'd been in time. *This* cat was still alive.

As the wounded panther—a good-sized male—lifted its head to snarl, Ethan drew his lips back from his teeth and preempted the cat's defiance with a warning growl of his own.

"Sorry, my friend, I know you're hurting," he said, pitching his voice to the low rumble of an alpha male asserting its dominance over a pack member. "But if you won't let me get close enough to help you, we're going to have to go the tranq dart routine."

Lifting his head, he scented the air again, memorizing the rank odor that had assailed his nostrils as he approached the clearing. His shape-shifter senses were preternaturally sharp, but even in his human shape, Ethan could track a scent trail. This one was distinct from any of his own pride, but it was somehow oddly familiar.

The cat on the ground snarled again, weaker this time. The

gouges clawed out of its side and belly glistened a deep crimson-stained black in the moonlight.

Ethan took one last, long look around and dropped down into a crouch next to the animal. "It looks like the bastard who did this to you is gone. So let's get you to someone who can help."

The panther bared its teeth in one final act of defiance before Ethan grasped the sides of its face in his hands and stared into its eyes. He sent a mental touch into the cat's mind, simultaneously muting the pain the animal was suffering and delivering a simple message: *Pride-brother. Alpha. Help you.*

As he lifted the heavy body into his arms, careful not to jostle the cat more than necessary, he uttered a grim promise. "I'll get him for you, friend. Believe me, he'll pay."

TWO

Marie stood on the emerald-hued grass and stared, nearly transfixed, at the white marble temple inlaid with jade, sapphires, and amethyst, memorizing it anew, though she'd lived and worked within it for more than three centuries of days. She wanted to burn its image into her very being, in the event—the almost impossible event, she reminded herself—that she were never to see it again.

Her temple. Her sacred responsibility.

The one she was abandoning.

Her breath quickened, and an obstruction the size of one of her favorite sea sapphires lodged in her throat. "Erin, I—"

Beside her, Erin sighed and shook her head, her blonde curls shimmering in the magically created sunlight that replaced the rays of a sun that had never dared venture so far beneath the sea. Erin put her hands on her hips in that peculiarly human gesture that both she and Prince Conlan's beloved, Riley, favored when they were frustrated.

Humans. Marie marveled anew at the idea that she had two human friends, when no human before Riley had set foot in Atlantis for more than eleven thousand years.

"Not again, Marie," Erin said firmly, tapping her foot in mock impatience. "We are not going over my duties in the temple one more time. As First Maiden of the Nereids for more than three hundred years, don't you think it's time you had a vacation?"

"But Lord Justice—"

Erin sobered, the playfulness fading from her face. "No one wants to find him more than Ven and I do, Marie. You know that Conlan and Ven and all the warriors have done nothing else but search for Justice since he . . . since he . . ."

Erin's voice trailed off, as she visibly fought for control. "He sacrificed himself to that monster to protect *me*. To protect Ven and me. We will never give up."

Marie hugged the shorter woman, offering up yet another silent prayer that Lord Justice yet lived. After admitting to the shocking truth that he was half brother to Prince Conlan and his brother, the Lord Vengeance, Lord Justice had offered himself to the vampire goddess Anubisa in exchange for his brother's life. Marie had heard the tale of it many times but still could not comprehend the courage it must have required to voluntarily submit to the goddess of all Chaos.

Especially knowing of Conlan's seven years of torture at her hands.

Erin took a deep breath and stepped away from Marie's hug. "But life goes on. It always goes on. Women still come to the temple for help with their pregnancies and childbirth, and even though I am no temple-trained midwife, the gems give me the healing power to help them."

Marie smiled at the understatement. "You are our gem singer, Erin. You sing the healing power of the stones to our women and babies. You healed Riley and the unborn heir to the throne of Atlantis. Do not discount your Gift."

"I don't discount it, or I never would have agreed to this. The responsibility for the unborn children of Atlantis is an enormous one, far too much for a single witch," Erin replied. "Or at least it would be if you hadn't trained me yourself, surrounded me with your very knowledgeable temple acolytes, and watched as I used my Gift to sing healing and peace to women in labor."

Marie's desire to visit her brother, Bastien, and meet his new love, Katherine, pulled at her, but still she was torn. "I feel as though I were abandoning my duties at a time when all Atlantis must work together."

Erin's blue eyes softened with sympathy. "I know. But you deserve this time, Marie. And your brother and Justice were very close, weren't they?"

Marie's lips curved into a smile. "Yes, always. Thick as jellyfish, those two."

"Thieves."

"What?"

"We say 'thick as thieves,' " Erin said, laughing. "Although I must admit that thick as jellyfish makes more sense."

Marie studied the witch who had captured Lord Vengeance's heart and restored the glory of the Temple of the Nereids through her gemsong. Abruptly, she nodded. "Yes. You are correct. Bastien will be nearly insane with rage and worry for Lord Justice, and even more so from the frustration that he could not immediately join the search. I must go to him."

Almost as if on cue, an icy wind swept between and around them and resolved itself into the shimmering form of Poseidon's high priest, Alaric. He wore his customary black clothing, and the fire in his green eyes burned starkly in his drawn face. "Are you ready for the journey, Lady Marie?" he asked, his voice raspy as if little used in recent days.

"I am," she replied, inclining her head to the priest. He carried such a weight of bitter anguish with him, but it was not the pain of injury or illness. She sensed it was an emotional suffering but would never presume to impose upon his privacy by asking, no matter the whispers that had circulated about Alaric and Quinn, the sister of the prince's beloved.

If Alaric ever chose to share his anguish, she would listen. It was her role in life, and she had been content with it. To watch, to listen, to heal as best she could. Such a life was not without its rewards. She glanced at the temple one last time and smiled, then lifted her small travel bag from the grass at her feet and nodded again. "Please call the portal, if you would."

Alaric merely stared down at her for a long moment before he spoke. "Know that I am against this journey, my lady. We face more danger Above than we have for millennia, so now seems to be a ridiculously foolhardy time for you to venture from the safety of Atlantis."

Marie answered him with the respect due a warrior priest who had fought with and healed her brother and the rest of the Seven countless times, even though she'd thought this discussion finally put to rest when he'd agreed to call the portal for her. "As always, your opinion and advice are valuable. But I am not without defenses, as First Maiden. The goddess will not abandon me should danger threaten."

When he looked as though he would interrupt her, she held up a hand to touch his arm. "I know, Alaric. I *know*. But he is my brother, and he has need of me, though he would never admit to it. I must go."

He tightened his lips, and she saw the muscles in his jaw clench, but he said no more, merely lifted his hands in the air, closed his eyes, and called the magic. The magic of a high priest who was more powerful than any ever before anointed by Poseidon was truly mesmerizing to behold. The portal, sometimes capricious in how and when it responded, would never dare to disobey Alaric. On his command, the shimmering oval appeared first as a tiny gleam of light no larger than the palm of her hand then widened and expanded into an ovoid sphere sparkling with the effervescent colors of a thousand gemstones.

She'd seen it before, of course. She'd watched her brother and his fellow warriors, those elite who formed the Seven and protected High Prince Conlan, travel through the portal nearly as many times over the centuries as there were gemstones in the Temple. But the sight never failed to amaze her, and today even more so.

Today *she* was finally the one who would travel through the portal.

There were no farewells remaining to be said. No final instructions to be dispensed. She was simply ready, and so she smiled her thanks to Alaric and Erin and stepped into the portal. Into her new adventure.

Even as the magic surrounded her, Marie wondered at the chill that swept over her skin. The swirling winds of the transference whipped the murmured words from her lips as she spoke them. "Am I excited? Or simply afraid?"

Big Cypress National Preserve,
in front of Kat's cabin

Ethan leaned against a tree about as far as he could get from Bastien without displaying overt rudeness, but he met the huge Atlantean warrior's gaze in a shared moment of utter disbelief after Kat pulled the silver tube out of her pocket for the eighth or ninth time. The completely professional, cool, calm, and collected Katherine Fiero, highly regarded National Park Service ranger and daughter of the late alpha of the Big Cypress panther pride, was actually checking her lipstick in a hand mirror.

Like some kind of . . . *female.*

Then she bit her lip in a nervous gesture, and Ethan nearly laughed. He coughed, catching it in time, but she rounded on him and glared. "If you're going to mock me, get the hell out of here. I don't need any more witnesses to me making a fool of myself in front of Bastien's only sister."

Bastien blinked and then patted her shoulder as if she were an unruly cub. She whirled, her tawny hair flying, and snapped her teeth at the Atlantean, reminding both of the men that Kat Fiero was also a shape-shifter with the newfound ability to transform into more than one hundred fifty pounds of feral panther.

"Stop patting me. What if she doesn't like me?" She'd tried to hide the fear behind her words, but Bastien clearly had heard it, too, since he stopped trying to talk to Kat and swept her up into a fierce embrace. The love and passion in Bastien's expression made Ethan wish he were somewhere else.

Anywhere else.

Since Bastien and Kat had mated, or reached some Atlantean magical state that the warrior called the "soul meld," the two had been inseparable. Their hunger for each other was so powerful that Ethan was sure even a man who *wasn't* the alpha of Kat's pride would have been aware of it.

Since Ethan *was* the alpha and had once entertained hopes that he and Kat would someday settle down with each other, being around the pair was something akin to taking a serrated blade to the gut. He gave them another minute, then growled his displeasure. "If you're done groping each other, how's the cat doing?"

Bastien released Kat but shot a warning glance at Ethan. "Perhaps you should concern yourself less with us and more with whoever or whatever is attacking your cats."

Ethan snarled at him. "Don't push your luck, Atlantean. I may respect your fighting ability and our alliance, but don't even think about questioning my concern or efforts on behalf of my panthers. Shape-shifter or the single-natured."

Bastien inclined his head. "As you say. None can doubt your commitment to the members of your pride or to your panther counterparts."

Kat's eyes narrowed. "Do I have to toss a little of my mojo your way, boys?"

Both men stepped back from her, lifting their hands in

surrender. Kat's Gift calmed aggression and sent waves of peace flowing through even the most antagonistic predators, and Ethan suspected Bastien didn't want it used on him any more than Ethan did.

Ethan wasn't in the mood for peace. "About my cat?"

"His injuries were really severe, Ethan," Kat said. "Dr. Herman is the best, but he said it's touch and go." She shook her head. "If you hadn't gotten there when you did . . ."

"Yeah. I'm a big hero." Ethan forced the words out through clenched teeth. "Such a big damn hero that I've let five of our cats die. Maybe six now. Six out of a total population of Florida panthers of maybe ninety, max. At this rate, they'll be facing extinction again, like they were back in '55."

"We'll find him. Or them. Or it. Whatever is doing this, Ethan," Kat promised.

"I, too, will assist you in your search," Bastien added. "Until such time as my prince releases me from these political negotiations to join the search for Justice."

The fury that burned in Bastien's eyes at the mention of his friend and fellow warrior reminded Ethan that he was glad to have the Atlanteans on his side. "I understand what you mean about politics. But we have to lock in support among all the Florida shape-shifter coalitions so that they ally with us against the growing vampire threat. Organos proved that the vampire master plan to enthrall the shape-shifters has advanced far beyond what we'd suspected."

Bastien's eyes gleamed. "Organos died for his temerity, and so will any others that oppose us."

Ethan started to agree, but Kat cut him off with a loud hissing noise. "Is that . . . is that it? Is that her?" she whispered, pointing to a spinning sphere of light that had suddenly appeared in front of them.

Bastien put an arm around her shoulders and pulled her to him. "So it is. Finally you will meet my sister."

The sphere stretched and lengthened into a tall, oval shape, and a fractured kaleidoscope of light shimmered like a starburst in the center of it. Suddenly, near the bottom, one delicately shod foot stepped through the portal and onto the grass, followed closely by the rest of the tall woman in her white dress. Ethan barely got a glimpse of the side of her head, her glossy dark hair bound up in some kind of intricate braid thing, before she hurled herself at her brother. Bastien whooped and yanked her off her feet and swung her around, shouting with joy. But Ethan's attention snapped back to the portal when a second figure stepped through, this one ominously familiar: Alaric.

As Ethan nodded his head briefly to the Atlantean god's high priest, the portal's light winked out of existence. "Alaric. Be welcome among the pride," he said in the formal words of greeting.

"I come as an ally and friend," Alaric said, nodding in return. Ethan supposed after he'd seen the priest a few more times, he might get used to the man's bizarre glowing green eyes.

Maybe.

Alaric suddenly froze, his entire body stiffening as his eyes focused on some faraway sight. Nearly a full minute passed before Bastien, caught up in greeting his sister, noticed.

"Alaric?"

Bastien finally allowed his sister's feet to touch the ground again and hugged her, then looked at Alaric over her head. "What news?"

"We may have a lead, Bastien," Alaric said. "Conlan just contacted me. We need you now in the hunt for Justice."

"Of course," Bastien said, all but baring his teeth, his stance going to full-on alert. Ethan thought, not for the first time, that the warrior would have made a good panther.

"Marie, you must return to Atlantis and take Kat with you, so you'll be safe while I'm gone," Bastien continued.

Kat and Marie, whose face Ethan still hadn't seen, both spoke at once.

"I'm not going anywhere," Kat said.

"I only just arrived," Marie pointed out.

Ethan raised one eyebrow. "Certainly my protection extends to your sister while you search for your pride-brother, Bastien."

"Pride-brother? What a fascinating term," Marie said, stepping out from behind Bastien. "It appears our societies have much in common, as the warriors in the Seven are as close as brothers, as well."

Ethan had mere seconds to think that her voice sounded like crystal infused with laughter, and then he saw her face.

Enormous dark blue eyes gazed up at him out of the most beautiful face he'd ever seen. Her creamy pale skin begged to be caressed, and her mouth was wide and generous, with full, sensuous lips that sent a shiver of dark desire spiraling down his spine.

Marie was ethereal, almost otherworldly in her beauty. Equal parts of awe and craving shot through his nerve endings, and he struggled to put a tight leash on his inner cat, who wanted nothing more than to haul her off to a dark lair somewhere far from any others. But he was alpha, and he'd won fiercer battles against more desperate opponents than his own hungers. Convinced he'd tamed his beast, he held out his hand in greeting.

Marie smiled up at him, and the bottom dropped out of his world.

THREE

Marie's senses sharpened to painful clarity as she locked gazes with the shape-shifter, and her breath caught, trapped in her throat and somehow entangled with the rapid beating of her heart. Her vision telescoped until Ethan and only Ethan was framed within it, the others having vanished into the perimeter of the sparkling haze swamping her whirling thoughts. Ethan stood before her, holding out his hand, and courtesy dictated that she take it in greeting.

But fear drowned out all thoughts of courtesy. Somehow, instinctively, she knew that by touching him, some hidden stillness inside her soul would be disturbed. Raucously awakened, perhaps never again to find quiet. An inner voice mocked her girlish tremors, and sheer pride and force of will combined to overcome her hesitation.

Bastien's voice rumbled out from somewhere to her left. "Is there a problem?"

Marie lifted her chin, ignoring the concern in her brother's voice. "I am Marie, First Maiden of the Temple of the Nereids," she said to Ethan, proud that only the faintest tremor lay within the syllables of her speech. "I am honored that you welcome me to your lands." She briefly touched her hand to his but pulled it away before she could react to his touch.

Ethan's sensual lips had tightened at the sound of her voice, and he stared down at her with golden eyes darkened by some unknown emotion. The tawny hair, so similar to Kat's, framed his face in thick waves that might have looked feminine on any lesser man, but only highlighted his stark masculinity. His sharp cheekbones, strong chin, and proud, straight nose all stated without words that this man—this shape-shifter—was a warrior, born and bred.

How fortunate that she was not drawn to warriors.

Especially not tall, lean, hard-bodied warriors who looked at her as though she were some particularly delectable dessert.

Ethan smiled slowly, a dark, dangerous smile that spoke of pleasures whispered in the shadows. Heat swept through Marie, and her lips involuntarily parted on a small sigh. Ethan's gaze whipped down to her mouth, and he pointedly stared at it, his smile fading. The heat between them was palpable, cutting through the biting winter wind that carried hints of swamp and sea. Marie shivered, though whether from the chill or from the expression on Ethan's face, she could not tell.

Or, at least, she would not admit. Not even to herself.

She deliberately turned her back on Ethan and faced Kat, the lovely, tall park ranger who was clutching Bastien's hand and chewing the glossy polish off her lips. Marie held out her arms. "Forgive me, my new sister. The journey through the portal seems to have tired me. I am so pleased to meet you at last!"

Kat hesitated for only a moment and then flashed a dazzling smile that gave Marie much reassurance as to her brother's choice.

"I'm so happy you're here!" Kat said and then rushed forward to envelop Marie in an exuberant hug. "We have so much to talk about. I can't wait to show you around." Kat glanced at Bastien, smiling. "Bastien told me that this is your first trip out of Atlantis, ever. I can't even believe how much you need to catch up on! We're going to have a blast!"

Alaric cleared his throat. "Yes. Well. We must offer our farewells now, then. Bastien?"

Bastien's eyes narrowed, and he crossed his arms. "Marie, you know I would prefer it if you return to Atlantis and reschedule your visit for a time when I could be here to protect you."

From behind her, Marie heard an almost inaudible growling sound. Startled, she quickly turned around but saw only Ethan. However, it was a very different Ethan from the man who'd greeted her mere minutes ago. Gone was the sexy, speculative smile. His eyes were glowing golden flame, and his fists were clenched at his side. She blinked and watched the panther as he visibly forced himself to calm, straightening his hands and quirking his lips into a semblance of a smile as he stared at Bastien.

"As I said, Atlantean, I will protect your sister as my own. Do you doubt my word or honor?" His words dropped like heated stones into the sudden silence, and Marie felt the tension between the men shoot up to an unbearable level. "Even now, my pride-brothers surround this area to guard and protect."

"I doubt neither, shape-shifter, but you would feel the same about Kat, and you know it," Bastien returned, in a tone far more reasonable than Marie had expected from him. Evidently the liaison role he'd undertaken had affected him in more ways than merely touched the surface. The brother she'd always known would have led with his fists. This new brother used logic. Marie smiled at Bastien, delighted at the change.

"And yet Kat is now under *your* protection, and I am at peace with her decision, however wrongheaded it may have been," Ethan said smoothly.

The interplay between the men was fascinating to observe, but for once in her centuries of existence, Marie was impatient with merely acting as observer. She held her arms out at her sides, palms up. "I find I have tired of being talked about as though the decision were not my own. Lady Kat, perhaps you will take me into your lovely home, so I might freshen up and be settled?"

Kat grinned and gestured to the small cabin. "It's Kat. And I'd be delighted to, Marie. I have a feeling we're going to be great friends."

Marie crossed to her brother and stood on the tips of her toes to press a kiss onto his cheek. "Be well, and find Lord Justice. Do not worry about me. As I have repeatedly told Alaric, Conlan, and what seems to have been three dozen of your fellow warriors, I am not defenseless. The goddess protects her own."

Bastien lifted her off her feet in a strong embrace. "I know this is true. Be well, and I will return as soon as we find Justice and free him from—"

Marie touched his lips with her fingers. "Do not speak her name here in this place. Names hold power, and I do not wish to attract her attention to your beloved's home."

Bastien nodded and stepped back, then bowed. "I will return as soon as I may," he repeated.

Alaric, who had remained uncharacteristically silent, spoke up. "Send a message should you have need of me, First Maiden." He bowed to her, then gestured with one hand to draw the portal to open for his and Bastien's return to Atlantis.

Marie nodded her thanks, then turned to walk toward the cabin and give Kat and Bastien a moment for a private farewell. Ethan, who had remained standing behind her as if frozen into place, now blocked her path. He stared down at her, and the heat she'd felt earlier at his mere glance intensified until she wanted to lean into him and soak up his warmth, wrap herself in the flames that the touch of his skin must surely generate in her body.

She drew in a deep breath and forced her expression to one of calm amusement. "Must I have the same talk with you that I have had with my brothers so many times over the centuries? The one about individual responsibility? Where I explain in very simple words that I am no fragile Atlantean flower to be cared for and coddled in a hothouse?"

Ethan leaned forward slightly, his hands behind his back, and raised one silken, dark eyebrow. "Simple words might be a really good idea, beautiful," he said softly. "Because I'm having a hell of a fight with my inner cat right now, who wants to carry you off, strip you bare, and lick all of that deliciously creamy skin of yours."

She inhaled sharply as his words sent tsunami waves of shock and heat slapping through her nerve endings. Before she could summon a properly stinging response, he lifted a hand and touched a curl that had escaped her braids. "And as for individual responsibility, I intend to be *completely* responsible for seeing this glorious hair unbound and spread all over my bed. So consider that, Lady Marie, and maybe you'll be the one who wants to run back to your hothouse."

Her much-prized serenity completely deserted her. "You . . . you—"

"Yes," he said firmly. "Me. Remember it." Then he bowed to her, flashing another of those mocking smiles, and strode off, sketching a half salute toward Bastien and Alaric over his shoulder. Marie glanced at her brother, wondering if he'd caught the interplay between her and Ethan, but Bastien was talking intently with Kat. When she looked back toward Ethan, she saw nothing but a tawny blur disappearing through the trees. She finally let out the breath she had not realized she was holding and continued toward the cabin on knees gone suddenly weak.

Life with the landwalkers was going to be far more fascinating than she had ever imagined.

E than leapt into the trees, shifting as his feet left the ground. In panther form, he ran as far and as fast as he could, determined to outpace the overpowering hunger she'd awakened in him.

Marie.

The mere thought of her name sent another rush of heat through him, and the cat he'd become snarled and pushed harder, lengthening his strides, escaping from the subtle scent of sea and flowers that had surrounded her.

Needed to run. Further and further. Needed to run away from the woman who'd destroyed his equilibrium in sixty seconds flat.

Strip her bare and lick her skin? What the *hell* had he been thinking? Not two minutes after swearing his protection in front of her brother and the priest, he'd insulted and threatened her. He snorted and drew his lips back from his fangs, snarling again as he ran. Not only was he a damned fool, but he'd probably incited some kind of international incident.

Panting, finally nearing exhaustion, he slowed to a walk, padding on four powerful legs that were trembling faintly from the strain of the run. He looked around and stopped, recognizing the woods behind his house, the big-ass mansion that served as home and headquarters to the alpha of the Big Cypress pride. No wonder he was short of breath and suffering from a little muscle fatigue. He'd never run ten miles in such a short time.

Maybe lust was good for the metabolism.

He called to the magic that infused both halves of his dual natures and lifted his head to receive the transformation. As always, the shift came to him effortlessly, and he stood fully clothed in his human form afterward. Ease of performing the shape change was one of many indicators of shape-shifter strength, and he was alpha. Strongest of all the shape-shifters in Big Cypress. Rumored to be the strongest in all of Florida; perhaps in all of the southeast region.

"Yeah, big, tough alpha cat, running away from a female," he muttered in disgust.

But some trick of the wind brought the faint scent of the sea to his panther-enhanced senses and—just like that—it was as though she stood before him again. He clenched his jaw as his cock hardened painfully in his suddenly too-tight jeans, and he realized that he'd been fooling himself.

Alpha or not, there was no way he'd be able to run away from this woman. Every fiber of his being was commanding him to turn around and run right back to her, but he refused to surrender to the impulse. Grimly determined to put the insane attraction behind him and get back to the serious business of discovering who or what was stalking his panthers, he strode toward his house.

So she was like some kind of crazy Atlantean catnip. He could resist catnip.

His cat snarled inside him, then rolled luxuriously, sending Ethan the sensation of warmth and silken fur curled around a blaze of feral hunger. The image of Marie's creamy skin and dark, drowning blue eyes flashed into his mind, and he nearly stumbled.

Dammit. He was toast.

FOUR

Marie sat in a chair at the kitchen table, hands folded in her lap, still trying to retrieve her usual calm, when Kat entered the cabin a few minutes later. Kat hesitated briefly in the doorway before seeming to come to some internal resolution. She stalked across the cabin's warm and inviting living space, lush with wooden furniture and yellow and red overstuffed cushions. The sunlight from the window gleamed on Kat's golden hair, as it had done with Ethan.

Ethan.

Stop thinking of him.

Kat stopped a few paces in front of Marie and took a deep breath. "Okay, here's the thing," she blurted out. "If you're here to tell me I'm not good enough for him, well, I kind of know that. I mean, you guys are Atlantean nobility and all. Denal filled me in on how Bastien is really Lord Bastien and you're Lady Marie. But I love him, and I'm going to fight for him."

Marie raised one eyebrow and studied Kat for nearly a full minute before responding. Finally she smiled and stood so she faced Kat, their eyes on a level. "And of course that is all I need to know about you. You love him, and you're willing to fight for him. From what I have heard, you were willing to die for him."

Kat's face reddened, but she didn't lower her gaze. "He nearly died for me. Do you think I could do less?"

Marie hugged the woman who was truly worthy of her brother. "I thank the Goddess for you, Katherine Fiero, and that my brother has found you. Be welcome to our family."

Something tense seemed to relax in Kat's body, and she returned Marie's hug. "Well . . . wow. Thanks. And welcome to my family, too. Which mostly consists of my pride, but I'm sure Ethan already welcomed you to that, as well."

A rush of heat swept through Marie, and she looked down quickly before Kat could see the evidence of it on her face.

"What? What did he say to you?" Kat asked, suspicion heavy

in her tone. "I know he can be kind of rough-edged, but he is a good man. I'm sorry if he gave you a bad impression—"

"It was nothing. I am, after all, accustomed to warriors and their arrogance." Marie lifted her bag. "Perhaps I could settle in, and then we can have a talk?"

"I guess he's not the only one with rough edges," Kat said, grinning. "I'm sorry. Let me show you the guest room, and I'll make some coffee. Then we can have a nice long chat."

"I look forward to both the coffee and the talk," Marie said, returning her new sister's smile. As she followed Marie down the narrow hallway to the guest room, she reminded herself that she had more than three hundred years of practice in self-control. No arrogant alpha shape-shifter would be a match for her. Perhaps she would take him for a lover. He might be amusing for a few days.

A shiver raced down her spine at the thought of bedding all that lean, hard muscle. Staring into those burning golden eyes while he drove his body into hers.

No, she was candid above all things, even to herself. *Especially* to herself. There was definitely nothing *amusing* about him.

Marie filled her third cup of the rich Irish cream coffee that Kat had brewed, then replaced the glass carafe in its position, closed her eyes, and held the mug near her face to inhale the luscious aroma. "This is truly magnificent. I must bring some of it home with me when I return to Atlantis."

Kat laughed and shook her head. "Better wait first and see what kind of reaction you have to that much caffeine. Three cups in an hour and a half may have you crawling out of your skin."

They'd fallen into an easy friendship, as was only to be expected from two women who both loved her brother. Kat was passionate about her work, and her stories of life as a park ranger were fascinating and so completely different from Marie's own secluded life in the temple that they raised a feeling akin to envy.

"You are so fortunate to have been brought up to such independence," she said, placing her mug on the table. "The Goddess placed her mark on me when I was yet a child, and my family knew I was destined for the temple. My life was a regimented one of study and apprenticeship."

Kat bit her lip. "I'm so sorry. Was it awful?"

"Oh, no, no. I don't mean to give that impression. Free will reigns in Atlantis; though the Goddess marked me, I could have declined life as her maiden. But from the moment I stepped foot in the temple, her power infused me. My Gift is to heal and assist those women who are with child and their unborn children, and I am honored to fulfill that role."

"Bastien said you were the boss?"

Marie laughed. "Boss? Not exactly. I am First Maiden, and my role is to lead and train the acolytes. *Boss* is such a funny human word, but I suppose some aspects of it apply."

"Hey, don't knock it," Kat advised. "On Bosses' Day, I send my supervisor a box of Godiva chocolates."

"Chocolate? I could get used to the word *boss* for chocolate . . ."

A loud ringing interrupted their shared laughter, and Kat rose to pull a small silver telephone from her jacket pocket and snap it open. "Fiero. Yes. No, I have—but, that's . . . Yes. Yes, of course." She sighed. "Fine, I'll be there in two hours."

She closed her phone and muttered something under her breath, then turned to Marie. "I'm so sorry, but that was *my* boss, coincidentally. We've got a regional meeting tomorrow morning, and the person in charge of putting on an important presentation can't make it. His wife just went into labor with their first child."

Marie smiled. "Certainly that is more important than any meeting."

"I agree, but it puts me in the hot seat. My boss wants us to meet tonight and go over his presentation so I can give it in his place tomorrow. I hate to leave you alone like this, but—"

"Do not give it another thought. I would love the opportunity to explore your beautiful lands, and I am very comfortable with my own company," Marie said, attempting to reassure Kat even as she tried not to think about how vastly different her visit was turning out to be from what she'd imagined. Perhaps her misgivings back in Atlantis had been well-founded, and she should contact Alaric to return. She could visit another time, she tried to console the empty space inside herself. Just because her first adventure was not unfolding as planned—

Kat cut into Marie's dejected thoughts. "I feel awful. We had so many plans—Bastien and I were going to take you to dinner at Thelma's and introduce you around, and . . . Wait! I know. Ethan can take you. He told me last week he wanted the chance to get to know you while you were here."

The floor under Marie's feet seemed to shift at the sound of his name. Definitely not a good idea. "No," she protested. "I'm sure he has many important duties. I can remain here or go for a walk by myself or even return to Atlantis and visit you when Lord Justice is safely returned home. It's—"

Kat wasn't listening, though, and was already speaking into her phone. "Ethan? Look, I've got to run out to an unexpected meeting, and I'll be gone all evening. I was wondering if you—"

She flashed a brilliant smile at Marie. "You will? That's great. I'll . . . An hour? Sure. I'll tell her. We were going to eat at Thelma's and . . . Sure . . . I'll tell her. Thanks!"

Kat snapped her phone closed. "He offered to show you around Big Cypress and take you to dinner before I even asked. You must have made some impression on him."

"I don't . . . Kat, I'm not sure . . . Ethan and I—"

Kat's eyes narrowed. "What did he say? Was he rude to you? I'll kick his ass for him, alpha or not, if he offended you. Ethan has this 'all arrogant, all the time' thing going on, because everybody bows down before him, and he needs to get over it. It's nothing personal, though, if that matters."

Marie laughed a little wildly. Nothing personal? He wanted to lick her skin! It could not be more personal than that, could it?

She needed to pull herself together. She was First Maiden to the Goddess of the Nereids, and she would not be thrown off balance by one . . . one . . . surly kitten.

"On second thought, Kat, exploring and dinner with Ethan would be lovely. I'll just go change my clothes while you get ready for your meeting." Marie rinsed her coffee mug in the sink, her thoughts already on what she would wear. So he liked her hair, did he? Had fantasies of it spread across his pillows? A slow, wicked smile spread across her face. Perhaps she'd let him see exactly what he'd been fantasizing about. As she walked down the hall to her room, her fingers were already busy undoing the dozens of intricate braids.

FIVE

Ethan knocked on Kat's door a good thirty minutes earlier than he'd planned to be there. So much for casual nonchalance. He'd tried to do some work, but memories of his too-brief contact with Marie had insinuated themselves into his mind. Flashes of her skin, her hair, her ocean-colored eyes.

That smile that had knocked him on his ass, figuratively speaking. He planned to have the upper hand this evening, though. Be the perfect gentleman. Calm, cool, and completely unflappable.

The door opened, and Marie stood there, smiling that perfect, kissable smile again. But he was prepared. He was unflappable. He glanced down, and the waves of her blue black hair and the dress she was almost wearing finally registered, and he sucked in a sharp breath.

"Holy shit!" Okay. He was flappable. He was flapped. He was what-the-hell-ever, but no way was she going out in public like that.

"Is that a common greeting among your people?" Marie asked, raising her chin and smiling. But underneath the smile was a hint of something else. Hurt, maybe. Nervousness.

"Damn. I mean, no, that is not a common greeting. I'm sorry, you just knocked me a little off balance," he admitted. Then he stepped forward, forcing her to let him enter the cabin. He closed the door behind him and took another step toward her.

The polite thing would have been to maintain a courteous distance.

When she put that dress on, she should have known he'd have no chance at polite.

He deliberately dropped his gaze from her face and scanned her luscious curves in the silky dark blue dress. The neckline dropped low in some kind of draped fold, and the rest of it wrapped her waist and hugged her breasts and hips like it had been sewn around her body. The swing of the skirt caressed her legs just above her knees, and he wanted nothing more than to drop to his own knees before her, push the fall of fabric slowly up those silken thighs, and discover what exactly she was wearing underneath.

He lifted his head and stared down into her eyes. "Did you wear that for me?" he said, almost not recognizing the raspy words as his own voice.

The brave smile trembled on her lips, and she began to answer, then abruptly turned away from him and walked toward the kitchen. But the view from behind was just as sexy, and he had to shift his legs as he hardened painfully inside his pants. Waves of dark silken hair tumbled down over her shoulders and back, brushing against her rounded hips. The vision he'd had earlier of her hair spread over his bed came back to him in full force, and he had to remind himself to breathe.

She stopped on the other side of the table, as if using the furniture as a barricade between them. "It was simply a dress I brought to wear for dining," she said. "Is it inappropriate?" She'd uttered the words in a tone of bored indifference, but the rapid pulse of her heart told him it was an act.

"You can't lie to a shape-shifter, darlin'," he said, putting a little southern drawl in the words. "I can hear your heartbeat. If you want to play games with me, I'm all for it. But be advised that I'm alpha for more reasons than physical strength. Are you sure you're up to playing games with me?"

He'd moved closer to her as he talked, stalking her. His cat had the scent of prey in its nostrils. No. Not prey. Something more primal. More visceral.

Mate.

Ethan stopped midstride as the realization came to him. His cat wanted to lay mate claim to this woman. This Atlantean who was not even a shape-shifter.

No.

Hell no.

"No, I am not sure that I am up for your idea of games," Marie said. "If you prefer, we can cancel our dinner plans, although I'm sure it would have been . . . pleasant . . . to spend time with you. But if the idea distresses you . . ." She shrugged. "Far be it from me to cause distress to the alpha of your pride, as you so continually remind me you are."

He weighed and discarded responses and finally settled on the simplest. "Do you have any idea how beautiful you are?"

It was her turn to be caught off guard. He watched, entranced, as rich, rosy color swept up her neck to her cheeks and burned there. She tilted her head and examined the wood grain of the table, which was evidently fascinating. "I . . . No, you . . . Thank you. That is very kind of you."

"No. It's not," he said flatly. "It's not kind at all. It's the truth, and I'm just wondering how many fights I'm going to get in if I take you out in public wearing that dress. You look like a man's hottest fantasy come to life, and I know more than one of my pride who would lose their senses over you."

She fisted her hands on her hips and glared at him. "Is that what women are to you here on the surface? Possessions over which to be fought by brainless men?"

He laughed. "Nice grammar, ocean girl. 'Over which to be fought,' huh? Never thought proper syntax would make me hot."

Marie blinked, opened her mouth, and then closed it. Finally she started laughing. "You are incorrigible," she said, her eyes sparkling with the shimmering depths of the sea at midnight under a rising moon.

He took a step closer and held out his hand. "I can live with incorrigible. How about I apologize for my unforgivable rudeness and we start over? I'm Ethan. Welcome to my territory. Would you like to have dinner with me? Somewhere away from any brainless men? Well, any brainless men besides me, of course."

She hesitated, then placed her slender hand in his. "I am Marie, and I would be honored to have dinner with you."

The touch of her hand sent something shining and razor-edged skimming through his nerve endings. His cat snarled and paced inside him, demanding to be let out to play.

To claim. Mate-claim.

But Ethan forced his animal half down and back, determined that the man would enjoy this evening. There was no possibility of laying mate claim to a nonpanther, let alone a woman who was not even a shape-shifter. This would simply be a pleasant meal among friends.

As he followed Marie out the door of the cabin, unable to look away from her gently swaying backside, he clenched his hands into fists and focused on the essentials.

Control.
Pleasant dinner.
No pouncing on the Atlantean.
Marie glanced back over her shoulder and smiled at him, and he stumbled, his inherent feline grace deserting him. Screw *that*. There was definitely going to be pouncing.

M arie tried to slow her breathing as she pulled her wrap around her shoulders against the chill of the late afternoon.
In. Out.
Calm. Focus.
She concentrated on the breathing exercises she'd so often taught to women who were with child. In. Out. Measured, even tempo. No flutters or hitches or gasps, no matter that the man following her was burning holes in her back with those shocking golden eyes of his.

She'd worn the dress in an attempt to get a reaction from Ethan, and it had worked so well she'd been caught completely off guard. She'd lived her life surrounded by warriors, so why was this one—this man who wasn't even Atlantean; wasn't even fully human—so different?

Maybe because Poseidon's warriors treated her as a cherished sister, due to their friendship with Bastien. They admired and respected her, certainly, but none had ever desired her. At least not that she'd ever known. Her few love affairs had been with men from the scholarly life. Philosophers and historians. Gentle, learned men.

None of them had ever made her blood race the way this panther did. A thrill of pure electricity had sizzled through her blood at his touch when she'd finally dared place her hand in his. She'd pulled away from him as quickly as courtesy would allow, but not before she'd seen the shocked expression on Ethan's face. This attraction traveled both directions on the path between them, and she was unsure if she could resist it for long.

She glanced at him again and wondered how simple black trousers and a white shirt could be so elegant, when she had seen the high prince dressed in full royal attire on ceremonial occasions. Ethan walked with the pure grace and deadly determination of the ultimate predator. Every line of his body flowed with sinuous movement, and if she narrowed her eyes, she could almost visualize the cat that he could become.

They stopped at his car, some sleek black vehicle that looked fast and expensive, based on what little she knew of cars, and she stared at him as he walked up next to her to open her door. Her breath caught in her throat as he approached, and she blurted out the first thing that popped into her head. "Will you show me?"

He raised an eyebrow and folded his arms across his thickly muscled chest. "Show you what?"

"I . . . Is it rude? Perhaps . . . never mind," she said, then blushed as she realized that she was actually babbling for the first time in her life.

"We don't stand on ceremony around here, Marie. Just tell me."

He'd moved closer, so that he stood so near that his breath feathered across her hair, and the spicy warm male scent of him filled her senses, nearly making her forget what she'd been about to ask. She shook her head a little, to counteract the hypnotic effect he had on her, then drew up her courage and asked. "Your panther. I was wondering . . . Is it rude to ask you to show me the shape change? Or perhaps you would shift your shape in private and then show me the other of your dual natures?"

She was breathless by the time she finished, both from her own temerity and from his nearness. The heat of his body was enchanting her, calling to her, beckoning her to wrap herself in his arms and his warmth. She suddenly felt as if she'd lived her life in the cold and only he could rescue her from it.

Madness. She dug her nails into her palms to shake off the fanciful imaginings and return to normalcy, but he moved even closer until she was backed up against his car. He placed a hand on the metal on either side of her, bracketing her body between the heat of his arms and chest and the icy chill of the car's metal.

"You want to see my cat, ocean girl? That's a very personal request," he murmured, leaning forward and breathing the words into her ear. She shuddered helplessly as heat flamed through her, then put her hands up to his chest to push him away. She was tall, and she was strong, but pushing against his chest was like pushing against the rock wall that bordered the palace garden.

He lifted a hand and tilted her face up to his with one finger beneath her chin. She looked into his eyes, unable to utter a word, and he searched her face for something, then stared fixedly at her mouth. Moments passed, and finally he stepped back from her, muttering an oath under his breath. "Maybe later," he said roughly. "You make me forget myself, Marie. I'm not sure how to handle that."

He yanked the car door open for her, then leaned in to show her how to fasten the seat belt, but his touch was brisk and impersonal. When he carefully closed the door and walked around the car to the driver's side, Marie stared at him through the window and finally released the breath that had been trapped in her lungs.

"As to forgetting yourself, Ethan, you are not alone," she whispered, wondering what she'd gotten herself into.

Wondering why she didn't want to get out.

SIX

As they drove through the breathtaking lands of the Big Cypress Swamp, Marie spent several minutes acclimating to the novel experience of riding in a car. When she was sure her stomach would not rebel against the motion and the bumpy ride, she asked Ethan to tell her about this place that he and his kind called home.

"It's a national preserve, protecting over 720,000 acres of swamp. Basically, the swamplands are crucial to the health of the Everglades, because they support the marine estuaries along Florida's southwest coast."

"It's beautiful, and so diverse," she observed. "I am so accustomed to the plant life in Atlantis that this seems very exotic to me."

He pointed to a stand of trees along the side of the narrow road. "Those are dwarf cypress trees. We have a mixture of tropical and temperate plant life, but it's not just the green and leafy stuff that's so exotic around here. We've also got gator communities, bears, and, of course, panthers."

She smiled. "Of course. Tell me about the panthers. I have access to your encyclopedias and other reference texts, but I do have some questions. Are panthers the same as cougars?"

"The Florida panther is a subspecies of cougar that has adapted to the temperature here. We've fought our way back from extinction for the panthers, but there are still fewer than a hundred remaining."

She turned her head to look at him. "But surely there are others elsewhere?"

A muscle tightened in his jaw. "A few in zoos. But the Florida panther is still one of the rarest and most endangered animals in the world. Unfortunately, developers don't care about that. Fortunately, on the other hand, we have Big Cypress. An adult male needs two hundred seventy-five miles of territory, but that can overlap with the females."

Marie looked out the window, wondering why the subject of male territory was causing heat to rush into her cheeks again. "Females, plural, you said? And is that true of the male shapeshifter as well?"

"For some, it can be," he said flatly. "I'm not one of them."

Marie winced, remembering what Bastien had told her of Ethan's mate who'd been killed by the vampire. "I am sorry, Ethan. I was not thinking. My condolences on the loss of your mate."

There was a long silence, then finally he spoke. "Yeah. Well. Fallon deserved better than what I had to offer her and certainly better than how she died."

Marie caught a glimpse of something large and golden red moving through the trees as they passed. "What is that? Is that one of your panthers?"

Ethan whipped his head to the side and then yanked the steering wheel to pull the car to a sudden stop on the side of the road, knocking Marie forward against her seat belt.

"I'm sorry. Are you okay?" He leaned over and grasped her shoulders, raking her with that intense golden gaze.

"Yes, of course. But why have we stopped?"

"We're having a problem with someone or something attacking our panthers, and I'd like to check this one out. I'll just be a few minutes. Stay here with the doors locked," he commanded.

His tone conveyed his expectation of perfect obedience, and for some reason it irritated her. "Fine. I'll stay here. But you might remember in the future that I am not a member of your pride, and my submission is not your right," she snapped.

The edges of his lips quirked into a grin. "I'll be glad to submit to you, ocean girl. Just name the time and place." Then he leaned into her and pressed a quick, hard kiss on her lips. "I'll be right back."

In seconds he was gone, and Marie leaned back against her seat, pressing her fingers to her lips. She was, perhaps, in more trouble with this man than she'd realized.

She shook her head, suddenly remembering what he'd said. Lock the doors. She examined the side of the door, wondering which of the many buttons was the lock, but suddenly the door jerked open and a pair of denim-clad legs stood in front of her. Startled, she stared up and into the grim face and crazed eyes of a man who was very definitely not Ethan. "What—"

"Get out of the car," he said, his quiet voice almost shockingly contrasting with his wild-eyed demeanor. "Now."

"But—"

He leaned into the car, unfastened her seat belt and ripped it off of her, then grabbed her arm and forcefully pulled her out of the car. Marie fell hard onto the gravel road when her legs tangled as he pulled her off balance. The immediate sharp pain focused her thoughts and snapped her out of the dazed state of shock the man's presence had caused. She evaluated him carefully. Taller than her, he was all muscle. Not someone she could hope to overpower. Dark auburn hair twisted in unkempt strands down to his shoulders, and his oddly pale yellow eyes burned with hate or some other equally intense emotion.

And—for whatever reason—it was directed at her.

"I'm not playing with you," he said, still in that calmly polite tone that was so at odds with the fury raging in his eyes. Then he fisted his hand in her hair and yanked her head up painfully. "Stand up now, or I'll kill you right there on your knees."

Marie called on the Goddess for strength and courage and forced an expression of calm to match his to her features. "Of course," she said, as she pushed up off the ground, ignoring the burning pain in her knees and hands where she'd scraped the skin off them. "Although I think perhaps you have the wrong—"

"Shut up." He released her hair and lifted his hand, clenched into a fist. A hint of madness twisted his features into a caricature of their former calm. "I've never punched a woman in the face before, but I can make an exception for Ethan's newest whore. Are you the slut he turned to after he let my pride-sister die? Or were you fucking him while she was still alive?"

Marie blinked, completely lost. "What? I don't understand what you're talking about. I only met Ethan today, and—"

He smiled at her and shook his head. "Wrong answer," he said, almost patronizingly. Then he pulled out the knife.

Ethan ran into the trees, following the strong scent of panther. More than one—some were shape-shifters. Maybe he'd finally catch them. He leaped into the air and shifted, landing on the ground on powerfully muscled panther legs. The scent immediately intensified, since his animal senses were far superior to his human ones. There were many of them, and they'd been congregating in this area recently. The scent was different from that of his own pride, but familiar.

Maddeningly familiar. He stalked around the area, head down, trying to make sense of the myriad individual scents, when he heard a female scream from the direction he'd left Marie in the car.

Marie.

He snarled and raced back toward the car, feral thoughts of ripping his prey into shreds whirling in his mind. Rage nearly blinded him as he crashed through the brush with no thought of stealth.

If they'd hurt her, they would die.

He whipped through brush and bounded around trees faster than he'd ever moved before, heedless of the branches and thorns slicing grooves in his side through his thick fur. Throwing caution aside, he leapt through the grasses bordering the road and landed in front of the car, scanning the area as he did.

There were four of them. Three surrounded the car, while the fourth held Marie with an arm banded around her waist. He had a knife to her throat.

He had a *knife* to her *throat*.

Ethan screamed with primal fury, his panther nearly insane with a murderous rage. But he stopped where he was when the bastard pressed the tip of the knife into Marie's tender flesh. Blood trickled down her neck, and Ethan swore he would exact vengeance upon them for every drop of it.

Every single drop.

The man holding her stared at Ethan and smiled. "Stay right where you are, Ethan. You wouldn't want my knife hand to get slippery and press harder into her neck, would you?"

Ethan snarled again but held his position. He was fast, but not fast enough to get to them before that knife would slice through Marie's carotid artery. She stared at him, fear and helpless anger on her face, and he wanted to kill them all for causing it. His panther wanted to rip their heads from their bodies and eat their hearts.

But then Marie would look at *him* with that same terrified expression.

He shunted the thought to the side. Focus. Get her to safety and then worry about the rest.

The man nodded. "Good boy. And I know it's you, so why

don't we dispense with the bullshit and you shift back into your human shape, Ethan. We have a little business to discuss."

Ethan knew that what little advantage he held in panther form was destroyed by the point of that knife against Marie's neck. He instantly shimmered into the shape change and stood before them, fully dressed, in his human form seconds later.

The man whistled. "Very nice. Fallon told me you were the fastest at the change of any shape-shifter she'd ever met. Even faster than me, I'll give you that. But not by much."

The connection clicked in Ethan's mind. "Fallon. That's why your scents are so familiar. You're Fallon's pride-brothers."

"Ding, ding, ding. Two points for the *former* alpha of the Big Cypress pride. I'm Travis, and I owe you blood feud for allowing Fallon to die," Travis snarled.

Ethan inclined his head. "It is your right. She was under my protection when she died at the vampire's hand, and I take full responsibility. But this woman has nothing to do with any of it. She is merely a visitor who arrived today."

The three men surrounding the car had been edging their way toward Travis and now stood fanned out in a loose semicircle around him, staring at Ethan.

Travis laughed, the sound a chilling mockery devoid of humor. "You lie. I can smell you on her. You're fucking her, aren't you? How does it feel to know somebody you care about is hurting? That she might die?"

Marie started to speak. "You gain nothing by threatening me. He spoke the truth. I—"

Travis dug the point of the knife further into her throat, and she broke off with a strangled moan. Ethan roared out his fury and started toward them, but the three thugs blocked him from Travis.

Travis shouted his command. "Stop or I'll kill her now. Just like I killed your precious panthers. Did you get my message? Or, wait, was it my half-dozen messages, delivered in the form of dead cats?" His chilling laughter rang out, and Ethan noticed that even Travis's henchmen shuddered. A panther shifter who could murder cats of his own kind was worse than the lowest kind of scum.

Ethan froze, gaze locked on the knife point where it was sunk into Marie's skin. "What do you want, Travis? Tell me now, and leave the woman alone."

"I want *you*, alpha," Travis said. "I call blood feud and alpha challenge upon you. Tomorrow night, under the full moon, we will battle for your title, your lands, and your pride. Dare you to refuse?"

Ethan stared at the Texas shape-shifter, assessing strengths and weaknesses. There was no option. Alpha challenge could never be refused. But if Travis harmed Marie any further, Ethan would kill him now.

He'd kill them all. Four to one was just another way to say good odds to an alpha who'd been trained by the best.

"I accept your alpha challenge, Travis, pride-brother to Fallon," he said in the formal words of acceptance. "The blood feud will resolve itself at the challenge. Now let the woman go."

Travis moved the knife away from Marie's throat and shoved her at Ethan so hard that she fell, then signaled to his men and turned to run. "Enjoy your woman and your land while you can," Travis shouted. "In twenty-four hours, they will all be mine."

Ethan leapt the distance to Marie, lifted her off the ground, and cradled her in his arms. "How badly did he hurt you? Your neck, your hands, and your knees are bleeding. He's going to die painfully for this, I swear to you," he vowed, his hands almost compulsively clutching her to him.

"Ethan, please. It is not . . . I am not severely injured. Merely surface wounds. But I would like to return to the cabin, if you do not mind." She was trying so hard to be brave for him, he could tell, but her breath caught in a hitching sob at the end of her sentence. She pressed her face into his chest, and he felt something cold and hard in his heart soften even while rage pounded through him.

Protective instincts far older and more primitive than any he'd ever known, even in his role as alpha, swamped him. He would protect this woman, no matter the cost. His cat snarled its agreement inside him, roaring out its claim. Marie was theirs to protect.

As he carried her to the car and placed her gently into it, he surrendered in his internal battle. No matter that it didn't make any sense at all. Marie was his, and he would avenge every scratch, every bruise, every touch from that knife.

Travis was going to die screaming.

SEVEN

While Ethan made several phone calls warning his pride members of the danger and informing them of Travis's alpha challenge, Marie spent the time in the car on the ride back to the cabin trying to overcome the terror that had frozen her into immobility in the encounter with Travis. Gradually, fury—both at herself and at Travis—won out over the fear.

By the time Ethan whipped the car into the small driveway in front of Kat's cabin, anger definitely held the upper hand. She shoved the door open and stumbled out of the car, barely taking a step before Ethan was there, scooping her into his arms again.

"I am able to walk. These are minor injuries, Ethan. Please put me down," she said and was dismayed to hear the tremble in her voice.

"Humor me," he said, striding up to the door. He gently lowered her to stand at the door, then quickly opened it and lifted her again, not letting go of her until he reached the overstuffed couch. For a moment his arms tightened around her, and he dropped his forehead to hers. "Never again," he muttered, and it had the ring of a promise or a threat. "Never again."

He gently lowered her to the couch and headed for the kitchen. "I know Kat keeps a first-aid kit around here somewhere." He flung open cupboard doors with barely controlled ferocity, and Marie sat where he'd placed her, just watching him, the tension in all that lean muscle somehow mesmerizing her.

"First-aid kit," she murmured, realizing what he must mean. "Does that contain medicines to render assistance? If so, it is unnecessary. I have some small skill at healing even in matters not related to childbirth. Perhaps you could find a cloth for me to clean these wounds, though?"

He ran water in the sink and brought a small wet towel to her. "Here's the cloth. But are you sure? You need antibiotics. Hell, you need to go to the hospital. What was I thinking?" He dragged a hand through his hair, looking every bit as wild-eyed as Travis had. Marie shuddered, not wanting that particular memory to surface just yet.

"No, I do not need the hospital or one of your human doctors. Although they are quite fine at their craft," she tacked on, not wanting to offend him.

As she wiped the gravel and debris out of her wounds, she fought to keep from wincing too much, since every involuntary flinch seemed to sear through Ethan, as well. "It looks worse than it is, perhaps," she lied.

"He hurt you," Ethan said in a feral tone of voice she'd never heard from him before. "There could be nothing worse."

Her anger at herself returned. "I was useless. I have the ability to call water, and I never thought to use it. I was rendered completely immobile from shock and fear."

He lifted a dangling strand of her hair and tucked it behind her shoulder. "That's nothing to be ashamed of, Marie. You're not used to violence. I was damn near frozen, too, when I saw that knife pressed against your throat."

She shuddered. "I have never been touched in anger of any kind, let alone harmed or threatened. The violence of it is soul-deadening, is it not?"

Ethan stood, clenching his fists and paced back and forth in the small space, as if the fury riding him needed some outlet before he exploded. "Yeah. It is. And those of us who live by violence wonder sometimes if there is anything left of our soul."

She finished cleaning her wounds and folded the towel and placed it on the floor. "You echo the concerns my brother and his fellow warriors have all shared at times. But when there is no recourse but for violence, and it is done in the name of protecting the defenseless, surely the gods will forgive any stain upon the soul caused by the doing of it?"

He crossed back to her and crouched down next to her. "I don't know the answer to that. The doings of gods are far above my territory. But we need to get you to a hospital, please, Marie. Your neck is still bleeding."

She drew a deep breath. "First may I hold your hands?"

He unclenched his hands and held them out to her. "That's the best offer I've had all day."

She smiled a little at his attempt at humor, then took his hands in her own. The healing was fairly minor, but she was weakened by the residual fear and the pain. She could amplify her healing powers through the strength of another, and she suspected Ethan's strength was far and away powerful enough to assist her. "Please hold still and do not remove your hands while I do this. You will feel a faint warmth."

He nodded, and she closed her eyes and called to the Goddess. "O, Goddess of the Nereids, it is your First Maiden who calls upon you. Please lend me your strength and your healing and your power, through my own small means and through the freely offered power of this man before me. Heal my injuries that I may serve you in full measure, O Lady."

For a moment, there was nothing but the pain in her hands, knees, and throat, and the rapid beating of her heart, caused as much by the feel of Ethan's hands in her own as by her injuries, she suspected.

Suddenly, the warm glow she'd experienced before in hundreds of healings swept through her body, focused and concentrated on the wounded areas of her skin. Even as the healing sent shimmers of sparkling heat through her, she watched the abrasions and cuts heal before her eyes. Ethan made some small noise, and she looked up to find his face mere inches from hers, his eyes wide.

"It's like magic," he murmured.

She smiled at him, invigorated by the healing power of her Goddess. "You who are part human and part beautiful, lethal cat would doubt the existence of magic?"

"Any man who looked at you could not doubt the existence of magic, Marie," he said. His eyes darkened to a burnished gold, and he leaned forward and kissed her.

He kissed her, and the healing warmth exploded into an inferno. Flames swept through her body and her blood, and she was helpless to do anything but lean into his kiss. He never released her hands, but somehow she was on his lap and felt the hardness of his desire pressing against her.

Ethan's tongue pressed against her lips, demanding entrance, and she could do nothing but accept him, surrender to the passion of his kiss, and moan at the rightness of it. He kissed her until she could not breathe, and then he lifted his head to stare at her, shock plain on his face.

She began to pull back, suddenly shy, still dazed from the intense hunger sweeping through her merely from the feel of his mouth on hers. But he shook his head and, releasing her hands, caught her around the waist and pulled her to him until not even a breath of air could have found passage in the space between them.

"Oh, no," he said, voice husky. "Let's try that again on our own, okay?"

She had a fraction of a heartbeat to realize that the Goddess had gone—the healing was complete—and then he caught her lips with his own again.

This time the fire was generated solely between the two of them, and she could not blame any of it on the healing warmth. Ethan kissed her as if she were a feast and he a starving man. He kissed her as though she were the prey and he a stalking predator. She succumbed, surrendered, clutching at his shoulders, wondering who was making that whimpering noise and then finally realizing it came from her own throat.

He left her mouth and pressed hot kisses to her throat, exactly on the now-healed spot where the knife blade had cut into her skin. "Never again, ocean girl," he murmured so softly she almost didn't catch the words. "Never again will anyone harm you. I swear this on my oath as alpha."

He lifted his head and stared into her eyes, and something of enormous importance passed between them, but she could not decipher it.

Refused to decipher it.

Fear of drowning, of entangling herself in the depths of a passion so far beyond any that she had known, shivered a sheet of ice through her, and she pulled away from him. "Ethan. No, Ethan, stop."

He instantly pulled back from her, his breathing harsh in the quiet room. "I didn't mean to scare you, Marie. I'm so sorry. Damn, I'm no better than . . . Please forgive me."

She lifted a hand, wanting to touch him, then clasped her hands together to resist the urge. "No, stop. You have nothing for which to apologize. We were both present and willing in that kiss."

As the heat stained her cheeks, she forced herself to continue, cloaking herself in the protection of knowledge. "It is a normal response to the release of adrenaline in the body. Similar to the fight or flight mechanism. Attraction . . . magnifies in the face of danger."

Ethan lifted one of her long curls into his hand and brought it to his lips, then let it fall back against her breast. "Trust me, beautiful," he said, voice husky, "there is nothing normal about my reaction to you. And it started way before we faced any danger."

He stood up and stared down at her, then shook his head. "Attraction. Now *there's* a tame word. My insides are going to explode if I don't lay you down right here and fuck you until you scream my name."

Heat shot through her and pooled between her thighs as her body responded to the sheer hunger in his words. "I . . . I . . ."

"No. Don't say anything. I'm sorry to be so crude. Pack up your stuff. You're coming with me to my place until we can get you back to Atlantis and out of the way of Travis and his blood feud."

"But—"

He sliced a hand through the air. "You're going. I command you to leave my territories while there is danger to you."

Anger shot through her, but she silently stood to comply with his command. As a visiting Atlantean, she could not jeopardize the treaty between their people by defying a command from the alpha.

He started to turn away, then whirled around and yanked her to him, controlled violence in his movement. "But hear me well, ocean girl. When this is over, you're coming back, and we're going to explore this thing between us."

She lifted her head and gave him her iciest glare. "Hear *me* well, shape-shifter. You do not command the First Maiden of the Nereids. I am not one of your little kittens to be ordered about. You should consider that when you are issuing your various arrogant demands."

"No, you're definitely not a little kitten. But either you come back, or I'm coming after you, even if I have to swim the whole damned way. You should consider *that.*"

With that, he kissed her again, a fierce, claiming kiss that left her senses whirling and her resolve splintered. Then he pulled away from her and strode over to the door, pulling his phone from his pocket as he walked. "The sooner you're packed, the sooner you can get away from my arrogant demands, Marie," he said, and then began snarling orders into the phone.

She stood there, wanting nothing more than to slap his egotistical, superior face.

Wanting nothing more than to kiss his egotistical, superior face.

She did neither but simply turned to retrieve her bag as ordered, accepting the truth behind his words. There was certainly something between them that needed to be explored.

If she had the courage to do so.

EIGHT

Ethan led Marie through the throng of silent, wary shape-shifters clustered around the entryway to his headquarters and home. He nodded to William, his second-in-command. "My office in ten minutes. Try to reach Kat. Her cell was turned off when I tried. If it's still off, track her down."

Marie lifted her head, the strain of the afternoon evident in her pale and drawn face. "She's with her . . . boss, if that helps, planning a meeting for tomorrow."

William nodded and headed toward the back of the mansion and Ethan's office, opening his phone as he went. Ethan stopped, realizing the necessity of introductions and some sort of explanation. He put his arm around Marie's shoulders and scanned the group of his pride members who stared at her; some hostile, some neutral. All curious.

"This is Marie, Bastien's sister from Atlantis. She came for a visit and is having the worst damn vacation on record," he said bluntly. "I'm sure William has told you that Fallon's pride brother, Travis, called alpha challenge upon me."

He looked around, meeting each gaze, noting and appreciating the anger and loyalty on every face. "We need to return her to Atlantis until I take care of this little problem," he continued. "In the meantime, I charge every one of you to protect her as if she were your own litter sister."

A few gasps met his words and more than a few speculative glances were cast Marie's way. But nobody even thought about arguing with him. Gregory, one of his fiercest pride-brothers, stepped forward. "I will guard her with my life, Ethan," he vowed, dropping to one knee before his alpha and bending his head to bare his neck. "For the honor of the Cypress pride."

Every panther there echoed the call. "For the honor of the Cypress pride!"

Marie stared around at them, eyes widened and lips parted slightly. She tilted her head to look into his face, and the floor shifted underneath him when his gaze met hers. The echo of passion from her kisses resonated through his body so hard and fast it was like a body blow. Only the presence of half of his pride prevented him from throwing her over his shoulder and carrying her to his bedroom to continue what they'd started on Kat's couch.

He took her hand and headed down the hall toward his guest suite, then changed his mind and veered off to the left toward the master suite. "Now I'm a damn caveman," he muttered. "Next I'll shift into some kind of saber-toothed tiger."

He realized Marie was almost running to keep pace with his long strides, so he slowed but did not release her hand.

"What did you say?" she asked.

"Nothing important. This is it. You can stay here until we can reach Alaric to come get you," he said, flinging open the doors to his rooms.

She followed him into the room, then stopped. "It's very . . . elegant," she finally said.

He laughed. "Smooth and diplomatic, I'll give you that. It's a damn bare room."

He looked around, trying to see the room through her eyes. Devoid of furniture except for a bed covered by a plain blanket, the space was huge and barren.

"Why does the prince of cats lead such a stark existence, I wonder," she murmured, but she wasn't mocking him. She'd spoken with concern and warmth in her tone. Two emotions he'd never expected to find in his bedroom.

He'd found lust there. He'd found callous indifference, spite, and—finally—hatred from Fallon. After she'd been murdered, he'd returned to the room in a killing rage and taken it out on the furniture. Every rug, painting, or piece of furniture she'd touched. He'd destroyed it all, clawing it to shreds in a towering fury. No matter what a heartless, cold woman she'd been, she'd been under his protection.

He'd failed Fallon.

He wouldn't fail Marie.

"I got rid of anything she'd touched. Couldn't stand to see it," he admitted, walking away from her. Anything so she couldn't see his face.

"You loved her that much?" The sympathy in her voice was like salt on the bloody wounds of his conscience.

"No," he confessed, the words wrenched from a black and twisted place in his soul. "I didn't love her at all. That's why I couldn't stand it. Maybe if I'd loved her, I'd have found a way to protect her, even from herself."

Marie stepped up beside him and placed her hand on his arm. "Bastien told me of Fallon and her plot to work with the vampires against you and Kat. As a leader, you must know that you cannot save everyone. Some are destined to walk a dark path."

Ethan stared down at her hand on his arm where it burned through his sleeve to his skin. To his nerve endings. "I don't need your sympathy, Marie. I made my choices, and I have to live with them. But you don't. Call Alaric, and let's get you out of here."

She jerked her hand away from him as if stung. "I did not offer my sympathy but my understanding. I see, though, that you require neither."

Whirling around, Marie walked to the center of the room, graceful even in her anger. He wanted to race after her and yank her into his arms and never let go. Inside him, his panther purred its agreement with that plan.

Instead, he stood his ground and watched her retreat. She closed her eyes and lifted her face toward the ceiling, raising both hands, palms up, at her sides. A faint silvery blue glow whispered around her still form until she was bathed in light. A nymph rising from the sea in starlight.

He suddenly wanted her with a painful urgency. His body hardened to the point of pain. He scrubbed his face with his hand, disgusted with himself.

I'm nothing if not the king of bad timing.

After nearly three full minutes, Marie opened her eyes. She bit her lip and shook her head, then stood there heaving in deep breath after deep breath.

"What? What's wrong?"

"This has never happened to me in three centuries," she said, visibly trembling. "Alaric's mental pathway is shut down. I cannot reach him. For good or ill, I cannot return to Atlantis."

Marie sat alone in the vast, gleaming steel and stone kitchen, toying with the remains of a sandwich. She'd eaten nothing all day, but worry and concern had robbed her of what little appetite she'd been able to muster. The mug of hot tea failed to soothe her, as well. The abyss gnawing at her insides had nothing to do with food or drink but everything to do with her inability to contact Alaric or Bastien. Granted, her mental reach did not extend far enough to contact Bastien if they were more than a few hundred landwalker miles apart. But Alaric was so powerful that even the suggestion of contact from a fellow Atlantean was sufficient for him to receive the message.

Always in the past the high priest had immediately opened the pathway between them at her call. Now there was nothing. No sense of being blocked, simply nothing at all. As if . . .

As if Alaric no longer existed.

But she refused to even countenance that thought.

Ethan's voice came from the doorway in that lazy drawl that he turned on and off seemingly at will. The mere sound of it shot liquid lightning through her.

"You hold that mug any tighter, and you're going to break it."

She refused to look at him, afraid her face would betray her reaction to him. "Then I will go to the mug store and purchase you a new mug. Conlan made sure I had some of your currency before I left Atlantis," she said lightly.

"Really? How much do you think a special mug like that would go for?" He walked over to where she sat on a high stool, not stopping until she could feel his breath in her hair. "That's a unique, genuine *Miami Vice* commemorative mug from 1985. Probably irreplaceable."

She lifted the mug and examined it. "Who are these men with the oddly laquered hair? Are they heroes among your people?"

He threw his head back and laughed, and Marie watched him, fascinated. "Do you know that I have not seen you laugh like that before now? You become a different person when you laugh so freely," she said, lifting a hand to touch the dimple that had appeared on his cheek.

The smile faded from his face. "I haven't had much to laugh about, beautiful. I think, under different circumstances, being around you might change that."

The room closed in on her, making the simple act of breathing difficult, but she decided to be bold, no matter the consequences. She would soon leave, never to return, more than likely. Her duties would not allow frequent or extended absences.

"I would enjoy the opportunity to bring you laughter. Under different circumstances, as you say," she whispered.

Calling on the Goddess for quite a different kind of courage, Marie stood and took his face between her hands and drew it down to her own. "I'm going to kiss you now," she said.

"I'm going to let you," he replied.

Then she lifted her face and kissed him, but it was vastly different from the kisses they'd shared before. She touched her lips gently to his, coaxing and then persuading his response. He stood rigidly in her grasp, hands clenched at his sides, as though afraid to touch her and break the moment.

She reveled in the power of taking the lead in their caress and lightly licked the seam of his lips. He groaned in the back of his throat and immediately opened his mouth, tilting his head to more fully meld his lips to hers. She twined her fingers in his thick, silky hair and pulled him even closer, making a quiet humming sound of contentment as the kiss deepened.

The tiny sound seemed to unleash something in Ethan, because he burst into fervent motion, clasping her waist with his hands and lifting her back onto the edge of the kitchen table. He thrust one muscled thigh forward to part her legs, then moved so that he was wedged between them, all the while still kissing her. One of his big hands shifted down to her bottom and pulled her still closer so that her dress rolled up and he pressed firmly against the heat at the juncture of her thighs, nothing but his trousers and the silk of her underclothes between them.

She put her arms around his neck and murmured some sound that meant, *Yes, definitely yes, oh please yes,* and he wrapped his other hand around the nape of her neck and deepened the kiss.

When they finally broke free to catch their breath, Ethan wore the same shocked expression he'd had before when they kissed, and she hiccupped a little as her laughter fought its way out past her gasping breaths. "You look like I feel, shape-shifter. Did the world tilt on its axis a little for you, too? Or docs my penchant for drama, as my brothers call it, overtake me?"

His sensual lips curved into a smile, and she tried to stop thinking about how she'd like to feel those lips all over her body. She had to focus. They were in crisis from all sides, and thinking about how good all that lean muscle would look—totally nude— was not helping.

Heat rushed through her at the thought, and her body convulsively jerked against him. He literally growled, like the panther that he was. "You need to stop doing that, or I'm going to take you right here on this table, ocean girl. And drama, hell. The world didn't just tilt, it bounced clear off the damn axis."

She flashed a seductive smile at him, filling it with the promise of everything she wanted to do to him. She knew the timing was bad. She knew the adrenaline response might be responsible for his reaction to her.

She wanted him anyway.

"If circumstances were different, as you say, I might take *you* right here on the table," she whispered.

His eyes gleamed, then narrowed, and his hands tightened on her. "Just what am I? Some kind of vacation fling?"

She blinked, dumbfounded, then began laughing helplessly. "Vacation fling? What does that even mean? This is the first occasion on which I have ever left Atlantis in the more than four centuries of my existence, so that would not say much for my powers of attraction, would it?"

His jaw dropped open. "Four centuries? You're more than four hundred years old?"

Her laughter died in the face of his obvious disbelief. "I have four hundred and seven years. Are you disgusted with the idea of kissing one so much older than yourself?"

"I suddenly find the idea of doing it with an older chick quite appealing," he said, an evil grin lightening the planes and angles of his face.

"An older chick? That cannot be an appropriate term, *young man*. Perhaps you should learn to respect your elders." She tried for a stern voice, but the fact that she couldn't seem to stop running her fingers through his hair may have ruined the effect.

He put his hands on the bottoms of her thighs and lifted her up off the table, still grinning. "Can I respect you while you're naked?"

She heard the wildness in her laughter and realized she walked the edge of hysteria. "Ethan, please. We need to figure out what to do."

He gently let her down, still holding her so close that she had to slide down the length of his body. Both of them were breathing hard by the time her feet touched the floor. But he stepped back from her, evidently agreeing with her assessment. "You're right. We need to figure out our plans. The first thing we need to do is get you out of here."

They both turned toward the kitchen doorway at the sound of

pounding feet approaching. Ethan pushed Marie behind him and pulled a very lethal-looking dagger from a sheath at his side.

William burst into the room. "I'm sorry to disturb you, Ethan, but we've got trouble. Travis called for reinforcements. He sent a message that the representatives of all the prides in the western region are on hand to make sure we follow the ancient rules of alpha challenge. Nobody gets in or out of pride lands until only one of you is left alive."

NINE

Ethan held the phone a good six inches away from his ear. "Kat. Kat. *Kat!*"

On the other end of the line, Kat finally quit yelling and took a breath. "Yeah. Sorry. But this ignorant fool says they aren't going to let me back onto Big Cypress for two days! He actually had the nerve to knock me aside when I tried to get my Jeep past him. What exactly is going on?"

Deadly rage raced through Ethan at the thought of one of them harming Kat. "Are you hurt?"

"What? No. No, it was nothing. He just kept telling me to 'phone home,' for whatever that's worth. What is going on, Ethan?"

He filled her in on the attack on Marie, the alpha challenge, and the rules about any of them leaving or entering pride lands. Kat started swearing. In spite of everything, he had to laugh. "Kat, those are words I didn't even know you knew."

There was a silence on the phone. "Do you really want to discuss my language right now?"

The brief flicker of amusement died, and the alpha in him took command. "No, I don't. But here's what I want you to do. Can those thugs hear my side of this conversation?"

"No," she replied. "In fact, I've been walking back to my Jeep while we talk. What's up?"

"I want you to find somebody impartial. Maybe Jack. We need a witness who doesn't belong to any of the factions that have wanted to take over pride lands in the past."

"Jack the weretiger? The one Bastien knows?" Her voice cracked on her mate's name. "Oh, Gods. Bastien. When he finds out I allowed his sister to come to harm . . ."

Ethan snarled. "I'm the one to blame, and I'll take any punishment he wants to dish out. I deserve it. But believe me when I say that no one else will lay so much as the tip of a claw on her skin and live."

There was another silence on the line. "Ethan? I've known you since I was a child, and I've never heard that in your voice. What exactly is going on between you and Marie?"

He turned his gaze toward the chair where Marie sat wrapped in the blanket from his bed, and she looked up at him at that instant, as if his thoughts had called to her. She was so beautiful it almost hurt him to look at her—art made flesh and infused with grace.

He'd failed her.

He could never deserve her.

"Ethan?" Kat's voice in his ear yanked him back to more pressing matters.

"Find Jack," he repeated. "I want a neutral observer. They'll be forced to let him in. You've got less than twenty-four hours, Kat. Do your best."

"I'll find him," she promised. "If you hear from Bastien—"

"Marie hasn't been able to establish contact with him or with their priest. When she does, I'll get a message to him to contact you."

He could almost hear through the phone lines her battle to focus on what needed to be done. "Fine. Call me if you can. I'll get Jack here if he's anywhere on the eastern seaboard, Ethan."

"I know I can count on you. You've always been one of the strongest of the pride, even before you discovered your ability to shift, Kat Fiero."

"Take care of her for me, Ethan. She's my sister now."

He looked over at Marie again. "I will protect her with everything I am, Kat."

As Ethan clicked his phone closed, he repeated his promise. Turned it into a vow. "With everything I am."

S everal hours later, Marie struggled to wake from a dark and terrifying dream in which bears battled panthers, and the strange lizardlike creatures the landwalkers called alligators snapped at the flesh of the vanquished. She abruptly sat up on the couch where she lay, realizing that it would not take a dreamspeaker to translate that dream for her. She was caught in a battle between opposing predators, and her gentle gifts of healing wouldn't be of any assistance at all to him.

To Ethan.

She watched as he stood at the table in his starkly furnished strategy room. Other than the couch where she'd finally dozed off, only a few scattered chairs, a desk, and a large table covered with charts and papers decorated the spacious room. He'd called it his office, but she'd been in the palace war room and recognized this place as its twin in purpose. Ethan's men surrounded him, discussing strategy and plans for the upcoming challenge. As if he felt the weight of her gaze upon him, he turned those golden eyes toward her, and his heated stare pinned her in place, stealing the very breath from her lungs.

He'd spoken truly when he named attraction a tame word for what lay between them. If attraction were a single hearth flame, this was a conflagration. An inferno of raging desire. It made no sense at all, and yet it made all the sense in the world.

Some attractions defied logic. Isn't that what the women who came to the temple had told her time and again? Even her brother, when he'd described his newfound love for Kat, defiance mingled with hope that she might understand and embrace her new sister.

Bastien, who'd always underestimated himself, finally came fully into his own when he found a warrior woman to stand at his side. But she, Marie, was no warrior. The best she could manage was a few simple tricks with the calling of water.

Her gift was to heal and to aid in childbirth. So unless Travis decided to go into labor during the challenge, she thought bitterly, there would not be much she could offer.

A noise alerted her to movement, and she looked up to see the pride members filing out of the room, nodding as Ethan issued last-minute instructions.

"William, take a team and relieve the first watch," Ethan said.

William nodded. "Get some rest. You'll need it. The intel says Travis is one of the most powerful alphas in the central part of the country."

Ethan bared his teeth in a terrifying mockery of a smile. "Then maybe he'll offer some sport before he dies."

Marie gasped at the overt ferocity in his voice, and he stood, head bowed, for a long moment before he turned to face her. As he crossed the large room toward her, she shivered at the intent plain on his face. He wanted her and was prepared to lay siege to her defenses.

She was unsure if she had any defenses left to raise against him.

He sat next to her and lifted a hand to twine in her hair. "Did you get a little rest?"

"I think I must have slept for a while. It has been a very long day, and I did not sleep well last night, with the excitement of the journey ahead of me."

His lips tightened. "Not exactly what you thought it would be, is it? I'm really sorry, ocean girl. Once we get this little problem out of the way, I'll wine and dine you in the very best restaurants."

She considered the leap for a moment before deciding to brave it. Life was fraught with potential danger. This courageous man would fight for his pride members, his lands, and even his life in fewer than twenty hours.

In the end, the leap was really only a very small step. She leaned her face into his hand and pressed a kiss to his palm. "I don't need the best restaurants, Ethan. Right now, I would be honored simply to be alone with you."

A crystalline moment stretched between them, lasting so long that she was afraid her offer had been misguided. Then something in him seemed to snap, and he lifted her onto his lap, pulling her to him so tightly that she could barely take a breath.

"Are you saying what I think you're saying, Marie?" he said, rasping out the words. "That you will be mine, if only for this night?"

The moment was too huge to comprehend; too crucial to some inherent need in her soul to acknowledge. Instead, she found refuge in levity. "Well, perhaps. But only if you will respect me while I'm naked."

He shouted out his laughter and jumped up with her still in his arms, as though she weighed nothing at all. Then he bent to kiss her and poured so much longing and hunger and need into the kiss that she was dizzy long before he released her to stand on her feet.

"I want you right now, ocean girl. But I won't take you here in my office. I want you in my bed."

She nodded, and he caught her hand in his own and pulled her, half running, down the hallway to his rooms. When they arrived, he kicked the door shut behind him and then locked it. She caught her breath, transfixed at the predatory cast to his face as he stalked her across the room.

"Wait," she said, breathless with anticipation, with longing, with a trace of fear. "I want . . ." She ran to her bag and dug in the bottom for the colorful scarves of Atlantean silk she'd brought with her, thinking perhaps she would wear them to some event with Bastien and Kat.

She tossed the scarves, rich with gold, silver, turquoise, and so many other jewel colors, onto his bed and spread them on his stark white pillows and sheets.

"Let me bring some color to your life, Ethan of Florida, as you have brought heat and desire to mine." Her words were brave, but she stood trembling. Afraid the flames that ignited in her body whenever he touched her would consume her.

Afraid that one night would never be enough.

Knowing that one night was very likely all they could ever have.

But desire triumphed over fear, and she held up her arms to him. "Be mine for this night, Ethan. Let Atlantis meet the dual-natured, and both be the better for it."

He did not say a word but started toward her. Slowly, stalking her. Letting her see the full weight of his hunger on his face. He pulled his clothes off as he came, so that by the time he reached her he was entirely nude, his enormous erection jutting up between them. Her eyes widened at the sight of his powerful body sculpted into lean muscle.

"It's time, ocean girl," he whispered. "I want to kiss every inch of your skin right this minute. In fact, I may very well die if I don't get my hands and my mouth on you in the next sixty seconds."

She leaned forward and traced one finger down the planes of his chest and abdomen, and he shuddered. She bit her lip and took the leap over the precipice.

"Then perhaps you should remove my dress."

E than stared at Marie, unable to believe his ears. Unable to believe that the most beautiful woman he'd ever seen was offering herself to him with the same courage she'd shown when she'd questioned his authority. When she'd defied him. When she'd laughed at his attempt to order her around.

Somehow, this gentle healer had displayed greater strength than the meanest and baddest of his pride-brothers. Maybe it was her gentle touch that had stolen its way into his heart.

"Your dress. Right. I might be able to manage that." He reached out for her, hoping she didn't notice that his hands were shaking. Touched the silken folds of her dress and, underneath, the silken curves of her skin.

"I love this dress," he said. "But it has to go."

He bent to grasp the hem of the dress on both sides of her endless legs and then stood, pulling the fabric with him. She moved to make some adjustment, and the top of the dress fell open, helping his clumsy fingers complete the job. In seconds, the dress was up and over her head, and she stood in only a few tiny scraps of dark blue lace.

The sight of her sent all the blood in his body rushing to his cock, which jerked and strained toward her. His inner cat agreed with the sentiment, growling its hunger and need.

"Holy crap," he said, grinning like a damn fool. "If that's the Atlantean version of ladies' underwear, I bow down to your superior race."

She tilted her head and flashed a smile filled with the power of ages-old feminine seduction and newly discovered heat. "Do you like it?"

"It makes me want to purr."

Marie laughed. "I'd like to make you purr, warrior. But first, I'd like to feel you touch me."

He didn't need to be asked again. Ethan swept her up and onto the bed, rolling with her as they fell so that she landed on top of him, trapped by his arms. "I plan to touch every part of you," he promised.

"Less talking, more touching," she said, and then she nipped at his bottom lip. The sharp touch of her teeth ignited the flames that had been stirring in his blood, and he pulled her head down to his and took her mouth.

The predatory heat in his eyes exhilarated Marie. No gentle coupling, this—she wanted flame and fury and the sea-struck lightning of tempest-force winds. He'd torn her undergarments from her body as if he had to see her totally nude or he'd die from the wanting. Then she'd taken the aggressor's part, she who had never taken the initiative in bed sport, and actually bitten him. She felt as though the panther side of his nature had communicated itself to her soul, and she, too, wanted to snarl and bite and dig her nails into his back, leaving no doubt in his mind that she was laying claim to him as well.

For one terrifying and thrilling moment she rose over him to conquer him, but then the predator in Ethan took command, and he growled low in his throat, then roared out a feral claim. He was alpha and master of his domain; he was fiercely primitive.

He was everything she'd never wanted and never known, and she was drowning in the sensation of him.

Ethan set his mouth on her and licked and kissed and bit her skin from her lips to her chin and then down to her neck. He bit the juncture where her neck met her shoulder, and she cried out at the electric current that sizzled down through her body. Her nipples tightened and hardened nearly to the point of pain, and then suddenly he moved down again and ran his tongue across one stiff point, and she cried out again. He lifted his head, a look of such fierce triumph on his face that the mere sight of it caused creamy heat to pool between her thighs.

"I warned you I would taste every inch of you," he repeated, his voice so rough that the sound of it rasped across her sensitized nerve endings. "I always make good on my promises."

He lowered his head to her breast and sucked one nipple into his mouth, licking and kissing it, then sucking it so hard that she cried out as the shock waves from the pull of his mouth sent arrows of knife-edged desire driving through her body. With his fingers, he caressed and pinched her other nipple, switching back and forth between the two until she was writhing on the bed beneath him, nearly mindless with hunger.

"Please," she moaned. "Please, it's too much, Ethan. Please."

"Not yet," he said. He moved back up the bed and kissed her again, eating at her mouth until she thought he'd devour her, his hands stroking and caressing every part of her except for the center of her need. She returned the favor, frantically shaping his rock-hard biceps and the sculpted muscles of his back and bottom with her hands. Every inch of him was lean and hard and purely male.

He drove her to a fury of desire and insanity until she finally grasped his thick, glossy hair with both hands and yanked his head back from hers. "I need you now," she said; it was her turn to issue commands.

Victory shone in his eyes, but she did not feel conquered by it. Rather, she felt herself the victor as well.

"I need you, too, ocean girl. I need to taste you and make you scream my name."

She shook her head and tried to prevent him from moving down her body. "No, there is no . . . That is not necessary. Although that form of lovemaking can be pleasant, I—"

He froze, and stared at her in patent disbelief. "Pleasant? *Pleasant?* Who have you been . . . ?"

Then his eyes darkened to the color of molten gold, and he bared his teeth in a grimace. "Never mind. I don't want to hear about any other man in your bed. Not now, not ever. Instead, I'm going to make you forget any other man ever touched you."

In a swift motion, he settled himself between her thighs and draped them over his shoulders. Before she could say another word, he put his mouth on her.

She screamed his name when she came.

Ethan didn't give her time to float back down from the spiral. Marie's body was still spasming with aftershocks when he positioned himself between her legs and held his cock so that the thick head nudged its way into her creamy liquid heat. She tasted like spice and honey, and every muscle in his body was demanding that he drive every inch of his cock as far into her as he'd go.

But he waited, muscles trembling from the effort it took to hold back. Hunger and violent urgency raged inside him, but he refused to *take* her.

He wanted her to surrender.

"Marie? Beautiful, you need to open your eyes and tell me yes right now before the animal takes over from the man. Because I need to be inside you more than I have ever needed anything in my life."

She opened those glorious eyes that shone like the midnight sky and, for one terrifyingly long moment, she didn't respond. When he was damn near frantic, she slowly smiled at him. "That was far more than pleasant; you spoke truly."

He laughed, but it was wild laughter that skirted on crazed. "Marie? Honey?"

"Yes, Ethan. I say yes."

He roared some unintelligible sound as he drove into her so far and so fast that his balls slapped against her ass when their bodies met. She bucked, arching up against him, and cried out.

But what she cried out was, "More."

He thrust into her, desperately urgent, riding her body to the heights of an ecstasy he'd never known. Every inch of his body strained to press against her lush curves. Every inch of his cock strained to press into her welcoming sheath. He felt her body tense under his and slipped his hand between their bodies, rubbing his fingers against her slick wetness and then finding her clit and pressing it rhythmically as he continued to drive into her.

She cried out again when he touched her, and then her movements grew more and more frantic. "Ethan, Ethan, Ethan."

He closed his eyes to focus on the feel of her, the silk of her skin against his. Her soft wetness as it welcomed his hardness. She arched into him, and he felt the orgasm wrenching through her body, and then she put her teeth on his shoulder and bit him as she came.

The feel of her teeth called to his inner panther, and it screamed its pleasure and approval. Ethan felt his body tighten and harden further than he thought possible. Then the world did bounce clear off its axis, and something inside him shattered. He exploded inside her, coming so hard that he cried out from it, shooting hot jets of his semen deep into her womb.

When he finally collapsed beside her, his softened cock still inside her body, he took a minute to try to remember how to breathe. He lay there, dazed, wanting nothing more than to fall asleep with this woman and then wake up still inside the warmth of her body. As the smile spread across his face, a gentle, cool wetness distracted him, misting across his head and body. He blinked his eyes open, and immediately regained full awareness.

Because Marie was glowing again; shimmering with that silvery blue light that had surrounded her when she'd healed herself. Except, this time, she also seemed to be making rain fall.

From his ceiling.

TEN

Marie swam up through waves of sated pleasure and contentment to the sound of her name.

"Marie? Ocean girl? We seem to be having a little unexpected weather pattern," Ethan said. His voice was full of laughter, and she opened one eye to see what had amused him so. A drop of water splashed on her nose, and she gasped, then sat up in the bed and stared around, bewildered.

It was raining. Indoors. She lifted a hand to feel the raindrops and realized a second truth. She was glowing.

"Oh! It's me," she gasped.

Ethan laughed out loud, then pulled her back down into the circle of his arms. "I kind of figured, with the Atlantis thing and all," he murmured into her ear. "It's fascinating, but maybe you could stop it before the bed gets soaked?"

She felt the heat sweep through her face as she blushed. "Of course." It was only a matter of a moment to focus on cutting off the water she'd unconsciously channeled. Then she turned her focus inward, and the glow on her skin faded.

"I'm sorry. I never . . . I've never done that. Called water without knowing it. I don't know how—" She stopped babbling, caught by a random thought. "It is true that intense emotion can sometimes trigger our abilities, so perhaps passion? I should write this down."

Ethan's arms tightened around her. "I have a better idea, my beautiful scholar. Why don't you write it all down later? The adrenaline reaction stuff you told me about earlier, the raining, the glowing. All of it."

He smiled, and there was much of smug male triumph in it. "Be sure to spell my name right in the 'passion causes rain' part, okay? E-T-H—"

She shoved at his chest, smiling in spite of herself. "I think I'll remember your name. I've certainly used it enough times this night."

He rolled onto his back, pulling her with him, and she felt his penis hardening against her leg. "How is that possible? Are you able to rouse again so soon due to your dual nature?" she wondered aloud.

"No, this is all you," he said, tangling his fingers in her hair. "Why don't we see how many more times you can call my name?"

She kissed him until she was breathless, then lifted her head. "You are very arrogant."

"Yeah, I am," he agreed lazily. "But maybe this time you'll call a thunderstorm."

Then he rolled her underneath him and was anything but lazy for a very long time.

Ethan stood at the window, looking out at the spectacular view of Big Cypress. Dawn's first warm glow touched the tops of trees, ribbons of light with gilt edges, like packages waiting to be opened by eager children.

The comparison led him to thoughts of the children of the pride, who looked to him as a role model for how a modern shape-shifter could interact with other shape-shifters, with the humans and, now, with the Atlanteans. Trying to work toward common goals and against common enemies.

What if Travis's mind worked like Fallon's had? What if he planned to take Ethan's pride and turn it over to the vampires? Organos was dead, but it never took long for another bloodsucker to pop up and fill a vacuum.

"A peacock feather for your thoughts." Her warm voice soothed and caressed him, bringing a smile to his face and a shimmer of interest to parts of his body that should have been limp with exhaustion.

He turned away from the window and took a moment to study her. In the faint morning light, she glowed like a jewel among her colored scarves that lay scattered across his bed.

He'd always have fond memories of those scarves.

He leapt across the space that separated them and dove onto the bed, catching her in his arms. "Peacock feather? We say *penny*. Don't the peacocks protest?"

"We only offer peacock feathers that are found lying about, silly man. We don't go around plucking palace peacocks."

"Plucking palace peacocks? Now say *that* three times fast," he murmured, bemused by this woman and her exotic expressions. Her exotic experiences. Hell, she'd made it rain in his bedroom.

Three times.

He kissed her neck and inhaled deeply, drawing the scent of warmth and sex and ocean-kissed skin into his nostrils. His scent was on her, too, he realized. The thought of it pleased him more than it should have.

He was getting possessive about her, and he had no right.

Which pissed him off.

"What does time have to do with it, anyway?" he demanded.

She blinked. "I beg your pardon?"

Cursing himself for a fool, he jumped up and off the bed. "You should. Beg my pardon, that is. If you think you're going to just use me for sex and abandon me. Go back to Atlantis."

A slow smile spread across her face, and she sat up, not bothering to lift the sheet to cover herself. He found himself hypnotized by the sight of her creamy breasts, their rosy tips pointing up at him.

"I confess I am delighted at the idea of being thought seductive enough to use you for sex," she purred, laughing at him.

But, no. She was laughing *with* him, he realized, and it was very different. Her laughter was inviting and welcoming, not mocking. He suddenly felt a cold, black mass in his chest rip open and let air and warmth and her own gentle summer rain into his heart.

It scared the crap out of him.

But it was a day for courage. He almost laughed. Facing Travis didn't scare him at all. Putting his heart on the line terrified him.

"If I win this challenge, will you give me a chance? Will you promise to give us time to know each other?"

There. He'd said it. Now the ball was in her court. If Atlanteans even played ball in courts.

"*When* you win this challenge," she replied, "we will take all the time we need to know each other. You have my word."

He nodded, a fierce joy rushing through him. He would win this challenge, and he would prove to Marie that she belonged with him. Easy.

"So now I prepare," he said.

She lifted her chin and tried to smile. "Now you prepare."

ELEVEN

Marie spent every one of the hours from dawn until midnight with Ethan. She watched him as he ran command sessions concerning everything from evacuation of the women and children to more mundane issues, such as emergency plans for the enormous business infrastructure that he and his team administered for the pride.

Kat called in every hour, reporting on her quest to find Jack, asking how Marie was faring under the strain, and inquiring about Ethan. Marie recognized Kat's ever-deepening worry for her pride members and friends and attempted to give solace. But there was little she could do over the telephone, and the barriers were still in place that blocked Kat from returning home.

She used Kat's phone calls as a reminder of sorts, and attempted to contact Alaric and Bastien each time she hung up with Kat. But every try was met with the same blank deadness. Empty space with no trace of either of them. She pushed the fear aside, to worry about later. First she had to get through the day and Ethan's challenge. Then she would find a way to contact Atlantis.

Alaric and Bastien were still alive. She *knew* it.

If anything about that long, long day surprised Marie, it was discovering the presence of so many moments of peace in the middle of planning for a war. For war it would be, she discovered, were the unthinkable to happen and Travis to defeat Ethan. William and the other warriors of the pride made it clear that they would challenge Travis, one after another, until he lay dead on the ground of the challenge circle.

She'd thought there would be more bluster. More of the hearty "Of course you will win, Ethan" directed toward their alpha. But the panthers were nothing if not pragmatists, as she supposed should be expected from a species walking the edge of extinction. If the pride alpha fell, another would take his place. It was the natural order of things.

"Damn the natural order of things!"

"So fierce, ocean girl," Ethan said softly from behind her, startling her. "What's on your mind?"

She whirled around. "*You're* on my mind. This stupid challenge is on my mind. It's only two hours until midnight, and you're talking about bank accounts with William. Shouldn't you be training or something?"

A fleeting smile crossed his face, then he stared solemnly into her eyes. "I love that you're worried about me, but there's no need. I'm going to make damn sure that Travis doesn't live through this. He sealed his fate when he put his hands on you."

"Stop it! It was nothing," she insisted. "You saw how easily those scratches healed. Do not risk yourself for such a petty reason."

He bent to kiss her. "It wouldn't be a petty reason, trust me. But there is so much more to this. The alpha challenge is a longstanding tradition among my kind. I can't refuse it, or my own pride would relieve me from command. Survival of the fittest applies to shape-shifters more than to any others."

"Ethan, I feel so useless. Please give me something to do."

"You mean something more than you've already done? Like helping that woman who was having labor pains? Or comforting the children who've taken refuge here with their mothers? Or offering logical, calm advice in any of a dozen discussions I've had today?"

She shook her head. "They were false labor pains brought on by stress. It will be more than a month before she delivers that baby, the Goddess willing."

Ethan took her shoulders in his hands. "Here is what you can do for me. Get out. If the worst should happen, and—"

"It won't. Don't even think it," she said, refusing to hear him say the words that spoke of his possible defeat and death.

"Maric, you have to listen to me. If the worst should happen, the new alpha must offer safe passage to anybody who wants to leave the pride. Travis is insane, but the reps from the other prides will force him to do this. That's one of the reasons I'd hoped to get Jack here, too, but it doesn't matter. There are enough of them with honor that you'll be safe."

She shook her head wildly, not wanting to hear it. Unable to bear the thought that the man she'd only just discovered could be torn from her after only the span of a day.

He caught her head, trapping it in his hands so that she was forced to look at him. "If I'm defeated, promise me you'll get out."

She stared into his golden eyes that burned with determination and realized her assent would relieve some measure of his burden. "I promise."

He studied her as if to measure the strength of her promise, then, evidently satisfied as to her sincerity, he nodded. "Then now we prepare."

Two hours later, Ethan strode past the ring of shape-shifters who surrounded the newly formed arena. They'd carved the space out of a dense spot of swamp forest only a few miles from his headquarters. He spared a moment of regret for the fallen pines and dwarf cypresses that had been hastily chopped down to form the challenge circle.

"What part of nature *preserve* don't you bozos understand?"

Travis laughed that high, skittering laugh of his again. "You won't have to worry about little details like that after tonight, Ethan. You'll be as extinct as your pathetic Florida cats."

A deep rumbling voice thundered from out of the shadows. "Neither of them are extinct yet, Travis of the Texas panther pride. And if you keep talking so casually about the extinction of your own kind, you're going to piss me off."

Travis snarled at the sound of the newcomer, but Ethan threw back his head and laughed. "Jack! Never thought I'd be so glad to see a tiger."

The hugely muscled weretiger strode into the circle as the wary panthers backed away from him. No matter how fearless, no panther was going to be a match for a shifter whose true shape was a five hundred pound tiger.

Jack shook Ethan's hand and then turned to greet Travis. But Travis snarled at him and backed away. "Get away from me. You stink of the jungle."

Jack's eyes narrowed, but his smile never slipped. "Nice manners. Lucky for you I'm Switzerland in this challenge."

Travis stripped off his shirt and threw it to the ground. "What are you talking about?"

"He's neutral," Ethan said. "Just here to observe and make sure that all the rules are followed."

Travis sneered at them. "Is that so? Maybe Switzerland is a little too late."

The sound of dozens of guns being cocked echoed through the clearing, and Ethan, Jack, and Ethan's pride members all crouched into position, ready to shift and face the threat.

"Oh, better wait for your girlfriend to join us, Ethan," Travis said, his eyes glittering with malice as he pointed to the path Ethan had just traveled.

Ethan sensed her before he saw her. *Marie.*

The bastards had Marie.

Primal rage poured through his body at the sight of the two men dragging her into the circle, her beautiful hair tangled around her. They shoved her to the ground, and Ethan moved to help her, but Travis wagged a finger at him as the two thugs both pointed pistols at her head.

Marie held up her hand as if to tell him to stand down, no sign of fear on her face this time. She was far tougher than she knew.

"They can shoot faster than you can leap, Ethan," Travis said. "So now we fight, without the help of your tiger buddy. And after I rip your intestines out and wrap them around your head, I'm going to fuck your woman right here on the ground next to your dead body."

A red haze of intense fury washed over Ethan's vision until he was nearly blinded from it, but he forced it back. Forced cold logic to wrest control from his rage.

He couldn't make a single mistake in the coming battle. More than his own life depended on it. If they hurt Marie . . . But he forced the thoughts back. He needed icy logic and cold control.

Ethan looked at Jack and made a nearly imperceptible gesture, subtly signaling that he didn't think they could rush the guns and win. Jack returned the gesture, agreeing.

"You want to fight or stand around boasting, Travis?" Ethan went for the emotional reaction. "Fallon always said you were all bluster and no balls."

Travis screamed a high, thin scream of pain and anguish. "I loved her! I loved her, and she left me for you. You never loved her, you bastard. You let her die. So now I'm going to kill you, and my men are going to shoot every member of your pride if they so much as twitch."

Marie spoke up from where she knelt on the ground. "Is this

your idea of justice and fair alpha challenge? Even I, who am new to your ways, know better."

Travis raised his hand into a fist and started toward her, and Ethan charged him. But before he could reach her, Marie rose fluidly, lifting her hands into the air. "You will never strike me again," she said, and a wall of water sparkled into the air surrounding her, appearing from nowhere, and burst outward in all directions, throwing the two thugs backward and to the ground and knocking Travis back a half-dozen feet.

Travis regained his footing quickly, though, as the sounds of fighting overwhelmed the circle. Ethan's pride-brothers had taken advantage of the momentary distraction to turn on the interlopers and disarm many of them. A few scattered gunshots split the night air, but screams and snarls predominated.

Ethan leapt to Marie and pulled her into his arms, relief swamping him. "I think *you* might be alpha, ocean girl," he said, keeping an eye on Travis to make sure he didn't pull any guns from hidden pockets.

Before she could answer, Jack was there next to them. "I'm guessing you have some unfinished business over there. I'll watch out for your woman."

In an instant, Jack shimmered into his tiger shape and curved his giant form around Marie.

"Stay with the tiger, Marie. This won't take long," Ethan promised. Every instinct he had demanded he stay with her, but honor and tradition forced him to finish it.

"You demanded an alpha challenge," he called out to Travis, who was clearly preparing to run away. "Now that we're back to even odds, you've got one."

Travis stopped and stared at him, suspicion twisting his face. "It's a trick. Why would you agree to the challenge after this?"

Ethan stripped off his shirt. "Because those ancient traditions you corrupted actually mean something to me."

"Fool! All that stupid honor. Fallon always said it would get you killed," Travis taunted him, circling around, looking for an opening.

"We'll see, won't we?" Ethan waited for the challenger's leap and followed it, shifting in midair, as Travis did the same. They were well-matched, he observed with a coldly detached corner of his mind. But then he didn't have time to think anything else, because the battle was on.

M arie watched, awestruck, as the two mighty cats met in a resounding clash of sound and fury. Ethan's tawny panther was slightly longer than Travis's red cat, but they were closely comparable in breadth and muscle. Terror for Ethan paralyzed her even with the tiger preventing her from moving.

She gasped as the two panthers rolled over and over across the circle, biting with deadly fangs and tearing with lethal claws, until both of them were bloodied and torn. Travis smashed a paw across Ethan's face, and Marie's legs moved as if to take her to them, but she found her way blocked by a quarter ton of snarling tiger. For a moment, her heart leapt into her throat, but Jack looked up at her out of the tiger's eyes, and she calmed.

Somehow the sounds of fighting from outside the circle didn't register with her enough even to make her fear stray bullets. Every ounce of her consciousness was fixed on the life-or-death battle taking place in the circle before her.

The red panther screamed again and managed to escape from underneath his golden foe, and Travis started running, trying to escape. Ethan chased him down and pounced, and again the battle was joined as the two tried to literally rip each others' throats out. Claws flashed silver and ivory in the moonlight, and blood stained the cats' fur with black shadows.

Marie raised her hands to call water again, unable to stand idly by and watch Ethan die, but the tiger butted against her legs with its huge head. As much as she hated to acknowledge it, she understood what Jack was trying to tell her. For her to interfere would be just as wrong as it had been for Travis's villains to do the same.

"But he'd better finish this quickly, Jack, or I'm going to do what I can. I'm past caring about ancient rules," she said, not knowing if the tiger could even hear or understand her. Every slice of claw or fang in Ethan's flesh screamed pain in her own.

The red cat gathered itself for a mighty leap and landed on Ethan's back. The golden panther fought madly, twisting and bucking to get his deadly enemy off his back, but Travis sank his fangs into the side of Ethan's neck, and Ethan crashed to the ground, hard.

Marie screamed as Ethan fell, but before she could move, the golden cat rolled his body over with a jerking motion and ripped his neck out of Travis's mouth. Then Ethan reared back on his hind legs and smashed a mighty paw across Travis's neck, ripping his throat out. The gushing spurt of arterial blood seemed to draw attention to itself by its very silence, and the sounds of battle around the circle slowly faded away to nothing.

Travis fell to the ground, obviously dead. As he fell, he slowly shifted back to his human shape. Ethan, still in cat form, stood near the body, head hung low, panting heavily.

Marie shoved past the tiger and ran to Ethan, falling to the ground in front of him. The cat raised its head, and Ethan stared out at her through its eyes.

"Now I may finally offer assistance," she said, and she put her hands on him and called to the Goddess. As the healing warmth spread through her hands and into his body, she watched as the vicious wounds in his sides healed. The silvery blue light of her Gift combined with the golden shimmer of his shape-shift, and he returned to human form.

For several frozen seconds, kneeling on the ground in the middle of the blood-scented darkness, Marie tumbled over the edge of conscious reality and into Ethan's soul. Images from his life rushed through her, and she felt his anguish at Fallon's death and his self-loathing at having failed to protect so many of his pride from the vampires and from Travis. She gasped as the window to his deepest emotions opened up to her, and the strongest image she encountered was her own face.

She fell back as the healing ended, staring at him in shock. His own expression mirrored hers. "I saw your soul, Marie," he said in a hushed tone. "I fell into your *soul*."

Then he seemed to snap out of a trance and leapt to his feet, pulling her with him, while he scanned the circle for further danger. Jack, again in human form, and William, sporting a bloody scratch down the side of his face but otherwise apparently unharmed, strolled up to them.

"Report," Ethan snapped out, staring at his second-in-command.

"We kicked their asses," William drawled. "I'll give you a full report tomorrow, but we're going to turn these lawbreakers over to the reps from the other prides."

Jack nodded in agreement. "They claim they had no idea what

Travis was planning, which is probably true. Anyway, if they take Travis's goons off our hands, there can never be any suspicion of unfair dealing on your part."

Ethan considered their words, then nodded. "Fine. Casualties?"

"Nothing but a few scratches on our side," William said. "Nothing, at least, that the change didn't heal."

"If I can be of service, I have some skill with healing," Marie offered.

"Nope. You're done doing anything but resting, ocean girl," Ethan said, all the arrogant command back in his tone.

Marie bristled and started to argue, but he bent down and put an arm under her knees and the other one around her shoulders and scooped her up against his chest. "Please," he murmured, for her ears alone. "I need you."

"Well, since you put it that way," she said, putting her arms around his neck, "how can I refuse?"

TWELVE

A week later

M arie awoke slowly to the smell of coffee and stretched luxuriously before she opened her eyes. She sat up and looked around Ethan's bedroom, pleased anew at the changes to the formerly stark and barren space. She'd cajoled and teased her panther into painting and hanging light fixtures, though he'd left the shopping to her and Kat. Now warmth and color filled the space, and it was a retreat that they'd enjoyed for many hours of the night and even occasionally during the afternoon, after they made their daily trip to Dr. Herman to visit the now nearly healed panther.

Since she'd heard five days earlier from Alaric that he and Bastien were safe but still on the trail of Lord Justice, she'd been able to relax and enjoy this respite from worry. She'd firmly placed to the side any thoughts of what would happen between herself and Ethan when she had to return to Atlantis.

The door opened, and the coffee smell that had woken her entered the room in the form of a tray carried by a very sexy alpha male panther. "Good morning, ocean girl. I thought you might need some caffeine, after you kept me up all night."

"I kept you up? Whose idea was it to try out every item of furniture?" She tried to sound indignant, but it came out as sleepy satisfaction. How the man could be so deliciously edible even in simple jeans and a white shirt was beyond comprehension. She tried not to think about how she must look, with her bed-tangled hair.

He placed the tray on the bedside table and leaned over to kiss her, then sat back, the smile fading from his face. "This is it, then."

A sudden lump formed in her stomach. "Yes, this is it. Alaric arrives to transport me back to Atlantis this night. So we have several hours."

He swore under his breath. "I don't want several hours with you. I want several years. Several lifetimes, even."

She caught her bottom lip in her teeth, then sighed. "I feel the same way about you. I never thought—you are the alpha, and Kat warned me—"

He interrupted her. "Kat warned you because of the way I was before I met you. But now I could never touch another woman, Marie." He took her hands in his. "You've touched my soul, ocean girl. I don't know how it happened, or even how it happened so fast, but there it is. I don't know how I'm going to let you go."

"The soul-meld takes whomever it will, Ethan, as you know. But free will reigns over all. You are . . . You may seek another if my absence—"

He cut her words short, his golden gaze burning into her as he frowned. "I don't *ever* want to hear you say anything like that again. Whether you're in my bed or thousands of miles away, you're still mine. Don't even *think* about forgetting that."

She tried to smile. "Still such a surly kitten, *mi amare*. I thought I'd tamed some of that arrogance by now."

"Never tamed," he said, his voice husky. "But always yours."

She felt the tears spill over her eyelashes. "But I must leave. My duties . . . I cannot abandon the temple, even if some part of me might wish it."

He pulled her into his arms. "And as much as I might want to, I would never ask you to abandon your responsibilities. If anyone can understand responsibility, it's me. But somehow it helps to know that some part of you thinks about it. For me."

They'd discussed the matter frequently enough, and sometimes with Kat, too, that they both knew how unlikely it was that Poseidon would ever allow him entrance into Atlantis. Perhaps at some time in the future. Certainly not now.

"I offer you my vow, Ethan of Florida," she said, putting all of her love for him into her gaze. "We will find a way."

"We will find a way," he repeated. "I offer you my vow, as well. I love you, ocean girl. Remember that every time you look at that ring."

She glanced down at the flawless diamond on her left hand, a symbol of a promise, he'd said when he'd offered it the night before. A tingle of curiosity made her wonder how it would resonate with the gems in the temple and what song Erin could sing from it. Surely such a beautiful gem, which held the promise of unending love, could sing powerful healing.

"You've got your scholar face on again," he said. "What's percolating inside that beautiful head?"

As his laughter rumbled in his chest against her cheek, she looked up to find his golden eyes filled with heat. Shimmering silvery blue light began to sparkle and swirl around her, and she fell back onto the bed, pulling him down with her.

"We have all day, my beautiful, fierce panther," she said, lifting her face for his kiss. "Can you think of any way we might spend it?"

He kissed her with leisurely skill and tenderness until she gasped for breath beneath him. "Oh, I've got an idea or two," he drawled. Then he cast a glance up at the ceiling. "Do you think I should get an umbrella?"

It took her a moment, but then the peals of her laughter rang through the room.

Together, she silently vowed, they would refuse to be daunted, no matter what peril the future might hold. Love and laughter would help them to surmount any obstacles. The shape-shifter had found his lady, and she had finally come home.

Sea Crossing

Virginia Kantra

For Kristen

I am a man upon the land;
I am a selchie on the sea
and when I'm far frae ev'ry strand,
my dwelling is in Sule Skerry.
—Traditional Orkney ballad

ONE

He had not come.

Emma March drew a quick, relieved breath. Or as much of a breath as she could manage. The steerage passengers squeezed together against the ship's rail. *Like so many sardines in a tin,* she thought with a flash of humor. The stink of wool and unwashed bodies mingled with the reek of the harbor, overwhelming the salt breeze running up the river from the sea.

On the Liverpool dock, a ragamuffin gang of boys whistled and waved their caps at the departing ship. A gray-haired matron sank into the stout, supporting arms of her companion like a tragic music hall heroine. Emma almost smiled. And then she glimpsed a gentleman's tall hat and cane descending the straight stone steps, and her heart knocked uncomfortably against her ribs. Her breath caught in panic.

Paul.

She squeezed her eyes shut. Against her closed lids, an image burned: Sir Paul Burrage, adjusting his gray top hat in the cloakroom's spotted mirror.

Tumbled among the students' boots and umbrellas, Emma had watched him, stricken, her body aching and her heart sore.

His gaze had met hers in the glass. *"The first time is always a disappointment, I hear."* He'd turned to her then, flicking a careless finger down her cheek. *"Next time will be better, I promise you."*

She had slapped his hand away. *"Next time? Do you think I would marry you now?"*

"Marry?" Paul had stared at her, stunned.

And then he'd thrown back his handsome head and laughed. *"Good God, I never intended to marry you."*

Standing at the ship's rail, Emma trembled with rage and a deep, remembered shame.

She forced her eyes open to search the crowds again.

But the gentleman in the hat was not Paul Burrage. He had not followed her.

She was glad.

Paul would not hesitate to denounce her to the steamship line's recruiting agent. The papers she had signed in return for her passage to Canada stipulated that she was of "strong constitution and good character." And her character was ruined, as Paul knew very well. He had ruined her. The bastard.

He was a governor of the school. She was merely a teacher. *Had* been a teacher. If he exposed her, if she were thrown off the ship by an irate matron, what choice would she have but to do as he demanded and become his mistress?

She shuddered again.

The large woman beside her turned with a sympathetic smile. "Cold, ducks?"

Oh, dear. Emma ducked her head. She was less in control of her emotions than she thought.

"I—yes, a little."

The woman pursed her lips at Emma's educated accent, but her expression remained friendly. "It's this wind, I 'spect."

"Yes," Emma agreed gratefully.

The woman continued to regard her with eyes black as currants in her pale, doughy face. "Mary Jenkins," she announced. "That's Mr. Jenkins with the children over there."

Emma glanced at the harassed-looking man in the brown coat pulling a boy down from the rail. She smiled. "Emma March."

Mrs. Jenkins nodded and waited. For the rest of the introduction, no doubt.

There was none. There was no one, Emma thought bleakly. Most of the steerage passengers were farmers and their families, lured across the Atlantic by the promise of homesteads in the Canadian west. But Emma was alone.

Her heart twisted. She had not expected her family to come and see her off. Hadn't her father told her she was dead to them now? And her mother would never defy him to make the journey from their farm on the coast of North Devon. Six years ago, Emma's determination to remain at Miss Hallsey's School for Girls as a junior teacher rather than return to her family's farm had created a deep and permanent rift with her parents. Her father always said education would be the ruin of her.

How humiliating to accept that he was right.

Emma drew a steadying breath.

"I am going into service," she explained.

"Ah." Mary nodded. "Well, plenty of opportunities where we're going, eh? Pretty puss like you."

Emma's smile froze. She knew her looks attracted attention. Her hair was too red to escape notice, Paul had told her. Her mouth was too wide, her bosom too generous to seem completely respectable. But . . .

Plenty of opportunities? Bitterness assailed her. Dear God, she had left work she loved and the only people she cared for to travel three thousand miles across the Atlantic as an indentured servant.

She did not see opportunities. Only exile.

Emma gave herself a mental shake. Better to scrub floors than earn her living on her back as Paul had offered. She had made her choice, driven as it was by panic, pride, and desperation. She could not afford the luxury of regret.

"You are very kind," she said. Surely the woman meant her remarks kindly.

The woman clucked. "And nobody, no sweethearts, to see you off?"

"No," Emma said firmly. "No one."

Her throat ached. No one at all.

The brown river rushed between the ship and the shore. The deck shuddered and surged underfoot. She watched—she felt—everything she had known sliding away to starboard. The great clock tower, the Custom House's dome, the spires of St. Nicholas's and St. Peter's, all the familiar landmarks disappearing forever because Paul had been a villain and she, a trusting fool.

Emma swallowed the lump in her throat. She would not give in to tears. She would *not*. She had wasted tears enough.

She caught herself straining for one last glimpse of the school, as if she could see beyond the bustling dock and busy streets to pick out one tiled rooftop among hundreds of other tiled rooftops in the city. Ridiculous. And yet . . . There was the promenade where she walked sometimes at the head of her girls, a line of bobbing baby ducks in blue wool uniforms.

The wind kicked up. Among the squawking, darting kittiwakes, a gannet soared, its wide wings flashing in the sunlight. The gray ocean rolled over the brown waters of the river, the waves adorned with foam like dirty lace.

An aching sense of loss weighted her chest.

A solitary seal heaved its head above the choppy water, braving the harbor traffic all around. Emma caught her breath. The massive dark body wore a thick band of scars like a necklace. The seal stood a moment against the wash, regarding the ship with dark, clear eyes, almost as if it marked Emma's passage. Emma stared back, wondering at the seal's boldness. Oddly comforted by its presence. As a girl walking along the cliffs of North Devon, she used to watch the seals hauled out on the rocky shore. But she had never seen one here before.

Just as suddenly, the great, sleek body disappeared. Disappointed, Emma squinted a long time at the moving water, willing the seal to surface.

When she looked again toward shore, the city and all the remnants of her past life had slipped away.

The wind blew from the west, retarding the ship's passage. The engines labored through long, heavy swells. After five days at sea, the ship was barely midway through the voyage, and most passengers had lost their stomach for adventure . . . and everything else.

The stench belowdecks was terrible.

Emma braced fourteen-year-old Alice Gardner in her bunk as the girl retched violently into a bucket. The child had been separated from her family and quartered aft with eleven other single women under the watchful eye of Matron. It should have reminded Emma comfortingly of school, but with so many seasick and bedridden, the area between decks felt more like one giant infirmary.

At least Emma had some experience nursing pupils. Alice was the same age as many of her students. Emma wiped the girl's face with a damp handkerchief, murmuring some soothing nonsense. She was grateful for something to do, for the opportunity to feel needed. She could not teach. That did not mean she could not be useful.

Matron—jealous, perhaps, of her own authority or suspicious of the color of Emma's hair—had initially spurned her offers of help. But the surgeon's time was taken up almost entirely with the twenty-six first-class passengers, and as conditions deteriorated in steerage, Matron relied more and more on Emma to help her with the younger girls.

After several days, Emma struggled simply to keep her eyes

open. She moved through a viscous fog of exhaustion. Her arms and legs felt weighted. Her stomach felt like lead.

The cabin pitched and tossed.

Alice shrieked and wept.

Up and down, up and down, the creaking ship rode the crests in time with the angry sea.

Up and—

A crack like thunder exploded from the hold, slapping Emma from her stupor. The ship shuddered, suspended, and then plunged.

The bucket slopped. Her stomach lurched. She grabbed the rail to avoid being tumbled to the floor.

Nineteen-year-old Cora Poole, in the bunk above, began to cry. "We're going to die. We're all going to die."

"I wish I was dead," another girl groaned.

Foreboding tightened Emma's chest. The roar of the engines still shook the air and vibrated the walls all around. But something was different. Something was . . . wrong. The ship lolled and rolled, no longer fighting the waves.

Emma clung to the bunk with sweaty palms, her heart tripping in her chest. She was almost as close to hysterics as her charges.

As if bursting into tears ever did anyone any good.

"That's quite enough," Emma said in her schoolmistress tone. If her voice trembled slightly, no one appeared to notice. "No one is going to die."

She hoped.

She mustered her charges, struggling for balance in the narrow, pitching cabin, bundling and buttoning them into cloaks and jackets and boots in case it became necessary to go—

Dear God. Emma closed her eyes a moment, fighting panic. Where could they go? They were in the middle of the ocean.

A new sound—a deep, rhythmic rattle—rumbled from the bowels of the ship, almost drowning the crash of the waves.

Matron appeared, her face as gray as a sheet.

Emma stood, her knuckles white on the bunk rail. "What is it?" she asked quietly. "What has happened?"

"The shaft is broken. We've lost the propeller."

Without the propeller, the ship was unmanageable. Helpless in this sea. Emma felt her knees fold like string and fought another wild surge of panic.

"But that sound—" She forced the words through numb, stiff lips. "The engines . . ."

"The pumps," Matron said. "Captain is pumping water from the hold."

Their eyes held a moment in silent communication. They were taking on water, then. Emma's heart plummeted.

"What can be done?" she asked.

Matron shrugged. "Wait for another ship."

Emma's throat constricted. Another ship? But that meant . . . That must mean . . .

Dear God.

They were sinking.

Hours passed. The ship bounced and rolled like a log in a river. Emma staggered through the single women's quarters, wiping faces, holding hands and buckets. As long as she kept busy, she did not have to think about the ship's fate.

Or her own.

No one ate or slept. Emma coaxed the girls to take sips of fetid water. She could not even brew a cup of tea in the tiny galley without setting fire to the ship or herself. The incessant clanking of the pumps pounded in her head, penetrating the babble from the main steerage compartment. Children screamed. Men grumbled. Women moaned and prayed.

Emma thought the noise would drive her mad.

Until it was replaced by something worse.

Silence.

Emma hurried in search of Matron and met her own fears reflected in the other woman's eyes.

"The leak in the hold has put the fire out." Matron's broad, country voice was sharp and raw. "There is no steam to drive the pumps. We're done."

The word tolled like a church bell at a funeral: *Done, done, done . . .*

Emma's mouth went dry. She wet her lips. "Has the captain—"

"Captain gave orders to abandon ship."

Emma braced on the rolling bow, light-headed with terror, struggling to keep her huddled girls together and upright. The wind lashed her skirts and tore at her bonnet. Her wet boots sucked at her ankles. Waves buffeted the ship's sides, washing over the stern. Spray shot halfway to the masts and fell like cold, hard rain.

Abandon ship?

Abandon hope, more like.

The lifeboats tossed on the towering waves, insubstantial as the paper boats with their cargos of pebbles and sticks that schoolboys sailed from the riverbank. Fragile. Perilous.

The heavy seas rendered the ship's ladders useless. The boats could not come near without crashing into the ship's sides. So the passengers had to be loaded in baskets, swung over the angry water and lowered by rope thirty feet to the rising, falling boats. Women first, in groups of three or four, and their children after them.

Emma held her breath as Mary Jenkins stretched out her arms for her youngest son and pulled him into the rocking basket. Her husband's pale face ran with spray or tears. His fists clenched at his sides.

"Careful, Mary!" he shouted.

The ship rolled, the stern wallowing in the water. The girls shivered and wept. Emma hugged fourteen-year-old Alice tight. Giving comfort. Taking courage.

"We're lost," one of the waiting men groaned. "All is lost."

All. The word struck Emma's heart. Keepsakes and clothing, the little package of books wrapped in oilskin to protect them for the journey, the few belongings she had salvaged from her former existence, everything she possessed to launch her new life, all gone, all lost forever.

"Lord, Lord, I don't want to die," Alice sobbed.

Emma got a grip on herself. "Well, of c-course not." Her teeth chattered. "Everything will be all right. Our turn is coming."

"One more," a sailor shouted from below.

The officer on the bow, a boy not much older than Alice, beckoned to Emma. "You, miss."

Alice clutched her. "Don't leave me."

Emma did not think. "No. No, I won't." She pried the girl's fingers from her cloak. "Here, sweetheart, you go first."

"But—"

Emma thrust her at the young officer. "Go!"

Alice stumbled forward, toward the waiting ropes.

Emma watched, her heart in her throat, as the basket bearing Alice was lowered jerkily by bowline along the side of the ship.

Was she . . . ? Emma strained over the rail to see the girl caught and pulled safely into the boat.

Emma inhaled in relief and satisfaction, straightening her back. The ship lurched. Off balance, she teetered and clutched at the rail. Her wet boots skidded on the slippery deck. *No. Oh, no.*

A cold wave rose and crashed over her, smashed over her, sluiced over her, ripping the rail from her grasp and sweeping her feet from under her.

Voices shouted. Hands grabbed. Too late.

She heard a rushing in her head, a roaring in her ears. The wave dragged her from the ship, and she toppled down, down into the cold, hard sea.

The shock knocked the air from her lungs and jarred her to the bone. A raging chaos engulfed her. She was numb. Blind. Cold. Her mind froze. She could not breathe. Water pulled at her skirts, dragged at her boots, spun her this way, tugged her that. Her petticoats floated and clung, trapping her like a fish in a net.

The boat. She needed to reach the boat. She was rolling, tumbling, sinking in the surge.

She was drowning.

The realization stabbed her like a knife. Like the lack of air.

She struggled, kicking with her sodden boots, flailing with her feeble arms. Something smooth and heavy glided against her legs, a shadow moving under her in the clear, cold dark. Horror clawed her.

Shark.

It circled higher, brushed by her, pushed more insistently. Terrified, she struck out, as if she could push the monster away, and touched fur, slick and flowing against her hands. She tightened her grip reflexively, dug her fingers into soft, thick pelt. Muscle rolled, flexed, and surged. Her arms jerked. Her shoulders strained as it pulled her through the freezing dark, towing her with fluid power. Up and up, the heavy, sleek body moving under her own, lifting her, supporting her, carrying her toward . . .

Light.

Her head broke the surface of the water. Her hair plastered her face like seaweed. She gasped, choked, inhaled.

The cold, briny air seared her throat and burned her lungs.

She retched and would have gone under again.

But her rescuer was there, big as a horse or a mattress, bumping and rubbing against her, bearing her weight. She clung instinctively to its bulk, felt its breath hot in her face, felt its . . . *whiskers?*

She blinked salt from her eyes, struggling to focus. Roman nose, round, dark eyes, thickset, powerful body—

A seal.

Wonder bloomed in her chest. She had been saved by a giant seal. With a band of scars around its neck. Its breath flowed over her again, warm and salty sweet, drugging as wine. Her senses swam.

No, she thought. She must swim. The boat. She had to reach—

The world whirled away from her, flowed away from her in streams of green and gray. Her vision was shot with gold like the sea on a sunny day. The ocean rushed in her ears, its melody rising in her blood, humming in her head, muffling the frantic beat of her heart.

Her lips moved soundlessly. *No,* she tried to say. *Really . . .*

Darkness.

Quiet.

Nothing.

TWO

Her bed was wide and soft. Emma drifted, floating with fatigue, buoyed by a dream. She didn't want to wake up. She was warm and dry and—

Naked.

Her stretching foot paused. Gooseflesh tingled her arms. Emma had not slept naked since . . . She never slept naked. The school was too cold. Her musty mattress at the boardinghouse had been infested with vermin. Even on board ship, she had—

The ship.

Memory flooded back in a rush: the ship, the broken propeller shaft, the sea. She had fallen into the sea. Emma remembered the weight of her boots, her petticoats dragging her down . . .

She inhaled sharply and opened her eyes.

Dear God.

She bolted upright in bed, grabbing for the covers.

A man loomed by her bed, a big man with a broad, bare, hairy chest. No shirt. No shoes. Not even stockings. Emma's heart pounded. She had never seen so much solid muscle, so much male skin in her life. Even Paul when they had—when he had—

But thinking of Paul brought a fresh surge of panic.

Her fists clenched on the covers. "Who are you? Where am I? Where are my clothes?"

The half-naked man stood quiet and unmoving, regarding her with dark, fathomless eyes. Dry-mouthed with fear, Emma fought to shake off the remnants of her dream. Did he understand? Perhaps he didn't speak English. He didn't look English.

She gulped. He barely looked civilized. His mane of thick, unruly hair was caught in a leather thong and tied in a stubby ponytail at his nape. His face was strong and raw, its lean planes broken by a brawler's nose. Silver glinted in the hollow of his throat.

A chain. He wore a chain. Like a dog, Emma thought.

Or a Viking.

She licked her lips nervously. She felt dazed. Almost drugged, as if she'd drunk too much wine or taken laudanum for a toothache. She didn't know where to look. All that skin . . . Her gaze dropped to his feet, broad, bare, masculine feet with a sprinkling of dark hair.

Her stomach clenched. Quivered.

There was something strange and almost unbearably intimate about those naked feet standing so close to her bed, the long pale arches, the jutting anklebones, the firm, muscled calves. His toes.

Emma frowned, convinced her mind was playing tricks on her. Something about his toes . . .

"They were wet." The deep, burred voice broke her distraction.

She jumped, her gaze flying back to the harsh-planed face of the man beside her bed. "What?"

"Your clothes," he explained. In English, thank goodness. "They were wet. You were cold."

Her skin prickled. Her chest felt tight. "I—"

"You could not wear them," he said patiently.

"No," she agreed faintly.

Oh, no. She fought another sudden wash of panic. She was not going to overreact to the notion of a man—this man—touching her, undressing her.

Memory engulfed her like a wave.

"Don't overreact, darling," Paul had said as he buttoned up his breeches. *"I thought you wanted it. You were certainly asking for it."*

Her throat froze. She could not move.

The man frowned and leaned closer. "Are you all right?"

Emma gasped and raised her hand to hold him off. *Don't touch me, don't touch me, don't . . .*

"Don't," she managed to squeeze past her throat.

He stopped instantly, his dark eyes watchful. "It's all right. You are safe now."

Safe. *Saved.*

She trembled in relief and reaction. What on earth had happened? She was dreaming. Drowning. She had fallen into the sea. And then . . . And then . . .

"What about the others?" she forced herself to ask. "Alice. Mrs. Jenkins."

"I do not know them."

Panic welled. "The other women on the ship. There was a girl, Alice Gardner, traveling with me in steerage. She was only fourteen."

Sudden understanding widened his eyes. "The girl who took your place in the lifeboat."

How did he know?

"Have you seen her?" Emma asked eagerly. "Is she here?"

"No. You are the only one."

Emma's heart failed. "But . . . all those people in the lifeboats . . ."

All drowned? All gone? Every one?

"They were rescued by another ship," the man said. "A cattle ship on the same route. The captain saw your distress signal and took the passengers on board."

Emma sagged with relief. Until a new worry stirred in her chest, like a worm at the heart of a rose.

"Then . . . what am I doing here?"

"You are safe here," the man repeated.

Safe, warm, dry . . .

Naked.

Emma tightened her hold on the covers. Rich covers, velvet and fur, smelling of lavender and the sea. The candlesticks on the mantel had the gleam of tarnished gold. But the grate below was empty. The flagstone floor was bare. Except for the extravagant bed and one heavily carved chest, the small stone chamber was as stark as a crofter's cottage.

"Where am I?" she asked.

Did she imagine it, or did he hesitate slightly? "We call it Sanctuary. You will be cared for here."

"Is this a hospital? Have I been ill?"

Perhaps that explained her odd flashes of memory, her fevered dreams. Images swam in her brain, flickering through the swaying darkness like fish darting through strands of kelp. She was dreaming. Had been dreaming.

Or delusional. She'd thought . . . Her heart stuttered. She had dreamed she was rescued by a *seal*.

Her head pounded.

"You are tired," the man said. "I will leave you to rest."

No, she thought. Said?

He looked at her, his eyes as deep and enveloping as the sea.

Dry-mouthed, Emma resisted the pull of that cold, clear, dark gaze, fighting her sudden sleepiness, struggling to understand. "My clothes . . ."

"Will be here when you wake," the man said. "Sleep now."

Emma scowled. She didn't want to sleep.

She wasn't going to sleep.

She did anyway.

G riffith watched the woman's blue eyes slide closed, aware of a faint, unfamiliar regret. The command to sleep was such a little magic, a minor imposition of his will compared to what he had already done. What he was prepared to do.

The future of his people was at stake, he told himself. The fate of one mortal woman hardly weighed in the balance.

He did what was necessary. Whatever his prince commanded. And yet . . .

Her face was smooth and freckled as an egg, her lips closed and composed. He wondered at the discipline she imposed on that soft mouth, even in sleep. Her red gold hair spread wantonly, luxuriously across the bed. All that brightness tangled with the sleek dark fur of her covers, the contrast of colors, the mingling of textures, tugged at his senses. His body tightened in unwelcome arousal.

He had not brought her here for this.

But the image of her body, soft and white and pink as he undressed her, burned in the back of his brain. Her scent—potent, hot, *female*—curled around him, heady and unmistakable. Every male within miles of Sanctuary would be drawn to her like sharks to the promise of fresh blood.

Griff's lips drew back from his teeth. Despite the fear in her eyes—perhaps because of it—he would protect her. As long as she slept covered by his pelt, she was safe.

But she could not sleep forever. The sooner he turned her over to the prince, the better.

He left her and descended the steps to the great hall.

Children and dogs drowsed together in a pile before the fireplace, where a sullen blaze produced more smoke than heat. Most of the children were very close to Change, ten or twelve years old in appearance. Born of human mothers, fostered in human households, they were only brought to the selkie island of Sanctuary as they neared puberty and could take their seal form, their proper form, in the sea.

Unfortunately, the magic of the island that kept their elders from aging prevented the young selkies from reaching maturity for a very long time.

And so they grew as lean and wild as the dogs, and fought as viciously for whatever scraps the adults threw their way.

A shaggy-haired boy raised his head at Griff's approach, his eyes the same calm gold as the prince's hound's. "Did you bring her?"

Griff nodded.

"To read to us?"

"Aye."

"I would rather she fed us," the boy said and laid his head back down.

Griff sympathized. He *remembered*. But the prince had instructed him to fetch a teacher, not a cook.

He padded up the circular stair of the prince's tower, his bare feet silent on stone.

Selkies shed their sealskins to walk on land, to play at politics or sex, and—rarely and reluctantly—to give birth. The water was their life and their home. Who would trade the bliss and oblivion of the ocean for the dreary duty of raising whelps on land? The sea king himself, old Llyr, had abandoned his human form and all responsibility to dwell in the land beneath the waves.

So it was the king's son, Conn, who ruled from this isolated tower, insulated by thick stone walls and a hundred-foot drop from the siren call of the sea below.

The prince's study was lined with books and piled with scrolls. Windows pierced the round room, north and south, east and west. The last red glare of the sun spilled from the sky, reddening the prince's strong, pale face like a fever.

The prince himself sat at a desk of carved walnut and iron plucked from a Spanish wreck off the coast of Cornwall. The entire castle was furnished with the salvage of centuries.

As if, Griff thought, gold and wood and crumbling pulp could compensate the selkie ruler for the time he must spend on land.

Griff entered the room silently, a big man on bare, webbed feet.

Conn looked up from the book on his desk, his eyes as clear and cool as rain. "The woman?"

"I put her to sleep."

The prince frowned. "It's been over eight hours."

"She's had a rough day," Griff said dryly.

"And she is only human." Conn smoothed a page of his book. "I suppose I must be grateful she isn't hysterical."

She had been frightened. Her pulse had beat in her throat like a caged bird. But she had swallowed her fears enough to demand her clothes and ask after her companions. Griff admired courage, even in a human woman. "She was asking questions. I did not know how to answer her."

"Tell her the truth."

Griff snorted. "That we wrecked her ship and plucked her from the wreckage because the little savages downstairs require a keeper?"

Conn shrugged. "Perhaps she would take pity on them."

"Aye, maybe," Griff said. Her feelings were not his responsibility. Neither was her fate any longer. So he was even more surprised than the prince to hear himself say, "She is worried about the other passengers."

Conn raised his eyebrows. "I sent them a ship."

"Without adequate food or water."

"That is the captain's problem. As soon as the passengers were plucked from the sea, their fate was in human hands. We do not interfere in mortal affairs."

"We interfered when I broke the propeller shaft."

Their gazes clashed, the prince's cool as frost.

Damn it, what was he doing? Griff wondered. He was the prince's man. He did not argue.

Neither would he beg.

But the memory of the woman's wide blue eyes slid into him like a knife, loosening his tongue. "It would be"—*What? Just? Compassionate?*—"expedient to restore the balance by seeing the other humans safely to their destination. With calm seas and favorable winds, they could reach land before their provisions run out."

Conn's long fingers drummed the desk. "Very well. Calm seas and an easterly wind to the Azores. And in return, I will have my school."

Griff bowed. He had won his point. The prince had granted his request. So why did he feel so uneasy?

"You cannot force her to teach," he said.

Conn smiled thinly. "Then you must persuade her."

E mma's heart pounded. Her nipples pebbled in the cool sea
draft that flowed over the stone windowsill. She shivered.

She needed clothes.

And answers.

She could wait for the tall, half-naked Viking to bring them to
her, or . . .

Hands trembling, she threw back the carved lid of the chest at
the foot of her bed.

Or she could seek them herself.

The other ship passengers had gone on, the man said. But there
must be someone—a doctor, a magistrate, a shipping line agent—
who could tell her where she was and how she was to get—

Not home, she realized bleakly. But to Canada, at least.

She dragged a length of warm red wool from the chest, measur-
ing the garment against her body. A skirt? A long cloak, and under
that a pile of thin, yellowed shifts. Hastily, Emma pulled an under-
garment over her head before tackling the line of cloak buttons.

Her stomach rumbled. She had not had a meal, a decent meal,
in days. If she had been ill, her sickness had not affected her appetite.

Just her mind.

Emma bit her lip.

She could not have been rescued by a seal. She must have
imagined it, conjuring the beast out of homesickness and terror
and her glimpse of the seal in the harbor.

But she had not imagined the man by her bed.

Who was he?

His broad, furred chest and dark, impassive face made her
heart skitter in pure feminine panic. Yet his voice, she remembered, had been deep and soothing, his eyes almost kind.

In some ways, he seemed the opposite of Paul, whose smooth
good looks and easy charm had masked a callous indifference to
her dreams and ambitions. To her comfort. To her feelings.

When Paul first sought her out, Emma had been flustered.
Flattered by his attentions. Sir Paul Burrage was a gentleman, a
governor of the school. She had believed he loved her. That he
wanted to marry her. And instead—

Instead, he had manipulated, hurt, and betrayed her.

She would not let herself be misled so, used so, ever again.

She reached for the door; hesitated. The Viking had not told her to stay in her room. She was safe here, he said. She smoothed her hand down the long line of cloak buttons to ensure they were all securely fastened. Taking a deep breath, she pushed open the door and went in search of food and answers.

*P*ersuade her?

Griff scowled as he descended the steps of the prince's tower.

He was a bull. He did not persuade. He enforced the prince's will among the males and took what was freely offered from the females.

The human woman stirred him, he admitted. Challenged him. He did not believe she was going to offer up . . . anything he wanted. Not without a lot of words and reasons.

Neither of which he had.

What was Conn thinking?

A scuffle in the hall below jolted Griff from his thoughts. A yelp, a low laugh, a rush of swift, padding feet . . .

Scattering whelps, Griff thought, *running for food or from a fight.* When the older bulls came in from the sea, they were not tolerant of young ones underfoot.

The hair rose on the back of Griff's neck. *When the bulls came in from the sea . . .*

He ran down the remaining steps to the hall, taking in the situation with a single, experienced glance.

The young selkies had cleared out. Only the boy with the golden eyes hung back, his hands clenched into fists at his sides.

Two selkie males had backed the human woman against the wall, crowding her like mating bulls on the beach. Their faces were flushed. Their eyes glittered. Their intent hung musky on the air, already ripe with the woman's scent and the sharper tang of fear.

Griff's lips peeled from his teeth.

The bigger bull—Murdoc—sniffed the woman's cloudy red hair.

She jerked her head, evading him, and her skull clunked against stone.

"Easy," Kelvan crooned. "We don't want to hurt you."

Murdoc laughed. The woman's face went white.

Cold rage rose in Griff. He growled. "Enough."

"We saw her first," Kelvan said without turning. "Find your own to play with."

Murdoc closed in, palming her buttocks through the rough fabric. She spun, jabbing his ribs with her elbow, and bolted.

Bad move.

He caught her easily, hauling her into his arms.

And Griff slammed into Kelvan, hooking one arm around his neck and grabbing his balls in the other hand.

"Drop it," Griff barked. "Or your friend will never use these again."

Murdoc grinned. "You must be joking."

Kelvan clawed at the arm around his throat. His bare feet scrabbled against the floor. "He means it," he said hoarsely. "Let her go."

"Why should I?" Murdoc asked. "They're your stones."

"Yours next," Griff promised grimly.

He could not fight Murdoc as long as there was a risk to the woman. But as soon as the other bull let her go . . .

Veins popped out on Kelvan's forehead.

The woman held as still as a doe surrounded by dogs. At least she had the sense not to struggle and aggravate the situation.

Murdoc sighed, glancing down at the woman in his arms. "Pretty hair. I suppose she is Conn's."

He should say yes, Griff thought. She would have Conn's protection. And she did belong to the prince, after a fashion. Conn had brought her here.

"No," Griff said. "Mine."

THREE

E mma's heart beat like a frightened rabbit's. She wrapped her arms around her waist, tucking her hands under her armpits to hide their trembling.

She was a teacher in a girls' school. She was not used to violence. Male violence. The men's casual assault and her rescuer's swift reprisal had shocked and shaken her.

The bigger man—the one who had grabbed her—led his limping companion away. Emma fought a shiver of reaction. Revulsion. They were no worse, really, than the men in the boardinghouse she had learned to lock her door against each night or the ones who called and whistled after her on the street. No worse than Paul.

They had not raped her.

Although they could have.

Another shudder shook her. Thank God she had been rescued. *He* had rescued her. Again.

He stood planted, unmoving, his eyes narrowed as the other two men staggered from the hall. Emma's gaze slid over the hard slabs of his torso to the ridges of his abdomen and felt a clench in her stomach that might have been fear. He wasn't even breathing hard. If not for the dark hair covering his powerful chest, the breeches clinging to his thighs, he might have been a statue.

"You," he barked.

Emma jumped.

But his attention was on the boy, the one with the odd-colored eyes. The only one who hadn't run when those two men cornered her.

"What in Llyr's name were you doing?" the big man demanded.

Emma moved instinctively closer to the boy. He was only a child. He—

"She was all alone," the boy said with dignity. "I thought—"

"You did not think. Murdoc could swat you like a fly. Next

time you see the prince's peace disturbed, you call me or one of the other wardens, understand?"

Wardens? Emma shied at the word like a horse from the bite of a lash. What was this place? A jail? An orphanage?

Her chest hollowed. An *asylum*?

The boy's thin face flushed. "Yes, sir."

Emma's protective instincts roused. Orphaned or crazy, the child meant well. "He was only trying to help."

Her rescuer turned his dark, brooding gaze on her, and she felt again that quick clutch in her belly. Tension rose off him like steam.

Her mouth dried. She should *not* have come down. She was *not* safe here.

She lifted her chin, refusing to be cowed.

"You wanted to help," he said without expression.

He was speaking to the boy. Emma gathered she was irrelevant.

The child straightened his narrow shoulders. "I—yes."

"Right. Make yourself useful, then. Fetch a girl to attend the lady."

The boy nodded and darted away.

"Wait!" Emma called after him.

The child paused, almost quivering in his desire to be gone.

"What is your name?"

He shifted his weight from foot to foot. "Iestyn."

"Thank you, Iestyn," she said gently. "I am Miss March."

"Yes." His smile flashed. "Thank *you*, miss."

He ran off.

Her Viking was still watching Emma with an intent, cat-at-a-mousehole look that made her palms grow damp. She clasped them together very tightly in front of her.

"Miss Emma March," she repeated. "Formerly of Miss Hallsey's School for Girls."

"Aye, I know."

Emma frowned. Had he read the ship's roster list? "You have me at a disadvantage, sir."

His full mouth quirked slightly. "I know that, too."

Hot blood flooded her face. "I meant . . ." Indignation struggled with gratitude. Had he no manners at all? "What is your name?"

"Griff."

"Just . . . Griff?"

His thick, dark brows rose. "Griffith ap Powell ap Morgan ap Dafydd."

It sounded Welsh. And unpronounceable. "Thank you, Mr.—"

"Griff will do. You left your room."

A mistake, she thought now. But she had been searching for answers.

She had—she acknowledged to herself—gone looking for him. Intimidating as he was, she drew an unexpected comfort from his presence.

Admitting that to him, however, would put her at an even greater disadvantage.

"I was hungry," she said and waited for his roar.

He scowled. "I would have brought you food."

"I didn't know that. You didn't tell me anything. What is this place?"

"Sanctuary." He guided her toward the stairs without touching her, herding her back to her room. "I told you that."

Emma sniffed. "You said I would be safe here."

"So you will be. Now."

She stopped with one foot on the stairs. "Those men—"

"Will not bother you again." He shifted his weight, urging her upward. "They would not have troubled you at all if you had stayed in the room."

"I thought you wanted it," Paul's voice whispered in her head. *"You were certainly asking for it."*

Emma bit her lip hard. "If you are accusing me of inviting their attentions—"

Now he stopped, looking down his big nose at her in apparent surprise. "I did not."

"No, but you said—that is, you implied—"

"I do not blame you, lass," his deep voice rumbled. "You cannot help the way you smell."

"What?"

He sighed and placed one hand at her waist to guide her down the hall. "Never mind. Kelvan was ever a manwhore, and Murdoc is an ass. It is not your fault they forgot the hospitality due a guest."

She stared at him, her mouth open, surprised and moved almost to tears by his reassurance. All her life, she had been blamed for attracting unwanted masculine attention. As if she could help the size of her bosom or the color of her hair. The devil's color, her father called it. Letitia Hallsey had cautioned her repeatedly about leading men into temptation.

Emma had been more amused than offended by the head-mistress's strictures. There were no men at Miss Hallsey's school except for the porter and an occasional visiting father or governor. Who would take notice of one red-haired mathematics and drawing instructor?

"Of course I noticed you, sly little thing," Paul had said. *"I couldn't help it. You invite men's attention."*

And yet this man—Griff—had just said what had happened was not her fault.

Their eyes held until his pupils widened, dilated, black on black, and her blood drummed in her ears.

Emma caught her breath. He was still a man. She must be careful. "Is that what I am?" she asked pointedly. "A guest?"

"My guest." He nodded, holding her gaze. "Aye."

"Mine," he had said.

The word shivered between them.

She tore her gaze away. "I don't understand. You called yourself a warden. Is this a jail?"

"It is not," he said firmly.

The pressure eased in her chest. "So I'm—" Heavens, how to ask without offending him? "—free to go?"

He nudged open the door of her room and held it for her. "Where would you be going?"

Not home. She frowned. She had no life, no work, no family to return to.

"Canada," she said. "I signed a contract. I owe the shipping line twelve months' domestic service in return for my passage to Halifax."

Griff shrugged and followed her into the room. "Then you owe no one anything. You did not reach Halifax."

"No, I—" She faced him, hands on her hips. The room seemed much smaller with him in it. "You didn't answer my question. Where am I?"

"North and west, beyond the Hebrides. Conn ap Llyr is lord here. This is his house. His holding. I am the castle . . . overseer."

His blunt explanation did not satisfy her. But it mollified her a little.

"What about the children?" she asked.

She had been shocked to find them in the hall, eight or twelve of them altogether, thin and sleeping in rags. She was sadly familiar with the sight of beggar children on the streets of Liverpool. But beneath their rags and dirt, these children were obviously healthy. Beautiful, even. Their eyes shone. Their skin was without blemish. Their teeth were sharp and white as cats'. Emma did not know what to make of them.

"They live here," Griff answered.

"All of them? With their parents?"

"Their parents are . . . gone."

Again, that odd pause. Not like a lie. More as if he had to search his vocabulary for the appropriate word. And yet he spoke excellent English.

"Conn takes them in until they can fend for themselves," he explained.

So they were orphans. Emma's heart contracted in quick sympathy.

"That's very good of him," she said. "But children need more than a place to stay. They need structure. Discipline."

And care and kindness, she thought. But it was not her place to say so. At least Conn provided a roof over their heads. At least these children were not laboring in factories or underground in the mines.

"They should be in school," she said.

Griff gave her a dark, unreadable look. "Aye. If we had a teacher."

Emma blinked. "Surely if you advertised—"

"We are isolated here. Not many would give up life on the mainland to work on an island without doctor or priest. We have not . . . attracted the right person for the post yet."

A lump rose in Emma's throat. Of course she wouldn't want to— She could never—

Even the most casual employer in the most remote corner of the world was bound to require references.

And she had none.

G riff waited, hoping she might take his bait.

Her pretty lips parted, as if she would speak, and then she pressed them together.

She was too canny for him. Or maybe, he thought with regret, too fearful.

She had spine. She had stood up to Murdoc's handling without falling apart.

But she did not trust him.

"Persuade her," Conn had said.

Griff let his gaze travel from those wide, wary blue eyes to the delicate line of her lips and further, to the pale constellation of freckles that starred her collarbone. He thought of all the ways he could bind her to him if he were willing to use his kind's usual methods of persuasion.

He could make her or any human woman respond to him.

Dubh, Murdoc could have made her respond if he weren't a ham-handed ass with no thought beyond his own satisfaction.

But something in Griff rebelled at taking even that small choice from her.

He must win her trust some other way.

"I will leave you now," he said.

"Where are you going?"

He was not used to having his actions questioned. "To get you food."

"And clothes," she said. "My own clothes, please."

Spine, he thought again, amused and appreciative. "What is wrong with the clothes you have on?"

"Nothing. They are very nice, thank you. However, the, um, castle is rather cold."

Selkies, even in human form, did not feel the cold. But of course she was not selkie.

"Iestyn will build you a fire."

"And there isn't much to them," she continued as if he hadn't spoken.

Griff narrowed his eyes. The long red cloak draped her from her slender white neck to her pretty bare feet. "You look covered to me."

"Well, I'm not. Not underneath. I don't mind giving up my corset, but I can't run around without a petticoat and stockings. Oh!" She pressed her palms to suddenly rosy cheeks. "I cannot believe I am discussing undergarments with you."

Griff grinned. He did not understand her embarrassment. Hadn't he seen her naked? But he took her frankness as a good sign, an indication she was slowly lowering her barriers with him.

"It was your petticoats that nearly drowned you," he said. "But you can have them if they make you comfortable."

Opening the trunk at the foot of the bed, he rummaged under layers of linen and wool until his hand closed on a hard, solid object at the bottom. He withdrew a knife in its sheath and offered both to her.

"Maybe this will make you more comfortable, too."

Her eyes widened. She regarded the dagger in his hand as if it were a sea urchin or a spiny lobster or some other creature dangerous to touch. "You said I would not be bothered again."

Griff scratched his jaw with the hilt. Any bull could disarm her before she inflicted a scratch. But they would recognize the blade—and the woman—as his. "If you say 'no,' they will hear 'no,'" he promised. "But you may need to get their attention before you say it."

"With this." She took the broad black hilt in hand as gingerly as a virgin with her first lover.

Griff felt the pang in his belly. Shaking his head at them both, he adjusted her grip. He showed her how to draw smoothly and guided her hand through the thrust. "Like that."

She sheathed the knife and smiled at him, her blue eyes rueful. "I don't feel very dangerous."

The look, the tone, cut him to the heart. So beautiful, she was. So achingly human.

He sucked in his breath. "More dangerous than you know, lass."

E mma watched from her window as the sun stained the western sky, setting the ocean on fire.

She breathed deep. After the vermin-infested boardinghouse in Liverpool, after her cramped and stinking quarters belowdecks, it was a relief to fill her lungs with crisp, clean air. To be standing in a castle by the sea as the sun went down in a welter of crimson and gold.

It felt good to be alive.

The boy Iestyn had kindled a fire and provided her with a bucket of warm water to wash in. The girl with him—Una, all glossy brown curls and dark, sidelong glances—brought her clothes and a comb. Emma had been surprised no trace of salt or moisture clung to her skirts. Or to her hair, she realized belatedly. As if it had been washed while she slept.

The burning fire warmed the room, creating a flickering illusion of home. All the room wanted to be completely comfortable was a rug on the floor. Emma rubbed her arms. And perhaps glass in the windows, to keep out the rain and hold the sea at bay.

The rich salt-brew sea smell poured through the casement, pushing back the heat from the fire. The boom and hiss of the waves rose from the rocks below. She could see seabirds, wheeling and dipping in the pink-streaked sky, and—she caught her breath in mingled pleasure and dismay—seals in the water. She watched them, wondering at their fluid grace as they plunged and played, their big bodies perfectly at home in their element. She groped her way through a swaying forest of half-remembered impressions, dark and tangled as kelp.

What had she seen?

And how much had she imagined?

The door to her room bumped open. Emma whirled, her heart crowding her throat at the large, male silhouette filling her doorway.

Griff.

He waited, a smile in his eyes and a tray in his hands, and her heart jumped again for a different reason.

Awareness filled the room—along with a strong aroma of grilled fish.

Emma's stomach rumbled.

A corner of Griff's mouth lifted. He set the tray on top of the chest. "Dinner."

She flushed. "It smells wonderful."

"It's not much." Four small, dark apples, an enormous fish cooked whole, and a handful of raw oysters gleaming in their shells. "Not what you are used to."

He sounded gruff. Defensive.

"For the past four days, I've been on a diet of stale bread and foul water," she replied frankly. "This is better than what I'm used to."

His smile warmed her from the inside out.

"Will you join me?" she asked. And then realized, too late, there was no place to sit but the bed.

"I have eaten," he said politely in his deep voice. "But I will take a glass of wine."

He sounded so civilized.

Emma clasped her hands together. She did not entertain strange men in her bedroom, she certainly did not drink wine with them, she was a teacher—

Had been a teacher, she corrected crossly. She was ruined now. She could hardly be ruined twice.

While she debated with herself, Griff folded his big body and lowered himself to the floor.

Well.

That took care of the seating problem.

She perched on the edge of her mattress, watching him pour wine from a crusted bottle into deep-bowled glasses. Two glasses. Her eyes narrowed as he handed her one, shifting forward in the firelight so that the lovely warm glow slid over his smooth shoulders and hard, furred chest. Her mouth went dry.

She gulped her wine.

No gentleman of her acquaintance would sit down to dinner without his coat, much less his shirt. Yet Griff seemed perfectly at ease in her room. In his skin.

His skin . . .

She had barely been able to look at him before. Now she found it difficult to look away.

"You do not touch your food," he said softly.

She grabbed her fork and stabbed at the fish. "It's delicious. *Oh.*" She closed her eyes a moment in appreciation. "It really is. Thank the cook for me."

"You are welcome."

"You? But . . ." She hid her confusion in another sip of wine. *"No doctor,"* he had said. *No priest. No cook, either?*

"We live simply here," he said.

Emma scowled into her glass. Simply, fine. But even the most modest households had one female who could cook.

A horrible thought struck her.

"You're not—" *Dear God.* "You're not smugglers, are you?"

His low laugh reassured her. "Not smugglers or pirates."

Relief made her giddy. Or maybe it was the wine on her empty stomach. "Too bad," she teased. "I always thought being kidnapped by pirates would be very romantic."

"Kidnapped," Griff repeated without expression.

She set her glass down. "I didn't mean—I hope you're not offended."

"No."

"Because you didn't kidnap me. You rescued me." *Or the seal did.* She was a little confused. The wine must have gone to her head.

He handed her an apple. "Eat."

She bit obediently. The fruit was crisp and tart enough to pucker her mouth. She took another sip to wash it down. "So . . . You grow apples."

He did not look like any farmer she'd ever known. His skin was smooth and the same warm gold all over. Cream and honey.

The corners of his eyes crinkled. "The apples grow," he said. "We are sea folk. We take what we need from the sea."

"And that's enough for you? You said yourself you were isolated here. Don't you ever want to see the world?"

"All of us may roam. But this is our home. Our way of life. I belong here."

Emma sighed. "That's nice. I never belonged at home. Or at school either, really." A red-haired charity student with an impulsive streak and dreams beyond her station had not always fit in at the solidly middle-class girls' school. "But I love to teach."

Griff watched her, an elbow on his knee, his long body absorbing the heat of the fire. She shivered.

"And that is all you want," he said. "To teach?"

Emma blinked. No one ever asked her what she wanted. "I wanted what every girl wants, I guess. Marriage. A family. A home of my own."

Paul's voice jeered in her head. *"Good God, I never intended to marry you."*

"You wanted," Griff repeated, picking up on her use of the past tense.

She raised her chin. "No point in crying after what you can't have."

His eyes darkened. "I am sorry for the . . . change in your circumstances."

"Don't be. It's my own fault."

His brows lowered. "How is it your fault?"

"I'm ruined," Emma explained, and maybe it was the wine talking, and maybe it was relief that she was alive and not headed to Canada, after all, to work twelve months on a farm, and maybe she was just tired of pretending she was in control and everything was all right.

Griff said nothing.

"I thought he loved me," she bumbled on. "I thought—" Her throat closed with remembered pain and embarrassment. Tears pricked her eyes.

"I wanted to," she insisted. "He said I did. But he didn't love me, after all, and it was horrible. Disappointing, he said."

Her voice broke on the word. Her vision blurred. She did not see Griff move. But somehow he was there beside her on the bed, his arms warm and strong around her, his chest hard and close. She turned her face into his smooth, warm throat and cried.

His large hand cradled her head against his shoulder. He didn't say anything, only held her as she gasped and wept, her hot tears smearing her face and his throat. She inhaled the musk of his skin and let everything else boil out, all her pain, her rage, and her grief. She cried for her lost dreams and her violated trust. She cried for her friend and mentor Letitia, who had turned her out, and her family, who had turned their backs on her. She cried until she was heavy and hollow and limp, lying against him.

He never spoke a word. And his silence gave her courage to admit the secret she had not confessed even to herself, the betrayal more shameful than Paul's.

"I'm ruined," she said bitterly. "And I didn't even enjoy it."

Griff was silent.

Humiliation seared her. Women were not supposed to enjoy it.

It was only her own perverse nature that led her to imagine she might.

"I wanted to feel close to him." As if any explanation could excuse her. "And instead I felt used. Empty."

Griff got up, the mattress shifting from the sudden removal of his weight, and set the tray outside in the hall.

Emma stared at him, her throat aching and her eyes puffy. Confused and bereft. "What are you doing?"

He shut the door and smiled at her, and the warm intent in his eyes thumped her in the stomach. "Let me fill you, lass. I will not disappoint you."

FOUR

"*L* *et me fill you.*"

Emma gaped. Impossible to mistake his meaning. Irresistible to imagine, for one taut moment, how it might be, his body covering hers, his legs pressing and parting her thighs, his weight pinning her as he stretched her, filled her, *hurt* her—

The memory clenched her body. *No.*

"No!" She scrambled off the bed in panic.

Griff didn't move.

Her heart pounded. She struggled for composure. He was in her room, where she had invited him. She was to blame, just as Paul had said.

But Griff was not Paul. Emma was sure—almost sure—he would not take advantage of her momentary weakness, her lapse in judgment, to force her.

"It's all right, lass," Griff said, his very dryness soothing. "I can hear 'no' even without the knife."

Emma flushed. "It's just—" *I'm afraid.* Of him, of herself. "I won't be used again."

He remained by the door, watching her with heavy-lidded eyes. "Then use me. Let me give you comfort."

His deep voice resonated in the pit of her stomach. But she had felt these lovely little rushes and flutters before, in the early days of Paul's courtship, and her feelings had betrayed her. The reality had been messy and violent, over quickly and best forgotten. Anything less comforting would be hard to imagine.

"Comfort?" The question should have been scornful. Instead, she sounded uncertain. Even, God help her, intrigued.

Griff nodded. "Comfort, aye. And pleasure."

She thought of what had been done to her on the cloakroom floor and shuddered. "How could there be pleasure in that?"

His dark eyes lit with . . . laughter? "Let me show you."

Emma licked her lips nervously. She had risked and lost everything—her position, her family, her hope of marriage, her self-respect—without feeling even a fleeting pleasure in return, without once experiencing the intimacy she longed for. She had nothing left to lose. Did she dare take one more chance at finding . . . What? Comfort and pleasure in the arms of a stranger?

"It's a risk," she said.

A terrible risk for any woman, but particularly an unmarried one. That fear, piled on top of all her other fears, had haunted her in the boardinghouse. What if Paul got her with child? For days afterwards, she had watched for her courses and prayed. Her prayers had been answered a week ago. But what if—

"I will not do anything you don't want me to," Griff said. "Let me take care of you."

Oh. Longing stabbed her.

He was a careful man, thoughtful, thorough. He had already fed and clothed her, protected her, and held her while she cried. And now . . . Could he really care for her that way, too? Could he care for her at all?

He watched her, patient. Waiting.

Emma trembled. She desired him. Or rather, she desired what he could give her: a memory to blot out that other memory, the closeness she yearned for and had not found with Paul. Had never felt with another human being.

She forced herself to meet his gaze. "Why?"

"Because I know you." His rough voice ran over her nerves like sandpaper, smoothing, soothing. "Because in one day I have seen the spirit and the spine and the heart of you. You showed courage on the ship and kindness to young Iestyn. Let me show you some tenderness in return."

The brilliance in his eyes pierced her heart. Her chest ached. She had refused the security Paul had offered with its strings and conditions. She might have resisted comfort. But *tenderness* . . .

She trembled. When had anyone touched her in tenderness?

Griff stalked across the room toward her, all male strength and animal grace, and panic rose like a bubble in her throat.

"I have seen the spirit and the spine of you . . ."

She swallowed hard and held her ground. She was already ruined. Was it so wrong to wish for something else, to grasp at something more, before she went back to exile and indentured servitude? Griff at least would be gentle. She was sure of it.

He stopped in front of her, close enough for her to feel his heat.

She faced him, thrumming with anxiety and desire, her nerves stretched and humming like cello strings.

If he did not touch her soon, she would scream.

She bit her lip, an inappropriate bubble of laughter rising in her throat. Of course, if he did touch her, she might scream. That would stop him.

She did not want him to stop.

He raised his hand, his eyes dark and intent. This close she could see they were not black, not all black. A ring of deep, warm brown circled the wide pupils.

Emma braced, her heart hammering in hope and dread.

His thumb, warm and callused, rested on her mouth and rubbed lazily back and forth, freeing her lower lip from the grip of her teeth. She tasted him, his salt, his skin, there at the entrance of her mouth, and her stockinged feet curled against the cold stone floor. He cupped her jaw. She inhaled sharply in anticipation of his kiss.

And then his hand slid further, under her hair, against her neck, and his fingers dug into the tight muscles of her nape.

She almost moaned in relief.

He massaged tiny circles along the cords of her neck, the line of her shoulders, his thumbs pressing, his fingers stroking, his touch firm. Seductive. Under her bodice, her nipples beaded. But he did not touch her breasts, only tugged her, turned her, so that her back was to him. Heat flowed into her, his heat, moving through his fingers, loosening her stiff muscles. It blanketed her brain, smothering thought. There was nothing overtly sexual about his touch, and yet inside she was melting, desire pooling in her belly as she yielded to his hands. Her head dropped forward in surrender. She could feel him behind her, his breath warm on her cheek, the solid slab of his chest and abdomen, the blunt ridge of his erection against her buttocks. Lovely little thrills ran like fire under her skin. Her knees sagged.

He gripped her hands and raised them, flattening her palms against the tall wooden bedpost, holding them there until she clung. Combing his fingers through her hair, he gathered it up, letting the strands fall over her shoulder. His hands skimmed down her arms.

He moved on her, his chest supporting her back, his knee between her thighs. And all the time his strong hands worked their magic, rubbing, kneading, leaving her aching and limp as string.

Gently, so gently, he closed his teeth on her neck. She

shuddered in reaction. She felt the warm nip of his mouth, the cool kiss of air on the back of her neck and between her shoulder blades. Fabric sagged. Her dress. He was unbuttoning her dress.

Emma gasped and would have turned to face him, but he only pressed closer against her back, holding her in place with the weight of his body. She felt his rod, the promise and the threat of it, hard against her bottom, but his hands wouldn't leave her alone long enough to worry about what came next. They flowed over her, gliding, sliding, commanding her attention. Her response.

He reached through the open back of her dress, his hands skimming along her ribs, stroking over her shift to find and cup her breasts. His thumbs rubbed her nipples. His leg nudged, thrust, lifted, until she rode its muscled length like a pony. She squirmed, trying to find her balance or her breath, and his hands and voice soothed her.

"Easy now, lass. Be easy. I've got you."

She sucked in her breath. The air was close and thick with the smell of the fire, the musk of his skin, the scent of her own desire.

She flushed, relieved she could not see his face. She did not remember this embarrassing wetness from before. Only blood.

His hands stroked down and glided up, dragging her shift and her petticoat with them until the material bunched against the bedpost and spilled over his arms. Emma closed her eyes, overwhelmed by her own recklessness. Abruptly, all sensation sharpened and intensified. Her focus narrowed to his hands as they moved over her, learning her shape, discovering her secret places.

"I know you." And, oh, he did. Better, it seemed, than she knew herself. There was something reassuring—and terrifying—about his intimate knowledge of her body and its reactions.

His long fingers trailed along her thigh, traced between her legs, brushing just the ends of the curls there until she quivered. She squeezed her eyes tighter, squeezed her legs tighter, embarrassed at what he would find.

"So wet." A growl of masculine satisfaction. "So sweet."

Heat flooded her face, her breasts. He expected the dampness, then. Expected and approved. Another layer of doubt dissolved, burned away.

Griff eased the angle of his thigh, letting her down gently, freeing her, freeing himself to touch and explore. Emma moaned and moved instinctively, rolling her hips into his hand, feeling his touch everywhere, wanting his touch. Everywhere.

She gripped the bedpost as he pressed and probed, teased and stroked her wet, sensitive flesh. His arms were hard as ropes around her, his breath hot in her ear as he worked her with his fingers, around and around, in and out.

The fire crackled and popped. Behind her closed lids, red sparks rose and danced in the heat. Her nerves smoldered. Veins of heat shot through her. She was shivering, shaking, falling apart, and yet he held her, safe and close.

Sensation surged and crested in a dark flood inside her.

"Take it, lass," he murmured. "Take what you need."

Emma panted. Resting her forehead against the smooth, hard bedpost, she let his hands drive her, let her body take her where he wanted her to go, into the sizzle and the warm dark.

S he burned in his arms like liquid gold, the scent of her rising to his head like wine or the mist on the rocks at night. Griff breathed her in, her response rolling over him like the ocean, primal, powerful.

Satisfying.

Her smooth cheeks were flushed, her soft lips slightly parted. She was warm and damp and delicate all over, her skin as pink and polished as the heart of a shell. He wanted her naked, wanted to suck her pretty breasts and nuzzle the richness of her sex, kiss every freckle, lap her like cream.

Later.

Right now he wanted inside.

Her body still quaked with the tiny aftershocks of her release. He wanted to push inside her and savor her trembling, wanted to stroke her with his cock until she cried out and came again.

Griff reached for his breech flap.

And saw, beneath the dark fan of her lashes, the silver track of tears shining like the beach in moonlight.

His chest froze. "Lass . . . Did I hurt you?"

She drew a shuddering breath. "No."

Her pale fingers uncurled from the bedpost. Lowering her arm, she dragged the heel of her palm across her eyes.

His heart sundered. Catching her wrist, he replaced her hand with his lips, soothing her tender skin with his kiss. Tasting salt.

A choked sound escaped her throat. She turned to him, curled into him, in a trusting, nestling move that ripped him apart.

He gathered her close, cursing himself, smoothing a shaking hand down the long, silken fall of her hair. "Was it so bad, then?"

Her head moved against his chest. She lifted her face, her blue eyes lambent, glowing, setting his heart on fire with relief and . . . something else. Something he had no words for or experience of.

"It was that good," she said.

"There's more," he promised hoarsely. "Better."

Beneath his hand, her small shoulders stiffened. Straightened. "Yes."

He'd never heard a braver assent.

Or a more discouraging one.

For all her passionate nature, he knew she had not enjoyed her previous experience of sex. Horrible, she called it. He should have taken her when he had the chance, before she had a chance to remember, before he looked in her face and saw her tears, before he gazed in her eyes and found them blue and shining with promise like the sea at dawn.

"Lass—" Longing and frustration roiled inside him. He had claimed to know her. But at this moment, he barely recognized himself. "What do you want of me?"

"Oh." A rosy blush swept from the freckles on her collarbone to the roots of her hair. "You will think me foolish. Selfish."

He thought her adorable.

"Inexperienced," he said. "And ill-used. Tell me what you want."

"Would you—" Another blush, deeper than before. Anticipation licked along his veins and tightened his groin. Her eyes met his, defiant. Beseeching. "Would you hold me?"

He almost groaned. *Human females.*

"I am holding you," he pointed out.

"Yes." Her gaze skittered over the rumpled bed, the smooth silks tangled with the sleek, dark fur of his pelt. "Never mind."

Comprehension forced its way into his lust-fogged brain. "In bed, you mean."

She swallowed; nodded. "I know it's not fair. You must think— You must expect—"

"I did not ask for anything but your honesty, lass."

And if her honesty resulted in a miserable night for him, he reflected wryly, he was well-served for his lies.

She bit her lip. "You don't mind? Won't it be hard?"

"Hard as a rock and stiff as a mast," he assured her, grinning when her eyes rounded. He trailed his knuckle along the curve of her jaw, coaxing her head up, inviting her smile. "It's not such a terrible fate, to sleep with you in my arms."

She smiled tremulously. He felt almost rewarded for his sacrifice.

But he knew, in his heart and in his stones, he would get no sleep tonight.

E mma dreamed.

In her dreams, she walked the track that led to her father's farm, while the sea pounded the cliffs below. If she did not watch her footing, she would fall. But her gaze kept drifting, drawn by the waves and the promise of something just beyond the horizon, a vision broader and brighter than the rutted track and her everyday existence of boots and butter and eggs.

The water shimmered like a sheet of beaten silver. A sleek black shape broke the shining surface. She caught her breath in wonder. A seal. She turned her head to watch its sinuous glide. Distracted, she tripped, tumbled, toppled down and down from the cliffs into the cold, hard sea.

The shock knocked the air from her lungs and jarred her to the bone. Panic seized her. She could not breathe. Water pulled at her skirts and sucked at her boots. Her petticoats clung, trapping her like a fish in a net.

The seal reared up beside her, regarding her with dark, clear eyes. *"It was your petticoats that nearly drowned you,"* it said.

She was drowning. The realization struck her like a knife. Emma struggled, weeping, fighting the constriction of her lungs, the tangle of fabric around her legs.

And the seal bore her up, supporting her with its thickset, powerful body, speaking to her with Griff's voice, Griff's words. *"Easy now, lass. Be easy. I've got you."*

Gasping, she opened her eyes.

The room was dark. The fire had died to sullen red embers. The bedcovers tangled around her legs.

Griff lay beside her, behind her, his chest warm and solid against her back, his arm heavy about her waist. Her heart hammered.

"It was only a dream," he rumbled. "Easy, lass. I've got you."

Only a dream.

Tension escaped her on a sigh. She subsided against her pillow.

Not a pillow. Griff's muscled arm supported her head. His rod, hard and ready, lodged against her backside. Emma sucked in another breath, a different kind of tension seizing her muscles. She shivered in longing and trepidation.

He stroked back her hair with his free hand, tucking a strand behind her ear. "It's all right. Sleep."

She relaxed, but she could not sleep. Visions of her dream lingered like the mist over the ocean, fogging her thoughts, but her body, primed by his touch, was alert. Aware. Her senses hummed. Her nerves tingled. Griff cocooned her in warmth, surrounding her with his undemanding strength. Only the nudge of his erection against her bottom issued its own demand, a silent declaration of intent. She curled into him, settling more firmly against that intriguing ridge, and felt his breathing change. His arm flexed beneath her cheek, but he did not move, did not reach or grab. Emboldened, she shifted, brushing against his hot satin length, feeling him just . . . there.

"I will not do anything you don't want me to."

His assurance freed her to discover, to feel, without expectation of pain or shame. She wiggled experimentally. Her toes explored the top of his foot, stroked his hairy leg to the knee.

"Lass." His voice shook with laughter and desperation. "You do not know what you are inviting."

Her heart pounded. She knew enough to experience a moment's panic. But he did not roll to crush her, covering her body with his own, his weight pressing her legs, her stomach, until she could not breathe. He lay still on his side, his body heavy with sleep and smelling of musk. His big frame curled protectively around her own—naked, warm, animal, relaxed.

Not so relaxed. His arm was dense with muscle. His member was hard and thick. She was seized with a terrible lassitude and an even more terrible longing. Curiosity and need rose and trickled within her. She felt suspended in time like an insect in amber, caught in the dark and honeyed now. There was no tomorrow. Only this man, this moment, this one opportunity to have and hold. Inside, she was loose and liquid, tight and aching. She pressed against him, shameless in the faceless dark, and the arm at her waist slid down, his fingers skimming over her quivering stomach, parting her thighs. With a moan, she turned her face into his hard biceps and opened for him, let him pet and stroke her as he had before, her body eager for more touches.

The blunt head of his penis nudged the curves of her buttocks, rubbing, seeking entrance from behind as his fingers soothed and readied her from the front, dipping into her moisture, spreading it through her slick folds. Emma stiffened. He should not . . . She must not . . . But her body moved blindly of its own volition, wriggling against him, wanting, seeking . . . He bent her forward over his arm, tilting her hips for his penetration, and slipped into her a little way, his smooth, thick head filling her, stretching her, making her gasp and want.

For, oh, she wanted this. Wanted him. Wanted more. Her need pulsed inside her. She tightened around him. With a grunt, he entered her in one smooth, hard thrust.

Yesss. Her inner muscles contracted.

No pain, she thought, dazed and relieved. Only this aching sense of completion. Of satisfaction. Of wonder that he could do this thing with such care and patience, and she could receive him with such pleasure.

He began to move, and she stopped thinking at all, completely taken up, taken over by the sweet friction, the slow, deep thrust and slide of him pumping in and out of her body, moving within her. She was filled with him, wrapped in him, as his rhythm quickened. Her breathing shortened. He nuzzled the curve of her neck, and she reached back, desperate to hold him, her nails digging into his smooth, taut flanks. He bit her softly—her ear, the side of her neck—gripping her hips, imprinting himself on her flesh, holding her hard and tight. She quaked and contracted around him. Her release spilled from her in an overwhelming flood, catching him up like a wave, dragging him with her.

He exhaled into her hair. She felt the warmth of his breath on the back of her neck and the hot gush deep in her body.

Emma meant to rise and wash. She fell asleep instead, lulled by Griff's weight warm behind her and his hand toying with her hair.

When dawn came, he was gone. Dimly, she recalled the sudden coolness beside her in the bed. He had murmured something—"my lord" and "duties"—before he kissed her and left her.

Now she stood at the window, concentrating fiercely on the fastening of her gown as if aligning each button in its appropriate hole could somehow restore her to her proper guise as mistress of mathematics at Miss Hallsey's School for Girls.

Useless.

Absurd.

She sat on the edge of the bed to roll on her stockings. She would *not* regret what Griff had done—what they had done together.

She had been numb, closed in on herself like a hand curled to protect the wound at its palm. Now every inch of her felt open and aching and alive. Her collar chafed the faint abrasions on her neck. The linen shift teased her sensitive breasts. And every rasp of fabric against her skin, every shiver along her nerves, reminded her of Griff.

Emma sighed.

He had lavished her with patience and with wicked skill, healing and transforming her. She was grateful for his care. Everything had changed . . . and nothing had.

Emma yanked on her other stocking. She was no longer so naive as to equate sex with marriage, or even tenderness with love.

Griff had not said he loved her. She would not have believed him if he did. Why, they barely knew each other.

The memory of his deep voice rolled through her. *"I know you, lass. In one day I have seen the spirit and the spine and the heart of you . . ."*

Her heart shook. Her hands trembled. She folded them together in her lap.

She had given him more than her body last night. But she could not, did not, expect any more from him. Men, Emma assumed, did not feel these things as women did.

The daylight had returned, and with it, reason. She would not make the mistake of relying on someone else to care for her. She was responsible for her own choices. Her own feelings. Her own future.

Dismally, she wondered when the next boat departed for Canada.

FIVE

"Canada?" Griff relieved Una of the tray and nodded for the girl to depart. "You do not want to go there."

Emma stared at him, broad and rough and male, and wished the sight of him balancing her breakfast tray in his big hands didn't make her heart stumble. She did not want to go anywhere. But neither could she stay in his bedchamber, blushing every time a child came to the door.

"I signed a contract," she said. "A year's service for passage on the ship."

His thick brows rose. "The ship sank."

He set the tray on the chest. More apples, Emma noted, and a thin gray porridge that shamed the silver bowl it came in. What kind of household couldn't produce porridge?

She dragged her mind back to their discussion. "Nevertheless, there are people expecting me."

"Not any longer."

He was probably right. By now, she would be considered lost at sea. And yet—

"My parents should not have to read about my death in the newspaper."

"You are close to them." It was not a question.

She shook her head. "Before I left, my father informed me I was already dead to them." Impossible to keep the bitterness from her voice.

"I am sorry, lass." His voice was deep and sincere.

His sympathy eased the hurt at her heart.

"It doesn't matter." But of course it did. "I planned to write to them when I reached Halifax."

"You cannot go."

Her heart leapt. Would he miss her? Did he want her to stay? Not that she could, under her present circumstances, but his apparent reluctance to see her leave was balm to her bruised heart.

"Why not?"

"This is not Liverpool. There are no steamships to take you clear to Canada."

Emma raised her chin. "You cannot tell me we are on an island with no boats."

Griff scratched his jaw with his thumb. "No, I cannot tell you that. But a ship large enough to bear you safely across the ocean . . . You could wait weeks for a vessel that size."

"Weeks," Emma squeaked.

"Aye. Months, maybe."

"But . . . what am I to do? How am I to live in the meantime?"

Griff appeared genuinely puzzled by her question. "You will live here."

"I can't." A familiar panic beat in her throat. "I have no money. I have nothing."

"You do not need money. You are my lord's guest."

"I cannot rely on the charity of a stranger." She could not rely on anyone. Paul had taught her that. Her parents, Letitia . . . "There must be something I can do to earn my keep." Inspiration struck as her gaze fell on the bowl of porridge. "Perhaps he would hire me as a cook."

"A cook," Griff repeated without inflection.

She nodded eagerly. "All the girls at Miss Hallsey's learn domestic management, along with history, science, geography, and—"

"Lass, you do not need to work to keep the roof over your head," Griff said wryly. "But if you did, you have talents of more use to my lord than cooking."

Her gaze flew to his. She trusted him. She did, with her body and a share of her heart. He could not possibly be suggesting—

"You could teach," Griff said, shattering her assumptions. "The castle needs a teacher."

Emma caught her breath. The offer, following so closely on her half-formed suspicions, left her stunned. "Teach," she said, in the same flat, disbelieving tone Griff had used for *cook*.

"You said you wanted to." He watched her, his dark gaze intent. "It would pass the time. Until you go."

The possibility swelled her chest like a balloon. She felt buoyant, almost dizzy. To teach again . . .

She bit her lip. "My reputation—"

"Does not matter. That is past."

"Not that past," she muttered. "I slept with you. Here. Last night."

Griff's mouth quirked. "We do not regard these things as you do. No fault attaches to either of us because you graced my bed last night. Both of us are free to choose. Your choice honors me. Mine protects you."

Memory closed like a fist in her throat, blocking her air: Paul, his handsome face flushed and sulky, saying, *I am offering you my protection. You should have the good sense to accept it and be grateful.*

"If I were to accept your offer . . ." Her cheeks heated. Her voice shook. "Where would I sleep?"

"With me."

"No."

"Why not?" He sounded baffled. Frustrated. Angry? She could not tell.

Emma clasped her hands together in her lap. She had given this man her body. She owed him her trust. Or at least an explanation. "Before I left England, a wealthy man—a governor of the school where I taught—offered to make me his mistress."

Griff's eyes narrowed. "The man who had you. Hurt you."

She inhaled. "Yes."

"I will kill him for you."

Her breath exploded in an appalled laugh. "No! He—I—he said I led him on. I didn't mean to. But I made assumptions, foolish assumptions about what he intended and what I wanted. It cost me my position at the school."

"He cost you your life," Griff growled.

"Yes." She closed her eyes in relief, at once vindicated and reassured. Not her fault, then. Not entirely her fault. "In one day, one instant, I lost my home and my livelihood. And then Paul told me all I had to do was make my body available to him at his convenience, and I would be fed, sheltered, secure. And . . . I could not do it. I could not be what he wanted me to be."

Her eyes opened, pleaded with his for understanding. "I cannot be what you want me to be, either," she said.

"You can. You are."

He tempted her to believe him. But she would not spoil what they had shared in the honeyed dark by dragging it into the daylight world of transactions and obligations. "I cannot eat the food from your table in return for—for—"

Griff scowled. "It is not the same thing at all."

"I know." And she did. From somewhere, she summoned a smile for him. Her decision was much easier—in a practical sense—because Griff was nothing like Paul. He was not like any man she had ever known before. He had lavished her with passion and tenderness. He was offering her an opportunity to do the work she loved.

Emma sighed. Of course, emotionally, his willingness to honor her wishes made her choice more difficult. "But I can't set aside everything I believe, everything I've been taught, simply because your employer might be willing to overlook our—our relationship. I can't risk making another mistake. I need time."

He shot her a sharp look, and she winced at what he would not say. She hadn't needed time last night.

"And if you are with child?" he asked.

Her heart pounded against her ribs. She raised her chin. "Are you offering to marry me?"

For the first time, Griff appeared disconcerted. "We do not marry. I would care for you. And the babe."

"Let me take care of you." The memory whispered over her skin like a touch, raising goose bumps.

Emma's throat tightened. She was vulnerable to him in ways she could never have guessed at before last night. Everywhere he had touched her, every place he had been, tingled from his possession. He was imprinted on her flesh, pulsing in her blood. Inside, she was softer, warmer, melting. She wanted him.

Still.

But in the pale, thin light of morning, she saw herself and her options clearly. The arrangement he suggested would leave her always doubting and unsatisfied. How could she face her pupils with confidence, how could she teach them with authority, when she was living openly with the castle overseer as his mistress?

She swallowed. "I will be your mistress, or I will be the children's teacher. I cannot be both."

She would never have made such an offer to Paul. But then, Paul had never offered her a choice at all.

Griff held her gaze, his dark eyes smoldering.

Her breathing quickened. If he touched her . . . If he kissed her . . .

But he did neither.

"Teach, then," he growled. "I will leave your bed. Until you ask me back to it."

He closed the door quietly behind him, leaving her alone with her cold porridge and her cooling thoughts.

G riff lurked in the great hall, listening for the sound of Emma's voice, cursing his duty and her stubbornness.

Conn had designated the antechamber as her schoolroom, furnishing it with mismatched tables and chairs, a globe, and a few—a very few—books. Emma had spoken with longing of a package lost in the wreck, *Paradise Lost* and *Jane Eyre* and *Mrs. Beeton's Book of Household Management*. But Iestyn had contributed a Bible, a parting gift from his human father, and today the class took turns reading, copying verses onto slates.

" 'There went in two and two unto Noah into the ark, the male and the female, as God had commanded Noah.' " Emma's clear, expressive voice rippled over Griff like the wind on water. He eased from the shadow of the doorway to watch her.

She stood beside the smoking fire, her sunrise hair confined at the back of her neck, her pretty breasts buttoned behind the ugly gray dress she favored. The selkies' enchantments did not affect her. But a week on Sanctuary had worked its magic anyway. Her face was faintly golden from science lessons disguised as long walks on the beach. The challenge of keeping a dozen restive adolescents interested and engaged had given new energy to her movements and a lilt to her voice.

Young Iestyn in particular looked at her like a milk-fed pup presented with a side of beef. Poor whelp. Griff wondered if his own face bore a similar expression.

"Iestyn, will you try the next verse?" Emma invited.

The boy bent over the tattered volume. " 'And it came to pass after seven days that the waters of the flood were upon the earth,' " he read slowly.

Emma smiled. "Very good. Roth?"

Reluctantly, the stocky boy beside Iestyn took the book. " 'And in the six hu—hun—' "

"Hundredth," prompted Emma.

" 'Hundredth year of . . . of . . . ' " Roth flushed and snapped the book closed. "This is stupid."

"You are stupid," Iestyn said.

"Sod off. I don't care about your dumb story anyway."

"Noah and the ark is a beautiful story," Emma said coolly. "And I appreciate Iestyn sharing his book with the class to read. Now—"

Griff marveled at her patience. His own was wearing thin, with her students, with her, and with himself.

"I will leave your bed," he had told her seven days and six long nights ago. *"Until you ask me to come back to it."*

Cocksure idiot.

She had not asked.

And he was aching for her.

Roth's chair scraped back, recalling Griff's attention. "I don't need to learn to read."

His defiance dropped into the classroom like a stone. Heads turned or lifted. Insubordination rippled outward.

"Sit down, please," Emma said, low and firm.

"You cannot make me."

Griff had heard enough. "I can."

He strolled forward, keeping his eyes hard on the boy until the whelp dropped his gaze.

"I don't see why I have to learn this stuff," Roth muttered. "After I Change—"

"You learn because my lord says you will," Griff said. "Because if you don't, I will crack your ignorant head. The same goes for the lot of you. Sit."

Roth sat.

Griff nodded to Emma to continue. She did so, without losing her composure or her place in the book, and he thought that was the end on it.

But when the story and the lesson were done and her charges were dismissed for the day, Emma looked at him, waiting at the back of the room as had become his custom, and raised her chin.

"In the future, I would appreciate it if you would let me handle discipline in my classroom."

If she was in the mood for a fight, Griff was ready to oblige her. Seven *days*.

He crossed his arms against his chest. "Handle it, how?"

"I would have spoken with Roth after class. He struggles with reading. He only needs a little extra attention."

"And if you could not find him after class? Or he would not listen?"

Her soft lips pressed together. "Then I would have addressed the matter with Lord Conn."

"Who would have told me to deal with it." Griff shrugged. "My way just saved you a couple of steps."

"And possibly cost me the trust of my students."

She did not back down. Stubborn. He tried not to like that about her.

"They trust you," he said. He figured she needed to hear it, and it was true.

"They like me because I feed them regular meals, which is not the same thing at all."

He grinned. "There is that."

"Thank you for the fish this morning," she added.

He moved closer so he could smell her hair. "You are welcome."

He thought her breathing hitched, but she did not move away. "About the students—" she said.

"Young bulls fight to establish their place. You outrank them. But they need to know if they step out of line, they deal with me."

Her lips curved before she shook her head. "They are children, not animals."

They were children who would grow up to be animals, who would learn to take their proper place and form in the sea. But he did not think she was ready for that explanation. Not yet.

He was silent.

"It's important that they respect my authority," she continued earnestly.

"Aye." His tone was dry. "So you said."

"I will be your mistress, or I will be the children's teacher," she had told him when she barred him from her bed. *"I cannot be both."*

He saw her remember, watched the wild color bloom in her face.

Standing this close, he could see the freckles on her nose, feel the faint warmth of her body, smell chalk and soap and the feminine perfume of her skin and hair. A strand had escaped its bounds to curl against her neck. He caught the curl between his fingers, watching the rise and fall of her breasts beneath the gray fabric of her dress. She did not protest, did not slap his hand away. So, brushing the strand aside, he pressed a kiss to the side of her throat.

Her pulse leaped wildly under his lips. Her hands reached up and clutched his shoulders. She tasted of salt and desire. He raised his head to look at her—wary, brave, determined Emma—and then kissed her as humans kissed, face-to-face, mouth-to-mouth, sharing his breath, stealing hers.

Her lips were moist and soft. His tongue stroked them, probed them, seeking entrance. With a little moan, she opened to him, tender, yielding. He fed on her response, her human heart, her human soul, there on her lips.

He raised his head with a groan.

"Emma." He gave her her name. He did not know what else to give her. He was not at all sure what she would accept.

He was a warden, a warrior. For centuries, he had battled the encroachments of demons with confidence and skill. Now, with her, he was as awkward and uncertain as a pup on ice.

Her wide blue gaze focused on his face, her pupils dilated. She looked as dazed as he felt.

"Are you—" *What?* "—happy?" he asked.

She blinked. "With our . . . arrangement, do you mean?"

With that, gods, yes. He wanted her to reconsider, to take him to her bed. He wanted to put himself into her so deep and so often he became a part of her, flesh of her flesh, bone of her bone.

He wanted more than that.

"With your life here on the island," he said.

Her chin firmed. "I am content. I am doing work I love with children I am coming to care for."

She would always, he thought, make the best of any situation. She was by turns fierce and determined, pragmatic and kind. Conn had chosen her well for her role as teacher of Sanctuary's children. Griff had chosen well.

The thought depressed him.

"And that is enough for you." His tone made the statement not quite a question.

Emma did not answer.

Griff tried again. "You said once you dreamed of a home and family of your own."

"I dream about seals."

His breath stopped. "What?"

She gave an embarrassed half laugh. "I've been dreaming

about North Devon. Not the farm, or my family. But walking the sea cliffs where I grew up, watching the seals on the beach below. Isn't that strange?"

"Not so strange, given that you spend your nights under a seal-skin." His sealskin. Did she ever dream of him?

"Is that what the fur on my bed is?" Her face clouded. "Poor seal."

"It gave its pelt to keep you warm."

"Yes." She sighed. "But they are such beautiful creatures."

"Emma." He paused, searching for words, for reasons that would convince her. "Conn is well pleased with your work. The children like you. If a ship comes—when a ship comes—you do not have to leave."

She regarded him steadily with her big blue eyes. "Would that be enough for you?" she asked, echoing him. "If I stayed for the sake of Lord Conn and the children?"

It had to be.

Among the children of the sea, alliances and affections were fleeting. Selkies might mate, but few pairings sustained for centuries.

Yet Emma, in the way of her kind, sought assurances. Commitment.

So Griff told the truth.

"I want you to stay," he said. "I miss you. One time only we had, and I cannot stop thinking about you. I have not had another woman since that night."

Her eyes narrowed, and he wondered if truthfulness was perhaps a mistake. Human ways were different. *Emma* was different.

"I do not want another woman ever," he added carefully. "Only you."

She tipped her head to one side. "Griff, are you . . . courting me?"

He held her gaze. "If that's what it takes to have you, aye."

"Well, then." Her smile danced across her face like sunlight on the sea. His heart turned over in his chest. "I suppose I will stay."

SIX

A home and a family of my own.

Emma stood on the tumbled shore as the wind whipped the waves to froth and chased the clouds like whitecaps across the sky. The castle on the cliffs reared at her back. She watched her pupils straggle in and around the tide pools, gathering mussels for dinner. Iestyn gazed out to sea with a pensive expression, the breeze snatching at his rags. Roth chased Una and another girl across the rocky beach, waving broad strands of kelp like battle flags.

The students were not really her children. She did not really belong here.

But after several weeks, Sanctuary felt curiously like the home she had always longed for.

Because of Griff. His attention made her feel appreciated, supported, accepted.

Loved.

Emma wrapped her arms about her waist, hugging her happiness to her. He had promised to join them on the beach this afternoon after his meeting with Conn. Emma could not imagine what the two men spent their time talking about. Most lords and stewards discussed land and tenants, livestock and crops. But the island appeared as poorly populated as the castle. She saw no old people and no very young ones. The hills and heaths produced nothing but wild oats and apples, and the only animals she saw, beyond the teeming colonies of seabirds, were small brown wild sheep.

It did not matter. Griff saw to it that she and the children were fed.

Emma had met her employer exactly twice, once when Conn had offered her the post of teacher, and again when she informed him of her decision to stay. The lord of Sanctuary was one of the handsomest men she had ever seen, with hair the sleek blue black of a mussel shell and eyes the color of rain.

He was also the coldest.

However, he told her, in his polite and formal way, that he was pleased to have her here and offered her the princely salary of forty pounds a year. Emma did not see how this bare estate could afford such a sum. But then, she couldn't imagine how she was to spend it living on this island, either.

Griff told her she had only to ask for anything she wanted. The island, he said, traded for what it needed and could not produce. And despite the noticeable lack of a harbor and his earlier warning about transport lines, Emma noticed there were frequent visitors to Sanctuary. She glimpsed them sometimes in the hall or the corridors that led to Conn's tower: broad-chested men and women with a great deal of bosom showing. Once she looked up from her teaching to find a woman watching her from the back of the classroom, a woman with Iestyn's golden eyes and a silver chain like Griff's about her neck.

For the most part, however, the castle visitors paid little attention to Emma. Clearly, a mere schoolteacher was beneath their notice. And she paid little mind to them. She preferred to concentrate on her students, her students and Griff, shoving away the occasional awareness, a growing sense that something was not quite . . . normal about her full, satisfying, productive life.

She hugged her elbows tighter against a sudden chill.

Foam burst against the rocks and drained away, revealing the white bones of barnacles and a spill of scarlet weed like blood.

Along the water's edge, the girls laughed and shrieked as Roth chased them with the flapping kelp. Their screams mingled with the call of the gulls. And then the tenor of their voices changed, became cries of alarm. Distress.

Dread shivered along Emma's arms. She shaded her eyes against the afternoon sun, squinting down the beach. Something was wrong. Una—

Emma began running, her boots clattering and sliding over the rocks, even before the girl screamed and fell to the ground.

The children stood like sheep around the body writhing at the water's edge. Una shrieked again, clutching her stomach, her lips drawn back in pain.

Emma's stomach rocketed to her throat. "It's all right, my dear. You're all right."

But she wasn't.

Una screamed again, panting like a woman in childbirth,

gasping, guttural breaths that ripped at Emma's heart. Beneath her simple dress, her body undulated. Heaved. A seam split, and fur, pale, brindled fur, poured through the opening.

God. Dear God. The girl was being swallowed alive, consumed by the beast coiling under her gown.

Emma dropped to her knees, fumbling in her pocket for the knife Griff had given to her. Una hissed. The children swayed and pressed closer with pale faces and glittering eyes.

"Get help!" Emma yelled at them. "Get Griff!"

Una moaned and clutched at her. Her nails drew blood.

Emma yanked the knife from its sheath. But she could not see where the girl ended and the beast began, could not risk plunging the blade through the straining fabric into the shifting mass where the girl's legs should be.

Sobbing in terror, she slid the knife through the garment's seams, ripping Una free from the constricting cloth.

"Warden's coming!" Iestyn shouted.

Thank God. Emma spared a glance from Una's twisting body.

Griff charged—naked, a shock among all the other shocks—from the direction of the castle, a dark bundle in his arms. A blanket? A cover. The fur cover from her bed.

Emma's jaw dropped.

He ran barefoot over the rocks, muscled legs flexing, broad shoulders gleaming, until he reached the edge of the sea. His strong feet gripped the rock. His arms extended over his head. Just for a moment, his gaze met Emma's, his eyes dark and fathomless, churning with emotion.

The fur swirled over his shoulders.

The air shimmered with mist.

And on the beach where he had stood, a gray bull seal reared on the rocks.

Shock slammed through Emma, exploded in her chest, burst in her head. Her vision dimmed. She cried out in loss and denial.

No. Dear God, please, God, no.

Una wriggled in her arms.

Shuddering, Emma glanced down—at the whiskered face, the round, brown eyes, the fat, sleek form of a young seal.

No, no, no, no, noo . . . .

She sat helpless, stunned, as a wave washed up and wet her skirt, as the children crowded around her, as the bull seal herded the young cow into the sea.

Leaving Emma kneeling on the shore, clutching the tatters of Una's gown and the shreds of her own illusions.

A candle burned, quiet against the dark. A single yellow flame against the starless night outside Emma's window, against the smothering numbness of her soul.

She had already cried—well, bawled, really—as she had not cried since that night in Griff's arms. The memory of his tenderness nearly set her off again.

But eventually her tears were done, gone, leaving her wrung out and hollow, and there was nothing, not shock or sorrow or fear or pride. Only this cold emptiness.

How could she not have known? How could she not have questioned? Blinded by happiness and her own desires, she had seen only what she wanted to see. She had made assumptions about Griff. About their future.

Just as she had with Paul.

She was a fool. But how could she possibly have imagined . . . this?

She shuddered and closed her eyes.

There were legends around the islands of Scotland and the Cornish coast, stories of beautiful creatures with powerful sexual allure who took the form of men and women on land and the form of seals in the sea, tales made up to while away a long winter evening in front of the fire—or justify an unexplained pregnancy.

Any village girl reluctant to name a married man as the father of her baby could claim she had been seduced by a stranger from the sea. Of course, everyone in the village knew such girls were foolish, deluded. Mad.

But now . . .

Emma had proved herself as foolish, as deluded, as any one of them. She could be the girl abandoned onshore while her belly swelled with . . . what?

She had seen with her own eyes what Una had become. And Griff.

She swallowed against the tightness in her throat. She would almost have preferred to be crazy. Instead, she was bereft, betrayed. Alone in the dark.

Alone.

Griff had deceived her. The man she loved—had trusted with her body and her heart and her future—was not really a man at all.

The door whispered open behind her. She felt his presence before she opened her eyes, like a rise in the temperature of the room or a weight pressing on her chest.

"The first Change is hard," Griff said quietly in his deep, burred voice. "Even when they know, even when they are prepared for it."

Emma turned to face him, afraid of what she might find. Dismayed by what she felt for him. Still.

He stood just inside the doorway, watching her in the dark, his eyes gleaming in the light of the single candle. Animal eyes, she thought.

"I was not prepared," she said.

He winced. "No."

"Why didn't you tell me?"

He cleared his throat. "There was no time—"

"You had *weeks*." Her voice rose on the word. She was almost shrieking. If she were not careful, she would start screaming, and then she might never stop. She gripped her hands tightly together at her waist. "Weeks of me living here, teaching here, talking with you—"

Loving you, she thought but did not say.

"You should have told me," she finished bitterly.

"Aye." He shifted, as if he were suddenly uncomfortable in his big, graceful body. "But I wanted you to stay."

Oh. A fissure opened in her heart.

She ignored it. She didn't want to fall into that chasm, into the emptiness and the dark.

"Where is Una?" she asked. "How is she?"

"She is well. As you can see." He moved aside from the door, and Una, bright-eyed and pale, rushed into the room and flung her arms around Emma.

Almost, Emma recoiled. But this was Una, a child, not a monster. A pretty adolescent who stumbled over fractions and flirted with Iestyn and had lent Emma her comb.

Her arms came up automatically to embrace the girl as Una turned her head against Emma's chest, her arms tight around Emma's waist.

Emma found it difficult to breathe.

"The first time is hard," Griff repeated. "They—we must generate our skins from within ourselves, the first time. But the change becomes easier with practice."

Easier for whom? Emma thought.

As if he heard her thought, Griff's mouth tightened.

"I was glad you were there," Una said against Emma's dress front.

Emma stroked the girl's dark curls. "I'm glad, too." Remembering the child's screams, how could she feel otherwise? And yet . . . "I wish I had known how to help you."

"You held me. And the warden brought me back." Una looked at him, her eyes shining. "The land beneath the waves . . . It was wonderful."

Emma had a sudden, uncomfortable vision of Griff's big body crowding Una into the sea.

Griff met her gaze stolidly. "The young ones need a guide the first time out. The call of the sea is strong in us. They must learn to find their way back to Sanctuary and human form."

They must find their way back.

Yes.

Only sometimes the things said and unsaid, the spoken lies and unuttered promises, formed an insurmountable barrier.

"Sometimes," Emma said, with a catch at the heart she refused to acknowledge, "there is no going back."

"Then we must go forward," Griff said. "Off with you now."

Una turned her head against Emma's breast, her curls tickling Emma's chin. "But I haven't told her anything yet about the surge or the sea forest or—"

"Tomorrow. You can tell her anything you like tomorrow."

Una practiced a pout and a flounce on her way out the door. Emma smiled faintly as she caught Griff's eyes. Apparently even a mythical beast was capable of behaving like an average thirteen-year-old when the mood struck her.

He smiled back, and Emma stiffened.

He knew she would be softened by seeing the child. He knew her. She was being manipulated. Again.

Her smile faded. "What *are* you?" she whispered.

He reached into the hall for something. His sealskin. Her breath caught as he tossed it onto her bed, as the rich, dark fur spilled over the frame and onto the cold stone floor. "I am that," he said.

He crossed to stand in front of her, opening his arms until she was compelled to look at him, forced to acknowledge him, his strong, hard face and broad, furred chest and overwhelming maleness. Her heart pounded. Her mouth was dry. She could feel the heat of his body.

"And I am this," he said in his deep voice. "I have not changed, lass. Nothing has changed."

She took a step back. "Rubbish," she said in her farmer father's voice. Judgmental. Accusing. She hated sounding this way. She hated feeling this way. But she could not help herself. "Unless by 'nothing has changed' you mean I've been living in a fantasy world all along."

Griff's arms fell to his sides. "It was no fantasy, lass."

She looked at him in disbelief. "You're a seal."

"A selkie. Aye."

Anger rose inside her, warming, burning. She did not want to feel it. She did not want to feel. The cold numbness hurt less than this. But she was furious with him. And with herself, for allowing her feelings to betray her into accepting an impossible situation. For trusting him. For loving—

No.

"Forgive me if I don't see the difference," she said.

"Seals are animals. Selkies are elementals. We are the children of the sea, formed when God brought the waters of the world into being, the first fruits of His creation."

"Not human."

"No."

"Not . . . mortal?"

Griff hesitated. "We can be killed. But we do not die as your kind understands death. As long as our bodies, our sealskins, return to the water, we are reborn again in the sea."

Emma's legs refused to support her any longer. She sank down on the bed. *The first fruits of God's creation . . .*

"How old are you?"

"There are older among us," he answered carefully.

Not lying, Emma thought bitterly. Just not telling her everything. "How old?" she insisted.

"Two thousand years," he admitted. "Give or take twenty."

She sat dumbly, her blood roaring in her ears.

"Our people are of two kinds," he continued, "sea born and blood born, those brought into being at the first creation and those born of a union between male and female, mortal and immortal. My mother was human. I can still give you children, Emma."

That roused her. She raised her head and glared at him. "Oh, no, you cannot. I'm not letting you touch me."

"Because I revolt you."

"No!"

She saw the faint easing of tension in his muscles, the subtle relaxation of his lips, and hated herself for her ready response, for her vulnerability, for her honesty.

Hated him for making her feel.

Because he did not revolt her. Far from it.

"A relationship between us is impossible. You must see that. I'll get old and wrinkled and die, and you'll always be . . ." She flapped her hand at him, one gesture encompassing his strength, his immortality, his perfect masculine physique. "Like this."

Griff took her hand. Held it, despite her attempts to tug away. "Not always. The island's magic keeps us young. That's why our children are fostered in human families and why they take so long to mature once we bring them here. But outside of Sanctuary, we age as humans do, for as long as we are in human form."

He sat beside her on the bed, lacing his fingers with hers. The mattress depressed under his weight until her thigh touched his. "We could grow old together, Emma. If we moved the school, moved with the children to a neighboring island, it would suit all our needs."

Emma's hand trembled in his hold. She wanted nothing more than to fall into the promise of those warm, deep eyes, to fall into his arms, to fall in with his plans. But something niggled at the edge of her consciousness, swayed below the surface of her thoughts, like a sea anemone swaying and retracting in the tide. Something about the school . . .

Slowly, she withdrew her hand from his. "What needs?"

"I need you," he answered so promptly she was almost disarmed. "The children need you."

His pelt still lay beside her on the bed. Dark, like the hair on his head and chest, and silky smooth. She ruffled the fur with her fingers and felt his sudden stillness, heard his breathing change.

"Emma . . ."

A scar slashed across the thick, smooth fur, a hard, silver ridge running like a road through a forest. She traced it with her finger. A scar . . .

"What is this?" Her voice was high. Tight.

"My chain." Griff touched the silver band around his neck and smiled ruefully. "It . . . rubs, under the pelt."

Emma looked at the braided silver chain, the stylized spiral medallion glinting against his warm muscle and crisp dark hair.

And saw the seal in the Liverpool harbor with the necklace of scars around its throat.

"It was you," she whispered. "The seal at the docks."

"Aye."

"You watched me."

"Emma—"

"You followed me."

"Yes."

Her voice rose. "My being here—it wasn't an accident, was it?"

"Lass—"

She felt sick. "The shipwreck wasn't an accident."

He was silent.

Dear God.

She stumbled to her feet. She wanted to throw up. "All those people on the ship—"

"—are safe. Not one life was lost." He stood, grasping her shoulders in his strong, steady hands, forcing her to look at him. "I swear it."

Mary Jenkins, little Alice, her books, all her things . . . "And that's supposed to make me feel better?"

"It should," Griff said grimly. "I did it for you."

Oh, God.

"Which?" she flung at him. "Saved their lives or wrecked the ship?"

A long pause, while their eyes warred and her heart broke all over again.

"Both," he admitted.

She was no longer numb. Numb was too easy. This . . . this was agony.

"You didn't do it for me." She was shaking, shivering, splintering apart inside. "You did it because your damned lord Conn wanted a damn teacher."

"The fate of our children was at stake. The future of our people." Griff's face was like stone. His voice grated like iron. "Nothing else could be of significance compared to that. You were needed." His eyes pleaded with her for understanding. "And you have been happy here. Emma—"

"But I didn't have a choice! Those poor people who lost everything on the ship didn't have a choice. I may be human and mortal and insignificant, but I know we deserve a choice."

He was looking at her as if she were the monster, as if she were a strange, rare beast who might suddenly sprout fur and flippers and swim away.

"A choice," he repeated.

Her chest felt tight. She stuck out her chin. "Yes."

He nodded slowly. "Very well. I will speak to my lord. Tomorrow, after you have said good-bye to the children, I will take you wherever you want to go."

Emma's mouth dropped open. Her chest caved in.

Why? It was what she asked for, what she wanted, what she had always wanted. Wasn't it? A measure of control over her own life. "You are not serious."

His mouth was a hard, tight line. "Never more so."

"But . . ." She struggled to organize her thoughts. Her words. "What about the school? The children? They still need a teacher."

"There are other teachers. Conn will have to find one."

She had been warm and angry. Now she was cold all over, her hands, her spine, the pit of her stomach. "And will you wreck her ship, too?"

He glared back at her, all the heat and frustration and anger she had felt burning in his eyes, and she said, "Or will you seduce her into doing what you want, the way you did me?"

"It's no concern of yours," he growled. "Or mine, either."

"What does that mean?" she snapped, still goading, still wanting . . . What?

"There are other teachers," he repeated. "There is no other woman. Not for me. When you go tomorrow, lass, wherever you go, I will follow you."

Emma looked stunned.

He might as well have clubbed her over the head, Griff thought. Her mouth opened and closed several times like a fish's, and her eyes and nose were red from the weeping she had done and the weeping she had not allowed herself to do.

He should not have found her beautiful.

He should not love her.

He should not abandon his home and his prince, his duty and his very nature to follow her around the world.

But he did, and he did, and he would.

Passionate, brave, determined Emma. He would follow her to hell if he had to.

Apparently the opening and closing got her mouth working again, because she asked, "You would do that for me?"

Hadn't he just said so?

His jaw set. "Aye."

Her blue eyes were wide and bewildered enough to break his heart. "But . . . why?"

"I told you. I am courting you."

"Oh." A jagged breath like a sound of pain. She shut her eyes. "It isn't fair to say such things to me."

"There is no 'fair' with the heart," Griff said. "Only what is."

He went into the hall and returned with a package. He pressed the gift into her hands, folding her fingers around it. "I have never courted a woman before," he told her gruffly. "So you must be patient with me while I learn."

Her eyes opened. "Two thousand years, and you expect me to believe—" Her gaze fell to the package in her hands. Her throat moved as she swallowed.

"A man who is courting brings presents. Or so I have heard," Griff said.

"My books." Emma smoothed the oiled paper back with trembling fingers. "You brought my books to me."

He shrugged, trying to hide the quick jump of nerves in his stomach. "You said you wanted them."

"Weeks ago. I can't believe you remembered." She looked up, her eyes shining with appreciation. He hoped it was appreciation and not tears. "Thank you."

"I could not find them until today." When he went into the sea with Una. Best not to remind her of that. "So . . . I am forgiven, then?"

"For always knowing what I want and giving it to me?" Her lips curved. His heart thumped in sudden hope. "That depends," she said.

"On what?" he demanded.

She clasped her hands tightly on the books. "On whether you will give me what I want now."

Griff's face, his mind, went blank. He had offered her everything, his loyalty, his life. He did not know what else to give.

"You," she told him, and took his breath away. "I want you."

He reached for her and then stopped himself, his hands hard on her shoulders. "Now? Because I do not think I can wait until we get to Canada."

"I don't want to wait. And I don't want Canada. I just need to know that you—" Her gaze dropped. She wet her lips. "—care for me."

Tenderness swelled his chest. "I love you, lass. And I want you willing. No more making the best of a bad choice."

Her throat worked. "You love me?"

"I do. And I always will."

"Even when I'm old?"

He heard the hope in her voice, and his own pulse surged and quickened. "I will love you until we both are old and gray," he vowed. "And I will hold you in my heart forever."

"Oh, Griff." It was the right answer. He saw it in her eyes. "I do not need to make the best of anything. Because I have the best of everything with you."

He cupped her face.

She smiled into his eyes.

He took her in his arms then, drawing her onto the bed, letting his weight down on top of her, spreading her thighs with his. He felt her stiffen, and he remembered that other one, the one who hurt her.

So he reversed their positions, pulling her on top, coaxing her to straddle him. "Better?"

She bit her lip. Nodded. Smiled. Relaxed.

He absorbed her hum of pleasure as he moved against her, as he rocked against her, as he lifted her hips and slid hard inside her, wet, slippery, hot. His shudder shook them both.

He loved her. They loved each other. Face-to-face, body to body, breathing and moving together in a rhythm as old as the sea, as compelling as the tides. Griff clenched his teeth, trying to hold back, trying to hold on, wanting this to last forever. Until Emma rose above him like a goddess, the moon burning in her hair, bright and beautiful and his. With a soft cry, she jerked and tightened around him. And again. Her peak surged through him like a wave, undulating, sucking him under. His blood roared in his ears. He gave himself up to it, gave himself up to her, releasing hotly, deeply at her center.

Afterward, she lay against his chest as he stroked her hair, listening to the sea break and break on the rocky breast of the shore below, eternally new, forever changed.

TURN THE PAGE FOR A SPECIAL PREVIEW OF

SEA WITCH

BY VIRGINIA KANTRA
COMING SOON FROM BERKLEY SENSATION!

If she didn't have sex with something soon, she would burst out of her skin.

She plunged through the blue-shot water, driven by a whisper on the wind, a pulse in her blood that carried her along like a warm current. The lavender sky was brindled pink and daubed with indigo clouds. On the beach, fire leaped from the rocks, glowing with the heat of the dying sun.

Her mate was dead. Dead so long ago that the tearing pain, the fresh, bright welling of fury and grief, had ebbed and healed, leaving only a scar on her heart. She barely missed him anymore. She did not allow herself to miss him.

But she missed sex.

Her craving flayed her, hollowed her from the inside out. Lately she'd felt as if she were being slowly scraped to a pelt, a shell, lifeless and empty. She wanted to be touched. She yearned to be filled again, to feel someone move inside her, deep inside her, hard and urgent inside her.

The memory quickened her blood.

She rode the waves to shore, drawn by the warmth of the flames and the heat of the young bodies clustered there. Healthy human bodies, male and female.

Mostly male.

Some damn fool had built a fire on the point. Police Chief Caleb Hunter spotted the glow from the road.

Mainers welcomed most visitors to their shore. But Bruce Whittaker had made it clear when he called that the islanders' tolerance didn't extend to bonfires on the beach.

Caleb had no particular objection to beach fires, as long as whoever set the fire used the designated picnic areas or obtained a permit. At the point, the wind was likely to carry sparks to the trees. The volunteers at the fire department, fishermen mostly, didn't like to be pulled out of bed to deal with somebody else's carelessness.

Caleb pulled his marked Jeep behind the litter of vehicles parked on the shoulder of the road: a tricked-out Wrangler, a ticket-me red Firebird, and a late-model Lexus with New York plates. Two weeks shy of Memorial Day, and already the island population was swelling with folks from Away. Caleb didn't mind. The annual influx of summer people paid his salary. Besides, compared to Mosul or Sadr City or even Portland down the coast, World's End was a walk on the beach. Even at the height of the season.

Caleb could have gone back to the Portland PD. Hell, after his medical discharge from the National Guard, he could have gone anywhere. Since 9/11, with the call-up of the reserves and the demands of homeland security, most big city police departments were understaffed and overwhelmed. A decorated combat veteran—even one with his left leg cobbled together with enough screws, plates, and assorted hardware to set off the metal detector every time he walked through the police station doors—was a sure hire.

The minute Caleb heard old Roy Miller was retiring, he had put in for the chief's job on World's End, struggling upright in his hospital bed to update his résumé. He didn't want to make busts or headlines anymore. He just wanted to keep the peace, to find some peace, to walk patrol without getting shot at. To feel the wind on his face again and smell the salt in the air.

To drive along a road without the world blowing up around him.

He eased from the vehicle, maneuvering his stiff knee around the steering wheel. He left his lights on. Going without backup into an isolated area after dark, he felt a familiar prickle between his shoulder blades. Sweat slid down his spine.

Get over it. You're in World's End. Nothing ever happens here.

Which was about all he could handle now.

Nothing.

He crossed the strip of trees, thankful this particular stretch of beach wasn't all slippery rock, and stepped silently onto sand.

She came ashore downwind behind an outcrop of rock that reared from the surrounding beach like the standing stones of Orkney.

Water lapped on sand and shale. An evening breeze caressed her damp skin, teasing every nerve to quivering life. Her senses strained for the whiff of smoke, the rumble of male laughter, drifting on the wind. Her nipples hardened.

She shivered.

Not with cold. With anticipation.

She combed her wet hair with her fingers and arranged it over her bare shoulders. First things first. She needed clothes.

Even in this body, her blood kept her warm. But she knew from past encounters that her nakedness would be . . . unexpected. She did not want to raise questions or waste time and energy in explanations.

She had not come ashore to talk.

Desire swelled inside her like a child, weighting her breasts and her loins.

She picked her way around the base of the rock on tender, unprotected feet. There, clumped like seaweed above the tide line, was that a . . . *blanket*? She shook it from the sand—*a towel*—and tucked it around her waist, delighting in the bright orange color. A few feet farther on, in the shadows outside the bonfire, she discovered a gray fleece garment with long sleeves and some kind of hood. Drab. Very drab. But it would serve to disguise her. She pulled the garment over her head, fumbling her arms through the sleeves, and smiled ruefully when the cuffs flopped over her hands.

The unfamiliar friction of the clothing chafed and excited her. She slid through twilight, her pulse quick and hot. Still in the shadows, she paused, her widened gaze sweeping the group of six—*seven, eight*—figures sprawled or standing in the circle of the firelight. Two females. Six males. She eyed them avidly.

They were very young.

Sexually mature, perhaps, but their faces were soft and unformed and their eyes shallow. The girls were shrill. The boys were loud. Raw and unconfident, they jostled and nudged, laying claim to the air around them with large, uncoordinated gestures.

Disappointment seeped through her.

"Hey! Watch it!"

Something spilled on the sand. Her sensitive nostrils caught the reek of alcohol.

Not only young, but drunk. Perhaps that explained the clumsiness.

She sighed. She did not prey on drunks. Or children.

Light stabbed at her pupils, twin white beams and flashing blue lights from the ridge above the beach. She blinked, momentarily disoriented.

A girl yelped.

A boy groaned.

"Run," someone shouted.

Sand spurted as the humans darted and shifted like fish in the path of a shark. They were caught between the rock and the strand, with the light in their eyes and the sea at their backs. She followed their panicked glances, squinting toward the tree line.

Silhouetted against the high white beams and dark, narrow tree trunks stood a tall, broad figure.

Her blood rushed like the ocean in her ears. Her heart pounded. Even allowing for the distortion of the light, he looked big. Strong. Male. His silly, constraining clothes only emphasized the breadth and power of his chest and shoulders, the thick muscles of his legs and arms.

He moved stiffly down the beach, his face in shadow. As he neared the fire, red light slid greedily over his wide, clear forehead and narrow nose. His mouth was firm and unsmiling.

Her gaze expanded to take him in. Her pulse kicked up again. She felt the vibration to the soles of her feet and the tips of her fingers.

This was a man.

Kids.

Caleb shook his head and pulled out his ticket book.

Back when he was in high school, you got busted drinking on the beach, you poured your cans on the sand and maybe endured a lecture from your parents. Not that his old man had cared what Caleb did. After Caleb's mom decamped with his older brother, Bart Hunter hadn't cared about much of anything except his boat, his bottle, and the tides.

But times—and statutes—had changed.

Caleb confiscated the cooler full of beer.

"You can't take that," one punk objected. "I'm twenty-one. It's mine."

Caleb arched an eyebrow. "You found it?"

"I bought it."

Which meant he could be charged with furnishing liquor to minors.

Caleb nodded. "And you are . . . ?"

The kid's jaw stuck out. "Robert Stowe."

"Can I see your license, Mr. Stowe?"

He made them put out the fire while he wrote them up: seven citations for possession and—in the case of twenty-one-year-old Robert Stowe—a summons to district court.

He handed back their drivers' licenses along with the citations. "You boys walk the girls home now. Your cars will still be here in the morning."

"It's too far to walk," a pretty, sulky brunette complained. "And it's dark."

Caleb glanced from the last tinge of pink in the sky to the girl. Jessica Dalton, her driver's license read. Eighteen years old. Her daddy was a colorectal surgeon from Boston with a house right on the water, about a mile down the road.

"I'd be happy to call your parents to pick you up," he offered, straight-faced.

"Screw that," announced the nineteen-year-old owner of the Jeep. "I'm driving."

"If I start giving Breathalyzer tests for OUIs, it's going to be a long night," Caleb said evenly. "Especially when I impound your vehicle."

"You can't do that," Stowe said.

Caleb leveled a look at him.

"Come on, Robbie." The other girl tugged his arm. "We can go to my place."

Caleb watched them gather their gear and stumble across the sand.

"I can't find my sweatshirt."

"Who cares? It's ugly."

"You're ugly."

"Come on."

Their voices drifted through the dusk. Caleb waited for them to make a move toward their cars, but something—his threat to tell their parents, maybe, or his shiny new shield or his checkpoint glare—had convinced them to abandon their vehicles for the night.

He dragged his hand over his forehead, dismayed to notice both were sweating.

That was okay.

He was okay.

He was fine, damn it.

He stood with the sound of the surf in his ears, breathing in the fresh salt air, until his skin cooled and his heartbeat slowed. When he couldn't feel the twitch between his shoulder blades anymore, he hefted the cooler and lumbered to the Jeep. His knee shifted and adjusted to take his weight on the soft sand. He'd passed the 1.5 mile run required by the state of Maine to prove his fitness for duty. But that had been on a level track, not struggling to stabilize on uneven ground in the dark.

He stowed the evidence in back, slammed the hatch, and glanced toward the beach.

A woman shone at the water's edge, wrapped in twilight and a towel. The sea foamed around her bare, pale feet. Her long, dark hair lifted in the breeze. Her face was pale and perfect as the moon.

For one second, the sight caught him like a wave smack in the chest, robbing him of speech. Of breath. Yearning rushed through his soul like the wind over the water, stirring him to the depths. His hands curled into fists at his sides.

Not okay. He throttled back his roaring imagination. She was just a kid. A girl. An underage girl in an oversize sweatshirt with—his gaze dipped again, briefly—a really nice rack.

And he was a cop. Time to think like a cop. Mystery Girl hadn't been with the group around the fire. So where had she been hiding?

Caleb stomped back through the trees. The girl stood with her bare feet planted in the sand, watching him approach. At least he didn't have to chase her.

He stopped a few yards away. "Your friends are gone. You missed them."

She tilted her head, regarding him with large, dark, wide-set eyes. "They are not my friends."

"Guess not," he agreed. "Since they left without you."

She smiled. Her lips were soft and full, her teeth white and slightly pointed. "I meant I do not know them. They are very . . . young, are they not?"

He narrowed his gaze on her face, mentally reassessing her age. Her skin was baby fine, smooth and well cared for. No makeup. No visible piercings or tattoos. Not even a tan.

"How old are you?"

Her smile broadened. "Older than I look."

He resisted the urge to smile back. She could be over the legal drinking age—not jailbait, after all. Those eyes held a purely adult awareness, and her smile was knowing. But he'd pounded Portland's pavements long enough to know the kind of trouble a cop invited giving a pretty woman a break. "Can I see your license, please?"

She blinked slowly. "My . . ."

"ID," he snapped. "Do you have it?"

"Ah. No. I did not realize I would need any."

He took in her damp hair, the towel tucked around her waist. If she'd come down to the beach to swim . . . Okay, nobody swam in May but fools or tourists. But even if she was simply taking a walk, her story made sense. "You staying near here?"

Her dark gaze traveled over him. She nodded. "Yes, I believe I will. Am," she corrected.

He was sweating again, and not from nerves. His emotions had been on ice a long time, but he still recognized the slow burn of desire.

"Address?" he asked harshly.

"I don't remember." She smiled again, charmingly, looking him full in the eyes. "I only recently arrived."

He refused to be charmed. But he couldn't deny the tug of attraction, deep in his belly. "Name?"

"Margred."

Margred. Sounded foreign. He kind of liked it.

He raised his brows. "Just Margred?"

"Margaret, I think you would say."

"Last name?"

She took a step closer, making everything under the sweatshirt sway. *Hell-o, breasts.* "Do you need one?"

He couldn't think. He couldn't remember being this distracted and turned on since he'd sat behind Susanna Colburn in seventh grade English and spent most of second period with a hard-on. Something about her voice . . . her eyes . . . It was weird.

"In case I need to get in touch with you," he explained.

"That would be nice."

He was staring at her mouth. Her wide, wet, full-lipped mouth. "What?"

"If you got in touch with me. I want you to touch me."

He jerked himself back. "What?"

She looked surprised. "Isn't that what you want?"

Yes.

"No."

Fuck.

Caleb was frustrated, savagely disappointed with himself and with her. He knew plenty of women—badge bunnies—went for cops. Some figured sex would get them out of trouble or a ticket. Some were simply into uniforms or guns or handcuffs.

He hadn't taken her for one of them.

"Oh." She regarded him thoughtfully.

His stomach muscles tightened.

And then she smiled. "You are lying," she said.

Yeah, he was.

He shrugged. "Just because I'm—" *horny, hot, hard* "—attracted doesn't mean I have to act on it."

She tilted her head. "Why not?"

He exhaled, a gust between a laugh and a groan. "For starters, I'm a cop."

"Cops don't have sex?"

He couldn't believe they were having this discussion. "Not on duty."

Which was mostly true. True for him, anyway. He hadn't seen any horizontal action since . . . God, since the last time he was home on leave, over eighteen months ago. His brief marriage hadn't survived his first deployment, and nobody since had cared enough to be waiting when he got out.

"When are you not on duty?" she asked.

He shook his head. "What, you want a date?"

Even sarcasm didn't throw this chick. "I would meet you again, yes. I am . . . attracted, too."

She wanted him.

Not that it mattered.

He cleared his throat. "I'm never off duty. Until Memorial Day, I'm the only cop on the island."

"I don't live on your island. I am only . . ." Again with the pause, like English was her second language or something. ". . . visiting," she concluded with a smile.

Like fucking a tourist would be perfectly okay.

Well, wouldn't it?

The thought popped unbidden into his head. It wasn't like he was arresting her. He didn't even suspect her of anything except wanting to have sex with him, and he wasn't a big enough hypocrite to hold that against her.

But he didn't understand this alleged attraction she felt. He felt.

And Caleb did not trust what he did not understand.

"Where are you staying?" he asked. "I'll walk you home."

"Are you trying to get rid of me?"

"I'm trying to keep you safe."

"That's very kind of you. And quite unnecessary."

He stuck his hands in his pockets, rocking back on his heels. "You getting rid of me now?"

She smiled, her teeth white in the moonlight. "No."

"So?"

She turned away, her footprints creating small, reflective pools in the sand. "So I will see you."

He was oddly reluctant to let her go. "Where?"

"Around. On the beach. I walk on the beach in the evening." She looked at him over her shoulder. "Come find me sometime . . . when you're not on duty."

ALSO BY
ANGELA KNIGHT

IN THE MAGEVERSE SERIES

MASTER OF SWORDS

Witch Lark McGuin has survived a vicious vampire attack that shook her confidence and left her struggling with feelings of helplessness and fear. The last thing she needs is a partnership with Gawain, a handsome vampire knight who means to seduce her every chance he gets.

MASTER OF WOLVES

The *USA Today* bestselling author returns to werewolves and a handler who's too hot to handle.

MASTER OF THE MOON

In the light of the moon, a sexy paranormal world awakens.

MASTER OF THE NIGHT

American agent Erin Grayson is assigned to seduce international businessman Reece Champion. But she's been set up. Reece is an agent, too—and a vampire.

"THE FUTURE BELONGS TO KNIGHT!"
—EMMA HOLLY

Available wherever books are sold or at penguin.com